Praise fo

THE SHARK
"This romantic thriller is tense,

—*Publishers Weekly*

"Precise storytelling complete with strong conflict and heightened tension are the highlights of Burton's latest. With a tough, vulnerable heroine in Riley at the story's center, Burton's novel is a well-crafted, suspenseful mystery with a ruthless villain who would put any reader on edge. A thrilling read."

—*RT Book Reviews*, four stars

BEFORE SHE DIES
"Will keep readers sleeping with the lights on."

—*Publishers Weekly* starred review

MERCILESS
"Burton keeps getting better!"

—*RT Book Reviews*

YOU'RE NOT SAFE
"Burton once again demonstrates her romantic suspense chops with this taut novel. Burton plays cat and mouse with the reader through a tight plot, credible suspects, and romantic spice keeping it real."

—*Publishers Weekly*

BE AFRAID
"Mary Burton [is] the modern-day Queen of Romantic Suspense."

—Bookreporter.com

THE
LAST
MOVE

MARY BURTON

THE LAST MOVE

Montlake
Romance

Published by Montlake Romance, Seattle

www.apub.com

Amazon, the Amazon logo, and Montlake Romance are trademarks of Amazon.com, Inc., or its affiliates.

ISBN-13: 9781542046923
ISBN-10: 1542046920

Cover design by Mark Ecob

Printed in the United States of America

THE
LAST
MOVE

THE
LAST
MOVE

CHAPTER ONE

When love is betrayed, there is nothing to contain the demons.

San Antonio, Texas
Sunday, November 26, 12:35 a.m.

He'd been following her for weeks. Watching. Observing. Loving the chase. The hunt. But he wasn't a monster, nor was he evil. He was a man with a narrowly focused plan that gave his life purpose and structure. Some doubted he had the backbone to see this new plan through. Some didn't think he had the balls. The commitment. But he did. He sure as shit did.

He waited in the shadows and watched as the silver four door pulled into the convenience store lot. Closed car windows barely muffled "Amor Prohibido" blasting on the radio as the woman in the driver's seat swayed, tapping her finger on the steering wheel.

When the song ended, she rose out of the car, moving to the pump and inserting the nozzle into the gas tank. This evening she'd chosen a black swing skirt, white silk blouse, and booted high heels. Her accessories were gold hoop earrings, a twenty-inch pearl necklace that nestled between her full breasts, bracelets on her wrists, and of course, her five-carat engagement ring.

She scanned the dark lot as if she sensed his gaze on her. She rubbed her hands over her arms, and then grabbing her purse, headed inside the convenience store.

She waved to the clerk behind the checkout counter. She'd seen him dozens of times before. His name was Tomas, and he owned the place. He had big dreams of building his business. She disappeared into the ladies' room.

He grabbed his kit from the stolen van's front seat and opened the door. The now-disabled dome light didn't click on, leaving him shrouded in the safety of shadows as he left the door ajar. Nerves gripping his gut, he jogged across the lot.

Kneeling at her back tire, he removed an ice pick from his kit. He tightened his grip around the wooden handle and jabbed the tip into the tire's tread, wiggling it side to side. When he pulled the pick free, the air slowly hissed out. She had maybe five to ten miles before the tire went flat and she would have to pull over. At this time of night, those extra miles on I-35 would put her farther south in a more isolated stretch of road, creating the perfect trap.

Light-headed with anticipation, he dashed not toward his van but toward the dumpster so he could blend into the shadows and watch as she emerged from the restroom into the glaring light of the convenience store. She had touched up her lipstick and fluffed her hair, and she was smiling as she paused by a display of chocolates. She never bought candy, only black coffee, but tonight she picked up a small bag of candies and clutched them close as if she were breaking a long-standing rule. She filled a to-go cup with her customary black coffee, paid as she joked with Tomas, and dumped several bills in a tip jar.

Outside, she ran long fingers through her dark hair. Gold bracelets, glistening in the gas station's lights, dangled from her wrist.

After replacing the gas nozzle and the cap, she slid behind the wheel, started the engine, and turned up the radio. Instead of driving off as she always did, she ripped open the bag of candy and dug out a thick piece of chocolate. The beat of Latin music pulsated as she sat for several minutes simply eating. Finally she put the car in gear.

His attraction to this woman had nothing to do with the gentle sway of her hips or the tilt of her head. He wasn't drawn to the shape of her ass in the dark skirt, the curve of her breasts in the white silk blouse, or the slender line of her calves.

That was all nice. But what made him really hard was the awareness that he was going to kill her.

Thoughts of leveling his gun at her heart made his erection pulse. He was in control of the last minutes of her life.

The power was intoxicating.

Her taillights clicked on, and she drove toward the I-35 south ramp. He dashed back to his van and followed, lights off until he reached the interstate ramp. He gripped the wheel as he trailed her, careful to remain several car lengths behind.

It was an unseasonably warm night, nearly moonless, and the stars were bright and clear. He turned on a country-western tune and rolled down his window, savoring the breeze on his face.

Three minutes of driving. The traffic around them was sparse. The tire was still rolling. Her car would soon slow. She'd drop back from the small herd of cars. They'd be alone.

Five minutes of driving. The taillights of the few cars had raced toward the dark horizon. Her car was slowing. The back right tire was already deflating. Seconds ticked by. He switched on his cell-phone jammer.

Seven minutes of driving. The tire was nearly on its rim. The car rocked awkwardly. Her right blinker flashed on, and she pulled to the side of the road. Gravel kicked up under her tires as dry Texas dust swirled up.

3

Mary Burton

He pulled in behind her, killing his headlights quickly as more lights glared in his rearview mirror. He waited. An eighteen-wheeler blew past him, the rush of air slightly rocking the van. Cars stopped on the side of I-35 often enough that not everyone paid attention.

Still, he needed to get moving. No telling who would come upon them or how long they would be alone. He had to move fast. It wasn't safe out here. But the risk of his own capture amped up the rush of adrenaline that snapped through his body.

His heart pounded as he checked his rearview mirror and saw only the dark stretch of highway. All clear, he clicked on a small camera sewn into his jacket and tucked the well-oiled Beretta into the waistband under his jacket. He got out of the van, his booted feet crunching against the fine gravel as he walked toward her car. His heart beat fast. His mouth was dry. His fingers tingled, and his gut tightened with eagerness he'd not felt in a long time.

Slowly he walked toward the driver's side window, and when he knocked on the glass, the woman flinched.

He smiled, dispelling the tightness in his expression.

She met his gaze and smiled.

This was going to be more fun than he'd imagined.

The game had begun.

CHAPTER TWO

The pills make the days' oppressive routines possible.

San Antonio, Texas
Sunday, November 26, 8:00 a.m.

Homicide Detective Theo Mazur parked on the side of I-35, twenty miles outside of San Antonio, behind the forensic van and the collection of Bexar County cop and rescue vehicles. Flares had closed the two southbound lanes, and a deputy was directing snarled traffic toward the access road that ran parallel to the highway. The morning sun cast a warm glow over the endless miles of brush, low prickly trees, and red dirt.

Mazur climbed out of his SUV, and immediately the midseventies temps reminded him he was far from home. No crisp bite in the air or scents of snow. No rumble of the L trains or the honks of cars in congested Chicago traffic. A transplant from the Chicago Police Department, he had joined the San Antonio force just six months ago.

Culture shock remained a daily annoyance, and today's weather was simply one aspect. What had been automatic to him in Chicago—navigating the streets, eating at a favorite bar or restaurant, hanging out with friends, or hell, even knowing the names of the beat cops—wasn't a given here. Every crime scene required a GPS. Every new uniformed cop was a test in name memory. What came naturally in Chicago took time here.

The move south came when his ex-wife, Sherry, had told him seven months ago she was moving with their daughter, Alyssa, to San Antonio. He and his ex had lost their son, Caleb, to crib death two years ago. They'd called him their bonus baby, a gift after years of infertility. The boy's death had devastated them both and shattered an already shaky marriage. After Caleb, when he and Sherry weren't with Alyssa, they were buried in their jobs. He'd made captain. She'd left city government for a law firm that paid mid–six figures—enough to set Alyssa up in private school and later for any college.

When Sherry announced the move days after they signed the final divorce decree, family, friends, and colleagues had expected him to stay behind and take frequent trips south to see his kid when he could. No one had predicted he would walk away from the job, the pension, and family. But he had only one surviving child, and he wasn't letting anyone take her away.

Gravel crunched under his loafers as he moved toward the yellow crime-scene tape and the uniformed officer standing guard. Across the highway on the northbound side, several news vans had already taken up their posts on the access road and were running film.

Mazur moved along the side of the road, nodding to the officer. His nameplate read *Jericho*.

"Nothing like pulling duty on Thanksgiving weekend," Mazur said. All cops worked some holidays each year, but as he was now low man, he was on all weekend. This meant his holiday had amounted to a drive-by to see his kid on the way back from investigating a stabbing.

The patrolman looked him over and shrugged, clearly not giving a shit about making small talk with the man whose arrival had snatched a local boy's spot on the homicide team. "It happens."

Mazur did what he did best when he was pissed. He smiled. "Maybe there's hope for the rest of us at Christmas. Personally, I'm angling for New Year's off."

"Right."

Mazur's smile vanished as he fished latex gloves from his pockets and slid them on. "Who was the first responder?"

"Me. I've been here since three a.m. Answered a call from the victim's husband."

"How did the husband know to find her here?" Mazur asked.

"She called him. Said her car broke down. Rattled off the last exit she'd passed before her phone went dead." He glanced at a small notebook. "Husband is Martin Sanchez. He says the victim is his wife, Gloria Sanchez."

"I've heard that name before."

"She and her husband own four car dealerships. She does all kinds of commercials. She's the Queen of Cars. Always spouting catchy sayings."

The association triggered the image of a sultry brunette in a red sequin dress holding a scepter and singing a slightly off-key song about Christmas in July. "Where's the husband?"

"In the back of the squad car."

He glanced toward the black-and-white and caught the silhouette of a man in the backseat. His head was tipped forward into his hands.

"Okay, I'll get to him in a minute. Any problems with keeping the scene secure?"

Jericho looked toward the access road on the other side of the northbound lane. "A couple of the reporters were trying to get under the tape, but we chased them off."

The I-35 Highway, or simply "interstate" to the Texans, ran north and south, stretching the fifteen hundred miles from Laredo, Texas, all the way up into Minnesota. The major trucking route was known for high-speed traffic and crashes. He'd responded to a few deaths on the strip in the last couple of months, but all had been accidental.

"How did she die?" Mazur asked.

"Shot point-blank in the chest."

He looked out over the endless horizon of orange-brown dirt and scrub trees. Miles back, there was an exit with a convenience store and a few fast-food joints, but here she was out on her own.

"She couldn't have picked a worse place to break down," Mazur said to no one. He turned back to Jericho. "Who's working the forensic investigation?"

"Jenny Calhoun. She's been here a couple of hours."

A familiar name. Friendly from what he remembered. Good. He'd had his fill of passive-aggressive bullshit for the day. "See anyone near the scene when you arrived?"

"Only the husband's car."

"Gloria Sanchez was driving the white four door?" Not the kind he'd expect a fancy auto dealer to drive.

"She was."

"Thanks, Jericho. Don't be such a chatterbox next time."

As his long legs chewed up the twenty feet to the car and Calhoun, he noticed the back right tire was completely flat. There were no other signs of damage on the car.

The forensic technician was a tall, lean woman with blond hair she'd pinned up in a tight bun. He'd worked with Calhoun on a couple of cases in the last few months and found her dedicated.

She didn't look up from the camera's viewfinder as she snapped pictures. It gave him a moment to study what remained of Gloria Sanchez.

The victim's white silk blouse was doused in crimson blood. Her right hand, draped over her left thigh, was ringed by a collection of narrow gold bracelets that winked in the morning light. A four- or five-carat diamond encircled her well-manicured ring finger, a pearl necklace hung from her slim neck, and her designer black purse lay on the floor of the passenger side. Her wallet was exposed along with a checkbook. Whatever the motive for killing her, it hadn't been robbery.

The chest wound had to have been instantly fatal. Bloody fingerprints smudged the outside of the door as well as the left side of her neck. He pictured a panicked husband yanking open the door and checking for a pulse. The driver's side window was open, but there were no bloodstains on the button. Had she opened the window for her killer?

Calhoun looked up and smiled. "Detective."

Latex snapped and crackled as he worked his fingers deeper into the gloves. "How'd you get so lucky to pull this shift?"

"I volunteered. No family. Might as well work."

"You're a good soul. Tell me what you have."

"As you can see, she was shot in the chest."

"I see bloody fingerprints."

"Husband panicked and touched the victim."

"Her window is open."

"It is." She wrinkled her nose as if it itched and rubbed it against her shoulder. "Husband said it was open when he arrived."

"She trusted the killer," he said.

"Out here, alone, with a broken-down car, what choice does she have?" She held up a plastic bag that contained a cell phone. "I did find this in her lap. I've dusted the phone and pulled a few prints. Husband gave me the pass code."

The phone's screen saver displayed a grinning Gloria Sanchez, standing beside the Texas governor. Her thick hair draped her shoulders and a blue dress hugged her curves. "Jericho said she called her husband but the phone went dead. What's the charge on her phone?"

She checked. "Fully charged. But it's not uncommon for calls to drop out here."

Calhoun nodded toward the passenger side of the car. "There was a second phone on the passenger seat floor. Less expensive. No pictures or screen savers. Fully charged."

"A burner?" Burners were prepaid phones that could be bought at any box store for cash. They could be used and tossed, leaving no trail back to the user.

She shrugged. "That would be my guess."

He studied it. "What would Mrs. Sanchez be doing with a second phone?"

"Maybe it wasn't her phone. The car is a loaner from the dealership. Maybe it was left in the car by the last person who drove it."

Mazur grinned as he nodded. "You sound like a detective."

"Making detective is just one rung on my way up the ladder to chief."

Mazur smiled. "Don't forget the little people."

A begrudging grin followed. "I won't forget you."

"Thanks, Chief." He studied the phone. "Have you checked it for incoming calls?"

"It has received eight calls from one phone."

One number.

"Maybe she was having an affair?" he asked.

"I'd say definitely hiding something."

Again he puzzled over the car. It was five or six years old. No scrapes or dents or signs of any kind of accident. But not the flashy kind of car Gloria Sanchez sold. She could have pulled any car from the lot, and she chose this one.

Mazur held out his index finger and thumb, mimicking a gun. "The shooter wasn't more than two feet away when he fired. Judging by the blood spatter, he was standing right here."

"One shot. The medical examiner will make the final call, but I'd say the bullet shredded her heart."

"He didn't try to take her jewelry or money."

"Something may be missing. Her husband might know."

There was an open bag of peanut-chocolate clusters on the seat and beside it a bloodstained, rumpled receipt. In the cup holder was a to-go cup. "Is the receipt from a local store?"

"It's going to take me a little time to figure that one out. Soaked in blood."

He leaned in and tested the weight of the coffee cup. It was full, and there was none of the victim's red lipstick on the cup lid.

"Any signs of sexual assault?" he asked.

"Not that I can see, but again, the autopsy will tell you more."

He popped the trunk, moved to the back of the car, and found the tire and jack in place. Nothing else.

He knelt by the back right tire, now resting on its rim, and ran his hand over the tread. No screw or nail. Likely the puncture was small enough to get her onto the interstate before the tire deflated. "Punctured just enough so that it didn't flatten right away?"

"Best guess."

"Once you've finished up here, we'll talk."

"You know where to find me."

Mazur crossed to the patrol car that contained a sturdy man with a thick mustache and tussled gray hair. He wore a gray T-shirt stained with blood, sweats, and expensive loafers with no socks. His head was tipped back against the seat, eyes closed, and his hands were balled into tight fists.

Mazur knocked on the window, and the man opened his eyes and sat taller. Briefly his gaze was lost as if he didn't know where he was, and then realization chased off the wild-eyed expression and replaced it with a scowl. Mazur opened the door and motioned for the man to get out.

"I'm Detective Theo Mazur," he said.

The man straightened and was almost as tall as Mazur's six-foot-four frame. "I'm Martin Sanchez."

"Gloria Sanchez was your wife?"

"Yes."

"I'm sorry for all this." He always started off nice. He wanted witnesses and suspects to like him because people, even murderers, opened up to those who felt like a friend.

"It's been a nightmare," he said in a thick Texas drawl.

Mazur angled his head down, and dropped his voice a notch. "Mind telling me what happened?"

Martin touched a thick cross that dangled around his neck. "She called me at one a.m. Woke me up out of a sound sleep. She told me she was having car trouble and asked me to come get her. She told me the exit before the line went dead."

"What was your wife doing out here in the middle of the night?"

"She was driving down to Laredo to see her mother, who's in a nursing home. Gloria drives to Laredo at least three times a month. Yesterday was very busy at the dealership, and she couldn't get away from the showroom until after eleven."

"Is that her regular car?"

"No. She drives a silver Mercedes. She texted me yesterday and said her Mercedes was being serviced and that she'd find a loaner for the trip."

"No disrespect, but this car is kind of plain and ordinary." With a chagrined smile he leaned in a bit as though they were friends. "It's the kind of car that I would drive, but not the Queen of Cars."

Martin looked back toward the vehicle but quickly shuddered and glanced away. "I don't know why she took that car. She usually goes for the luxury models. I guess she was in a rush, and it was available. She's always in a rush. Always so busy." He rubbed the back of his neck with his hand.

"How far is the dealership from here?"

"Thirty miles."

Mazur scanned the horizon before looking back at Sanchez. "So she takes a loaner, stops for chocolate and coffee, and ends up here with a sabotaged tire."

Sanchez looked the part of a grieving husband, but a lot of murderers were talented actors.

"I can't . . . I can't think about it." The anguish and disbelief that threaded around the words sounded genuine.

"And then she's shot point-blank in the chest. Hell of a bullet hole." The comment was intentionally blunt. He wanted to shock Sanchez, who as the victim's husband was top on the suspect list right now.

Tears glistened in Sanchez's eyes. "I'll never forget what she looked like when I came up to the car. So much blood. It doesn't make any sense."

"Anyone have a beef with your wife?"

"She was a tough businesswoman. There were people who didn't like her, but I can't think of anyone who would have gunned her down like this. This killing had to be random. Someone who happened upon her."

"Her window was open. Whoever shot her won her confidence." She definitely would have lowered the window for her husband.

"That's not like her. She's not a trusting sort."

"The flat tire wasn't by chance. It was intentional. And the longer I'm a cop, the less I buy into coincidence. Most people know their killers. It's rarely random."

Dark eyes narrowed as Sanchez ran his hand over the gray stubble on his chin. No wedding band. "What are you saying?"

"Were you and your wife having marital problems?"

"No."

He nodded toward Sanchez's rough, calloused hands. "You don't wear a wedding band?"

The man didn't look down. "I'm a mechanic. I often take it off. It's a hazard. I just forgot to put it back on."

13

"How much older are you than your wife?"

"Fifteen years."

"That's one heck of an age gap."

Sanchez lifted his chin. "The years didn't matter to us."

"You two have any financial problems? I mean, she's dressed real nice, but all that glitters is not gold."

"I run the garage. She took care of the sales and numbers. We always had highs and lows. That's the nature of business. But in the last year, she said it was all going well, so I didn't question her."

"How many phones does she carry?"

His brow wrinkled. "One."

"There was a second phone in the car. Know about that?" Mazur understood something about having a spouse with a wandering eye. The sad-sack husband was the last to know.

"I've never seen a second phone."

"Maybe it belonged to someone else."

Heavy brows knotted. "My wife loved me. And I loved her."

"You mind giving a DNA sample to Officer Calhoun over there?" His tone was always casual and keeping it friendly until the situation required a different approach.

"I let Officer Calhoun fingerprint me."

"Good. I appreciate that. We're going to be collecting a lot of forensic data from that car, and it would be nice to have your DNA and exclude you quickly."

"What kind of DNA?"

"A cheek swab. Takes just a second, and then we're done. Will save you time later. You won't have to come down to the station." Again the no-big-deal, let-me-be-your-pal tone.

Sanchez jutted his chin out as he looked at Mazur. "I didn't hurt my wife. I came out here to *help* her."

Insistence reverberated from the man's words, but Mazur didn't have a good enough read on him to determine if he was telling the truth or just a damn good liar. "Once you are eliminated as a suspect, we can get to the business of solving the case."

"I should call my lawyer."

"You can do that. Will just give the killer more time to get away." When Sanchez hesitated, he added, "This is all very routine. I do it in every homicide case."

The man shook his head. "Sure. Take my DNA. Do whatever you need to do."

Mazur motioned Officer Calhoun over, who set aside her camera on a temporary worktable. When he explained what he needed, she pulled a DNA kit from her forensic van and carefully swabbed the inside of Sanchez's cheek.

"I didn't kill her," he said. "I came to help her."

At least a third of murdered women died at the hands of a husband, boyfriend, or lover. "I'm going to do everything I can to catch her killer."

A sigh shuddered from Sanchez. "What will happen to her? Who will come for my wife? Where will they take her?"

"We'll send her to the medical examiner," Calhoun said. "Once medical professionals have examined her body, they'll call you and you can make arrangements with a funeral home." The technician secured the cotton swab in a glass vial, labeled it, and stored it in her van.

"Funeral home. Jesus. I was talking to her just a few hours ago."

Mazur studied the man's body language closely. Sanchez was wringing his hands and making eye contact with him, both signs of grief and truth telling. "When she called you, did she give you any idea that she was in trouble or that she was being followed?"

"No. She sounded annoyed. Pissed off. Gloria has been short tempered lately, and the flat tire made her furious."

"Why was she short tempered?"

"I asked her several times, but she said it was nothing. She's lost some weight, so I figured it was one of her crazy diets." He ran a hand through his hair. "This is a bad dream."

The sound of a cell phone dinging had Mazur checking his own and realizing quickly it wasn't his, but the victim's burner that Calhoun had bagged in plastic. She held up the bag. The display read **BLOCKED**.

Calhoun carefully opened the bag and then the phone. "It's a text with a video attachment."

Mazur turned to Sanchez. "I'm going to have an officer escort you home. We are also going to need your shirt for testing."

"My shirt?" Sanchez glanced down and saw the blood. More tears filled his eyes. "Yes, of course." The older man's shoulders slumped forward as the weight of his wife's death sank in. "You'll take care of my wife?"

"Yes, sir."

Again, Sanchez looked pale, upset, devastated. He was hitting all the right emotional high notes. But killers also felt regret. In the aftermath of a murder, especially of a loved one, many sincerely mourned the loss of the very person they had just killed.

When a uniformed officer escorted Sanchez to a different patrol car, the detective turned back to Calhoun and read the text. **Dr. Kate Hayden, you did not catch me.**

"Kate Hayden," Mazur said, trying to recall the person.

When he couldn't make a connection, he hit the icon for the video attachment. In this remote area, cellular service was spotty and slow, and it took nearly thirty seconds for the attachment to load. When it did, he saw the freeze-frame of Sanchez's car. He pressed "Play."

The camera images showed someone moving from the back of Gloria Sanchez's disabled car to the driver's side window. Gloria Sanchez startled as she looked up from her phone into the camera.

"Are you all right?" a man asked. *"Looks like a flat."*

Her gaze warmed and she smiled. *"I'm safe in my car and can wait until help arrives."* The closed window muffled her response as she gripped her phone.

"Want me to change the tire?"

"What? No." She looked up, blinked. *"You shouldn't have to do that."* She glowered at her cell phone and punched the numbers. *"I always have bars on this stretch of road."*

"I can check mine and call the cops or a tow truck."

Her smile widened. *"That would be great."*

A gloved hand grazed the edge of the camera as he raised a cell. Seconds passed. *"I've got nothing either."*

"You don't have to stay," she said. *"Really, I'm fine."*

"You have no cell service and your tire is flat. Leaving you like this would be wrong. I can drive you ahead to the next gas station and ask them to send a tow truck."

"Really?" She cracked her window a fraction.

"Sure. It's going to take about half an hour to get there and send someone back. Do you have a flare? Easy to get sideswiped when you're on the shoulder."

She glanced toward the darkness. *"I hate this stretch of I-35."*

"I'm not crazy about it either," he said.

"I should have been in Laredo by now. Work ran late."

"I'm in the same boat. Extra shift at the hospital. I'm buzzing on an extra-large coffee and a bag of vending machine cookies."

"Jesus, this is the last thing I needed." She reached for her phone, punched in more numbers, and cursed.

"Pop the trunk. Let me have a look at the spare."

"You know cars?"

"Enough."

Some of her tension visibly eased. *"If by some miracle you can fix that flat, I'd be in your debt."*

"Not necessary. Let me see what I can do."

As he moved toward the trunk, the camera caught the image of a blue van. The plates were blurred by the darkness.

The trunk popped open, and he ran a gloved hand over a full spare tire. His breathing was steady as he returned to her. *"Spare's flat."*

"What? That's bull."

"Have a look for yourself."

This time she rolled down her window. *"I don't mean to be rude. I'm just really stressed."*

"Just trying to be a Good Samaritan."

"Oh, you are."

And then the barrel of a gun appeared.

She braced. *"What the hell?"*

The muzzle flashed, and the bullet struck her square in the chest. She recoiled back as crimson droplets splashed her face, the steering wheel, and the dash. Blood soaked her shirt, skirt, and the seat.

"You're not alone. I'm here for you."

"Shit," Calhoun said. "He filmed the killing."

"Why the hell does he want us to see this?" Mazur asked, more to himself.

"Maybe he's bragging. Maybe he's proud."

He watched the video again, studying it closely. The killer gently wiped the hair from Gloria Sanchez's face.

"Seems pretty damn personal to me," Calhoun said.

"Or it's part of his ritual."

"The killer left the phone so he could communicate with us."

"Yes, he did," Mazur said.

"I can try and trace the incoming phone call."

"Go ahead and do it now. If this guy has any brains, he's using a burner and will have deactivated it right away. But sometimes we get lucky."

"I'll move fast." She reached for her cell. "Hoping for stupid killers right now."

A smile tweaked the edge of his lips. "I bet you've seen your share."

"And no doubt you saw a few in Chicago." She raised her phone to her ear.

"Something tells me this one is smart." Mazur looked up and down the stretch of highway. A memory sparked. "There were other killings on I-35. Women traveling alone, disabled car, and then shot point-blank. Serial killer or copycat?"

"It's been six months since that killer struck. The last shooting was farther north. And the FBI made an arrest in that case."

"All the killings moved progressively south on I-35."

Calhoun's call dropped. She cursed and redialed. When the second call went through, she turned from him and discussed a phone trace. Traffic on the northbound side was heavy and noisy, forcing her to cup her hand over her ear as she listened.

Mazur searched the Internet on his phone. The articles were slow to load but finally appeared on the I-35 killer, also known as the Samaritan. His memory had been correct. The five victims had been random, all were shot once in the chest, and each victim's car had suffered some kind of malfunction. One ran out of gas. One had a punctured tire. Another had a rag stuffed in the tailpipe of her car. The lead FBI investigators on the case were Agent Mike Nevada and Dr. Kate Hayden, profilers based at Quantico.

The killer was reaching out to Agent Kate Hayden.

Calhoun tucked her phone back in her holster. "The phone is being traced as we speak." She glanced at his display. "FBI? You really want to pull the FBI into this case?"

"Want to? No. But when is life ever about what you want?"

CHAPTER THREE

*The bait will be too enticing to resist. Get more flies
with honey than vinegar.*

Salt Lake City, Utah
Sunday, November 26, 12:10 p.m.

Agent Kate Hayden, PhD, was violating hospital visiting hours as well
as a direct order from her supervisor when she rolled up the sleeves of
the white lab coat and crossed the polished lobby toward the visitor's
station. Overhead lights hummed as the distant elevator doors opened
and a gurney disembarked.

Her phone buzzed in her pocket. The display read **Agent Jerrod
Ramsey**. Her boss. The guy had radar. She silenced the phone and
tucked it in her pocket.

An older woman wearing a blue volunteer's smock smiled and then
made a sad, pouty face when she didn't spot hospital identification
clipped to Kate's jacket. "Are you on staff?"

Instead of answering the question, Kate said, "I left my cell phone
and ID badge in the gift shop. They have the cutest sweaters, and I tried
one on. I just got distracted. You'd be doing me a big favor if you'd let

me sneak up there for just a minute." Her practiced go-to smile usually worked. "I know exactly where I left it."

"I need to see identification."

She glanced at the woman's name badge. "Delores, can you cut me a break? My attending will eat me alive if he finds out I left it." The store was just up the escalator within sight of the information desk.

"I don't remember you."

"I'll run up there very quickly and bring it back." Kate allowed some real worry to leak into her expression. "I'm in a rush."

A tall, broad-shouldered man approached the front desk to ask a question, and the brief distraction gave Kate the opening to start walking. The woman's answer was lost as Kate moved up the escalator and past the gift shop toward a second bank of elevators. As the doors of one opened, she slipped in behind two nurses dressed in scrubs and a man and woman in white lab coats. At each floor the doors opened and her fellow passengers got off, until finally she was alone.

At the sixth floor, she exited the elevator, moved toward the lockdown unit, and pressed the intercom. "I'm Dr. Kate Hayden. I'd like to speak to a nurse."

"Step away from the doors." The voice crackled from the speaker.

The doors swung open, and a young nurse in scrubs appeared. "What can I do for you?"

"I'm here to see Sara Fletcher."

The nurse studied her. "Are you medical personnel?"

"I'm a doctor." PhD in linguistics, but that was semantics now.

The nurse shook her head. "Morning visitation is over."

Kate held up her FBI badge. "I won't be long. It's important."

The nurse stood her ground in the open doorway. "Law enforcement has been here all morning. The poor girl is in critical care, exhausted, and she's still not talking. I've strict orders from local police not to let anyone in."

This case was turning into a jurisdictional tug-of-war. And Kate had not helped when a local detective had questioned her methods as if she were a child. She'd called him a moron, and the working relationship had soured from there. Now he was trying to cut her out of the case. "Your job is to help her body heal. My job is to catch the guy who locked her in a box in his barn for thirty-four days."

The nurse's gaze narrowed. "She needs rest."

"Her abductor needs to be caught."

The nurse hugged her clipboard close and leaned in toward Kate. "Did I see you on television? Were you the agent who found her?"

"I was."

The nurse's guard dropped for a split second, no doubt as the scene played in her head.

Kate took advantage of the other woman's distraction and stepped through the doors into the unit. She was short but moved very quickly when motivated. She walked toward the girl's room.

The nurse recovered and followed, and the automatic doors swung shut behind them. "Look, you really can't see her now. If you don't leave, I'll call security. You might be FBI, but while that kid is here, I'm in charge."

Kate didn't break stride. "Ever been in a wooden box the size of a coffin for a minute, an hour, or thirty-four days as in Sara's case?"

The nurse frowned. "I know it's been horrible for her."

"Do any of us really know? I sure can't say that I understand what she's endured."

"We're all devastated over the girl's trauma."

"You know Sara's skin is so raw because of the constant pressure of the wood scraping against her. She can't tolerate light thanks to the perpetual darkness. She can't walk because her muscles have atrophied so badly she'll need months of PT. And the STD she has came from repeated—"

The nurse moved in front of her. "I'm aware of her injuries."

Kate straightened herself to her full five foot two inches. "Have you heard about the other girls this monster locked in boxes? We found other coffins buried in shallow graves on his property."

Some of the nurse's fire cooled. "There were others?"

"Four others. Those girls weren't lucky." She glanced around and dropped her voice. "One victim didn't fit in her box. Want to guess how he got her to fit? He broke her legs."

The nurse drew in a sudden breath. "My God."

"He's going to do it again." She hoped the image of the girl, legs broken and suffering in a dark box, haunted this woman for a long time. It tormented her. "I just need to ask her one question."

The nurse's lips flattened. "She's not talking to anyone."

"Is she awake?"

"Yes."

"Then we'll be fine." Kate didn't bother with a thank-you as she moved past the nurse and down the hallway still decorated with paper Thanksgiving turkeys. When she reached room 602, she didn't knock but slowly opened the door to the dimly lit room.

Eighteen-year-old Sara Fletcher lay in her bed, a television remote gripped in her hands as she stared at the muted television screen. The girl was channel surfing, clicking from network to network without giving herself a second to see what was playing. The room was filled with flowers and Mylar balloons featuring Wonder Woman, who apparently had been a favorite of the girl when she was younger.

"Sara."

The girl gripped the remote. Sharp blue eyes locked onto Kate with the leeriness of an animal caught in a trap. Even if the girl could run, her muscles still wouldn't support her weight.

Sara Fletcher had long blond hair that framed a thin pale face with angled cheekbones and a pointed chin. She'd lost twenty-six pounds of fat and muscle during her ordeal, and it would take weeks, perhaps months, before her body recovered.

Kate stood still, giving Sara a moment to study her in the dimly lit room. Seconds ticked by, and though her suspicion didn't abate, some of her tension eased.

Kate closed the door behind her. "You recognize me, don't you? I'm Dr. Kate Hayden. I'm a profiler with the FBI. I found you."

Tears glistened and her chin trembled.

Kate held up her badge as she moved slowly toward the bed. "I know I don't look the part." The white coat billowed around her small frame but covered jeans still coated in mud from the crime-scene search.

The girl studied the badge. She'd trusted a stranger once, and it had cost her dearly. Good. She was wary. That meant she was smart, and her chances of surviving this mentally were better.

"I recognize the look on your face." Kate wasn't adept at levity but understood it had its place. "It's a 'you don't look like an agent' glare. I get it a lot." She was 101 pounds soaking wet, as her mother used to say. Her light-brown hair was curly and stayed scraped back in a ponytail most of the time. "Operation code names for me have run the gamut in the eight years I've been at this. Smurf, Munchkin, and my favorite, the Lollipop Kid."

Beyond the odd monikers, she had a few lame jokes but right now couldn't recall a single one as the guilt of not finding this kid faster pressed against her chest. The girl stared at her, silent, but suddenly observant.

"People think when you're small you aren't smart or aggressive. But we can be the toughest of the tough, right?"

Sara nibbled her chapped lip and stared back at the television.

"We acted on an anonymous tip that led us to the abandoned Anderson farm." The Anderson name carried weight in this county, and when the tip first came in, it had been discounted. Another two days passed before the local authorities had called the FBI.

Kate had traveled to the farmhouse within hours of being contacted. She'd quickly found Sara's box, and as she pried out the nails hammered into the lid, she'd heard the girl's faint cry for help. She'd felt exhilaration, anger, and sadness as she opened the lid and discovered the painfully thin, pale, and frightened girl. Sara hadn't been able to give Kate the name of her abductor before paramedics had taken the girl away in the ambulance. Kate was left to study the surrounding property and the abandoned wooden outbuildings, now graying and tumbling under decades of abuse from the harsh Utah winters. With the use of ground-penetrating radar, they'd found the location of other graves.

Upstairs at the farmhouse, Kate had discovered fast-food wrappers, receipts, stacks of newspapers, and Sara's purse. A rumpled hardware store credit card receipt for lumber, nails, and duct tape had yielded the name of Raymond Drexler Jr., a cousin to the Anderson family. Surveillance cameras from the hardware store had shown Drexler buying supplies. A background search of Drexler turned up mug shots, arrest records, and mental-health records for a man addicted to stalking.

Today, she didn't have all the answers. But she had Drexler's name and a picture that she hoped Sara would identify as her abductor.

She moved to the side of the bed but didn't pull up a chair. She respected Sara's personal space. "We haven't caught the guy yet."

Sara tightened her hold on the remote and turned up the volume of the television. She surfed faster, turning the channels into an unrecognizable blur.

This kind of avoidance was expected, and Kate didn't fault the girl, but she needed a suspect identification. If they couldn't communicate with words, then actions would have to do. She slowly crossed to the television and unplugged it.

Silence crackled in the room. Sara's brow knotted, a hoarse moan escaped her lips, and she tossed the remote at Kate. When it hit the floor, the back panel opened and batteries tumbled free.

Kate picked up the pieces and carefully reassembled them. "I need your full attention now, Sara."

Sara frowned, dropping her gaze to the blanket. Pale, thin fingers, with nails still brutally short and jagged from scratching at wood, rubbed a dirty, inexpensive Wonder Woman bracelet she'd been wearing since the day she'd been taken.

The bracelet's red, yellow, and blue paint and the *W* were worn down. When rescue crews had tried to remove the bracelet, the girl had howled and fought. The trinket wasn't expensive and had been a gag gift at a girlfriend's eighteenth come-as-a-sexy-superhero birthday party. But this insignificant bauble had been with the girl through the entire ordeal, and rubbing it had become a self-soothing technique that allowed Sara to cling to sanity. Kate had been the one who intervened with the rescue crew and told them to leave the bracelet alone.

"I've four pictures I'd like you to look at," Kate said.

She removed the pictures from her coat pocket, but kept them pressed to her chest. "All I want for you to do is look at the pictures. If you recognize one of the individuals just point, nod, blink, or grunt."

The girl's gaze remained downcast. Her hand trembled as she picked at an already threadbare spot on the blanket.

"He cannot hurt you anymore," Kate said. "Now it's my turn to go after him and make him pay. He needs to be locked in a small prison cell for the rest of his life. Will you help me?"

Sara stared into Kate's eyes as if searching for a lifeline. Her bloodshot eyes were dry, no hint of tears.

One by one, Kate laid the mug shots beside the girl on the bed as if dealing cards. She was also careful not to look at the pictures, fearing a glimmer or linger would prejudice identification. She didn't want the girl to parrot her thoughts. She wanted a legitimate ID.

"You need to look at the pictures." Kate checked her watch. "I shamed a nurse into letting me into this room, but she's going to shake it off soon, decide I'm trouble, and insist I leave. I'm breaking a few dozen rules just by being here."

Sara studied Kate.

"I know it won't be easy," Kate coaxed. "But you have to look. Point to any picture you recognize, and I'll take care of the rest."

The girl's blue eyes were wild with fear, but also rage. She was in there somewhere.

"I'll make him pay," Kate whispered.

Sara's brow furrowed before she scanned the pictures.

Immediately she locked onto the third image on the left. A sob caught in her throat as she reached for the picture. Slowly she brought the image closer, staring at the face of the man with the black beard and shoulder-length hair.

Sara swallowed, then crushed the image in her hand, squeezing until her knuckles whitened.

Kate gently laid her hand over Sara's fist and slowly unfurled her fingers. She took the crumbled image and smoothed it out. "I need you to tell me he's the guy who took you."

Sara closed her eyes. She nodded.

Kate studied the crinkled image. "You're sure?"

Another nod.

She'd identified Raymond Drexler Jr.

"You're sure?"

She opened her eyes and mouthed, "Yes."

Kate collected all the pictures and tucked them in her pocket. "Good work, Sara. I'll nail him."

A quiet desperation deepened the lines in Sara's forehead and around her mouth. She was eighteen but looked decades older.

"I'll catch him. I promise you." Promises were tricky, and Kate didn't make them often. But she would hunt this piece of garbage to the ends of the earth.

Kate wished she could tell Sara her demons would vanish when Drexler was caught and convicted. "I'm not going to kid you. Catching him will help, and it'll save other girls. But it won't make your nightmares disappear completely. Time will fade some of the memories, but nothing in this lifetime will ever purge those thirty-four days."

Sara's frown softened.

Kate knew the nurses, doctors, and cops were telling the girl she was safe now. They were doing everything they could to reassure her. Of course, physically she was safe. Her body would eventually heal. However, the psychological part of the equation was a different matter. Her life would never be what it had been. The old Sara was dead.

"I'm very proud of you, Sara. To survive what you did . . . well, you're amazing. You're Wonder Woman."

The first, very faint flickers of hope crossed the girl's gaze before a fresh frown scattered them.

Kate mentally distanced herself from the crushing sadness that always stalked her. "I'll be posting this man's face in every department in the country. It won't be long. In the meantime, you're safe here. It's a lockdown unit. No one gets in."

The girl glanced toward the door.

"I got in, yes. I not only have a badge, but I'm short and also very charming when I try."

A brow raised.

Good, she understood sarcasm. More signs of life. "Ah, you must remember how delightful I was with your rescue squad driver?" The attendant, after trying to remove the bracelet, had tried to take a picture of Sara, likely to sell to the media. Kate had snatched his phone away and ground it into the mud with her foot. "I think he called me a tiny-ass bitch."

The girl's lips twitched. A year ago the poor kid might have smiled or even laughed at the self-deprecating comment.

Kate plugged the television cord back into the socket and handed the girl the television remote. "I'll call you when we have him."

Sara grabbed Kate's wrist in a surprising grip. Kate stopped. Time stretched as she stared into the girl's eyes, so full of wrenching pain. Sara pulled off the Wonder Woman bracelet, and with trembling fingers she slid it onto Kate's wrist.

Kate reverently touched the bracelet, needing a second before she could steady her voice. "Are you sure?"

The girl nodded.

"I like it. In fact, it rather works for me." Kate tapped her finger on the worn *W*. "But when I catch this guy, I'm bringing it back to you, and you can decide what happens to it next."

The girl's nod was almost imperceptible as she relaxed back against the pillows and turned on the television. She switched the channels again.

Kate left her room and made her way off the wing and down the elevator. Outside, she spotted her partner leaning against an unmarked blue four-door FBI vehicle. Agent Michael Nevada stood several inches over six feet. He had broad shoulders, a bare-knuckle brawler's hands, and a perpetual scowl. He was handy to have when her five feet didn't intimidate skeptical cops and streetwise criminals. Words had power, but sometimes it could only take you so far.

Nevada pushed away from the car. "You made it past the nurses, I see?"

"The Lollipop Kid rides again." She shrugged off the white coat, balled it up, and shoved it in a backpack resting on the pavement beside him. "Thanks for distracting the woman at reception."

He tossed her the FBI jacket she'd left with him. "Did Sara make an identification?"

Kate handed him the wrinkled picture. "Raymond Drexler."

Nevada flicked the edge of the picture. "So, you were right?"

"Yes."

Nevada grunted when emotions got the better of him. "I'm looking forward to finding this guy."

"Damn right."

He grinned. "I'd do this part of the job for free."

As she glanced at her phone to check email, the display flashed an unknown name. Area code was San Antonio, Texas. Her mother lived there, which was reason enough to answer instead of letting it go to voicemail. She also realized she'd missed three calls while the phone was muted. "Dr. Kate Hayden."

"Dr. Hayden, this is Detective Theo Mazur with the San Antonio Police Department."

She stilled. A call from the cops never promised good news. "What can I do for you, Detective?"

"We've had a shooting on I-35. Woman traveling alone, car broke down, and she was shot point-blank in the chest. I understand you worked several cases like this one in the last year."

Her trapped breath bled through her lips. She'd arrested Dr. Charles Richardson six months ago. When Dr. Richardson had been actively killing, he'd reached out to the cops via texts on burners left with the victims. After her press conference in Oklahoma days after the third murder, he communicated with her directly via the burners.

The texts had contained a mix of well-thought-out sentences and odd misspellings. This had gone on for weeks. There'd been a fourth killing and then a fifth. And then Richardson had made a mistake. He'd texted her with a phone that was traced to his secretary.

Kate had Richardson brought in for questioning. She'd been all smiles and offered him coffee, which he'd accepted. After he left, she'd had his DNA tested. It matched touch DNA found on the first victim's car. That had been enough to get a judge to sign a warrant for his financials. Credit card receipts led to purchases of burner phones and bullets. And in victim five's case, an ATM camera captured a car following her. An enhanced version of the picture caught part of a license plate of a stolen vehicle. Several partial prints pulled from the vehicle's radio button and turn signal switch matched Richardson's.

Though she'd yet to find the gun, which would definitely link Richardson to all the killings, she could now connect him directly to two of the five killings and had investigators digging deeper into his past. In time, she expected she'd link all five murders.

Since Richardson's arrest, she'd had reporters and even Richardson's legal team call her trying to glean information. And this man's unlikely mix of a Midwestern accent and the San Antonio, Texas, jurisdiction did not sit well with her. "What do you need from me?"

"I know you worked the last few Samaritan shootings, and you made an arrest six months ago," Mazur said.

A quick Internet search could have told him that. "Go on."

"I don't know if we have a copycat or an accomplice or you have the wrong guy, but this shooter sent a text to a burner phone found with the victim. The text is addressed to you."

"All the details you mentioned were released to the media," she said.

"The medical examiner is going to do the autopsy tomorrow. Once we have the bullet, we'll be able to compare it to the bullets used in the other Samaritan cases." Every gun barrel has unique microscopic indentations, or striations, which imprint on each fired bullet.

He hesitated. "I've called your boss, Jerrod Ramsey. I'd like you to come down and review the evidence."

"Once I've heard from Special Agent Ramsey, I'll be in contact."

"When you have your flight information, send it to me. I'll meet you at the airport," Detective Mazur said.

Steel hummed under the soft-spoken tone. He spoke as if her arrival was a foregone conclusion, but there were several more hoops to jump through before she'd get on a plane. She checked her watch and calculated how long it would take her to change, pack, and catch a flight to San Antonio.

She'd not been there in years. Her trips to her hometown had been infrequent after she left for college, and in the last few years had dwindled to none. There was always a good work excuse to miss family gatherings that had been bearable only when her sister-in-law was alive.

After Sierra's death, there was no one to referee or smooth the waters between Kate and her brother, Mitchell.

Maybe five years was finally enough time for a little forgiveness and maybe some forgetting. Should have been. Would have been nice for their mother if she and her brother got along. But she doubted a truce was possible.

"You still there, Dr. Hayden?" Detective Mazur asked.

"I'll call my boss, and if he green-lights the trip, I can be there by morning." She wanted Drexler in cuffs and to close the chapter in this horror story. But this job expected her to shift focus on a dime.

"I've already spoken to him. He gave me your number."

Kate arched a brow as she studied Nevada. "I'll need to hear it from him. Stand by." She ended the call.

Nevada folded his arms over his chest. "No rest for the wicked?"

"Looks like there's someone posing as the Samaritan."

"Richardson is in jail, correct? I'm assuming he still hasn't made bail."

"He is in jail." She dialed Jerrod Ramsey's number.

Ramsey was head of their profiling unit at FBI headquarters at Quantico. Each member of the team not only was trained in profiling but also had a specialty. Nevada specialized in field tactics, ballistics, and weapons. Genovese St. John, PhD, was an art forgery expert, James Lockhart was capable of piloting multiple aircraft, and Ramsey had a PhD in forensic pathology.

Kate's expertise was in forensic linguistics, the study of words and crime solving. She analyzed letters, hate mail, ransom notes, even text messages. She examined word choices, letter shapes, punctuation marks, typos, and more. Every component of a written communication held insight into a suspect.

Nevada cursed. "Richardson's attorney, that prick Westin, is going to be on that shooting like flies on shit." The elongated last word hinted to a Georgian drawl.

"Right."

Ramsey answered on the third ring. "Kate, I'm on the phone with an angry hospital administrator. He wanted a pound of your ass when I put him on hold to take your call."

"I have an identification from Sara Fletcher. The man who took her is Raymond Drexler."

"She's sure? *You're* sure?"

"One hundred percent."

Silence ticked away a couple of seconds. "That helps."

No hint of apology in her tone, Kate asked, "You get a call from a Detective Theo Mazur?"

"I did."

"You gave out my number to Detective Mazur?"

In the distance, a dog barked and wind whooshed. "I verified his identity, and since you weren't answering your phone, I gave him your number. If I'd only known you were trespassing on hospital property and creating another mess for me to clean up."

"What about the Utah case?"

"I know you've worked hard on this, but Nevada can see it through. He'll find Drexler."

Logically it didn't require two agents to track one man, and Nevada was the best. But logic did little to soften the primal craving to see this creep in cuffs. "The shooter in San Antonio is a copycat or an accomplice."

"And until we have ballistics, it's anybody's guess which one it is. Right now we only have evidence linking Richardson to two of the five Samaritan cases. Yes, the bullets used in the five Samaritan murders were 9 mm hollow points fired from the same gun, but any good attorney could argue Richardson didn't pull the trigger in the other three cases. This San Antonio killing adds weight to that argument."

She sighed. "I know."

"Let me know what you find out there."

"Right." She ended the call and flicked the ringer back to the "On" position. "I'm headed south. You'll have to keep me posted on the Drexler case."

"I'll text you a picture of him in shackles and cuffs."

The Wonder Woman bracelet dangled heavily from her wrist. "No holds barred."

"Absolutely."

"All right."

Richardson had killed at least two women, and so far all her investigations hadn't suggested an accomplice. She had other agents digging into his past, but their work wasn't yet complete. Jesus, had he trained someone else?

"You okay with returning to San Antonio?" Nevada asked.

Few knew about San Antonio. She'd told Ramsey, knowing her history would pop up on a background check. And she'd laid it all bare to the team when they'd formed five years ago. She wanted to believe putting it out there herself would make it almost inconsequential. And for the team it had been.

Did this mean she was okay with a return to San Antonio? No. She was not thrilled.

"Ramsey can assign another agent," Nevada said.

"My case."

"What about—"

"That was seventeen years ago," she said. "It won't bother me." In a text, she instructed Detective Mazur to forward his information via telex to the local FBI office.

"I'll bet money it'll take me less than forty-eight hours to prove Mazur is wrong."

"Did I eavesdrop correctly? Did the shooter ask for you via a burner?"

"My name's been in the news lately. Anybody with half a brain could have read it. But I have to check it out."

Nevada didn't bother with "be careful" or "watch your back" good-byes. "Call me if you need anything."

"All I need is a texted image of Raymond Drexler. Dead or alive."

"Consider it done."

In her rental car, she wove through the center of Salt Lake City, managing to hit every red light until she exited onto the I-80 west ramp and wound down Amelia Earhart Drive to the gated entrance of the FBI office.

She'd been working out of this office since she arrived in Utah ten days ago and had barely been around enough for the receptionist to recognize her. She showed her badge. "I've paperwork waiting."

"Pulled it just now." She handed Kate a stack of papers. "I thought you'd be headed home soon. Heck of a find last week."

"Maybe I'll be home in time for Christmas."

She'd not been to her apartment in Washington in almost six weeks. Times like this, she wondered why she kept a place near Quantico, Virginia. In the eighteen months she'd leased the small apartment, she'd spent about a month's worth of nights there. Chasing the wicked never stopped.

She found a conference room and, shrugging off her backpack, located a coffeepot. An hour later, she received a call from Mazur.

"I'm still reviewing the case notes," she said as way of a hello.

"When are you coming?"

She ignored the question. "Do not speak to the press, and keep as many details quiet about this case as possible. If and when the media is addressed, I'll tell you what to say."

"I've no intention of speaking to the press." Again, his tone was even, steady, and steely.

"But they do have their place, and we might need them. Also, if an attorney by the name of Mark Westin calls, know that he's representing Dr. Charles Richardson, who has been arrested in one of the Samaritan shootings. Do not speak to him."

"Not my first party, Doctor." No edge sharpening the words, but he was firm.

It was natural to resent outside assistance in a high-profile case. Many local cops saw her as a threat. But she wasn't, of course, if they did their jobs well. "I'm simply conveying facts."

"When are you going to arrive in San Antonio?" Mazur asked.

She pulled up the airline flights. "There's a five a.m. flight out of Salt Lake that will put me in San Antonio at eight a.m. your time."

"I'll meet you at the airport."

"I'm familiar with San Antonio. I can rent a car."

"It'll save us both time if I pick you up."

Us. Both. He was already using words of team building and unity.

Outside of her FBI team, there was no *us* or *both*. However, no need to press the point. She'd give him this one. "Understood."

***

In front of him were four television sets, each playing a different broadcast. The evening news would be on soon, and he expected some mention of the crime. The last three Samaritan killings had stirred up concern and hysteria and were widely covered by the press. However, there had been next to no coverage on his killing so far.

While he waited for the broadcasts to begin, he replayed the video of last night's shooting. Each time he watched it, a thrill of excitement snapped through his body. It had been some time since he'd fired a weapon and watched someone die. He feared the old excitement and pleasure might have faded, but the sensations had hit him with full force when Gloria looked at him with such utter happiness and relief. Her savior had arrived. The entire experience was priceless.

And, as he raised the gun and pointed it at her, Gloria's smile had vanished. Facing death had been sobering, but she'd not cried or wailed. He'd found her composure vaguely disappointing, hoping at the end she would break. Beg. Plead. But she'd not done any of that. She was proud to the end.

Still, even without the tears, the feeling of superiority had been potent.

He'd been so juiced after the killing. He came home, stripped, and bagged his clothes. He'd showered, rinsing the blood spatter from his face, dried off, and changed into clean clothes. He'd tossed the towel in with the clothes and buried the bag on his property.

After, he'd poured himself a strong drink. When the booze hadn't taken the edge off, he'd ordered a hooker online: small, blond, and young, the way he liked them.

She'd met him at his home. Perhaps not the wisest choice, but he'd needed to exorcise the energy. When she'd arrived, she'd tried to look confident, but she was nervous. Her fear had jacked him up more, and he'd kept her for several hours. She'd left with a couple of grand in her purse, rope burns on her wrists, and lashes on her back.

That should have calmed him. But as he sat here, he felt the energy building again as he replayed the tape, watching the woman's smile fade, the gunfire, and the body recoil.

"It was a beautiful and elegant death."

He sat back and savored the feeling before he shifted his gaze to the two other screens, which broadcasted live feeds from cameras monitoring the living rooms of the next victims. There was Coffee Shop Woman and Law School Girl. He'd get to those two in time.

He leaned closer to one of the monitors. She wasn't home yet, no doubt still working in her shop. They'd crossed paths several times, and he liked her pretty smile. She smelled of perfumed soap and peppermint, and it was easy to think of her as innocent. But she was not.

"Soon, Coffee Shop Woman."

The evening anchors covered a robbery, a mall fashion show, and a dammed high school football game. Finally the anchor cut to a reporter on the side of the interstate. The neatly coiffed woman was on the other side of the highway, standing on the northbound access road, a good distance from the car.

He leaned forward and in the background saw police milling around the site as the reporter talked about an unexplained death.

"Unexplained, my ass. She was shot in the chest."

On another television, Channel Two projected Gloria's face. As the newscaster listed off her accomplishments, images appeared of her with politicians, school children, and in front of her car dealership.

Why hadn't the cops told the media more?

Gloria wasn't some low-class hooker or a junkie. She was the kind of woman people missed. All he could surmise was that the cops were scrambling as they tried to figure out if they'd arrested the wrong man or if there was another Samaritan. He didn't care if they were confused or bumbling around as long as they'd spoken to Kate. The point of the text was to alert Kate. She was the one who needed to be on the scene. It wasn't right if she wasn't in the mix.

Frustrated, he rose and paced around the room. He flexed his fingers as he tried to expel the nervous energy cutting through his body. Times like this, it was all he could do to contain the feelings and racing thoughts. He paced. Clenched and unclenched his fingers.

It would be so easy to upload the video he'd taken and show the world what he'd done. His footage would send a ripple effect through the city, the state, and even the country. The Samaritan would again be feared and respected. Think of the panic!

But as tempting as it was, he paused.

He didn't care about publicity or public fear. The goal was to control one particular person. He had to believe his text had reached Dr. Kate Hayden and she'd soon return to San Antonio.

This game, like chess, had to be played patiently and carefully. He didn't need to rush. All the pieces were in position, ready to play. Though the media wasn't covering him yet, they soon would.

He picked up the worn notebook, flipped to one of the last clean pages, and scribbled down the day's date.

You have no idea how long I have planned our meeting, Kate. It has been a long journey, and now the final match is upon us.

He studied the note and circled the word *final* several times with a steady hand.

It was a matter of time before Kate's return home.

CHAPTER FOUR

Her smile is sweet, and she thinks her sins are a secret.
But I know them all.

San Antonio, Texas
Monday, November 27, 7:45 a.m.

Mazur stood at Gate 6 in the San Antonio airport, knowing that Dr. Hayden's flight was several minutes early. He'd gotten home a few hours ago to shower, change, and grab a quick breakfast before coming here. Most of the night had been spent dealing with the chain of command, who were scrambling to handle a high-profile murder that they feared could go radioactive if the video clip hit the Internet.

His phone rang, and he was ready to send it to voicemail when he saw his daughter's name. "Hey, kiddo. You ready for the math test today?"

"Yeah," Alyssa said with a dramatic sigh.

Some of the fatigue bled away. "You sound disappointed."

"It won't be much of a challenge."

He rolled his neck, feeling his vertebrae crack. "Why do you say that?"

"Because all we've done is go over stuff I've already learned. I'm not crazy about this school, Dad."

It was an expensive private school, one of the best, which Sherry had insisted on. His pride had taken a knock because he wasn't the one providing for his daughter, but he knew the school would be good for Alyssa. "Then I'll talk to your teacher and get you bumped up a grade."

"Dad, *no*. I'm making friends in this class."

"You'll make friends in the new class." He was only half teasing.

"Dad, do *not* call my teacher."

He'd have pushed the point two years ago when she was in the school he was paying for. Alyssa was smart, and he wanted the best for her. "Understood. Is Mom driving you to school today?"

"Yes. She's getting dressed. She has a big meeting this afternoon."

His ex had warned him that San Antonio might not be her last stop in her climb up the ladder, but he'd still downshifted his career and moved south anyway.

"Good. Nice that you and Mom have this time in the morning."

"She's always on the phone. Her boss has already called once."

He swallowed bitter frustration. He'd asked his ex to let Alyssa stay in Chicago with him, but she'd refused, claiming his schedule was too unpredictable. And when he pressed, she'd confessed she couldn't lose another child. "She loves you. And things will settle down with her job."

"Yeah, I guess. Dad, don't change my class. No more changes right now, okay?"

The note of worry told him more than he'd expected from the call. Sherry must have made more noises about another move. She'd said nothing to him, but then communication between them had been shit since she'd moved out.

"I promise, Alyssa."

"Thanks, Dad."

The boarding agent opened the door to the sky bridge. "I don't hear enthusiasm. Remember, if you frown too much you might end up looking like me. Not good, kiddo."

"True. That would so not be good."

He liked his kid. She was as tough as him, maybe tougher. "What about the chess tournament?"

"I'm studying moves and practicing. There're a couple of games scheduled this afternoon at the library I might sit in on."

"Chess is your thing, kid. You're one of the best."

"Coach says I'm too aggressive."

"Take it as a compliment. Strategy can be taught. Aggression cannot." He checked his watch. "I've got to meet an incoming plane."

"Who?"

"FBI agent."

"Can you talk about it?"

"Not yet."

"Will you tell me later?" she asked.

Mazur worked hard to put distance between his work and family. "Maybe."

"I'm not a baby, Dad. I'm fourteen. You can tell me stuff now."

"Don't grow up too fast. I'll call after school and see how the test went."

"Stop worrying."

"Cut me some slack. It's hard seeing you grow up."

She groaned, but it was tinged with affection. "Okay. Love you."

"Love you, kiddo."

He rang off, wondering for the hundredth time if he was doing any of this fatherhood stuff correctly. There was a time when he'd thought he had it all figured out. Now, he had no idea.

He glanced at his phone and did a Web search for *Dr. Kate Hayden*, knowing at least on the job he was making a difference.

The search engine pulled up several video clips of the profiler as she stood at a podium with local law enforcement standing behind her. She'd worked several high-profile serial cases over the last five years. He chose the most recent, which dated back eight months and related to the last Samaritan killing.

"We don't know how he chooses his victims," she said. *"All the women were in their midthirties to early forties, and all worked in the service industry. We do know he disables the victims' vehicles while they're at a convenience store near I-35, and then he follows them until they're forced to pull over. I'm encouraging all travelers to check their cars before getting back on the road, especially if their destination is along I-35."*

Mazur hit the "Pause" button and studied Kate Hayden's mop of brown shoulder-length hair, which curled at her shoulders. Her trim, petite body and young voice didn't fit the FBI mold.

More searching painted the picture of a woman in her early thirties who graduated top of her class from the University of Virginia and earned her master's and doctorate degrees in linguistics from Yale by the age of twenty-seven. She had been working with the FBI for nearly seven years. Though she'd been associated with the high-profile cases, for the most part, she stayed in the background.

The first of the deplaning Salt Lake passengers appeared, and Mazur shoved his phone in his pocket as he waited for her. A dozen or so people filed off the plane before the short brunette appeared rolling a single carry-on with a worn backpack slung over her shoulder. Her slim figure was partially masked by a baggy black suit jacket, slacks, and white collared shirt. Her light-brown hair hung loosely around her shoulders, accentuating high cheekbones and a slightly sunburned face.

Walking with Dr. Hayden was an elderly woman. Dr. Hayden smiled as she pointed down the terminal, speaking until the woman nodded and walked off. The doctor quickly dropped her gaze to her phone and scrolled through what must have been emails that had accumulated during the flight.

When she looked up, her gaze searched and settled on him. She crossed to him as if they'd already met. "Detective Mazur."

"I look that much like a cop?"

She barely blinked. "You do."

If not for the suit, he'd never have nailed her as a Fed. She looked younger than her thirty-plus years, and picturing her small frame chasing a bad guy almost made him smile. "You need to make any stops before we hit the road?"

"No. Thank you. I assume the autopsy is still scheduled for this morning."

"It is." He checked his watch. "They're waiting on us, so when we can get there, they'll start. The victim was well known in the local business community. She had many friends on the city council and in state government." He reached for the handle of the suitcase. "I can take that for you."

"You don't have to."

Jesus, he hoped she was not one of those hard-assed feminists. "This is Texas."

"You're from Chicago."

"Accent gave it away?"

"Yes."

"When in Rome." That seemed explanation enough for her, and she allowed him to take the suitcase. He guided her through the busy airport and toward ground transportation and the parking deck. The November sun was already high in the sky, and the weatherman was promising another warm day.

"Different than Virginia, I imagine."

"I haven't been home in six weeks. Utah was my last stop. But I understand the leaves are changing in Virginia."

The hints of warmth he'd seen as she'd spoken to the old woman were gone. The pleasantry was spoken almost as an afterthought, as if she'd memorized the phrases from an FBI handbook on conversation.

Her small stature belied her stiff tone. And if he wasn't off the mark on his action heroes, she also wore a Wonder Woman bracelet.

But warm and fuzzy wasn't what he was looking for just now. He needed this case solved.

She had to move quickly to match his pace, and he slowed as they crossed the large parking lot. He clicked the lock open to a black SUV, raised the back hatch, and loaded her bags inside. She slid into the passenger seat, gazing again at her phone. As he settled behind the steering wheel, she typed a quick response, then fastened her seat belt.

"I understand the evidence you have on Richardson for two of the Samaritan murders is solid. Anything in his background to suggest an accomplice?"

"My profile of Dr. Richardson suggests that he's a loner despite appearing gregarious and outgoing. Outside of work-related activities, he mixes with no one. No wife, no girlfriend, no buddies. A forensic sweep of his computers revealed no other contacts. If he'd not texted me from his secretary's phone, I'm not sure when we would have caught him."

"Maybe he has fans?"

"Possibly. Likely, even." Absently, she touched the Wonder Woman bracelet on her wrist.

She tossed him a practiced smile and glanced out the window as he drove toward town. "The area has changed a lot in the last five years."

"I hear the growth has been good for the city."

She looked at him. "I'm not good at polite conversation."

"Really?" He appreciated the honesty, even if it was ham-fisted.

"I'll warn you now that I'm painfully honest at times. *Abrupt, rude,* and *bitch* have all been adjectives attached to me before."

"I'll take a straight shooter any day."

"Remember that when I become annoying, because that moment always arrives."

For a Fed, she was okay. "Noted."

"Do you know why she was going to Laredo?"

"There's no other reason than to visit her mother, who's in a nursing home. The company owned a dealership down there but sold it last summer. She visited her mother just last weekend."

"Was she having an affair?"

"Her husband says they had a good marriage."

"Do you believe him?"

He shook his head. "If they didn't he was likely the last to know."

"Why she was traveling on I-35 doesn't really matter. What would have mattered to someone who thinks of himself as the Samaritan is that she was driving alone on his own personal hunting ground."

"Samaritan. Hell of a nickname. When did the press start calling him Samaritan?"

"After the second killing," she said. "An eyewitness later said she passed a disabled motorist who was being helped by another man. When she slowed, the man waved her off and gave her the thumbs up as if he had the situation under control."

"If I remember my Bible, the Samaritans were outcasts and considered the unclean."

"That's correct," she said.

"Richardson sees himself as an outcast. I get that. But what is *good* about what he does?"

She shrugged. "Somewhere in his mind, he's a positive force to be reckoned with."

"How so? Do any of the victims have a history of abuse or trouble? Does he feel the need to end their suffering?"

She tilted her head and rubbed the side of her neck. "Two of the victims were divorced, but there was no history of domestic abuse. Another victim had some credit card debt but hardly crushing. Another had a son in juvenile detention. They had issues in their lives but nothing that was overwhelming enough to draw the notice of an outsider."

"You said they were in the service industries. Was there a common client?"

"None that I found. All the victims lived in different cities that were hundreds of miles apart."

"The final killing was last year?"

"That's correct. And Richardson was arrested six months ago."

Mazur took Loop 410 onto Babcock Road and wound his way toward the Bexar County Medical Examiner's office located in the University of Texas Health Science Center. He parked and they got out. The three-story building was constructed of plain reddish stone with smoked glass windows. Like most law enforcement offices, it could easily be overlooked by anyone driving by.

"I'll need my backpack," she said.

"Sure." As she reached for it, he was tempted to offer to carry it, but sensed that despite her small stature she was not the type to accept help gladly. As she slung the bag onto her shoulder, he wondered why he'd put so much thought into a simple exchange.

"Are there vending machines in the building or a place where I could grab a sandwich?" she asked.

"There is a small café on the third floor. You can get the basics there."

She checked her watch. "I shouldn't hold you up long."

"Better you eat. Five minutes here or there won't matter. Let's get inside."

He escorted her to the café, where she ordered a coffee and a bagel. When she paid and turned away, he couldn't help but ask, "That's it?"

"It'll get me through."

He ordered and paid for a cup of coffee. "Okay."

She sipped her coffee as they sat down at a table. "I would like to also see the crime scene and examine the victim's car. I noticed from the photos you sent me that the victim had bought coffee and chocolate. Do you know where she stopped?"

"A purchase receipt in the car was doused in blood and hard to read. I've got uniforms checking the nearby exits."

"The caliber of the Samaritan's gun, what the shooter was wearing, the way he disabled the cars were all posted on the Internet. So anyone could have copied him."

"Have you had copycat killings?"

"There was one man in Kansas City who attempted it. He shot and killed his wife. Tracing his cell phone GPS put him at the crime scene and the shooting. And he stood to inherit a lot of money if his wife died. He thought he was clever, but he was sloppy."

"Getting away with murder isn't as easy as it looks."

"No." She finished off her bagel and sipped her coffee.

"So I've an imposter on my hands?"

"I don't know. We'll first need to dig deep into the victim's past. Is there anyone who wants her dead?"

"I plan to look into that as soon as this exam is over."

"I'd like to accompany you as you investigate Gloria Sanchez's background. It'll help me make a determination faster."

"Sure." His phone chirped with a text from the medical examiner, and he responded back. "Dr. Ryland is ready for us."

She took one last sip of coffee and stood. "I'm ready."

Both tossed their cups, and she followed him to a bank of elevators at the end of the hallway. When the doors opened, they stepped inside and he pressed the button to the basement. She stood ramrod straight and made no effort at conversation. He supposed this type of antisocial quirkiness was part of a brilliant mind. Warm and fuzzy didn't figure into the Kate Hayden equation.

The familiar antiseptic smell filled the air of the autopsy suite. He'd seen more autopsies than he could count and had developed a detachment to death until Caleb had died. Since then, he found it harder to see the body on the table as evidence.

They moved down the gray tiled hallway under the ultra-bright lights toward Dr. Grant Ryland's office. He knocked twice on the closed door.

"Come in." The doctor's voice was deep and gravelly and perfectly fit the tall, broad-shouldered Texan who'd played center for the University of Texas fifteen years ago. Dr. Ryland looked up from a stack of papers and tugged off dark-rimmed glasses as he rose and came around the desk. "Detective."

"Thanks for working us in today, Doc. I'd like to introduce you to Dr. Kate Hayden with the FBI."

Dr. Ryland extended his hand to Kate. "Dr. Hayden."

Her grip appeared strong, and her eye contact had laser precision. "Dr. Ryland."

"This case is a hot one, Dr. Ryland," Mazur said. The fact that he'd landed a high-profile case had pissed off the detectives who wanted the attention and pleased the ones who had been waiting for him to get enough rope to hang himself. "Everyone from the governor's office down to my captain wants it solved."

Dr. Ryland shifted to Kate. "Anything I should be looking for when I autopsy the patient?"

"The Samaritan's bullet of choice is a 9 mm hollow point. He shoots one bullet to the heart, which does maximum damage as the bullet mushrooms on impact. My primary concern is the ballistics, which will tell me if this victim was shot with the Samaritan's gun."

"The Samaritan's gun was never recovered, correct?" Mazur asked.

"It was not," she said.

"Did all the Samaritan victims die immediately?"

"They were all shot in their cars and were dead within seconds. The medical teams estimated that each, with their catastrophic injuries, had bled out within half an hour to an hour." She touched the middle of her breastbone. "He targets the same area every time. Even though nearly point-blank, it's harder than you think to consistently hit the same area on a living target."

"Has Richardson hinted to why he chose a bullet he knew would shred his victims' hearts?" Mazur asked.

"He hasn't confessed to the killings. He still maintains his innocence," she said.

"I thought men like him enjoy talking about their crimes," Mazur said.

"He's not ready to talk," she said. "He would like to be freed and to kill again."

"Let's have a look," Dr. Ryland suggested.

The trio found their way to the locker rooms. As Mazur stripped off his coat and hung it in a locker, Dr. Hayden tugged off the large windbreaker, revealing a trim waist and full breasts. She quickly tugged on a gown, which swallowed up her small, very fit frame.

She rolled up the sleeves twice before they reached her wrist. With her hair clipped back and tucked in a cap, her face looked sterner. He suspected she understood a softer hairstyle and eye-catching figure weren't necessarily assets when dealing with law enforcement and sociopaths, both groups searching for weakness.

Another set of rooms led to the autopsy suite, equipped with four workstations, each outfitted with a stainless-steel table mounted to a large sink. A collection of instruments was lined up on a counter beside the sink. There was a whiteboard for notes, and across the room a CD player softly played country music.

The sheet-clad body of Gloria Sanchez was wheeled into the room on a gurney and positioned before Dr. Ryland's station.

The technician opened a sterile pack of instruments for the doctor and switched on the overhead light and microphone. Everyone donned eye protection.

Dr. Ryland pulled back the sheet just enough to reveal the pale drawn features of Gloria Sanchez's face. Her head rested in a cradle placed under the base of her neck. Her dark hair had been washed and brushed flat and her makeup removed.

He'd watched some of her car commercials on YouTube last night. All featured Gloria decked out in some kind of fancy outfit as she moved easily between rows of cars and pitched the latest deal. *Christmas in July. End of the Year Blowout.* She was comfortable on camera and seemed to relish its attention. There were other clips of her on local television as she discussed fundraisers she sponsored or the latest charity drive.

She was flamboyance and showmanship rolled into a tight, seductive bundle. She clearly enjoyed the limelight.

He refocused on the still, lifeless face now stippled with small brown spots, the skin drooping. In the nearly thirty-four hours since she'd died, rigor mortis had come and gone. If left alone, her belly would soon bloat as the microorganisms broke down all the tissues in her body. In a Chicago winter she would remain fairly intact for months. In Texas heat, her flesh would be stripped to bones in two weeks.

Dr. Ryland pulled back the sheet. The blood had been washed away from the single chest wound resting squarely between her enhanced breasts. The bullet hole didn't look savage or destructive, but if this killer had used a hollow-point bullet like the Samaritan, then her insides would be hamburger.

The doctor took several pictures for his files before tugging the microphone down a little closer to his mouth. He stated the date and time, named the victim, and listed the personnel present at the autopsy. "The technician pulled hair fibers from her body when prepping it for autopsy. The samples have been bagged and sent to the Forensic Department."

"Good," Mazur said.

After a detailed external examination, which inventoried a couple of scars on her left leg, an appendix scar, and a scroll tattoo at the base of her spine, he reached for the scalpel and made a Y-incision above her breasts and down the center of her stomach to her belly.

Kate watched without blinking as the doctor peeled away the flesh and cracked the exposed rib cage with a set of bone cutters. A couple of times she leaned in to get a better look, lingering until she was satisfied.

When Dr. Ryland lifted the rib cage away and set it beside the body, Kate tilted her head as she peered into the body cavity.

Dr. Ryland pointed to where the heart should be. The destruction was total. "No doubt a hollow point. Death was immediate."

"Why aim for the heart?" Mazur asked.

"There's symbolism in that," said Dr. Hayden. "I believe each woman reminded Dr. Richardson of a mother, wife, or lover. He doesn't damage their faces, but he obliterates their hearts."

"What's Richardson's love life look like?" Mazur asked.

"I've not been able to identify any girlfriends. He did frequent prostitutes, though none I spoke to reported any violent behavior."

"What about his mother?"

"She died when he was seventeen. No reports of abuse, but she was arrested for prostitution several times. There appears to be no other family to interview," Kate said.

Dr. Ryland probed his scalpel into eviscerated muscle until he located a flower-shaped slug. He dropped it into a stainless-steel pan for the detective to study.

"It's a hollow point," Mazur concurred. The slug had bloomed into razor-sharp petals, which on impact delivered all its kinetic energy to the target rather than punching cleanly through it. "It did its job. Ripped her apart."

Kate frowned as she stared at the slug. "Disturbing."

"You worried about your arrest now?" Mazur challenged.

She shook her head. "Richardson's attorney, Mark Westin, will use this to his client's advantage. Mr. Westin is always looking for an advantage when he bargains."

It always sucked when the guilty walked. "Whoever is copying your guy is doing a good job," Mazur said.

"Yes, he is," she said.

When Dr. Ryland examined the patient's uterus, he paused. "She had uterine cancer. The mass is significant and has metastasized. I don't think major medical intervention would have saved her."

"Is that a first?" Mazur asked.

"None of the other victims had cancer." Kate studied the woman's manicured hand. "They also didn't come from money as she clearly did. How old was she?"

"Thirty-nine," Mazur said.

"She looks older," Kate noted.

"She might have hidden the effects of her illness with makeup, but that would've soon changed," Dr. Ryland said. He studied the blue-green veins trailing her arms. "There's no sign of needles used for chemo or scars from surgery."

"Could the killer have known she was sick?" Mazur asked.

"I don't know," Kate said.

Dr. Ryland continued his examination of the subject's remains. There were no indications of recent trauma to the body. An X-ray revealed an old break and damage to her right knee, likely some early arthritis. There was no indication of sexual assault; however, he did find traces of semen in her vaginal cavity. She'd had consensual sex within twenty-four hours of her death. The samples were sent off for DNA testing.

The doctor shook his head. "Sexual intercourse wouldn't have been comfortable given the size of her cancerous tumor."

"Research shows sex is an affirmation of life," Kate said. "Run a toxicology screen. If she was as sick as you say, then she'd have needed heavy-duty meds to function. Dr. Ryland, will you call her doctor to see if she was under treatment?"

"Of course."

"Again, the victim's medical history was not the motivator for Richardson. Her driving on the interstate was enough," Kate said. "Again the ballistics report will be key."

The doctor concluded the autopsy, repacked the organs, and sewed up the chest. The examination had taken over four hours. "I'll keep you two posted."

"Thanks," Mazur said.

Mazur and Dr. Hayden moved to the outer locker room, stripped off their gowns, and met in the hallway. She dumped her surgical gown in the bin and reached for her backpack.

"So where do we go from here?" Mazur asked.

"Get me a strong cup of coffee and a conference room, and I'll brief you and your team on the Samaritan killings."

CHAPTER FIVE

We met in the café near the River Walk. I wanted peo-
ple to see us together and know that I can be fun and
kind. Especially when I want something.

San Antonio, Texas
Monday, November 27, 2:30 p.m.

Fatigue crept into Kate's limbs during the short drive between the medical examiner's office and the criminal justice building. Sugar and caffeine had kept her fueled for a short while, but until she had a decent
night's sleep, outrunning the exhaustion would be hard.

Out of the car, backpack on her shoulder, she followed Mazur to
the building where the police department was headquartered. After
another set of stairs, she arrived in the bull pen of the investigation unit.

The floor resembled countless other police department jurisdictions she'd visited. The same drab cubicles lined the walls, and similar
desks paired in half a dozen sets took up the center of the room. Worn
chairs for the detectives and slightly older ones for suspects had her
wondering what national clearinghouse supplied all these law enforcement agencies.

Fluorescent bulbs hummed above, casting an unnaturally bright light, and blended with the familiar sounds of phones ringing, chair hinges squeaking, and the jumble of quiet conversations and intermittent heated exchanges. Common smells of aftershave, bottom-of-the-pot coffee, and an occasional unwashed perp all collided to create their own unique funk.

She suspected the break room came equipped with vending machines to sustain cops during an investigation's long hours. If she wasn't dropping quarters and selecting chocolate or crackers, she was ordering a burger at a drive-through. High stress and long hours on the go mixed with sugary carbohydrates, smoking, and little exercise made for the perfect heart-attack cocktail.

Mazur was fit, and his trim waist was either a stunning stroke of genetic good luck or the result of self-discipline. She guessed the latter. His bearing and cropped hair suggested military service. His age she guessed to be late thirties or early forties, and a subtly confident swagger implied he'd been a cop for at least ten to fifteen years. He knew his job and didn't need to prove himself to anyone.

She noted no wedding band on his left ring finger, but many cops didn't wear a band. Less the world knew about them the better. Still, without realizing it, Mazur occasionally ran his thumb over the back of that finger. She suspected a recent divorce, which jived with the fit body. More time on his hands mixed with anger issues.

His clothes were neat, crisp, and in accordance with his salary: off the rack. He cared about his appearance because it instilled discipline, not because he was fussy. No signs of a tattoo, but of course the suit hid much, and calluses on his palms and his deep tan suggested he liked the outdoors.

"I require a fresh pot of coffee," she said. "If you point me in the right direction, I can make it myself."

"You're right to be cautious. These guys don't know how to make it."

"Few do, but I've mastered a variety of machines and make an excellent cup."

"That bravado, Dr. Hayden?" he asked.

"Do I strike you as a person given to exaggeration?" she asked.

A slight grin tugged the edges of his lips. "No, Dr. Hayden, you do not. I'm going to gather the troops," Mazur said.

"Perfect."

He was teasing her again. Establishing a rapport between them was important. Humor was his icebreaker. Coffee was one of her bonding strategies. Most cops lived on the sludge that passed for coffee, and a decent cup of joe was always a welcome treat.

A few officers glanced up from their work at her, and she sensed the judging process was underway. There were no smiles or welcoming comments, but frowns and a few eye rolls. No one relished bringing a Fed into his or her shop. Pride ran high in law enforcement, and no one wanted to admit they couldn't handle the job. The fact that Mazur had brought her in so quickly suggested an open-mindedness that his colleagues didn't share.

In the break room she passed the dented vending machine and set her backpack in a chair. She quickly cleaned out the black coating in the coffeepot and reloaded the machine. Soon fresh coffee perked. She moved to the machine and fished her credit card from her pocket. She chose crackers and a chocolate bar.

As the machine burbled, she washed the mugs in the sink and wiped down the counter. She chose the most generic mug, guessing it didn't belong to any individual. There were few transgressions worse than taking a man's coffee mug.

When Mazur reappeared she was sitting at a table, eating the chocolate bar and sipping coffee. Beside him was a tall redhead. She was early to midthirties with pale freckled skin, and she wore skinny jeans with a loose white blouse tucked only on her right side and brown cowboy boots. The identification badge hanging around her neck read *Detective Jane Palmer*.

Palmer and Mazur were an interesting mix. While Mazur appeared to be by the book, Palmer looked as if she didn't mind bending a rule or two. She was fit and, judging by her straight posture, proud of it.

"Dr. Hayden," Mazur said. "This is my partner, Detective Jane Palmer."

Detective Palmer extended her hand to Kate. "Pleasure to meet you. Sorry I missed you at the autopsy this morning. I was stuck in court."

Kate shook her hand, noting smooth palms and trim French-manicured nails. No sign of a wedding ring, but a gold-and-onyx college ring winked on her right hand. "Pleasure to meet you."

"I hear, and can now smell, that you know how to make coffee," Detective Palmer said. "That's a prized commodity in this shop." She moved to the counter and picked up a blue Disney *Frozen* mug. "And you clean. I could marry anyone who cleans." She paused to sip. "And makes great coffee." She nudged Mazur hard in the ribs with her elbow. "Why don't you ever make me coffee? You've been here six months and not one cup for me."

Mazur shrugged. Six months. So he was newer to the team than she'd realized. Perhaps the cool reception they'd received wasn't just a product of her presence. He was an outsider who'd brought in a Fed. She'd bet money his hire had sent ripples through this department, and though he was still in the proving stage of the job, he didn't seem to care about winning points with his associates. His heart was not rooted to this squad or this city.

"What's your secret to a great cup of coffee?" Detective Palmer asked.

"Cleaning the pot and machine," Kate said.

Detective Palmer laughed as she shook her head. "Who'd have thought?" Palmer's phone chimed with a text. She glanced at the words and frowned. "Dr. Hayden, you're the wordsmith, right?"

"Forensic linguistics is my specialty."

"What do you say to a guy who texts, *I might have time this weekend to see you?*"

Each detective had his or her own style of breaking the ice. While Mazur appeared easygoing and patient, Palmer used humor to build alliances. "Might? Does he have a job that keeps him on call?" Kate asked.

She cocked a brow. "He's an accountant."

"It's not tax season." Kate stared at Palmer. "You know what he's saying."

Palmer nodded, eyes narrowing. "But how do I respond?"

"Tell him, 'Making plans and with luck we might catch up. Have a great week.' And add an emoji. A smiley face."

Palmer typed the words, then hesitated. "The smiley face isn't my style."

"It's effective."

"Dating 101 over?" Mazur asked as he filled a paper cup with coffee.

Palmer shrugged, pushed a few buttons, and slid the phone in her back pocket. "Just because you don't care about a love life, Mazur, doesn't mean the rest of us live a monastic existence."

He stiffened a fraction as he filled his own cup. "The other detectives and cops are headed into the briefing room."

"Of course," Kate said.

She followed them into the windowless briefing room equipped with rows of chairs and desks, a podium for the speaker, and a whiteboard on the wall. Ten other officers, all in suits, filed into the room. Two older cops took seats in the front. They each had short gray hair, wore sport jackets, no ties, with khakis and cowboy boots. They were the veterans of the squad, the ones who didn't welcome change. A couple of other young detectives, who were introduced to her as Santos and Davis, stood in the back, arms folded. They were the young bucks in the proving stages of their careers. Still hungry, still aggressive, and most likely hadn't been happy when an older, more experienced detective from Chicago had joined their team.

Kate arranged files on the table beside the podium just as a six-foot-three man with white hair and a thick mustache entered the room. He wore a gray suit and cowboy boots.

"Mind telling me what a serial killer is doing in my jurisdiction, Agent Hayden?" the man asked.

"And you are?" Kate slid on dark-rimmed glasses.

"Chief Luke Saunders," the man replied.

"He runs the show," Mazur said. His tone shifted, not quite deferential, but respectful and suggestive of a paternal relationship. The chief, she guessed, had been the one to buck protocol and hire the outsider.

"I'm not sure what you have yet," she said.

"I thought you'd locked up this clown," the chief said.

"I have. You have a copycat or an accomplice."

The chief cursed. "So we're the lucky sons of bitches."

"That's correct," Kate said.

The chief frowned. "This isn't PC, but I'm asking the question anyway. How old are you?"

"I'm thirty-four." She spoke loud enough for everyone in the room to hear. "And in case you're wondering, I have a size five shoe and I wear a petite four in dresses. I'm five foot two and weigh one hundred and one pounds as of my last physical. If any of you have other questions or remarks about my size, please go ahead and ask now."

The chief eyed her, then grinned. "I like you. You've got grit."

Kate's gaze did not waver. "Thank you."

The chief took a seat in the front row and folded his arms over his chest. "Go ahead and get us up to speed."

Until Mazur's call yesterday, she'd been almost certain Charles Richardson had acted alone. She had suspected it was a matter of time before she found evidence linking him to the three other killings and disproving any theories that there could be a second shooter. Now, she had no choice but to admit he hadn't been working alone. What, or rather who, had she missed when she'd been digging into Richardson's background?

She lowered her gaze to her files, which were organized to the point of OCD. She'd been teased about them more times than her size, but she wasn't concerned. Given her constant travel, the system enabled her to juggle multiple cases at one time. She set up her computer and prepped it to show slides.

Mazur moved beside Kate, and the room grew quiet. "This is Dr. Kate Hayden with the FBI." He ran through her credentials and explained why he'd called her. "I'll turn it over to you, Dr. Hayden."

"Thank you, Detective Mazur," Kate said.

No welcomes, no smiles, no nods came from the group, so she pulled a green color-coded file marked *Samaritan*. Moving toward the whiteboard with it, she removed a picture of the first Samaritan victim and attached it to the whiteboard with a piece of tape. She repeated the process four more times until images of the five women were lined up in a neat column that stretched from the top to the bottom of the board.

She pointed to the first picture, which featured an attractive blonde with a lean face who wore heavy eye makeup and large gold hoop earrings. "Victim one was Delores Canon, a forty-one-year-old waitress who was shot on a deserted stretch of road fifty miles south of Duluth, Minnesota. She was last seen at a Quick Mart gas station, where she filled her tank and bought a bag of potato chips and a soda. That was May 1, 2015. A video of the shooting was texted to a phone left on the victim's lap. When local authorities inspected her car, they discovered a rag shoved in the exhaust. Initially, suspicion turned to her estranged boyfriend, but he was cleared after he proved he was in California during the shooting. The gas receipt put her at the service station an hour before her death; however, surveillance cameras at that station weren't operational. There were no witnesses to the shooting. The case soon went cold."

She pointed to the next image. "Nearly the exact same scenario played out in the next four cases. All these women were Caucasian with dark hair. They all worked in the service industry, from waitress to manicurist to dental technician. In each case, video footage of the murders was texted to a disposable phone." She selected a computer image that displayed a compilation of the victims' cars. "They all are white or silver."

Palmer folded her arms. "Could it be as simple as the color of their car?"

"Maybe," Kate said. She detailed the evidence she had on Richardson.

"Why would he send a text from his secretary's phone?" the chief asked. "Sloppy, given how careful he was before."

"I think he had become overconfident," Kate said.

"Did you find any video footage of the victims' shootings on any of his cell phones or computers?"

"No," Kate said.

"And no confession yet," Mazur said.

"Richardson still denies any wrongdoing," Kate said.

"He sure as hell didn't shoot Gloria Sanchez," Palmer said. "Maybe Richardson was set up by someone else."

When word of the shooting reached Richardson's lawyer, a frame-up would be his primary argument. "I can definitely link him to two of the shootings."

"We know Richardson isn't the San Antonio shooter, so let's keep the focus on *our guy*," Palmer said. "Like the Samaritan or *Samaritans*, our guy gets his rocks off helping women and then shooting them. Gloria Sanchez was no damsel in distress and could take care of herself. How did a stranger on a deserted highway win her over?"

"In the video, there's a glimpse of a blue van parked behind Sanchez's car," Mazur said. "I've put a call into robbery about missing or stolen blue vans. A minivan screams family guy a woman can trust."

"The van at your crime scene fits the Samaritan's profile," Kate said. "Richardson used not only a van with an infant car seat, but also a station wagon. These two vehicles were both stolen."

There was a rumble around the room.

"Was there ever a case of a Samaritan who fit the killer's MO helping a woman and not shooting them?" Mazur asked. "Sometimes guys like to have practice runs before they get their nerve up for the kill."

"We had several women who insisted the Samaritan had stopped and helped them on I-35. Each swore he fixed the problem and wished her a good night. They all met with police sketch artists. According to local law enforcement none resembled Richardson—however, one may be your shooter, so I'll have them sent here."

Several officers in the room murmured and shifted their stances, but none made a statement.

"What was different about the women who weren't shot?" asked Detective Palmer.

"Nothing. They all fit the profile."

"Gloria Sanchez doesn't fit the victim profile," Palmer said.

"No, she does not," Kate said. "She's affluent and well connected, though I understand she was driving an older car that may have caught the killer's attention."

"The Samaritan progressively moved south and never killed twice in one jurisdiction," Mazur said. "Safe to assume this killer will maintain the pattern?"

"Yes. If your killer sticks to script and continues to kill, he'll strike again farther south," she said.

"He only has a few hundred more miles before he's worked the length of I-35," Mazur said. "What happens when he runs out of road?"

"I don't know," Kate said.

"So what's next?" the chief asked.

She removed her glasses. "If this killer continues to duplicate the Samaritan's same pattern, you'll receive a typed letter via US Postal Service in the next two days."

Several of the officers asked questions to clarify what she'd just outlined. She answered each with succinct patience. She sensed her clipped tone was not doing much to endear herself to the San Antonio Police Department, but the feelings and egos of the personnel in the room were not her priority.

After the room emptied out, she gathered her files.

Mazur approached. "You know you'll get more from these guys if you aren't so abrupt."

Annoyance tightened her gut. "I don't care, Detective Mazur. Bruised egos and injured pride are luxuries."

She set her backpack on the table and carefully unpacked and opened six more files at random. Each represented an open case she was monitoring. "Let me show you why I can be abrupt."

Mazur looked at her, then moved forward. The lines around his eyes and mouth deepened as he studied the gruesome pictures.

"Cases like this one make it hard for me to care about other cops' hurt feelings," she said, tapping her finger on the first picture. "This is my newest case. I just came from Utah, where I left an eighteen-year-old girl's hospital room. She'd been rescued from a coffin-style box."

"Jesus."

"When I found her she was barely alive. Her abductor had raped her repeatedly and buried her alive. We only found her because we received an anonymous tip from a guy who overheard a drunk in a bar talking about burying women alive."

Mazur rubbed the back of his neck. "Tell me you caught him."

"He escaped. He's the one I was chasing when you called. While investigating the land around the abandoned farmhouse, we found four more graves. All recent and all filled with young females."

His jaw pulsed. "I have a fourteen-year-old daughter. And anytime there's a case with a kid, I think about her."

"It's hard not to personalize," she said softly. She moved to the second file. "This killer uses nails to restrain his victims."

He held up his hand. "Point taken."

"There might have been a time in my life when I was more open to holding the hand of a cop with hurt feelings over my abrupt nature, but I lost it a long time ago. All I care about is catching these animals."

"This is all you do?"

"It is."

"That's one helluva life, Dr. Hayden."

"I didn't choose it. It chose me."

CHAPTER SIX

Reliving the old kill is a satisfying addiction.

San Antonio, Texas
Monday, November 27, 5:15 p.m.

Kate and Mazur sat in the conference room and watched the video footage of the shooting on a big screen.

The shooter's camera jostled in time to the steady beat of footsteps as he walked toward the driver's side window. Dashboard lights silhouetted Gloria Sanchez's body as she held a cell phone to her ear.

"Are you all right?" the shooter asked. *"Looks like a flat."*

She glared at her phone before looking up. The closed window muffled her voice. *"I'm safe in my car and can wait until help arrives."*

"Want me to change the tire?" The footage ended. Neither spoke, but simply stared. Kate hit "Replay" and leaned in, scrutinizing every move the killer made. She listened to not only what he said, but also his tone of voice, accent, and inflections. She played it again. This time she closed her eyes.

"You're not alone. I'm here for you."

The voice jostled dark memories buried deep inside her, a connection she quickly dismissed as improbable. Whatever familiarity she felt must have likened back to the Richardson tapes.

"What were Richardson's tapes like?" Mazur asked.

She opened her eyes; she realized he was staring at her. She cleared her throat. "Very much like this. However, in three of the five cases, there is no audio."

"The cases that he can't be linked to."

"Correct." She rewatched the footage. "On all the first five tapes, the shooter stayed with the victim until she died. I believe on some level Richardson was concerned about how the world saw him. He's worried about his legacy."

"Why no audio on three of the five tapes?"

"Could be intentional. Could be technical issues with the tapes. Only Richardson can say for sure, and he's not talking."

Mazur drew in a breath. "A few kind words are supposed to negate putting a slug in a woman's chest?"

"We're dealing with psychopaths. There's often impairment in a psychopath's amygdala, the almond-shaped portion of the brain that generates emotion. They don't feel guilt as we do, and so they focus solely on what makes them feel good. Period. If looking like a knight in shining armor makes him feel better, that's what he'll do."

He sat back and shook his head. "I know one of the videos with audio was leaked."

The detective had done more digging than she'd realized. "To a reporter by the name of Taylor North."

"That would have given this guy a blueprint."

"And North has done a good job of unearthing a great many case details during his investigations. He's visited all the jurisdictions and spoken to as many people as he can. He knows this case as well as law enforcement."

"What's his angle?" Mazur asked.

"Attention. Book deal. Movie deal. I've no idea."

"This murder should be a boost to Taylor," Mazur said. "The Samaritan case faded away after the Richardson arrest. Once the details of the Sanchez murder get out, he'll be back in the spotlight again."

"That makes sense," she said.

"How much did you interface with Taylor?" Mazur asked.

"He was at each press conference ready with a question. He asked me for several interviews, but I declined them all."

"Whoever committed this murder wants you involved. He's calling you out. Could Taylor be involved?"

"He had solid alibis for the murders I've yet to link with Richardson." She shook her head. "Maybe we're all overthinking this. Maybe it's as simple as Martin Sanchez ordering a hit on his wife. He wouldn't be the first spouse to kill his wife and try to blame it on someone else."

"Believe me, that idea is still in play."

"I've spoken to all the other victims' families. And an interview with Mr. Sanchez will help me to gauge his guilt or innocence."

"I'm happy to set it up. Let me talk to Palmer."

Mazur caught Detective Palmer as she passed in front of the conference room and updated her on Kate's request to speak to Sanchez. He reentered the conference room. "Ready to talk to Sanchez?"

She looked up from the screen. "Is Detective Palmer joining us?"

"She's going to check with the Forensic Department and ask them about the bullet. She's also going to track down the sketches of those Samaritans who didn't kill their victims."

"You think this killer might have been making a practice run in those cases?"

"We need to look at this case from all the angles," Mazur said.

"Understood." She followed Mazur down the hall and into the elevator. The doors closed.

As they rode the elevator down, she was aware of Mazur looking at her. But neither spoke as they stepped off the elevator and crossed the lobby to the parking lot.

The sun hung low on the horizon and cast a rich burnt orange over the buildings of San Antonio. She'd forgotten how stunning the sunsets could be in Texas. The big open sky. Land as far as the eye could see. Bright bold stars. There were many magnificent places in this country, but none quite possessed the beauty of Texas. She missed that. Out here, of all places, she could breathe.

This newfound nostalgia was ironic. Living in San Antonio had not been a particularly joyful time. There had been happiness in her family when her father was alive, but after his death, the family had splintered. Maybe if he'd died in a normal way, such as a heart attack or cancer, the Haydens would have fared better.

Mazur parked the car in front of the Sanchezes' home and shut off the engine. "We're here."

She looked up at the five-thousand-square-foot brown adobe-style home. The rock and cactus gardens were neatly manicured, with a stone path that cut through the center of the yard.

"The car business has been very good to the Sanchez family," Mazur said.

"Have you checked their financials?" she asked.

He cocked a brow. "The judge signed the order about three this afternoon, so we should have numbers later tonight."

"All is rarely what it seems."

"Very true."

Out of the car, the evening air had cooled to a comfortable seventy degrees. They moved along the path to the large ornate, hand-carved front door. "Are the Sanchezes from this area?"

"They're local. Both were born to immigrants who worked hard and made good. Sanchez's first wife died in a car accident, and eight months later he married Gloria."

"Have you looked into the first wife's death?"

"Dr. Ryland is reviewing her autopsy report."

Mazur rang the bell, and seconds later it opened to a young Hispanic woman wearing a simple white dress. Long black hair was coiled at the base of her neck.

Mazur held up his badge as Kate reached for her own shield. "I'm Detective Theo Mazur. I spoke with Mr. Sanchez yesterday. Is he here?"

The woman nodded. "Yes, sir. He said you would return; please come in."

They followed the woman down a long well-lit hallway that opened up to a large room that overlooked the rugged terrain in the distance.

There were two gray-haired men in the room, but Kate sensed immediately that Sanchez was the shorter man on the right. His hands were thick and calloused like a man comfortable around a car engine, and though the fabric of his clothes was expensive, they were simple. He was from humble roots and looked slightly out of place in the richly decorated room.

The taller man wore a hand-tailored charcoal-gray suit. His red tie was fashioned into a Windsor knot, his watch was gold, and his shined shoes were made of fine leather. He could only be the lawyer.

Hanging on the wall was a tall portrait of Gloria Sanchez. She was dressed in a red gown. A diamond necklace encircled her neck. Her eyes stared boldly at the artist. The portrait exuded the woman's confidence and total comfort with the trappings of wealth.

The shorter of the two men moved to greet Detective Mazur. "Detective."

"Mr. Sanchez," he said.

"I'd like you to meet my lawyer, Roger Bennett. I called him a few hours ago."

Mazur didn't comment, but Kate knew he didn't like the addition of an attorney who represented an added layer between Mazur and his investigation.

"This is Dr. Kate Hayden," Mazur said. "She's with the FBI."

"FBI?" Bennett asked. "So it's true what I'm hearing."

"What are you hearing?" Mazur asked.

"That Mrs. Sanchez might have been murdered by a serial killer," Bennett said.

Mr. Sanchez gasped and shook his head. "When Bennett first suggested this idea, it seemed too far-fetched."

Bennett shrugged. "I know you don't want to hear this again, Martin, but Gloria's case is very similar to the Samaritan murders."

"That suspect is in jail," Kate said.

"Or maybe not," Bennett said.

"I'd like to ask your client a few routine questions, Mr. Bennett," Kate said.

"I'd like to help," Sanchez said.

When Bennett nodded, Mazur asked, "Mr. Sanchez, can you tell us about your wife's trip? You said she was traveling to Laredo to see her mother."

Sanchez looked at his attorney, and when Bennett nodded, he said, "Yes, that's what she told me. She was on the road so late because she'd worked a long day at the showroom. I never met a harder-working person than Gloria."

"And did she normally call the nursing home to let them know she was coming for a visit?" Mazur asked.

"Not every single time. Sometimes she surprised them. It was important to her that the staff stayed on their toes. She liked surprise inspections."

"Where did she stay when she was in Laredo?" Mazur asked.

"She has a condo there," Sanchez said. "It was easier for her to stay in the same place. In the last year, she had to be in Laredo for days at a stretch because of her mother."

Mazur pulled a small notebook from his breast pocket and made several notes.

"Was there any reason to go to Laredo other than to visit her mother?" Kate asked.

"We do have friends there, but her primary reason was her mother. We had a dealership there but closed it several months ago. It wasn't profitable."

"How was your wife feeling when you last saw her?" Mazur asked.

Sanchez's brow wrinkled. "Fine. Why do you ask?"

"The medical examiner theorized she couldn't have been feeling well," Mazur said.

"Why?" Sanchez asked. "She looked fine on Sunday." Again he looked to his attorney, but the man shrugged.

Kate found Sanchez's reaction interesting. He seemed genuinely taken aback with the question. "Did you know your wife was sick?"

Sanchez shook his head. "What do you mean sick?"

"She had cancer," Mazur said. "According to the medical examiner, it was advanced."

Sanchez shook his head, the color draining from his face. "No. She would have told me. The medical examiner has made a mistake."

"The medical examiner was certain," Mazur said. "She was a very sick woman."

"She'd not been to any doctors. She wasn't taking medicine. How could she have been sick?" Sanchez's brow furrowed as the weight of their words sank deeper. "She got tired, but she worked so hard."

Kate noted his voice inflection and facial expressions appeared genuine. "The doctor thinks it was a matter of time before she was going to be really struggling."

Tears glistened in Sanchez's eyes. "I don't believe it. What kind of cancer?"

"Uterine," Mazur said.

He cleared his throat. "No. She had the flu last month and a bad cold a couple of months before that, but not cancer. She would have told me."

"But she didn't tell you?" Kate said. Why wouldn't a woman share such grave news with her spouse?

Sanchez shook his head slowly as he made the sign of the cross. "Gloria hated any kind of limitations. Cancer would have been no exception."

Bennett placed a comforting hand on his client's shoulder. "My client can't speak to the motives of his late wife."

"Were you having marital problems?" Kate asked.

Sanchez looked as if he'd been struck. "Why do you ask that?"

"You still aren't wearing a wedding band," Mazur said.

He curled his fingers into fists. "After I found Gloria, I forgot to put it back on."

"Your fingers are perfectly tanned," she pressed. "If you wore it even some of the time, there would be a tan line." He certainly wouldn't be the first married man who didn't want to broadcast his status. Was he having an affair? Did Gloria know? Was that why she didn't tell him about the cancer?

Sanchez stiffened but didn't answer.

"Your wife was wearing a very expensive engagement ring," Kate said.

"Gloria's ring is a five-carat yellow diamond. She loved the way the light caught it. I gave it to her three years ago for our twentieth wedding anniversary. It was very expensive."

"What worries me is that the killer didn't take the ring or her wallet," Mazur said. "Robbery wasn't the motive."

Bennett shifted. "This certainly feeds into the serial killer theory. Which makes me wonder why a judge signed off on a warrant for the family financial records."

"I'm working all the angles," Mazur said.

"I did not kill my wife," Sanchez said slowly for effect.

"What was the financial state of your business?" Kate asked. "You said you closed the Laredo dealership."

Sanchez raised his chin. "The economy hasn't been kind the last year."

"That's not what you told me at the crime scene," Mazur said.

"Appearances were very important to Gloria. She wouldn't have wanted you to know the truth."

"And perhaps why she didn't want you knowing she was sick?"

Sanchez mumbled a prayer. "Maybe."

"Why did you close the Laredo shop?" Mazur asked.

"In the late spring, Gloria ran the numbers and said we might have to cut back on staff. Honestly, I was happy about cutbacks. I'm a simple man at heart. I like to work with my hands. Gloria was the one with big dreams." He shook his head, and tears glistened bright in his eyes. "Why wouldn't she tell me she was sick?"

"I don't know," Kate said.

He dropped his face to his hands and sobbed. "God, this is all too much."

"You told me yesterday that she called you from the road and said she was having car trouble," Mazur said.

"That's right. Why do you ask?"

Kate knew where Mazur was headed. In the killer's tape, Gloria never mentioned having called her husband. Wouldn't a frightened woman tell a strange man this, even if it weren't true?

"My client has had enough for today," Bennett said. "I'm not going to stand here while you go on a fishing expedition."

"I understand you and your wife have a daughter," Kate said.

"Technically, Gloria was Isabella's stepmother. But Gloria and Isabella were very close." The shift to his child sharpened Sanchez's tone.

"How old is she?" Kate asked.

"She's twenty-two."

"Does she live here?"

Sanchez closed his eyes. "She's in prelaw at Georgetown. She comes home from time to time."

"Where is she now?" Kate asked.

"She's on her way home. I called her this morning. Her flight was delayed," he said.

"I'd like to talk to her when she arrives," Kate said.

"Why?" Sanchez challenged. "She wasn't here when Gloria died. She's coming home to grieve for her stepmother and to support me."

"My questions are strictly background," Kate said. "And I'll do my best not to upset her."

When Sanchez readied to speak again, Bennett laid a hand on his arm, silencing him. "I'll want to be present when you speak to Miss Sanchez."

"Her first name is Isabella?" Kate asked.

"Yes," Sanchez said.

"And her biological mother was your first wife, who died in a car accident?" Kate asked.

"Selena's death was a devastating blow." Sanchez was clenching his jaw, an indicator of aggression. "And I don't see how her death is relevant now."

"That's enough with the questions," Bennett interjected.

Sanchez laid his hand on his lawyer's arm. "Gloria's death has torn me in half," he said. "But Detective Mazur, I won't let you traumatize my daughter."

As if the man had not spoken, Mazur glanced to Kate and in a pleasant voice asked, "You have any more questions? I'll stay as long as you need to be here."

"I've no more immediate inquiries for Mr. Sanchez," Kate said. "But I do want to talk to Isabella. I'll return when she's home."

Mazur nodded. "We'll be back."

CHAPTER SEVEN

The first kill is a rush of adrenaline, fear, worry, and elation all in one.

San Antonio, Texas
Monday, November 27, 8:45 p.m.

As Mazur pulled away from the Sanchez house, he was convinced Martin Sanchez had secrets. But being an adulterer didn't make him a murderer. "The first Mrs. Sanchez died in a car accident," Mazur said as he drove. "And Martin Sanchez is a car mechanic."

"And Gloria is much younger. It's a cliché because it happens a lot." Kate glanced at the clock on the dash and frowned. "I didn't realize it was so late."

"Time flies when you're having fun."

"What's your next move in this investigation?" she asked.

"I'm going to check in with the forensic team and see what they've found out about Gloria Sanchez's car. Jenny Calhoun said she'd have an update for me tonight."

"I'd like to hear it."

"Sure."

Five minutes into the drive, her phone buzzed. "My boss," she said as she studied the display. "I have to take this."

"Sure."

"Agent Ramsey," she said. "I have yet to draw any conclusions on the case."

She listened, frowning. "I promise you, we're moving as quickly as possible. Detective Mazur and I are returning to the forensic lab now to discuss the status of the victim's car. I'll call when I have information to report. You can do me a favor and check with the warden of Richardson's jail. Has he received any kind of communication from anyone?" She nodded. "Good. Also, do you have an update on the Raymond Drexler case?" Absently she angled her head and rubbed the side of her neck with her hand. "All right. Keep me updated."

When the call ended, she gripped her phone and stared out at the dark horizon. He understood what it felt like to want an arrest so badly it hurt to breathe.

"What's the deal on Drexler?" he said.

"He's still at large. Nevada, my partner, is following a southwardly trail through Utah. Drexler was spotted at a Utah gas station seven hours ago."

"Pressure from above on our case?" Mazur asked.

She leaned her head back against the headrest. "There's always pressure from above when I work a case. When I show up in your local jurisdiction, it's generally not a good day for anyone."

"You've worked a few high-profile cases, and from what I've read, solved several."

"Do you remember your solved cases or the ones you didn't crack?"

"Point taken."

She turned her head toward him. "I got the sense from the briefing today that you're not in the inner circle of your office."

"Why do you say that?"

"Body language is my thing. You received a few pointed stares during the brief."

"Par for the course with this crew. No one shoved a Chicago-style pizza in my hair or pissed in my Cubs mug today, so the way I see it, it's a good day."

"How long were you with Chicago PD?" The light from the dash caught the sharp angle of her cheekbones.

"Eighteen years."

"Most cops wouldn't walk away from that."

He cocked a brow. "Is this shrink time now?"

She shook her head. "I specialize in personality disorders, not family counseling. Just making conversation."

"Sounded like an interrogation."

She shrugged. "Interrogations are about the closest I get to conversations these days."

Silence settled for a moment, and there was only the rush of the wind past his window. "If you're making conversation and not analyzing, then yeah, the move has been tough. Still haven't sold the condo in Chicago, and if I have to use GPS one more time to find a crime scene, I might commit murder."

"Why did you move?"

"Divorce. Ex moved our kid to San Antonio." Despite his best effort, anger resonated behind the words.

"Staying close to your child is good. My dad died when I was a teenager."

"Must have torn you up."

"Of course. Devastated. He loved me and I loved him, but we didn't get each other. Lots of talking around each other."

"Alyssa is a little like you, Kate. She keeps it all inside. She hides her feelings. Makes jokes when she's worried."

"What makes you so sure I have feelings?"

That prompted a genuine laugh. "You're right. The jury is still out on that one."

She seemed unable to resist a smile. "What does your daughter like to do?"

"She's the smartest kid in the school. Band club. Chess club. Theater."

"None of the activities you can relate to?"

"No."

"Is she like her mother?"

"Has her brains, thank God. And her looks. But not her polish. Kid can't schmooze worth crap."

"A skill I've never mastered. Playing chess is a solid pastime. It teaches a great deal about strategy, but especially patience."

"You play the game?"

"I did when I was Alyssa's age. Not anymore." She stared up at the night sky. "There's too much light pollution in Washington to see the stars like I can out here."

"Why'd you give up the game?" He was more interested in her than the stars.

"I suppose I never had enough time once I left for college."

He shook his head. "There's always time for what you really want."

She smiled. "Nice, pivot. Should I start calling you doctor?"

"I'm a detective. I can smell an evasion a mile away."

When she didn't respond, he didn't make an attempt to fill the silence or backtrack. If he'd thought a heartfelt confession was on its way, then he was wrong.

"I believe Santos is the one who urinated in your cup," she said.

He shot her a sharp glance. "Why do you say that?"

"It's the brash move of a young man. He gestures with his right hand, the one holding his coffee cup. I suspect personal property—his territory—is important to him. Did he have a friend passed over for the team when you arrived?"

"He did."

"He'd strike back at something he'd deem important—your personal territory."

"How sure are you?"

"Ninety percent."

"Good to know."

The lights of San Antonio grew brighter as he steered the car toward the city, and the stars dimmed. He parked at police headquarters, and they made their way past the guard to the second floor. As she passed a vending machine, she dug her credit card from her pocket and bought two packets of Nabs.

"You should buy stock in that vending company."

She unwrapped the package and offered him a cracker. He took one.

"Keep the pack," she said. "One is enough for me."

He held one up. "The next two packs are on me."

"Done."

They made their way into a large garage-style room with cabinets and polished gray counters outfitted with an array of equipment.

A tall, trim woman dressed in a lab coat, blond hair pulled back, looked up from a microscope. "Detective. I wasn't sure if you could make it."

"Visiting Mr. Sanchez. Jenny Calhoun, meet Agent Kate Hayden with the FBI."

Calhoun rose and extended her hand. "The profiler."

Kate shook her hand. "Correct. Tell us what you've found."

"Cut to the chase, I like it." Calhoun led them through the lab to the forensic bay where Gloria Sanchez's car was now parked. "I dusted the car for prints in key areas: trunk, driver's side door handle, the radio buttons, gearshift, and the turn signal. I found prints in each spot, and 90 percent belonged to the victim."

"What about inside the trunk?" Kate asked. "I know we saw gloves on his hands in the tape, but we might get lucky."

"I did find two partial prints on the underside of the trunk."

"Have you taken Mr. Sanchez's prints?" Kate asked.

"I did, and they didn't match. His DNA, which I obtained from a cheek swab at the crime scene, is also being processed. I've fed the prints into AFIS, so we'll see if we get a hit. Also, the bloodstains on Sanchez's shirt were his wife's, but the smudge patterns aren't consistent with a close-range shooting, which would have sprayed him with blood."

"He could have changed shirts," Kate said.

"If he did, I haven't found it," she said. "And I searched the ground all around the car." And heading off the next question, Calhoun said, "Blood spatter on the windshield belonged to the victim." She waved them toward the four door and stood by the driver's side door. She pointed her finger as if it were a gun toward the window. "He was stand-ing within a foot of the car. As I understand it, the medical examiner removed a slug from her chest. I found no other slugs in, on, or around the car. I did find one shell casing under the car. I've dusted the end of the shell for a print but came up with nothing."

"The fact that you found a casing is interesting," Kate said. "That's inconsistent with the other cases."

"He's not left a casing before?" Mazur asked.

"No."

"I found tire marks behind the victim's car. I took casts and am try-ing to identify the manufacturer. I talked to robbery, and they reported two minivans and a Suburban with car seats stolen on Saturday night."

"What about the flat tire?" Kate asked.

"One puncture to the tread," Calhoun said.

Kate knelt by the tailpipe and studied it. She traced a gloved fin-ger around the pipe's opening. "Was this the first time Gloria Sanchez checked out this car?"

"I don't know," Mazur said.

She opened the back car door. "Have you searched the back seat for DNA or fingerprints?"

"No," Calhoun said. "I focused on the exterior, front seat, and trunk."

"Check every inch of the interior and the trunk."

"What are you thinking?" Mazur asked.

"People tend to be creatures of habit. If she checked out this car on Sunday, stands to reason she might have used it before. Maybe she likes not being noticed."

"She left a note for her husband that her Mercedes was being serviced."

"Be curious to know if that was the case," she said.

"Why did the killer key in on you?" Calhoun asked. "FBI is usually in the shadows."

"I gave press conferences and called the killer unemployed and impotent," Kate said. "I wanted to get a rise out of him."

"No pun intended," Mazur offered.

Kate blinked. "Correct."

Mazur looked at her, and when she didn't smile, shook his head. "You don't do humor well either, do you?"

"No," she said. "This killer is expecting a response to his text, but I'm going to make him wait. It's important he realize he is not in control."

CHAPTER EIGHT

*With age comes wisdom. And sometimes with wisdom
comes too much caution and fear. That is why it's
important to act no matter how much wisdom tells me
not to.*

San Antonio, Texas
Monday, November 27, 11:35 p.m.

When Kate sank into the hotel bed, her entire body ached from fatigue. She'd been going nonstop for eleven days with little sleep. And yet, as exhausted as her body was, her mind buzzed with the details of the day. She couldn't shake the feeling that something was off about this case. She could feel it, sense it, but fatigue had hazed over her thoughts. One way or another, she would have to sleep so that she could remain effective.

She checked her phone, hoping to see a picture of Drexler in cuffs from Nevada. There wasn't. Part of her was disappointed, and another part was hopeful she could still personally see this monster caged.

She fell back against the pillows. If the ballistics varied in the Sanchez case, then that would be enough for her to pull out and return to Utah. One more day in San Antonio to go. She'd not called her mother yet but could reasonably argue she'd been too busy. Still, to be this close, and not call, suggested personal issues bigger than a lack of time.

The shadows played on the wall, swaying back and forth as if they'd come to life. For centuries, the civilized were taught to not believe in monsters, but she knew damn well they existed. The horror they wrought upon the innocent was unspeakable in sane company. Images of them always came home to roost at night when she was alone.

Her chest tightened, and she looked toward the prescription bottle she always set out on her nightstand. The sleeping pills had been a big help when she couldn't shut her brain off after a case, but until last week, she'd been trying to wean off them. But as the muscles in her body begged for sleep, her mind still ran wild. Her skin tingled as if the shadows watched.

Clicking on the light, she reached for the bottle and took out one pill. Taking it felt like failure, but she knew she'd be good to no one if she were exhausted.

Kate swallowed the pill whole and with a deep sense of resignation lay back on the pillows. It took another thirty minutes for her mind to slow and her eyes to close, and when sleep reached out a welcoming hand, she accepted it even as she promised herself that next time she would not need the pills.

***

Mazur pushed through the front door of his house. The place was as he'd left it, fairly neat and tidy. There were a few pairs of Alyssa's socks that she'd discarded without thought the last time she'd spent the night. He never could bring himself to pick up her shoes because when he saw them he thought of her.

As he unclipped his gun, handcuffs, and badge and put them in the top drawer of his credenza by the front door, he studied the pictures always waiting for him in the entryway. There were pictures of his brothers and his mom in Chicago and another of him holding Caleb and Alyssa.

As he moved down the hallway, his phone rang. It was Alyssa. "What are you still doing up, kiddo?"

"I can't sleep."

He shrugged off his coat, switching the phone to his other ear as he did. "Why's that? Everything okay with Mom?"

"She's on a conference call to New York."

He checked his watch and frowned. The kid should be asleep. "How did the math test go?"

"I don't know."

He sat on the edge of his bed and kicked off his shoes. "Sure you do."

"Easy."

"How easy?"

"Like a ten out of ten."

"Good."

"Catch the bad guy yet?"

"Not yet. But I'm working on it."

"Still working with the Fed?"

He chuckled. "The Fed?"

"I keep up with the lingo. What's he like?"

Since Alyssa was eight or nine, she'd asked questions about his work. At first she worried about his safety and the late-night hours. His answers were always honest, if not measured. In the last year or two, she'd become curious about the cases. "She's interesting. Smart. Dedicated and a little quirky."

"Quirky in a good or bad way?"

"Good way."

"What's her name?"

"Dr. Kate Hayden."

"Let me check her out." Alyssa typed on what he suspected was the laptop he'd given her last year. "Wow, she has dealt with some real bad guys."

"I know."

"She also plays chess."

"She mentioned that. Said she doesn't play anymore."

"Wow. She was one of the best. Grand champion when she was in high school. Quit after her father died."

"She mentioned her father died when she was a teenager."

"She tell you he was shot in the street? So was she."

"Really?" Jesus, she'd been a victim of violence. What had she said to him earlier? *This life chose me.*

"It's on the Internet so it must be true," she joked. "Can you tell me more about her?"

When he'd searched Kate's name, he'd focused on her career, cases, and education, not her past. The more he learned about her, the more he wanted to know. She was a survivor, professionally accomplished, and attractive. He loosened his tie and glanced at the clock. "You need to go to bed, kiddo."

She groaned into the phone. "See you this weekend?"

"It's a date."

When she'd been little, he'd kiss her good night. Since the divorce, most *good nights* happened over the phone. "Love you, kiddo."

"Me, too, Dad."

He ended the call and changed into jeans and a faded Bulls T-shirt. He grabbed a pizza box and went to the dining table that served as a makeshift office.

A computer search of Kate Hayden revealed much of what Alyssa had just relayed. A young man who'd gone to school with Kate had gunned her and her father down in the parking lot of the civic center where she'd attended chess practice. Her father had died at the scene, and Kate's injuries were critical. The shooter was sentenced to fifteen to twenty years in prison.

The Internet search gave him the basics, but if he wanted the whole story, he'd have to pull the murder file. Her past was none of his business, but cops were nosy by nature. It kept them alive.

He imagined Alyssa seeing him gunned down and then getting shot herself. The thought made him sick. "Shit," he muttered.

No wonder Kate was an odd duck. But though she was closed and guarded, she was direct. There were also traces of humor. And if she wore anything other than the severe black FBI suit that swallowed her whole, he could easily find her way too attractive.

Amused by the train of thought, he switched his focus back to the real priority: solving the Gloria Sanchez murder.

Martin Sanchez was hiding secrets, which led Mazur to focus on the man's daughter, Isabella, who might know what had been happening in her father's marriage. He searched the young woman's name on the computer and quickly learned Isabella was accomplished in her own right. She'd graduated top of her class at Sacred Heart Catholic School, and she was now in her third year of prelaw. There was next to no information on Mr. Sanchez. He didn't appear in any of the ads, nor was he at any of the charity events covered by the press. No scandals. However, two dead wives was more than enough for most people.

By all accounts, Gloria Sanchez had a solid family life, and she had made a success of herself. She had everything to live for. The cancer must have been a real kick in the gut.

"Could you have been killed at random?"

Mazur checked his email and discovered a message from Palmer. The subject heading was *Financials*. As he sipped his beer, he opened Palmer's email.

Sanchez family and the car dealership were in real trouble. In the last year the company lost

money steadily. In the last three months their
bank accounts were on vapors. Checking on
life insurance policy. JP

He reread the email. The best way to murder a high-profile individual was to hide the murder in plain sight.

Kate's doubts about Sanchez might have hit their mark.

Blame it on a faceless serial killer who hadn't been caught and no one was the wiser.

***

Raymond Drexler pulled into the gas station in southern Utah, knowing he'd have to ditch the truck he'd stolen a couple of hundred miles back. If it weren't reported as stolen yet, it would just be a matter of time. He parked his truck in a spot hidden by the shadows. With luck no one would find it until morning.

Using his shirtsleeve, he wiped the steering wheel clean as well as the knob on the radio. He grabbed a small go bag he always kept packed. Better safe than sorry.

As he got out of the vehicle, the cold nipped at his face and the wind swept under his flannel shirt. He liked the cold. It, like death, energized him.

He stretched, his body aching from the driving. Already he missed his home. His land. It was about this time of night when he'd open his box and take Sara out to play. She'd been a favorite of his. Pale, thin, and blond. Just as he liked. Drexler had decided not to starve her too quickly as he had the others. Still, withholding food had made her docile. And in the last weeks, she'd grown so easy to handle. She'd do anything for him or to him for a few extra french fries.

Now she was gone. And he was on the run. Alone.

He'd texted his cousin, Richie, who'd told him Hayden had left Utah. What the hell? She turned his life upside down and then she went on as if she'd done nothing wrong.

News reports revealed his worst fear. They had found his Sara, and then they'd found his other girls. Beth. Cici. Debby. Naomi. They were all gone now.

The idea that they'd dug up his girls made his stomach twist and turn. Angry. No respect for the dead.

Last week he didn't know Kate Hayden's name. Now all he could think about was putting her in a box that was a few inches too short for her little body. That would teach her some manners.

In the convenience store, he nodded to the clerk but kept his gaze low as he moved to the coolers and pulled out a couple of energy drinks as well as a six-pack of beer.

He spotted a man, who had parked by his vehicle, stagger toward the store and straight to the beer case.

Drexler kept his gaze averted from the security camera and, tossing a pack of jerky on the counter by the drinks, dug twenty bucks out of his pocket. The clerk took the twenty and scooped his change out of the register.

"Thanks," Drexler muttered as he shoved the rumpled bills and coins in his pocket.

He returned to his car and set his purchases on the ground. If the cops weren't looking for this truck yet, they would be soon. Time to ditch it. He glanced back toward the store and watched the other lone customer pay for a twelve-pack of beer.

Drexler looked around, making sure no one saw him, and dropped to his knee. He flicked open a switchblade. Taking the car parked next to his would fix at least one of his problems.

After several minutes, the drunk staggered out of the store, the twelve-pack in hand. He was older, lean, and dressed in a mechanic's jumpsuit. The man swerved when he walked across the lot. He sang some country song as he fumbled for his keys. Drexler's heart beat faster, and his palms began to sweat. He wasn't fond of using a knife.

The other man didn't see Drexler crouched by the front of the car until he all but tripped over him.

"What the fuck?" the man asked, staggering back a step.

Drexler rose up quickly and jabbed the stranger in the gut several times. Drexler found the sensation of metal cutting into flesh nauseating. He didn't like blood or killing with his hands.

Blood oozed out of the man's gut as he stumbled and collapsed into Drexler's arms. The beers dropped to the ground with a hard thunk.

Drexler grabbed the man's keys and patted him down for a wallet. He found a money clip securing a hundred dollars' worth of bills and a phone. Drexler shoved his victim onto the passenger-side seat of his stolen truck. The man groaned. Drexler pulled the blade over the man's neck, severing his carotid artery. Hot, sticky blood was slick between his fingers as it gushed down over the dead man's white oval nameplate that read *Jimmy*.

Drexler swung Jimmy's legs in and turned his head away from the window. The dark seats and rug would hide the blood, at least until morning. And if anyone glanced in before sunrise, they'd see a drunk sleeping it off.

Drexler checked Jimmy's phone and discovered it was locked. He grabbed Jimmy's right thumb and pressed it against the "Home" button. The phone opened.

Drexler slammed the door closed to his truck, grabbed all the beer, and slid behind the wheel of the black Dodge truck. The truck was at least ten years old, and it smelled of old fast food and booze. But the engine cranked immediately, and the tank had enough gas to get him at least three hundred miles farther south.

The cops would find Drexler's vehicle and the man's body, but he figured he had about eight to ten hours before anyone figured out what had happened. By then, he'd find a new vehicle.

As he drove, he removed the security settings on the phone and searched for Kate Hayden. Immediately an article by Taylor North popped up. According to North, Kate Hayden was working a case in San Antonio.

As he drove, he kept searching, learning that Kate had been raised in San Antonio where her mother still lived.

When he'd first run from his property, he'd had no other plan than survival. Now he had a plan.

"San Antonio, Texas, here I come."

CHAPTER NINE

*When dropping a trail of bread crumbs, it is important
that the crumbs are the right size. Too small and they
could be missed. Too large and they look obvious. But
when they're just right . . . it's magic.*

San Antonio, Texas
Tuesday, November 28, 7:00 a.m.

When Mazur pulled up to the hotel, Kate was waiting for him in the
lobby. She was dressed in the same shapeless black suit, and her hair was
pulled back into a tight ponytail. However, her face had more color in
it, and she'd put on a bit of makeup. When she shifted her stance and
slung her backpack onto her shoulder, her jacket moved and he spotted
the outline of nicely rounded breasts.

Her pace was quick, determined, and restless. No mind reading
necessary to know she was anxious to wrap up this case and return to
Utah. She was a balled-up tangle of energy.

She set her backpack in the backseat, then slid into the passenger
seat. "Good morning."

The soft scent of soap mingled with a subtle perfume. "Get a good
night's sleep?"

"I did. You?"

"Enough." Sliding on his sunglasses, he pulled into traffic. "Jenny Calhoun called me about five minutes ago. She wants us to stop by the lab."

"Did she say why?"

"No. Said it was important."

Her brow wrinkled. "Curious."

"I've known Calhoun only a few months, but she's a straight shooter. If she's got something to say, she says it."

"Unlike Santos."

He grinned. "What do they say about revenge?"

"It's a dish best served cold."

"Damn right." He signaled to change lanes. "I received a report on the Sanchez family's financials. They're in worse shape than Martin indicated. Land assets and brokerage assets have been liquidated. Second mortgage taken out last month on their home."

Her phone chimed with a text, and she glanced at it, her brow furrowing as she read.

"That doesn't look like good news." Her business was none of his, but being around her kept piquing his interest.

"My partner, Agent Nevada, thinks Drexler ditched his truck and stole another one."

"Where was Drexler last seen?"

"Near the New Mexico border. That's where he stole a truck and stabbed the vehicle's owner, who was found in Drexler's vehicle. There was a lot of blood at the scene, so the vehicle he's driving is likely covered in it as well."

"Does he own any other properties or have friends in that part of the state?"

"Parents are dead. No siblings. A cousin whom I interviewed. Though the cousin defended Drexler, I suspect he's the one who called in the tip that led to the arrest. We're still digging into extended family connections."

"Can you prove the cousin called it in?" Mazur asked.

"No. It's a hunch. I did a baseline interview with him. We didn't talk about the case. His job. His house. Basic things so I could see how he reacted when there was no need to lie. When I asked him about the tip on Drexler, he leaned back as he spoke. He also crossed his legs and looked away or checked his watch. Several closed-posture gestures that deviated from the baseline suggested he was hiding secrets."

"He involved in his cousin's deeds?"

"I don't think so. I think Drexler got drunk and talked more than he should. I also think the cousin, though he made the anonymous call to local police, is clearly troubled by the fact he turned in family."

"I know what it's like to catch a guy that insidious. For me, it was Frankie Munroe. A piece of shit from the South Side of Chicago. Developed a taste for killing young prostitutes. One was thirteen. The way he cut them." He paused, pushing the image from his mind. "Took me nine months of tracking. But putting him down was all I drank, ate, and slept." Caleb had recently died, and the chase had been the only way to salvage his tattering sanity.

"And you caught him."

He tightened his hands on the wheel. "A couple of uniforms rolled up on him while he was cutting a woman's throat. Shot and killed him." Later that day, he'd returned home and Sherry announced she and Alyssa were moving out.

Kate didn't press him for details, instead turning her gaze toward the highway and the faceless businesses.

They finished the trip in silence, each lost in thought. At the station, she moved beside him, hurrying to match his pace. Normally his pace was steady, but the telling of his story ginned up urgency.

They stepped off the elevators and made their way to the forensic lab. They found Calhoun leaning against a counter, her arms folded over her chest as if she'd been waiting for them.

"Have you found something in the backseat?" Kate asked.

"I did find fresh stains on the seat, and preliminary tests suggest human bodily fluids, which I've sent for testing. And I can tell you the receipt in Gloria Sanchez's car proved she was at a convenience store named Lucky's shortly before she died."

"Good work," Mazur said.

Calhoun shook her head. "That's not why I called."

She held up the plastic evidence bag containing the burner cell phone left behind by the killer. "I had barely sat down this morning when I noticed this."

When Kate and Mazur had both gloved up, Calhoun removed the cell phone from the evidence bag and handed it to Mazur.

The new text read: When is Dr. Hayden going to make a statement to the media? Do I have to kill again?

"Did you put a trace on it?" Mazur asked.

"The message came through at 4:50 a.m., a couple of hours before I arrived. I called in the number right away, and tech support said they couldn't get a ping on it. You were my first call after they notified me."

Mazur showed it to Kate. "Who knows you're working this case?"

"Mr. Sanchez and his attorney, your department, and my people."

"So if I'm Sanchez or his attorney, would it be smart of me to send a text like this?" Mazur asked. "Or is this Samaritan nut watching?"

Kate studied the message. "His question implies knowledge. But I've been a background player on this case since I arrived in San Antonio. He's either guessing I'm here or is watching this building. Did you have an officer taping the crime scene and the people watching it?"

"Calhoun had a couple of squad cars with dash-cam videos running and aimed at the traffic passing by. She knows killers often return to the murder scenes."

"Excellent," she said. "Smart. Can you get those for me?"

"Will do, Agent Hayden," Mazur said.

Kate frowned. "As I've said, he wants to control this situation. So giving a press conference right now is the last request I'll grant him."

It was Mazur's turn to frown. "Looking to make him mad?"

"That's the point," Kate continued. "Killers like him are egocentric. They like the limelight. Like to manipulate. They also can have very thin skin. If I ignore him, maybe he'll get angry and make a mistake."

"Or he'll kill someone," Calhoun said.

"He'll kill again regardless," Kate said. "He won't stop until he's put down."

"You're talking about him like he's the Samaritan," Mazur said.

She studied him a beat. "He just might think he is the new Samaritan."

"And Sanchez? He didn't shoot his wife?"

"I've not ruled him out either."

***

He used the hotel pass key and opened room number 351. He knew Kate was out for the day and at police headquarters with Detective Mazur because he'd been watching the hotel.

She'd looked almost sweet and childlike in her dark suit that fit her so poorly. Like a child pretending to be an adult. Hiding under all the layers of fabric. Fearful of a world that she knew was a very wicked place.

He moved to the unmade bed and to the suitcase that sat open on the stand across from the bed. He picked up a pair of panties and held them to his face, inhaling her scent.

He'd dreamed about Kate relentlessly over the last few months, and now, being this close to her made his skin shiver with excitement. The panties clutched in his hand, he moved to the closet where she'd neatly hung her extra suit, still encased in plastic from the dry cleaner in Salt Lake.

Beside the suit hung a simple white silk blouse and crisp jeans dangling from a pants hanger. His heart beat faster as he ran his hand along the blouse's soft fabric. She hung her clothes in the same order regardless of where she stayed, a fact he'd picked up on over the last few months. On the closet floor, her running shoes stood next to black ankle boots.

He turned and moved toward the bed. The outline of her head still creased the pillow, and the covers on the left side were still rumpled. The other half of the bed was smooth, and he guessed she'd had a solid night's sleep.

"Enjoy the sleep while you can."

He touched the sheets and sat down on the edge of the bed. Unable to resist, he laid his head back on the cool sheets, imagining her naked body. He grew hard thinking about her. He ran his hand over his erection. He reached for the button on his jeans, undid it, and slid his hand around his erection. He moved his hand up and down the hard shaft, imagining Kate lying under him, naked and moaning. His fantasy fixated on the image of her, spreading her legs wide so he could drive deep into her. He pushed all of himself into her hard and slow, knowing it hurt her and enjoying the flicker of fear on her face.

The image tipped him over the edge, and he exploded in a rush of ecstasy that shuddered through his body. He wiped himself clean with her panties and lay still for a moment, savoring the rush.

Footsteps in the hallway brought him back to the moment, and he quickly righted himself, zipped up his pants, and stuck her panties in his coat pocket.

There were so many things he wanted to do with Kate Hayden.

He moved to the bathroom. He studied the cosmetics lined up in a neat row on a carefully folded washcloth. She always lined up her cosmetics in the same way. He reached for her perfume and inhaled the scent. Neatness and organization were quirks of hers.

Someone who didn't understand her would call her OCD, but he understood the rigors of travel and the importance of simple routines that created a sense of home and familiarity in what was an endless stream of generic hotel rooms.

He sprayed a quick burst of her perfume on his wrist and held it to his nose. He would carry her scent with him for the rest of the day.

Meeting his reflection in the mirror, he wondered if she'd recognize him when they finally came face-to-face. Would she find him attractive or lacking? He wanted her to like him. Wanted her to need him.

They were meant to be together. They were two very smart people addicted to the chase.

The hunt.

Before he revealed himself, he had to show her he was the alpha partner. He had to show her, no matter how hard she worked, he would win in the end.

CHAPTER TEN

*"Will you walk into my parlor?" said the Spider to
the Fly.*

—*Mary Howitt*

San Antonio, Texas
Tuesday, November 28, 1:00 p.m.

Mazur and Dr. Hayden arrived at Lucky's off exit 140 on I-35. He parked at the far end of the lot and took a moment to study the scene. The station had four pumps and a small convenience store. Midday, there were cars at each of the pumps, and he suspected they did a steady stream of business.

"This is very typical of the other gas stations targeted by the Samaritan," Kate said.

Mazur nodded toward a small lot across a narrow side street. "Easy to park over there."

Once out of his car, they walked to the vacant lot. Kate studied the vantage point of the convenience store. "Anyone parked here late at night would have a clear view of the pumps," she said.

The gravel in the lot was fine and prone to tire impressions. Because the spot was well used, it had multiple tire tracks.

Kate knelt down. "The killer didn't find this place by happenstance. Send a uniform to the area businesses and see who has cameras. Pull the footage from the last two weeks. See if there was anyone who returned to the spot more than once. My guess is he scoped this place out first and got comfortable with the location as he studied potential complications and victims."

"Will do."

Mazur and Kate returned to the Lucky's lot and pushed through the front door of the convenience store. Bells jingled above his head as he paused and allowed her to pass him. The place was small. A silver Christmas holiday garland draped the wall of cigarettes behind the cash register at the front of the store. Beer and soda coolers were along the wall near a unisex bathroom.

A young, thin Hispanic man turned from the register toward the door. His name badge read *Tomas*.

Mazur removed his badge from his pocket and identified himself. "I'm trying to retrace the steps of a woman who passed through here on Sunday night. Do you know who was working that night?"

"It was me," Tomas said. "I own the place. Is this about the woman shot nearby?"

"It is."

"I've seen her before. She stopped here whenever she drove to Laredo. She was always nice."

"How often did Mrs. Sanchez come into your store?" Kate asked.

"About once a week. Travelers like this place because we offer easy access on and off the interstate."

"Do you have security footage of her last visit?" Mazur asked.

"Sure. I keep the recordings for a month. Not everyone keeps 'em that long, but I'm a magnet for trouble this close to the interstate. You're not the first cops who've come looking." He rubbed his nose. "What time are you looking for?"

"About twelve thirty at night on the twenty-sixth," Mazur said.

Tomas turned to his right and squatted to inspect a computer attached to a small television screen located under the counter. Mazur leaned over and saw that the screen showed four black-and-white angles: two focused on the gas pumps, another on the register, and the last on the lot behind the store. Tomas typed in the time, and the screens blinked back to early Sunday morning.

For several minutes the camera caught no activity, and then at 12:32 a.m. Gloria Sanchez's four door pulled up to the outside pump. Out of her car, she ran a credit card through the gas pump, lifted the handle, and stuck the nozzle in the tank. Grabbing her purse, she hurried inside.

"I was dozing that night. It had been a long day because the kid opening for me didn't show," Tomas said. "You can see I was startled when she comes inside."

Mazur watched the view of the gas pumps and her car. Seconds pass, and then a man wearing a black hoodie walked up to her car and jabbed something into the rear tire. The man glanced toward the store and slowly walked off screen, careful to keep his face hidden from view.

The next camera caught Gloria moving toward the bathroom, and minutes later, appearing with her makeup refreshed and her hair brushed. She stopped at a rack of candy and chose a packet of chocolate before heading to the coffee station and then the front counter. After speaking with Tomas for a moment, she shoved several bills in the tip jar and left the store. Outside, she replaced the gas nozzle and sat in her car eating chocolate before she drove off down the access road and onto I-35 south.

Mazur kept watching, and fifteen seconds after Gloria drove off, headlights appeared from the parking lot where he and Kate had just stood. A blue van with Texas license plates pulled out. He leaned in but could only make out part of the plate. *IVR* . . . He knew enhancement of the image by his computer guys was possible. He might get a full license plate.

"Can I get a copy?" Mazur asked.

"That was the killer?" Tomas asked.

Kate ignored the question, her expression again giving no hint of what she was thinking. "I'm going to need copies of all you have."

***

Detective Mazur called headquarters as they were pulling out of the gas station and followed up on an early query about blue vans reported stolen. He supplied the partial plate. Five minutes later he received a callback. "We have a hit. The van was found in the parking lot of a strip mall."

"Excellent." Kate looked impressed.

He plugged in the location of the mall in the GPS. "Bear with me."

"Take a left up ahead. I know the mall. I went there as a teenager."

"Lead the way." He followed her instructions, even trying a shortcut she suggested that saved them from hitting interstate traffic. Fifteen minutes later they pulled into a lot where a uniformed officer was parked by a blue van.

Mazur retrieved latex gloves from the trunk, where he kept an assortment of supplies that included MREs, basic forensic testing kits, winter boots that he wondered if he'd ever use again, and extra ammunition.

Kate pulled on the gloves that all but swallowed up her hands as he made introductions to the officer who walked them over to the 2010 light-blue Dodge van. "Your timing is perfect," the officer said. "It was on the list given out at the briefing this morning and reported as stolen. Owners were out of town. Husband is a long-haul trucker, and he took the family with him on the last run. When they arrived home early this morning, they realized the van was gone. Car's registered to Bob and Lynda Thompson of Bexar County."

"Do you have their home address?" Kate asked.

The officer rattled it off, and Mazur scribbled it down on a small notebook he carried. "I actually know that area."

Mazur looked in the driver's side window and saw the keys lying on the front seat. He tried the door handle. It was locked. "Locked the keys in the car."

"This is consistent with the Samaritan," Kate said. "Again, he sees himself as a good guy and doesn't want to destroy property if he can avoid it."

Mazur shook his head as he reached for his phone. He called Calhoun, and after a quick exchange they agreed she or one of her technicians would come straight away. "Did any of the people who reported stolen cars used in the Samaritan killings have any kind of trouble with the law?"

"No. I investigated them all. But that doesn't mean we shouldn't talk to the Thompsons."

"Long-haul trucker would know his way around the interstates."

"Yes, he would."

Mazur and Kate drove to the home of Bob and Lynda Thompson. The house was a one-story brick home that looked no bigger than fifteen hundred square feet. There were toys in the front yard and a dog sitting on the front steps.

They walked to the front door. Kate stood to the right of the door while Mazur rang the bell. He moved to the left side. Both had heard of too many cops who had been killed making routine calls.

The front door opened to a plump redhead with a toddler on her hip. "You must be cops. You here about my van?"

"We are," Mazur said, holding up his badge. "We found it. Are you Mrs. Thompson?"

"Yeah, that's me." She grinned and stepped out onto the porch. "Thank God. If I have to bum one more ride with my mother today I might go nuts. When can I get it back?"

"We have a forensic team going over it now," Mazur said.

"That's kind of intense for a stolen van, isn't it?"

"We think the car was used in a murder," Kate said.

"Murder?" Lynda shook her head, her eyes wide. For a moment she stared at them, like she expected a punch line. When one didn't come, she asked, "Who would use a minivan for that?"

"Someone who didn't want to look dangerous," Kate said. "Is your husband home?"

"No, he's traveling. He dropped us off this morning and then had to leave again when the boss called and had a last-minute load for him to deliver. Won't be back until Friday." The toddler grabbed her hair and pulled hard, making the woman frown and push his hand away.

"Where is he now?"

"Five hours from here. I never know where he is half the time. He works a lot. We're saving for a bigger house with another baby on the way." She set the toddler down. "Why're you asking all these questions about us?"

"We're just trying to determine who shot the victim," Kate said.

"Well, if you need to blame anybody for that van being stolen, it's me. I was distracted right before we took off, and I left the keys in the unlocked car. Bob wasn't thrilled, but he knows I get spacey when I'm pregnant." She patted her gently rounded tummy. "We headed out of town and didn't realize it was gone until this morning."

"Do you have security cameras around here?" Mazur asked.

"We don't, but the guy across the street does. But you can save your breath. Bob already asked him for the tape, but the guy said his machine wasn't working."

Mazur looked over his shoulder at the brown stucco home with weeds and overgrown bushes in a front yard covered in scrub and red dirt.

The toddler tried to get around Mazur, but he laid his hand on the boy's shoulder without a second thought. The boy looked up at Mazur, smiling.

"Thank you, Mrs. Thompson. We're just trying to cover all the angles." The edges of his lips lifted as he stared at the boy.

"When can I get my van back?" Lynda asked again.

"It'll be a few days," Mazur said.

"A few days?"

"Our forensic team may come by here and roll your prints." Taking her prints was routine procedure, and given her open and relaxed demeanor, she wasn't involved.

"Why?"

"To eliminate all the people who were normally in the van. Same goes for your husband."

"All right," Lynda said.

Mazur and Kate crossed the street, and he knocked on the neighbor's door. As they waited, he stared up at the camera. No one came to the door, so he tucked a business card in the crease where the door pressed against the jamb.

After they settled back in his car, he stared at the small house for a long moment as Lynda walked her son inside.

His breath stilled.

"You okay?" Kate asked.

He cleared his throat. "Yeah, sure."

She stared ahead at the house. "He reminds you of your son?"

"They all do." He pulled on sunglasses and started the car.

***

105

He sat in front of the televisions searching the channels for any sign of Kate and her news conference, but so far, there was no sign of one. Surely she'd received his text by now?

He rose and paced the room. What was she waiting for? What . . .

The letter. She was waiting for the letter. This was a test to see if he knew about the Samaritan. He checked his watch. The letter would arrive within the hour, and then he'd get his press conference.

He keyed up a recording of her news conference in Oklahoma City. The briefing had begun with the local chief of police, who had turned the podium over to Kate. She stepped up, so assured and confident.

He leaned forward, and freezing the image on her face, traced the line of her jaw and her lips. At the time of this conference, there'd been three confirmed kills, and she'd been playing a game of give and take with the Samaritan for months.

Her goal then had been to piss off the killer. She wanted the shooter to question his manhood. React like a fool. And that's exactly what Richardson had done. He knew better than anybody how easy it was to pull Richardson's strings and make him dance.

If Kate thought she could goad him into acting rashly and making a rookie mistake, she was wrong. She was playing on his terms, and nothing she could say would change his plans.

"Okay, Kate, I'll wait for you to get my letter. Then you'll see you're dealing with the real deal."

CHAPTER ELEVEN

There is more to life than money. There is retribution.

San Antonio, Texas
Tuesday, November 28, 3:00 p.m.

As Mazur drove, Kate dialed Dr. Ryland's number. She said she was curious about the toxicology tests run on Gloria Sanchez.

He picked up on the third ring. "Dr. Hayden."

"Dr. Ryland, did you speak to Gloria Sanchez's family doctor yet?"

"I did."

"Was he treating her for cancer?"

"He diagnosed the cancer about a year ago, but she never came back to see him. He said he followed up and called her; she said she was seeking other treatment. He pressed for details, but she said she had it under control."

"Who was the other doctor she was seeing?"

"He didn't know."

"Is there any record of treatment?" Kate asked.

"Not that I found."

"Did you test her blood for narcotics?"

"I did. I should have results back in about a week."

"And no record of prescription pain meds?" she asked.

"No."

"Thanks, Dr. Ryland." She hung up.

"Why all the questions about Gloria Sanchez's health?" Mazur asked.

"How did she look in the most recent commercial clips?"

"Great. Healthy as a horse."

"I'm just wondering why she hid her disease from her husband and stopped seeing her doctor."

"Fear. Vanity. Who knows?" he said.

She frowned. "Did you ever find out the cause of the car accident that killed the first Mrs. Sanchez?"

"Let me check with Palmer." He dialed her number, and when she picked up, he switched to speakerphone. "Palmer, I have you on speaker with Kate Hayden. Any more information on the first Mrs. Sanchez?"

"She died twenty-one years ago in a car accident on I-35. According to the police report, Selena, aged thirty-nine, was driving late at night when she lost control, ran off the road into a ravine, and hit a tree. The medical examiner reported she didn't die right away. She suffered major internal injuries. Took her several hours before she expired."

"Detective Palmer," Kate said. "Was there a life insurance policy on Selena Sanchez?"

"There was. Fifty thousand dollars."

"Not a huge sum," Kate said. "And Martin Sanchez married Gloria eight months later."

"Correct," Palmer said.

"What did he do with the insurance money?" Kate asked.

"From what I can tell, he started the dealership with it."

"Did anyone check out Selena Sanchez's vehicle to see if it had been tampered with?" Kate asked.

"The police report didn't indicate a problem. But I doubt they'd have been looking for one. The car was all but destroyed, and she didn't have the kind of clout to trigger an intense investigation."

"Okay," Mazur said. "Thanks, Palmer."

"Here to serve," she said.

After he hung up, he angled his head toward Kate. "So what's the connection?"

"Right now, I don't see one." She rubbed her eyes. "I suspect something is off about Gloria's illness, but I'm just not seeing it."

"How about a break? I'm starving. I'm getting a burger."

"Sure."

"I assume you eat meat."

"I do."

"Good. You can eat, too."

She rubbed the back of her neck. "You're always trying to feed me."

"Call it self-interest. You can't think if you're exhausted and starving. When was your last meal?"

"Yesterday."

"The crap from the vending machine?"

"Yes."

Shaking his head, he pulled into a drive-through and ordered two number-three burgers, fries, and sodas. As he pulled to the next window, he fished out his wallet.

"I've got this," Kate said.

"You get the next one." He paid, accepted the bag of food, and parked in a nearby spot. He handed her the bag.

When she took a bite, he nodded. "Not sure I would totally trust a vegetarian."

She pulled off a pickle. "I eat everything but vegetables. Though if they came in vending machines, I might try them." She took another bite. "Eating hot food is a moment to be celebrated."

He smiled and took a bite of his burger. After a moment, he asked, "Do you think Martin Sanchez knew about Gloria's cancer?"

"He looked surprised when you told him."

"You think he killed her?" Mazur asked.

She pinched a piece from the bun. "If he really didn't know about the cancer and he thought she had many more years to live, Sanchez could have hired someone to kill his wife."

"You must be reading my mind." He nodded toward her half-eaten burger. "Finish up."

"This is good," she said. "Thank you."

"I'm still getting to know the area, and the best burger joints are hidden. Haven't found a pizza place that rivals what we had in Chicago. You're from this area, do you know any?"

She picked up a fry. "My restaurant information is outdated."

"You said your mother lives in town."

She arched a brow. "Why the curiosity about my family?"

He smiled. "It's called making conversation, Kate. You must have learned about that in your volumes of profiling books."

If she noticed he had dropped her formal title, she didn't seem to mind. "I skipped that lecture."

He feigned shock. "Oh my, was that a joke?"

"No. It's a fact."

He laughed. "I don't doubt it."

They ate in silence for several minutes before she said, "We should talk to Martin Sanchez. There's more behind what we're seeing."

He wiped his hands on a paper napkin. "He can wait another ten or fifteen minutes. Eat."

She bit into the burger. "Right."

"So what made you choose the FBI, Kate?" he asked.

She set the burger down and wiped her hands on a napkin. "I was working on my PhD when law enforcement approached my linguistics professor with a letter from a stalker. They asked him to read it. He brought me in to consult, and based on the observations we made, the cops were able to catch the guy. The FBI was recruiting so I applied. I'm now a part of a team, and we're sent out to investigate complicated cases."

"You like it?"

"You know how it goes. There are times when you are witness to man's inhumanity to man. Other times when the rush is so exciting, you're on a high for days."

"I hear ya."

"Why'd you become a cop?"

"Couldn't imagine myself in a nine to five. And I wanted to make a difference." He studied her. "Did you choose the FBI because of your father's murder?"

She stilled, and for a moment he wasn't sure if she'd answer. "That was certainly part of the equation. His death devastated our family."

He heard the tremor in her voice. "I'm sorry."

For an instant, she closed her eyes. She then balled the remainder of her burger up in the wrapper. "I blame myself."

"Why?"

"I went to high school with the shooter, William Bauldry. We were in chess club together and got to be good friends."

"What was Bauldry like?"

"He was smart, funny, and very charismatic. I wouldn't call him a popular kid, but all the popular kids liked him."

"And you dated him?"

"As you may have noticed, I'm a geek. This trait is an asset now but wasn't so much in high school. He befriended me, which I found very flattering. When he asked me out on a date, I couldn't resist. I thought I was the luckiest girl in San Antonio."

Mazur was silent. "Why did you break up with him?"

"That niceness he projected to the world changed when we were alone. He became too controlling. He wanted constant affirmations from me, and I couldn't keep doing it."

"So you broke up."

"Yes. He was furious. At first my parents didn't understand why I broke it off. William was so very charming, but when I insisted this was the right move for me, they backed me up. When he called, my parents ran interference. When calling didn't work, he wrote me dozens of letters. The letters all seemed benign at the time, but if I were reading them now, I could point to all the warning signs. I wish to hell I had seen them then."

"You were a kid, how could you?"

"He shot and killed my father. I cannot forgive myself for not seeing the warning signs."

"What about your mother? They can't blame you."

"Mom's support never wavered, which made dealing with it all that much harder. My brother, Mitchell, blamed me for Dad's death. Honestly, I could deal with that better than Mom's understanding."

Mazur was silent for a moment. "Bauldry clearly had mental-health issues. That's not your fault."

She shook her head and tipped her chin up. "I've told my story to other victims of violent crime before. The hope to create a bond and to show them I understand. I'm usually good at distancing myself from the story and the words. But being back in San Antonio is making it difficult to keep that distance."

He knew when to press and when not to and realized now was not the time to dig into her old wound. He sat in silence for a moment, giving her a chance to regain control. And when they were finished, he gathered the trash and dumped it in the garbage.

As they settled in their seats his phone dinged with a text. "My daughter needs to be picked up at school. Do you mind?"

"No."

"It won't take much time."

Mazur moved in and out of traffic. A couple of times he had to think twice about street choices and happily chose correctly each time. Twenty minutes later he pulled onto the tree-lined campus that blended old and new architecture.

Alyssa was sitting in front of the school on a stone bench, her backpack on her lap. She was a petite girl with blond hair that brushed her shoulders and framed a round face.

When she saw Mazur's car, she grinned and hustled toward it.

As he got out of the car, she tossed him a pointed look that resembled many Kate had given him. "Thanks, Dad. We got out early and I didn't want to wait for Mrs. White."

He kissed her on the cheek and took her backpack as he opened the back door. "Going to have to put you in the back like a perp. Company today. Alyssa, this is Agent Kate Hayden."

Alyssa slid into the backseat. "Hi, Agent Hayden."

"Nice to meet you, Alyssa. Call me Kate."

"So, are you the Fed working with Dad?"

"I am."

"So what case are you working on?" Alyssa asked.

"Two murders," Kate said.

Mazur slammed the back car door and glanced at Kate as he slid behind the wheel. "She doesn't need the details, Dr. Hayden."

Alyssa rested her folded arms on the front seat. "*She* likes details."

"I have to honor your father's wishes, Alyssa," Kate said.

"Daaaad. I want to know about the case," Alyssa said.

Mazur shook his head as he circled the parking lot back toward the main entrance. "Dr. Hayden, keep it G-rated."

Kate frowned as if shuffling through her facts to choose the tamest. "Alyssa, we have one victim who was shot. I was summoned to town because there is evidence to suggest there might be a serial killer involved."

Mazur glanced in the rearview mirror in time to see the kid's eyes widen with keen interest.

"So, do you work cases like this all the time?" Alyssa asked.

"I do."

"How long have you been with the FBI?"

"Seven years."

"That is so cool," Alyssa said. "What kind of cases have you worked?"

Mazur's thoughts suddenly turned to the girl in Utah and the other horror cases Kate worked. He cleared his throat, determined to redirect. "What bit of advice can you give Alyssa about staying safe, Dr. Hayden?" Mazur inquired.

Kate turned in her seat and faced his girl. "Never, ever get into anyone's car, even if they threaten to shoot you. You have a better chance with the bullet than if you get in the car."

"Dad says that."

"And always have your cell with you and the GPS locater activated."

"Yes," she groaned. "Dad says that, too."

"If you're ever fighting for your life, don't get fancy and think a ninja kick to the groin is going to save you. He could grab your ankle, and then you'd be flat on your back with a cracked skull. A hard strike to the nose is effective, as well as biting. Play dead if you think it'll work to your advantage."

"Have you ever had to fight anyone off?" Alyssa asked.

"Once late last year. There was a man who was badly hurting women." She glanced toward Mazur. "He figured out I was closing in on him so he came after me."

"Did he hurt you?" Alyssa asked.

"He tried. But then I shot him."

"Wow. Dad, can I have a gun?"

"No."

Alyssa sighed. "Agent Hayden, you aren't much taller than I am," she said.

"Use it to your advantage," Kate said. "Your attacker will underestimate you."

Maybe, Mazur thought, but most people weren't prepared to survive a monster's attack. Adding fuel to his worries, his girl was pretty, outgoing, and not afraid to talk to strangers.

"Reverse pressure on a thumb works, or a punch to the throat," Kate added. "And if you're taken, try to leave clues behind for the people looking for you."

They drove in silence for less than a half mile before Alyssa asked, "How did you get that scar on your face?"

"Alyssa," Mazur said. "Don't be nosy."

"I barely notice the scar anymore," Kate said. "I was shot."

"Is that when your dad died?"

"You've been reading up on me," Kate said.

"Sorry. Curious."

"Curious is good. And yes, the scar is from that shooting."

Mazur pulled into the gated community, paused at the guard station to show his ID, and drove Alyssa to an elegant Spanish-style home. The front door opened, and an older woman with graying hair appeared.

"Good, Mrs. White is home. I forgot my key again." The words tumbled out of the girl as she got out of the car.

Mazur shook his head. "Not good, kiddo. Keep your keys handy."

She leaned in and kissed him on the cheek. "Will do."

He waited until she and the housekeeper disappeared into the house.

"Great kid," Kate said.

"The best."

***

At the Sanchez home there wasn't a collection of expensive cars parked in front of the house. A black sash had been draped above the doors. "Looks like there aren't a lot of people home," he said.

"It would be better if we could talk to Isabella alone."

He wasn't interesting in upsetting the young woman, but he wasn't opposed to pressing her for details. "Agreed."

Kate and Mazur walked up to the front door, but before they could knock it was opened by a young woman with ebony-brown hair and the rich-brown eyes she'd inherited from her father. Her full lips were pulled into a strained frown, and the furrows in her brow ran deep.

"You're the cops, right?"

Mazur pulled off his sunglasses. "Yes, ma'am. Are you Isabella Sanchez?"

"I am. Are you the two who talked to my father last night?"

"We are."

The young woman leaned in a fraction. "I'm not supposed to talk to you without an attorney present. Dad's pretty upset."

"Is he here?" Kate asked.

"No. My father and Mr. Bennett are at the medical examiner's office. They're trying to get Gloria's body released."

"If you don't want to talk to us, we understand," Kate said in a soft voice. "We know this is a terrible time. I've lost a parent, and I understand how painful all this can be."

"You lost a parent?" She slid her hands into her pockets. The gesture signaled she was closing off.

"My father," she said. "He was also shot to death."

"For real?"

"I was younger than you. Seventeen. We were in a parking lot, and a guy came out of nowhere and shot him. It's tough. Tore my family apart."

Kate's tone was almost friendly. There was empathy behind the words but not the softness he'd seen when she spoke to Alyssa.

Tears welled in the girl's eyes. "I don't know what I'd do if I'd seen it. I think I'd go insane."

Kate didn't speak, but she'd moved a half step closer to her as if trying to forge an invisible bond by simply creating closer proximity between them.

Isabella swiped a tear away as she glanced around. "Look, my father and Mr. Bennett aren't here so come inside. It's not like I've anything to give away."

"Thanks," Kate said.

Mazur allowed Kate to go first, and he trailed behind, happy to let her take over the line of questioning. She didn't appear as stiff and controlled as she had in front of the cameras, and some of the tension had melted from her shoulders. Still, she was wound tight.

They sat in the spacious living room, Isabella on the couch with Kate close by. He settled in the chair across from them to give them space.

"Isabella, I hate to ask questions." Kate absently touched the worn bracelet on her wrist. "But I have to."

"Ask," the girl said, shifting her body toward Kate.

"I was reading your father and stepmother's financial statements. Nearly all their money is gone. Did either of them talk to you about money troubles?"

"Gloria ran the money show. A couple of times I asked her about it, but she said I shouldn't worry. She said she had a talent for making money grow."

"But kids hear things," Kate said. "Surely Gloria and your father discussed money."

"I heard them arguing when I was home over summer break. Dad wanted to pull out some cash but said their joint account was almost empty. She wanted to know why he needed the money right now, and he said he shouldn't have to clear purchases with her. She told him he would have to wait a few weeks."

"Do you have any thoughts on what was happening?"

"I don't know. Gloria and Dad's relationship had been kind of cool this year. They seemed to annoy each other. Nothing big. Just lots of little things. I asked Dad, and he said not to worry. It was regular couple stuff."

"Was there anyone hanging around your father or stepmother who bothered you?" Mazur asked. "Anyone who would want to hurt them?"

"Not that I knew, but like I said, they always kept me separate from the business. I wanted to work in the dealership during summer breaks when I was in high school, but Gloria never would let me. She wanted me taking a class. Said my brain was my best asset."

"What about the trips to Laredo to see her mother?" Kate asked. "Your stepmother was driving down to check in on her mother weekly, correct?"

"Gloria was going to Laredo? That's weird."

"What's weird about it?"

"Gloria was always good about paying for Nina's nursing home, but she didn't visit her often."

"Did they have a falling out?" Kate asked.

"Gloria never talked about it except once about five years ago. She'd had too much to drink and said Nina never approved of her marriage to my father."

"Why was that?"

"My mom had only been dead about eight months when they got married. And Dad is fifteen years older than Gloria. Gloria said Nina thought it was a cursed match."

"Nina said *cursed*?" Kate asked.

"Gloria also said that Nina was old school and believed Dad should have been in mourning for at least a year."

"Do you remember your mom?" Mazur asked.

"Faint memories. I've pictures of us. In fact, Gloria took a bunch of pictures of Mom and me and put them in this beautiful scrapbook. It was really touching."

"Your father said Gloria had a condo in Laredo so she had a place to stay when she visited," Kate asked.

"Gloria has had the condo there for years."

"What was it for?" Mazur asked.

"Her trips into Mexico."

"Why did she go to Mexico?" Mazur pressed.

"She had clients down there who liked the high-end cars. Some paid top dollar, and when they did she sometimes would personally deliver the cars to them."

"That's some service."

"Some of the cars cost over one hundred grand. She took care of clients like that because she said they'd come back to her when they had more money to spend." The young woman frowned. "Do you think she was killed for one of the cars?"

"She wasn't driving an expensive car. It was at least six years old and very nondescript," Mazur said.

"Gloria usually doesn't drive old cars," Isabella said. "Not her style at all."

"How was your stepmother feeling physically?" Kate asked.

"Fine, I guess. I saw her a month ago when she came to see me in Washington, and she seemed fine. She got a little tired her first night in town, but said it had been a long day. By morning she was fine. Why do you ask?"

"The medical examiner found a mass in your stepmother's uterus," Kate said.

Isabella's head cocked. "What, like cancer?"

"Yes."

Isabella blinked. "She never said a word to me. Are you sure? She would have told Dad, and he can never keep a secret."

"The medical examiner is positive," Kate said.

Isabella shook her head. "Jesus. She looked fine the last time I saw her. She was her usual self. Always on, if you know what I mean."

"Can you explain?" Kate asked.

"I mean she was wearing makeup and had extra smiles. Although she could be like that when she was stressed."

"What do you mean?"

"When she was worried, she always tried harder to be perfect. When the tough gets going, she put on more makeup. I guess now that I know about the cancer, that explains why she was upset."

"When was she upset?" Kate asked.

"Christmas last year. I finished up exams early and arrived home a few days before they expected me. She was up in her room, listening to music and looking at pictures. I asked her what was wrong, and for a second I thought she was going to tell me. Then she smiled and said she was fine. I never saw her like that again."

The front door opened and closed hard. Hurried footsteps echoed in the foyer and into the living room. Mazur rose and faced Mr. Sanchez.

"What are you doing here?" he demanded as his gaze skimmed to his daughter.

"It's fine, Dad," Isabella said as she rose. "They were just talking to me about Gloria."

Sanchez crossed to his daughter. "I told you not to talk to them unless Bennett was here."

Kate seemed more interested in the man's mannerisms than his words. Her gaze focused first on his fisted fingers, then to the tension banding his shoulders.

"Why do I need an attorney?" Isabella asked. "The questions were straightforward. Did you know Gloria was sick?"

"You shouldn't have told her," Mr. Sanchez said to Mazur. "No good comes from telling her that."

"I still don't understand how your wife could have hidden her illness from you," Kate said. "Were you two living apart?"

"No, of course not." Sanchez sighed. "I had a sense she was off. She was quieter. More removed the last seven or eight months, but I didn't know about the cancer until you told me."

"You're sure you didn't know?"

"What does it matter now what was ailing my wife? It wasn't the cancer that killed her but a serial killer's bullet. The rest doesn't matter."

"Do you think that she knew the extent of her illness?" Kate asked.

He nodded. "Looking back now I think she did. When she was worried she tried extra hard at work, with friends, parties. She hosted several parties over the last couple of months."

"If she knew she was sick, why did she go alone to Laredo so late at night?" Mazur asked.

Sanchez twirled his worn wedding ring. "You would have to know Gloria. She never slowed down. And if there was an obstacle in her way, she didn't go around it. She went through it."

Gloria Sanchez was a type-A personality who didn't like limitations. Her husband might not have known about her illness, but Mazur wondered if she'd had a confidant. Since she worked eighty hours a week and was not close to her mother, it made sense she had friends at the office. "Which of your dealerships did she work out of?" Mazur asked.

"The one in central San Antonio," Sanchez said.

"And you?"

"My shop is twenty miles west of town."

"Did Gloria run all the offices?"

"She oversaw them. The day-to-day operations were handled by the individual branch managers."

"Who managed the central branch?" Mazur asked.

"Lena Nelson."

Mazur scribbled the name in a small notebook.

"Why do you want to talk to Lena? A serial killer murdered my wife."

"I'm looking at all the angles, Mr. Sanchez," Mazur said. "Thank you for your time."

CHAPTER TWELVE

I saw her today. And I smiled when she looked at me. When she was not looking, I stared at her and dreamed of wrapping a cord around her slender neck and strangling her until she died. I am good at that—smiling and planning.

San Antonio, Texas
Tuesday, November 28, 4:15 p.m.

Mazur and Kate arrived at the Sanchez car dealership located in central San Antonio. The glittering glass-and-chrome showroom featured expensive luxury cars. A red Ferrari 488 Spider was parked beside a black Lamborghini Aventador. There were a few more name brands Kate recognized, but the others were unfamiliar.

"Impressive," Mazur said as he ran his hand over the Lamborghini's polished hood.

"I'm not really a car person." Kate looked around the dealership, expecting a salesperson to appear. Their absence suggested news of Gloria's death had reached the staff.

He moved around to the driver's side of the car and peered into the window. "I bet you drive something compact and dependable. And I guess it's white."

"It's silver," she said.

"Were you walking on the wild side when you sprang for that color?"

He was teasing her again, and despite herself she smiled. "I like things plain and simple. Boring can be very refreshing."

"When you bought the car, was it the demo on the lot or the loaner the dealership gave to people when their car needed servicing?"

"I negotiated a good deal."

"I would expect no less. You rent or own the furniture in your apartment?"

"I own it."

He opened the car door and slid behind the wheel. "Standard, practical furnishings. I'm guessing small compact television, no cable, and lots of books." Reverently he palmed the gearshift. "Am I right?"

"Not too far from the truth." It was one thing to profile someone else, quite another to have it done so well back at her. "In my defense, I'm never there. It doesn't make sense to pay for cable." She looked past the car to the office.

With a sigh, he got out of the car. "I've been a cop long enough to know, I need a home that's separate and untouched by work. I had that in Chicago. It was a whole world that didn't revolve around work. Family and friends."

"And you gave it up for a town you've yet to commit yourself to."

He moved toward the Ferrari. "Ever wondered what it would be like to drive one of these?"

She allowed his deflection to stand. "No. And if we're playing guess-my-ride, I'd say your personal vehicle is American made. Dark. You keep the car clean and polished, but if you look on the undercarriage there's some rust from the Chicago winters. I'd also say you don't have subscription radio or personalized plates."

He grinned, reminding her of a kid getting caught with his hand in the cookie jar. "Go on."

"Your suit is older, but it's a classic style and well maintained. You tie your tie in a Windsor knot because you like to look professional. Even your police-issue car isn't the newest model, but again, it's clean and your files organized."

"I'm low man on the totem pole."

"Agreed, but the car doesn't bother you. I'd wager you like to watch classic football games. You wouldn't leave Chicago for San Antonio if family didn't matter. I'd also wager the divorce was not your idea."

"Why do you say that?"

"A few times you've touched your ring finger as if you expected the band to be there."

He laughed. "Pretty good. We could keep playing this game, but I'm afraid of what you'll say. You must be a hit at parties." He held up a finger before she could answer and grinned. "But I'm guessing you don't go to parties. You'd rather spend your time alone reading with your three rental cats."

She couldn't resist a smile. "I listen to audiobooks while I run or hike. I don't like being indoors."

"Why's that?"

"Don't want to waste the sunshine."

Some of his smile faded. "Because you spend too much time in the dark hunting monsters?"

"They're real."

"Yes, they are."

He reached for the door leading back to the offices and glanced down at her as she passed through first. His gaze lingered, and she sensed he wasn't trying to figure her out, but admiring her. It felt good to be noticed by him. He was an attractive man. Strong. Smart. Yearning tightened her muscles.

Inside, the showroom's soft music played. A young man dressed in an expensive charcoal-gray suit approached. He was smiling, but it lacked the warmth reserved for those who looked like they could afford the tab on one of the cars.

"I didn't hear you come inside," the man said. "We're all a little distracted here today."

Mazur pulled out his badge and introduced them. "We'd like to see Lena Nelson."

"She's on the phone."

"Tell her we want to talk to her about the murder of your boss. Now."

The man hesitated, then moved back toward an office with glass walls and vertical blinds that had been drawn shut.

"They've all got to be wondering if they're going to keep their jobs," Kate said.

"After what you told me about their financials, they would have been worried regardless. All this is a house of cards."

The click of heels had them both looking up to a tall, dark-haired Hispanic woman. She wore a red tailored suit that hugged her full curves, and polished black high heels.

She extended a manicured hand to Mazur. "I'm Lena Nelson."

"Detective Mazur."

"Agent Hayden."

Each showed their badges, which she inspected before saying, "Please come into my office." The trail of expensive perfume wafted around her as she led them to an office bearing the nameplate *Gloria Sanchez*. She motioned for them to have a seat at a small round table. She sat across from them. "As you can imagine, we're all in a state of shock. I heard late yesterday when Mr. Sanchez called me. It really hit me this morning when I came into the office and she wasn't here. She's always here."

"You are working in Mrs. Sanchez's office?" Kate asked.

"I tried to work from my own but spent the morning running up and down the hallway to check her files. Finally, I gave up an hour ago and started working from here. We've been inundated with calls from clients, even the media."

"Media?" Kate asked.

Ms. Nelson glanced down at a pink message slip. "Mr. North. I haven't spoken to him yet." She shook her head. "This is so tragic. And it's happened at such a terrible time."

North. It hadn't taken him long to dig into this story. "Why is the timing bad?" Kate asked.

"Well, the timing would never have been great. Gloria was the heart and soul of the business. But she had just negotiated a bank loan and was supposed to sign the papers tomorrow. But the papers aren't signed so now Martin is going to have to figure out what to do."

"The dealership needed a loan?" Mazur asked.

They'd been partnered less than a day and a half, but Kate already had a sense of his interview style. He was your good buddy and confidant. He had an easygoing style that masked a laser focus. She could alter her interview style based on the circumstance, but easygoing was not natural. Mazur had it in spades.

"It's more of a cash-flow issue," Lena said. "We have to pay out quite a bit to keep the dealership open. We have a steady stream of good clients, but there's often a lag time between purchase and payment. Sometimes the load is too much to carry until the cash starts flowing, so we need a little help from the bank. Gloria always saw to it that the loans were paid off within a year. She understood debt but didn't like it."

"What can you tell me about Gloria's background?" Kate asked.

"Gloria met Mr. Sanchez when she was twenty and he was thirty-five. He and his first wife ran a small garage and a used-car dealership.

The wife did the bookkeeping. But it wasn't until he married Gloria that the business grew. They were a good match, they worked hard, and"—she held out her hands—"they have a lot to show for it."

"What was she like to work for?" Kate asked.

"Driven and sometimes difficult to keep up with. She was the first in and the last out. But she was fair, and she rewarded the successful and the loyal. Loyalty was very important to her."

"And for those who weren't successful?" Mazur asked.

"She fired them. It wasn't personal, but she needed her sales people productive. If they didn't deliver, they were gone."

"And if they were disloyal?" Kate asked.

"She went out of her way to ruin them." She shook her head. "I don't mean to speak poorly of the dead. I was twenty-six and a single mother when she took a chance on me. When I came in for the job interview, I thought I was dressed up, but now when I look back I could cringe. I didn't have a clue. But she must have seen something, so she gave me a job in the back. I worked my way up to sales."

"How long have you been here?" Mazur asked.

"Fourteen years."

"Was there anyone who resented being fired?" Kate asked.

"No one likes it." Lena fingered a gold hoop earring. "She gave a lot and expected your loyalty in return."

The credenza behind the large glass desk was filled with dozens of silver-framed pictures. Most featured Gloria with some famous politicians, including the governor and a US senator, as well as a couple of very recognizable movie stars. One picture featured Gloria with her ten-year-old stepdaughter, husband, and a Boston terrier on the young girl's lap. Judging by Isabella's age, the picture had been taken about eight or nine years ago.

"Cute dog," Kate said. Most people dropped their guard when she talked about animals.

"Martin loved that dog. Her name was LuLu."

"I'm guessing LuLu is long gone," Kate asked.

"She died right after that picture was taken. I'd been here about five years."

"Old age?" Kate queried.

"Hit by a car. Whoever hit her just left her body in the driveway for Martin to find when he got home."

"They ever find out who hit LuLu?"

"No."

"Terrible," Kate said.

"Broke Martin's heart."

"Was there anyone who was unhappy with Gloria after she fired them?" Kate repeated the question, suspecting Ms. Nelson would dodge it if she could.

"There were a couple of men, of course. Lots of machismo in this business. Everyone says they can work for a woman, but not every man can."

"Such as?"

"Rick Dryer," she said. "He was fired about two years ago. Came by the dealership several times demanding his job back. The last time he was here he threatened to sue."

"What happened to him?" Mazur asked.

"Stopped coming around. For whatever reason, he let it drop and moved on."

"Who else didn't like Gloria Sanchez?" Kate asked.

"The only other guy that sticks in my mind is Dean Larson. He left about two months ago. Again a guy who knew cars but couldn't sell them. He and Gloria had a very heated argument before he left for good."

"Anything to warrant a call to the police?" Mazur asked.

"Gloria was not fond of involving the police. She was a big supporter of them, but didn't quite trust them."

"Why?" Kate asked.

"I think it goes back to when she was a kid. She never would say, but I think her brother had several run-ins with the cops."

"Where's her brother now?"

"I don't know. She hasn't talked about him in years. The only time she did mention him was after a holiday party. She'd had a couple of drinks."

"She say what the brother had done?" Kate asked.

"Nope. Only that the cops didn't understand him."

"Did Gloria and Martin Sanchez seem happy to you?" Mazur asked.

"Sure. Mr. Sanchez supported Gloria one hundred percent. We all understood that without her, none of this would last. She had a sharp mind for business. Always thinking ahead."

"He wasn't wearing his wedding band yesterday," Mazur said. "Was he having an affair?"

Absently she tugged at the cuff of her blouse. "He loved his wife."

"I'm sure he did, but that's not what I asked," Mazur pressed gently.

She drew in a breath. "He had a wandering eye sometimes. He would never have left Gloria, but he got around."

Maybe the right mistress had come along and Sanchez wanted out of the marriage. "Do you know who he was sleeping with?" Kate asked.

"No. And I didn't want to know. Gloria would not have been happy about that."

Kate nodded toward pictures on a side table featuring Gloria with a local charity. She was presenting an oversize check to a food bank. "She was involved in the community."

"God, yes." The words came out in a rush. "Huge donor, and most of the time no one ever knew she'd donated. When Isabella went off to college, she dedicated more time to several fundraisers. Literacy was her thing. She worked with kids, abused women, even prisoners. She believed reading was everyone's ticket to success."

"Did she have direct contact with those that she helped?" Mazur asked.

"She did. She visited several after-school programs and even sponsored former prison inmates in job programs."

"How did that go?" Mazur asked.

"Very well. We have a few working in our western office with Mr. Sanchez." She hesitated. "You don't think it was one of the ex-cons who shot her, do you?"

Mazur shook his head. "I don't know what to think at this point."

"I spoke to Martin this morning. The poor man is devastated. He can't believe a woman so full of life would be gunned down like that."

Kate didn't speak but noted the subtle shift in the woman's tone when she said *Martin*.

"He says the medical examiner hasn't released the body yet." Ms. Nelson shook her head. Tears glistened. "He started crying. I can't believe I'm even talking about bodies and a funeral. It's all just so senseless. Do you know when they'll release her?"

"I can't say for sure. The medical examiner is always cautious in the case of a homicide," Mazur said.

Lena fingered a thin gold bracelet dangling around her wrist. "I would hate to find a dead loved one."

"By the way," Mazur said. "Mrs. Sanchez was driving a white four door. Older car. Modest. Did she take that car out often?"

Lena shook her head. "No, but she did check that car out a few times last year and this past summer. Never said why."

Mazur removed a card from his breast pocket. "Call me if you think of anything that might be of help."

She glanced at the card, flicking the edge with a manicured finger. "Of course."

Mazur and Kate didn't speak as they made their way back through the showroom to his car.

"What do you think?" Mazur asked.

"She seems genuinely upset."

"I've seen killers mourn those they've murdered."

"True." She fastened her seatbelt. "Did you notice the way her voice softened when she mentioned Martin?"

"Not particularly."

"She was working hard to hide her emotions. But her voice did change when she talked about him. She also touched the bracelet on her wrist. I bet it was a gift from him."

"You think they were having an affair?"

"Likely, given the way she talked about him. If she said he had a wandering eye, that means there were others. A look into Mr. Sanchez's phone records might give you your answer."

"Already subpoenaed. Should be able to see those records today." Mazur checked his notebook. "Ms. Nelson mentioned the charities. I'd like to talk to the ex-cons she hired."

Kate nodded. "Mr. Sanchez works in the west-end office. He'd know who they are. We could call him and get the names."

Mazur shook his head. "I don't want contact with him until I've more information. A better plan is to pay the office a visit. I don't like to give folks too much of a heads-up when I'm coming."

CHAPTER THIRTEEN

*"Yet each man kills the thing he loves . . . The coward
does it with a kiss, the brave man with a sword."*

—*Oscar Wilde*

San Antonio, Texas
Tuesday, November 28, 5:15 p.m.

Half an hour later Mazur pulled into the parking lot of the Sanchezes'
west-end office. He glanced toward Kate as she appraised this simpler
office stocked with moderately priced cars designed for the average
consumer.

They walked inside. This time a young woman dressed in black
slacks and a white blouse greeted them. Her dark hair was pulled into
a ponytail, and her shoes were flat, as if she expected to cover a lot of
ground in a given day.

Mazur showed his badge. "Who manages this site?"

"That would be me. I'm Brenda Conner. Chief cook and bottle
washer."

"Sounds like you might be stretched thin."

Her smile was tense, nervous. "Staff cuts. Budget issues. I'm just glad to still have a job. Who knows now what's going to happen with the boss going down."

"Will Martin Sanchez be able to keep it going?" Mazur asked.

"Don't get me wrong, he's a nice guy. But Gloria was the engine behind it all."

"Did she come by here often?" Mazur asked.

"Not so much, probably because Martin was here."

"Did they work well together?" Kate asked.

"Each had their specialty and their way of doing things. Different styles. But it worked for them."

"I understand she was active in the community."

"Yeah. She helped in all kinds of ways. Kids, homeless, you name it."

"Also heard she reached out to ex-cons."

"She did."

"How did that work?" Mazur asked.

"For the most part, pretty good."

"Most part?" Mazur asked.

"Most of the guys are good workers. A couple were flakes. Got drunk, showed up late. One tried to clean out the register."

"How many of these guys did she hire?"

"Ten or twelve. But if you're thinking one of those guys shot her, you're wrong. They all adored her. Even the dumb ones who blew a second chance still respected her."

"How did they blow the second chance?" Mazur asked.

"Two got back into drugs. Couldn't stick with the program. Their drug tests came up positive, and she fired them on the spot."

"Whom did she fire?" Mazur asked.

"Harry Driver and Matt Jones."

"Where are they now?"

"Both have been gone a couple of months. They each came by here to pick up their final paycheck, so I couldn't tell you where they are now."

"Either make threats?" Kate asked.

"Matt made some noise. He wanted the test redone, so Gloria had it redone. He still failed. He wanted another chance to get clean. She told him to come back in six months and she'd retest him." Brenda folded her arms over her chest. "Gloria had a big heart, but she had little patience for weakness."

"That could make some people angry," Kate said.

"She could be exacting, but she was also generous. It was hard to stay mad at her for too long."

"We heard that Martin was having an affair," Kate said.

The abrupt shift seemed to catch Brenda off guard, and she looked flustered. "I heard rumors. And he liked to take afternoons off a couple of times a week."

"Do you know who he was sleeping with?" Kate asked.

"No." She shuddered. "Gloria's dead, but that information would bring her back from the dead to haunt Martin and whomever he was doing."

Mazur glanced around the shop, wondering what other angle to this case they were missing. "Where do the ex-cons work?"

"In the garage here. They were training to be mechanics."

"Can I get a list of the employees in this shop?" Mazur asked.

"Sure, I guess that's okay." She frowned. "Or should I ask for a warrant? I'm not sure how this works."

"I can get a warrant or you can make this easy," Mazur said smoothly.

Slowly she shook her head. "I should ask Martin. For now he's the guy in charge and I can't afford to lose my job. I'll ask him."

"Any of the ex-cons working now?" Mazur asked.

"Rocco's back there."

"Can I talk to Rocco?"

"Sure." She led them through the back toward a large building with six open bays. All were empty except the first one. There was a late-model red Ford truck on the lift.

The whirring of a pneumatic drill mingled with the sound of rock music rising from a cell phone on a workbench. Mazur approached the tall man with the short-sleeved T-shirt and muscled arms covered in tattoos.

"Rocco!" Brenda shouted over the music.

The man looked up from a ratchet set, and his eyes narrowed as he looked at Mazur. Rocco didn't need to see a badge to know he was face-to-face with a cop.

Still, Mazur held up his shield and identified himself and Kate. "We're looking into Gloria Sanchez's murder."

"Figured." He set down the tools and reached for a rag. "What can I do for you?"

"Know anyone who would want to shoot her?"

He shook his head. "Mrs. S was a class act. She was a good woman and took a chance on me when no one else would. I will always be grateful to her."

"Was everyone as grateful?" Kate asked.

Rocco shrugged. "She was a ballbuster. Some might not have liked it when she dropped the hammer, but they got over it." He shook his head while glancing toward Brenda before he commented in a lower voice. "She didn't have an enemy in this shop. But I can't say the same for her in the showroom."

"Who didn't like her?"

"She took risks both with a bunch of ex-cons and in business. Some were afraid her gambles might bring down the whole shop."

"What about Matt and Harry? They make threats?" Mazur asked.

"Sure, they made noise, but they're loudmouths. All talk, but neither one of them has the stones to carry it out."

"What about the guys who weren't loudmouths?" Kate asked. "Watch out for the quiet ones, right?"

He studied her. "I don't know what you're talking about."

"Sure you do. It's the ones you don't see coming who get you killed."

He wiped his hand with the rag. "Billy Boy was like that."

"Billy Boy?" she asked.

"William was the name he liked better. Made him sound smart. I called him Billy Boy just to get under his skin."

"What's his last name?" she asked.

"Bauldry. William Bauldry."

The color drained from Kate's face. She was rattled and for the first time at a loss for words. After a few seconds, she asked, "Are you sure about the name?"

Mazur had been a cop too long to believe in coincidence. Bauldry had shot Kate and now was linked to a crime that had brought her back to San Antonio. He shifted his gaze to Brenda. "What can you tell us about Bauldry?"

"He was here for the first six months of this year. He didn't like getting his hands dirty but knew a job was a condition of his release, so he did whatever was asked of him."

"Rocco, what didn't you like about William?" he asked.

"He didn't say much, but he was always looking and watching. He was good at buttering up Gloria. I think she might have known him from back in the day."

"What do you mean by back in the day?" Kate asked.

"From before she married the old man. Neither one ever mentioned it, but it was a vibe."

"Does Bauldry still work here?" Mazur asked.

"No. He did his six months of the work-release program."

"Has he been back since?" Mazur asked.

"Nope. Never heard another word from him again. I think his family has money. He doesn't need this gig."

"Thank you," Kate said.

"If I have more questions, I'll be back," Mazur added.

"I'll be here as long as I have a job," Rocco said.

Outside, Mazur thanked Brenda, and as he and Kate walked back toward the main building, he put on his sunglasses and studied the dealership for an extra moment. "What are your thoughts?" Mazur asked.

Kate frowned as she slid her hands into her pockets. "Rocco is nervous. He has a good thing and sees it going away. Brenda clearly sides with Gloria, who had enemies that were far more dangerous to her than a random serial killer."

"Agreed." He shook his head. "What're the chances that a woman deeply in debt, sick with cancer, who made regular trips over the border, would be gunned down on the side of I-35?"

"Low."

Mazur's jaw tightened. "Bauldry's the man we need to talk to now. Are you okay with that?"

"I see the logic."

"That's not what I asked. Are you okay with it? I can talk to him alone."

"No. I'm not afraid of him."

"You trying to convince me or yourself?"

"Myself. I'd be lying if I said I wasn't dreading seeing him again." She flexed her fingers. "I know where he lives."

"Really?"

She shrugged, but her color was still pale. "I've kept tabs on him."

His phone rang, and he snapped it free of its holster. "Mazur." His jaw tensed. "Okay." He settled the phone back in the holster on his hip. "Your letter from the Samaritan has arrived."

She checked her watch. "It's late."

***

Kate, Mazur, and Palmer watched as Calhoun dusted the envelope that had been addressed to Agent Kate Hayden in care of the San Antonio Police Department. The letter had come through the mailroom and had caused some confusion in the ranks when no one recognized her name.

Palmer caught the query from the mailroom and had immediately told them to set it down. She was there in minutes to bag it.

Calhoun swirled the brush with magnetic powder over the paper. It was a long shot she'd pull viable prints given that it arrived by US mail. She carefully sliced the very end off the envelope. Oddly the envelope was not self-sealing, which meant she would test the glue strip for saliva and DNA.

Calhoun tapped the envelope on the end, and the letter slid out. She photographed the folded yellow lined notebook page several times next to the envelope before opening the single sheet of paper.

The note was handwritten in a mixture of block and lowercase lettering in a black thick-tipped marker. The handwriting appeared crude and at first glance matched the other Samaritan notes.

But Kate realized immediately that the writing style was slightly different than the other Samaritan notes she'd analyzed.

Kate;
Your voice is always in my head. And all I hear are your lies. You are wrong about me. I am smarter than you. There will be more deths soon. I will show the world you aren't an Angel of Mrcy.
Samaritan

"He said your voice was 'in my head.'" Mazur's gloved fingertips held up the edge of the plastic bag that contained the letter.

"The Samaritan isn't the first killer to blame me for his actions." His clear, bold handwriting suggested anger and resentment. None of what this killer had done was her fault. *None of it.* And yet the burden of his sins would rest heavily on her shoulders until she caught him.

"Guy spells like I do," Palmer said.

Kate pulled out her phone and snapped pictures of the note. What was it about the letters that struck a familiar chord? "Don't be fooled by the misspellings. In letters like this they're often intentional. He spelled *are* correctly in one sentence and then incorrectly in the next. He wants us to think he's uneducated."

Palmer reread the letter. "He spelled *Samaritan* right. A word I find challenging without spell check."

A queasiness washed over Kate as Palmer reread the letter again. "The words remind me of William Bauldry," she said.

Calhoun photographed the envelope and letter. "I'll dust it for prints and compare."

"Who's William Bauldry?" Palmer asked.

Kate had shaken off some of the initial shock she'd felt when she'd heard his name at the garage, so it was easier to keep her voice even as she explained again what he'd done. "If you find any prints on this letter, compare them to Bauldry's."

"Having his name certainly will make the comparison easy," Calhoun said.

Kate snapped several more pictures of the letter. She turned from the group and studied the misspellings, the grammar, the phrasing, the word choices hinting of a neutral dialect. "Detective Mazur, would you read the letter out loud?"

"Sure, why?" he asked.

"It was written by a man."

"How can you be sure?"

"It's an educated guess based on the shape of the letters, which are very boxy. The pen was also pressed firmly against the paper."

He read through the letter.

She closed her eyes and listened to the inflections and the nuances of his Chicago accent, which naturally seeped into the neutral language. "Gloria Sanchez's shooter, who spoke briefly on the murder video, didn't have a deep Texas drawl. And none of the phrasing in the note hints at a dialect. Bauldry's parents were from California and he lived there until he was eight, so his accent was always neutral."

"What else do you see?" Mazur asked.

"All the positive statements are not contracted, but the one negative statement is contracted."

"What does that mean?" Palmer asked.

"It's an unconscious pattern that he might not be aware of," Kate said.

"How do these compare to the other Samaritan letters?" Mazur asked.

"They're almost identical. But Mr. North got a hold of two letters and published them. Anyone could replicate them."

"How did North get the letters?" Mazur asked.

"He said he bribed a forensic tech in Minnesota."

"Or Mr. North knew more about what Richardson was doing. Maybe he had an inside track with Richardson," Palmer said. "From what you've said, he seems to have a lot of intimate knowledge of the case."

"He does. And he's received a great deal of attention since he covered this case. The publicity had died down considerably since Richardson's arrest."

"What do you know about North?" Mazur asked.

"He received his journalism degree from Columbia twenty years ago. He's worked at several major papers, but two years ago left his job at the time after it was proven he manufactured and exaggerated facts while covering a criminal trial. When it all came out, he resigned. Shortly after that, he founded a news site that was doing moderately well until the Samaritan shootings."

"Could he have written these letters?"

"I considered that," she said. "No one has been able to link him to the letters. And I've tried, as well as a half dozen detectives just like you."

"I haven't tried," Mazur said.

CHAPTER FOURTEEN

I am my brother's keeper.

San Antonio, Texas
Tuesday, November 28, 7:15 p.m.

Mazur might not have been a genius like his older brother, Sebastian, a prosecutor in Chicago, or have the physical strength of his bull-in-a-china-shop brother, Samuel, a detective in the Windy City, but he did have the power to persevere. He'd done it several times when he'd been deployed in the Middle East, and he'd done it when his son had died and his ex-wife had announced the move south with his only kid. If he wanted something badly, he did what it took to overcome any obstacles.

Today he wanted the I-35 shooter. The Samaritan copycat or accomplice had pulled the trigger and killed Gloria Sanchez.

He stood with Kate and Detective Palmer just outside the press briefing room. The buzz of conversation on the other side of the door told him the media had shown up in large numbers. Good. He wanted the attention.

The firm click of boots connecting with tile told him the chief had arrived. The chief had no tolerance for bullshit rising in the ranks and enough backbone to support the men and women who worked under him. When Mazur had approached him about the news conference, he'd given his consent.

Chief Saunders's gaze swept over Dr. Hayden and moved to him. "Detective Mazur. Agent Hayden."

The chief wrapped a large hand around Kate's. She didn't shy away from the strong grip or the height difference, and he continued, "So, this nut has communicated with you?"

"Yes."

"How do you want to play this, Agent Hayden?" the chief asked.

"Your department is the lead in this investigation," Kate said. "Give a brief of the facts as you know them, and then introduce me. I'll make a short statement so that whoever sent me that text knows he's been heard."

"And then what, Dr. Hayden? The shooter is just going to come running from the crowd to confess his sins?"

"I'll make a few remarks designed to irritate him. Hopefully that will smoke him out." She pulled a sheet of paper from a leather notebook. "Talking points to consider."

"What about Richardson? He had any regular visitors in jail?" the chief asked.

"My boss called the jail, and they told him that the doctor has had no visitors or any kind of correspondence," Kate said.

The chief glanced at the notes and frowned. "Painting a target on your back, Dr. Hayden?"

"It won't be the first time."

"Detective Mazur," the chief said. "You going to keep this gal alive?"

"Yes, sir."

"I suggest you stick to my talking points," Kate said.

The chief arched a white brow as he shook his head and looked to Mazur and Palmer. "Does this sit well with you two? You're the investigating officers."

"It's an opportunity we might not get again, and Dr. Hayden is right," Mazur said, looking to Palmer.

Palmer nodded her agreement. "This is our best play."

"What if the killer turns out to be someone the victim knew?" the chief asked.

"We're chasing that angle, too," Mazur said.

"All right," the chief said. "I'll play along at your dog and pony show." He rolled the notes into a tight cylinder and, clenching them in his fist, walked out into the room. Mazur, Palmer, and Hayden followed.

The chief stalked up to the podium and stared down the room of two dozen reporters.

Dr. Hayden stood next to Mazur and Palmer behind the chief. Her face was as unreadable as always. She didn't sway, fidget, or shift her stance. If this bothered her, she gave no sign of it.

The chief cleared his voice and began the briefing. He named the victim and explained where she'd been shot. "There have been some media reports suggesting this case is linked to the I-35 killings, also known as the Samaritan killings. The San Antonio police are working closely with the FBI, specifically their profiler, Dr. Kate Hayden." Several reporters called out, raised their hands. He pointed to a dark brunette in a blue suit.

"Do you know where Mrs. Sanchez stopped and how her car broke down?"

"We do," the chief said. "But I won't share those details at this time."

The reporters fired more questions, all of which zeroed in on the details the chief would not confirm. Finally he held up his hands. "Let me turn the podium over to Dr. Hayden."

She moved up to the microphone, thanked the chief, and looked at the reporters, never flinching from the bank of cameras. She adjusted the microphone, paused, and then ran through the stats of the cases along I-35 before focusing on the Gloria Sanchez case. "We have solid evidence linking Dr. Richardson to two of the five killings and expect to link him to the other three. At this time, we're still trying to determine if or when this killer might have been in contact with Dr. Richardson. We have several leads regarding clandestine communication, but I can't discuss them now."

Mazur knew Kate's last comments were meant to catch the killer's attention. They didn't have much on the killer at this stage, but no one outside of the investigating team knew that. He shifted his body forward a fraction toward Kate, but said nothing. He wanted her to understand that he had her back.

"Evidence suggests this case is connected to the others," Kate said.

"How can you be sure?" another reporter asked.

"I can't discuss the details now." This new murderer was killing in the style of Richardson for a reason. "I can tell you that I believe this killer is a white male in his midthirties to midforties. I believe he either is underemployed or has no job at all. My guess is that he lives with family, or is very dependent on family money, and that he has no romantic interest in his life."

"In Oklahoma, you said the killer might be impotent. Did that turn out to be true?" the brunette asked.

"Yes."

"Any physical description of this killer?" another reporter asked.

"So far, no." She raised her gaze directly to the camera. "We have gas station footage of someone loitering around the victim's car and are still analyzing facial images." Not true, but the shooter didn't know that.

A dozen hands went up, and she answered more questions, many a reiteration of what she'd already said. Over the rumble of questions, a loud, deep voice from the back shouted, "How did Richardson make contact with this apprentice?"

She shifted her gaze and stared at the tall, bulky man with dark hair and brown-rimmed glasses. For a moment she didn't speak before she said, "Mr. North, you've been at this long enough to know I can't share specifics."

Mazur's attention zeroed in on the man in the back. Mr. Taylor North was the reporter who had followed this case so closely. Nothing remarkable about him at first glance. A second look revealed an intense gaze locked on Dr. Hayden.

"Can you tell us more about what you saw in the gas station footage?" North asked.

"No comment," she said.

"When you were brought into the original case, it took you almost a year to catch Richardson. Three women died while you headed the case," North said. "Do you really think you're the person to solve this case? How many innocent people are going to die before you crack it?"

Kate didn't waver. "Are those rhetorical questions?"

"No. I want to know," North said.

She drew in a slow breath. "I'm the best person for this job. Evidence led me to Charles Richardson. And it'll lead me to this killer. I strongly urge all motorists to check their vehicles before traveling on this interstate, and I'm here to make sure no more women die."

"What does it feel like to be back in San Antonio, Texas?" North challenged. "Have you been back since you and your father were gunned down here?"

She didn't blink or flinch, but he saw her right hand clench the podium until her knuckles whitened as she said, "That has no relevance here today."

"Are you worried about the man who shot you coming after you again?" North asked.

"No. He is irrelevant."

Kate Hayden gave the appearance of cool detachment, but he saw the way she still gripped the edge of the podium.

More questions rumbled from the crowd, including several more from North, but from everyone's vantage point other than Mazur's, she was rock solid.

Other reporters fired more questions, which were mostly a repeat of what had already been asked. Kate answered them all and gave no hint of frustration.

When the conference was finished and the press escorted from the room, he turned to her. "What's the deal with North? How did he end up knowing so much about you?"

Carefully she stacked her papers. "Mr. North is my number-one media fan. He believes if he insults me enough I'll blow a gasket and give him a quote."

Mazur wondered where she stowed all the emotions. He'd seen her reaction behind the podium, so he knew they were there. "He sure got down here fast."

"He monitors all activities on I-35. The shooting would have hit his radar almost immediately. I suspect he wasn't far away and knows I've worked all the cases."

"He doesn't bother you?"

"I didn't say that. He has a talent for finding the raw nerve. But he won't bully me into a quote."

Mazur found he liked Kate's professional style more and more. "And that bit about analyzing facial footage from the gas station. We never saw his face."

"I never said I didn't lie to the media, Detective Mazur. I know the traits liars project, which makes me very good at deception. I can play their game, too."

Shaking his head, he grinned. "Well played, Kate."

She checked her watch. "Who's watching the burner phone left at the crime scene?"

"Calhoun. She's plugged it into a charger and will call if anyone texts the number."

"Good. I think it's now time that we paid a visit to William Bauldry's house," she said. "Time to see what he's been up to."

"You can handle that?" Mazur asked.

"Of course."

Mazur angled his head as he studied a very genuine expression. "That a truth or a lie, Kate?"

"Doesn't matter. The job has to be done."

***

Mazur didn't speak to Kate as they drove across town to William Bauldry's house. She was glad for the quiet and the time to process the press conference and settle her thoughts regarding Bauldry. Dealing with Bauldry again bothered her very much, but feelings had no relevance in her line of work.

They parked in front of a large adobe-style home. "I'm doing the talking," Mazur said.

"But I know him. I should lead the conversation."

"You know him too well. You're not impartial regardless of how many times you say it out loud."

"I'm objective and can handle myself."

"This is my case. I do the talking." Steel underscored the words, and it gave her enough pause to take an emotional step back and see his logic.

He walked up to the front door and rang the bell. The chimes echoed in the house. Footsteps sounded, followed by the click of several locks, before the door opened to a young woman. She was small, in her midthirties, and her blond hair was pulled back into a tight bun. She wore a black shirt and slacks.

"Can I help you?" she asked.

Mazur held up his badge. "I'm here to see Mr. Bauldry."

"He's in New York right now," the woman said. "He'll return in two weeks."

"When did he leave?" Mazur asked.

"A week ago."

"Do you have a number for him?" he pressed.

She stood ramrod straight, but the tilt of her chin betrayed some of her nerves. "I'm not at liberty to give out that information, but I can give him your name and number when he calls in."

Mazur gave her his card. "Who are you?"

"Mr. Bauldry's housekeeper. Elizabeth Lopez."

"Have him call me as soon as you give him the message."

"Yes, sir." The woman moved to close the door, but Mazur blocked it with his foot. "Tell Mr. Bauldry he will not want to make me wait long."

She paled, nodded, and closed the door, and Mazur turned from the entrance, his jaw pulsing.

He inspected the large home. "Looks like Bauldry landed on his feet."

"It's family money," she said.

"Do you think he's in New York?" Mazur asked.

"No. William hates crowds. He couldn't handle the packed hallways of high school. New York would be the last place he'd go."

"Where else could he be?"

"Bauldry has a brother, Jeb, outside town," she said. "Jeb might know where William is."

"That's all he has in the way of family?"

"That I know of."

"Let's pay him a visit."

Twenty minutes later they arrived at Jeb Bauldry's house, located twenty miles outside of town on a sprawling ranch. Bald cypress trees lined an aggregate driveway that led through stone pillars toward an arched entrance.

"The family is more well off than I imagined," Mazur said.

"The old man made his money in oil in Houston. Invested wisely in real estate. Jeb then took over and had his father's knack for making money. He avoided the market meltdown in '08, then bought stocks afterward for a song and rode them higher. If you have investments, he's the man to see."

"Only investment I have is my condo in Chicago, which I'm still trying to sell. If I can't see it or touch it, I don't want it. What about you?"

"I'm in the markets."

"I bet with your brain you can see the trends."

"Sometimes."

"So what are you going to do with your millions?"

That prompted a smile. "I've no idea."

He paused. "First, you didn't discount the millions. Second, how could you not know?"

"Work gives me the most pleasure."

He shook his head. "All work and no play . . . how does that go?"

"I'm the first to admit I'm very boring. If you want excitement, find someone else."

Mazur rang the bell, and they waited in silence until the front door opened. Both showed their badges.

"Agent Kate Hayden to see Mr. Bauldry."

"One moment, please." The woman left and returned. "Yes, he's waiting for you in his study. Right this way."

They passed along polished marble floors through an arched passageway that led to an open room. A bank of windows opened up onto a lush stand of grass. The woman steered them to an office.

Jeb Bauldry rose and came around a large hand-carved desk. His gaze locked on Kate.

"The last time we saw each other in person was at my brother's sentencing."

"Yes," she said. She'd felt sorry for the family dealing with the wake of their son's violence. Bauldry senior had died a year later of a heart attack, and Mrs. Bauldry had passed five years ago from cancer.

"I supposed you've come about William."

"Yes," said Mazur. "Is he here?"

"I haven't heard from him in months. The family has had almost no contact with him since he went to prison."

"Have you seen him in the last year?" Kate asked.

"I have. And he's a different person now, Kate. He's not the troubled young man he used to be. My father saw to it that he had doctors while in prison. He would never hurt you again."

Kate's focused on showing no reaction, but it was harder than she'd anticipated.

"Has he mentioned Dr. Hayden?" Mazur asked.

Jeb drew in a breath. "My mother visited William while in prison. I wasn't happy about it, but he was her son and she couldn't abandon him. She said he mentioned you often."

"What did he say?" Kate asked.

"He was desperate to reach you and get your attention. I don't blame you for ignoring him, but it troubled him deeply."

"Makes perfect sense that I wouldn't engage him in a dialogue."

Jeb was silent for a moment, clearly rethinking the consequences of his comment. "We were all devastated when he shot your father. Our family grieved just as much as yours."

"I doubt that."

He shook his head. "No one has pity for the shooter's family. No one. I struggled for years to get beyond what William had done. I didn't do anything wrong, but I was punished."

She wasn't going to get into a discussion on who suffered most. "Where is William now?"

"I assume he's at his house. That's where he's basically been holed up since he got out of prison."

"He wasn't there when we paid him a visit," Mazur said. "Does he have other properties?"

"There's the ranch. It's fifty miles west of town. He was never crazy about it as a kid, but that would be the only other place I'd imagine him going. Why are you asking about William? Has he approached you?"

"His name came up in an investigation," Mazur said. "We just want to talk to him. We think he might have valuable information."

She suspected he'd avoided the mention of murder, knowing the word could likely silence a man worried about legal troubles. "I can't help you. Feel free to check the ranch. We don't keep staff out there since Mom passed. She was the one who loved that place most. But I can give you a key and permission to investigate."

"That would be helpful."

"Are you going to arrest William?"

"Right now we simply want to talk to him." Mazur was smooth, made it sound like they were looking to have a friendly chat and catch up.

Jeb moved to his desk and retrieved a key from the center drawer. "The place is a little rustic. It was Mom and Dad's first home, before Dad made his money. I guess that's why William likes it. Reminds him of simpler times."

Mazur accepted the key. "Does the family have a place in New York?"

Jeb's brow furrowed. "No. All our business is in Texas. Why do you ask?"

Mazur rattled the key in his fist. "I don't know. It's a big city. A good place for a guy like William to hide."

"That would be the last place William would go," Jeb said.

"Why would his housekeeper, Elizabeth Lopez, tell us he was in New York?" Mazur asked.

"She must have been mistaken," Jeb said.

"I'm not debating that with you now. If William is not at this cabin, where else would he be?"

"It's anyone's guess. William is smart. Knows how to set up dummy corporations that own multiple properties. If he doesn't want to be found, it's going to be tough to find him."

***

Kate was silent as Mazur drove on TX-173, bracketed by grassy flatlands and scrub trees and endless barbwire fencing. The sky was full of stars and the landscape full of scattered barns and farmhouses. A few trucks and cars passed them, but for the most part this stretch of road was quiet and dark.

Twenty minutes later they arrived at the entrance to the Bauldry property, marked by twin stone pillars and metal struts that supported a sign that read "Stone Horse Farm."

Dust kicked up around the car as they drove another ten minutes down a dirt road that ended at a one-level ranch built over one hundred years ago. It had a tin roof, a wraparound porch, and stone chimneys that hugged both the east and west sides of the house. The house was dark, the only sign of movement caused by the wind rustling through the trees near a horse corral.

Mazur left his car running and headlights shining into the house as they both got out of the car. Drawing his weapon, he moved in front of her and took the five stairs first. Kate also drew her weapon, and they stood on opposite sides of the door. He pounded on the door with his fist and called out, "Bauldry! San Antonio police!"

Silence answered them. It didn't appear that anyone was here, but a smart cop assumed trouble waited behind the door. A dark house and a man who didn't want to be found created a ripe scenario for trouble. Mazur banged again on the door, then tried the doorknob. It twisted open.

"It's common for folks out here to not lock their doors," Kate said.

"I never trust an unlocked door." He raised his gun and pushed open the door. Again silence. With the headlights shining into the house, now he had enough light to switch on the lights in the porch and main room. Reddish-brown tiled floors ran throughout a large den and into a connected kitchen. Twin guns hung over a stone fireplace, faded red Navajo rugs warmed the floor by a leather couch, and a collection of deer antlers adorned the wall. Off to the side stood a wide-screen television.

Again, Mazur shouted, "William Bauldry! San Antonio police!"

No response.

"Stay here," Mazur ordered. He moved into the house slowly, constantly looking left, right, and up toward the ceiling as he went through the den and kitchen and into the two bedrooms on opposite sides of the house. He shouted to Kate, "All clear!"

Her weapon in her grip, she moved into the house's center, noting the landscape oils on the walls, the rich brass light fixtures, and the ornate tile work in the kitchen. This might have been the senior Bauldry's first house, but they'd clearly upgraded it recently.

"I'm in the bedroom on the right," Mazur said. "Have a look at what I found."

She found Mazur standing by a desk. Centered on top was a framed picture of Kate and William taken when they were dating. They both were smiling. His arm was draped over her shoulder, and she stood close to him. "He's not forgotten you," Mazur said.

"That picture was taken when we were in high school."

"But the glass is freshly polished. And the image faces toward the bed."

She didn't want to touch the frame or get any closer to the image. "I remember the moment. The picture was taken at a concert near the Alamo." She glanced toward William's hand tightly clutching her shoulder. "I had to wrench free of his hold."

"How did he react?"

"He was frustrated. Wanted to know why I was so cold to him. He was only trying to show me how much he loved me. He ordered my meal for me at dinner. I didn't want to eat but he insisted and then was moody when I didn't eat. He kept interrupting me and telling me I was wrong. I broke up with him shortly after." An uneasy feeling clawed up her spine, but she pushed it aside. "Is there anything here that might link him to the shooting?"

"Nothing out in the open. If we want to search drawers and closets, it's smarter to get a warrant." He pulled out his phone and took a picture of Bauldry and Kate. "But that could change. I noticed a shed out back. I want to have a look."

"Of course." She followed him, grateful to turn her back on the room and step outside into the fresh air.

He retrieved a flashlight from the trunk of his car, and they followed a graveled path around the side of the house to the large shed. Mazur kept his gun drawn and the flashlight shining ahead.

At the shed, while she stood to the side, he pushed open the large sliding door. He shone the light inside the workshop, searching for any movement that would alert him to danger. But nothing moved. There wasn't a sound.

His light landed on a vintage red truck that looked like it dated back to the forties.

"He's always liked old cars," Kate said. "His father has a large collection as well."

"The advantage to old cars is they don't have GPS, making them impossible to track." He moved toward the truck and shone the light inside. "Where would he go if he's not here?"

"I don't know. His brother said he has many properties."

He nodded toward the door and closed it behind him. As he stared out over the vast land and the distant horizon, he shook his head. "Finding him is like looking for a needle in a haystack."

***

An hour later, Mazur dropped Kate off at the car rental place. As she pushed through the front doors, a clerk greeted her with a smile, which she made herself return. When given the choice of cars, her first inclination had been to choose white, but remembering Mazur's earlier teasing, she chose red. Hardly rebellious, even though for her it felt a little that way.

When she arrived at her hotel, she went straight to her room. The instant she opened the door, she hesitated. The hair on the back of her neck rose. Normally she didn't have cleaners come into her room. She hated having her space invaded. But today, she'd forgotten to remind the front desk.

She moved into the room, hand on her gun as she looked first in the closet and then under the bed. Nothing. In the bathroom, she reached for the shower curtain. Her heart pounded for reasons she could not quite explain. She tightened her hold on the grip of her gun and pulled back the curtain. Nothing.

She closed her eyes. "Not good, Hayden. Not good."

Chocking it up to fatigue and too much work, she opted to go for a run. Sweat and fresh air were the best medicine for anxiety.

She changed quickly. Normally she didn't carry her gun when she worked out. Its weight and bulk sometimes rubbed against her skin, but tonight she put up with the inconvenience. She clipped the gun at the base of her back and pulled an oversize T-shirt over it.

The night air was crisp. As a teenager, before things went wrong, she used to run. She'd loved the solitude. But now she had worry and stress weighing on her.

She grabbed her phone and shoved earbuds in before cutting through the lobby. With a nod to the woman working behind the desk, she headed outside. The run began slowly. But within minutes sweat beaded on her forehead and soaked her T-shirt.

Many of the old streets and buildings hadn't changed much in the last seventeen years. Sure, some businesses had traded hands, but the buildings and the street patterns had remained the same. Memories from the past flashed through her mind, and she recalled walking these streets with her mother, father, and brother. Before her father had died, they'd been a happy family. Her father had been the glue that held them all together. And with him gone, it all unraveled.

Her gaze settled on a too-familiar location. Breathless, she slowed her pace to a walk, pressing her hand to her side as she moved closer to the alley that she would never forget.

Usually she drove to chess practice alone, but that night her father offered to drive. It was dark when she came outside and saw her father standing by the car. As she approached him, William stepped out of the shadows. He hesitated when he saw Kate's father, then raised his weapon before her father could wrestle the gun away. The pop, pop of the weapon was loud, and Kate flinched as time slowed to a crawl and every detail came into perfect focus.

Her father sank to his knees, stared up at her, his eyes reflecting shock, anger, and fear. He mouthed, "Run," as the barrel swung toward her. Her life stilled. William fired.

The first bullet struck her in the thigh, tearing through flesh. The impact dropped her to her knees. The next rapid-fire shot hurled a slug toward her face. William never spoke as she tumbled back toward the ground.

She would later learn that a facial wound could bleed excessively, often looking far worse than it was. Unconscious and covered in blood, she must have appeared dead to William.

Her next memory was a siren blaring and William cursing her. "Why the fuck did you make me do this?"

The blast of a horn brought Kate back to the moment, and she realized several people were staring at her. Ducking her head, she turned and ran back toward the hotel. When she arrived, her hair and clothes were drenched in sweat.

She entered the lobby and was suddenly anxious for a hot shower to wash away the sweat and memories. She had just pressed the "Up" button on the elevator when she heard, "Kate."

She stiffened at the sound of the familiar voice. Activating mental armor, she turned to see her brother, Mitchell, crossing the lobby. It had been at least five years since she'd seen him. He was as tall and muscular as ever, but since his wife's death he looked tired. Silver now wove through his dark hair. A Texas Ranger's star pinned to his chest glinted in the lobby light, and he held his Stetson in his hand.

She didn't speak as she rubbed the side of her neck. "Mitchell. Is everything all right?"

"Mom is fine."

"How did you find me?"

"When I saw you on the news I figured you'd be staying close to police headquarters. I stopped by the police department and identified myself."

Annoyance scraped under her skin. "And they gave you the information?"

"I'm a Texas Ranger. And I know a lot of those guys."

Still, it didn't sit well. "Right."

"Mom also saw you on the news. She knows you're in town."

Guilt jabbed her. "I'll call her."

He traced the leather-and-silver-studded band of his Stetson. "Why haven't you gone by to see her?"

Visiting the family home where her mother still lived always churned up bad memories. Whenever Kate did have free time, she invited her mother to come see her wherever she was staying. Her mother always agreed, never once pushing Kate to visit the house.

"I said I would call her and I will." Her brother might be trained to interrogate, but she was adept at avoiding questions.

He glanced at the tiled floor and then looked back up. "Why're you staying here and not at the house with her?"

"That's not a good idea."

"Why not?" He leaned in, towering over her. But she had been playing this game with him since they were kids.

Standing her ground, she shook her head, feeling an old surge of bitterness. "I'm not interested in revisiting the past."

He ran his hand along the rim of his hat. For a moment, he didn't speak. "I don't remember exactly what I said after Dad died, but I know it was shitty. And I should have apologized to you a long time ago. Sierra's death has made me see a lot of things differently."

Her chin raised a notch. "You said I might as well have pulled the trigger myself."

His brow knotted, and he shoved out a breath. "I was young. Angry. Hurt. I didn't mean—"

"Of course you meant it, otherwise why say it?" Unshed tears choked her throat.

"What I'm trying to say is that I'm sorry, Kate."

She could still picture the hate in his eyes and the rage coating each of his words the last time they'd really talked before she left for college. "I'll call Mom. The rest of this is unnecessary."

His jaw tightened. "It's necessary, Kate."

"Why, Mitchell? Why after seventeen years is it necessary?"

The lines at the corners of his eyes and mouth had deepened. He was thirty-eight but looked a decade older.

"I was wrong. I wanted you to know that."

If he thought an apology would create some kind of family bonding moment, he was wrong. She appreciated the effort, but she couldn't accept his forgiveness when she couldn't forgive herself. "Thank you for the apology. Now, I've got to be going. I've an early call."

"Are you close to finding this Samaritan shooter?"

Feelings were off limits for the two of them, but somehow murder was a safe subject. "We're still waiting on the ballistics. I should have my answer by tomorrow or the next day."

"Mazur is a good cop. New to the area but seasoned."

His opinion of Mazur mattered more than it should. "Good to know."

He pulled a card from his wallet. "If you need me, call."

She flicked the edge of the card with her index finger. Her bruised feelings would have to wait. She lowered her voice. Her brother might have been an ass, but he had a reputation as a good lawman. "The victim knew William Bauldry."

Dark eyes locked on her. "What?"

"William worked for the Sanchez dealership after he was released from prison. Detective Mazur and I have visited his home. His housekeeper said he was in New York."

Mitchell shook his head. "That's not his style."

"No, it's not. So we visited his brother's home and the property near Medina. He's nowhere to be found."

"Jesus, Kate. You were just out running alone at night with this guy somewhere nearby."

"I've dealt with men like him before. But with William lurking around, maybe you should talk Mom into seeing Aunt Lydia."

His grip on the brim of his hat crunched the well-worn edge. "Mom won't leave town until she sees you."

"Talk to her. Convince her to leave."

"Go see her."

"I'm in the middle of an investigation."

"I'll try to talk to her, but go see her," he said more softly. "She loves you."

His words stung more than any insult. "I'll talk to Mom."

"What can I do?"

"I haven't even proven it's William," she said. "There're a dozen other reasons why Gloria could have been murdered."

"You're smart and you'll figure it out. Dad said you have a gift. If there's a pattern, you'll see it."

Fatigue was strengthening second doubts. She had to have more than a gut feeling about William. She needed facts. "Just keep an eye on Mom. I'll call her tomorrow."

He looked as if he wanted to say more but finally nodded. "You call me if you need anything."

"Sure."

"I meant it when I said I was sorry. I know I can be difficult. But we're family."

For Mitchell, this was a grand gesture. "Can I get the 'I can be difficult' on tape? Might be a good ringtone."

His posture relaxed a fraction, but a smile was still too much to expect from either of them. "It'll take a few beers before that happens."

"I'll keep that in mind," she said.

"You take care of yourself, Katie."

"You, too, Mitchell."

***

Raymond Drexler hadn't expected his life to turn to shit so fast. He still could not get over the fact that he had lost his sweet Sara thanks to the fucking cops and Kate Hayden. Nobody understood him.

He stopped in New Mexico and pulled into a truck stop. Keeping his head low, he bought a razor and scissors and went into the bathroom, where he showered and shaved his head and beard. After dressing, he put on an old ball cap he dug out of the lost-and-found bin. A few men passed by him, but he didn't look up. He wasn't the first man to shave and change his look in a place like this.

Tossing the razor and shaving cream back in his bag, he crossed the lot to his truck. Glancing in the rearview mirror, he skimmed his hand over his bald head. The new look would take getting used to. And without the beard, he wasn't sure if he even liked his face without it. Shit, he felt naked.

Exhausted, he drove another hour south before fatigue forced him to pull over. He parked in the shadows of a deserted parking lot off one of the interstate ramps and slept for what he thought would be a quick catnap.

When he startled awake a glance at the clock told him he had slept ten hours. "Shiiit!"

For a few gut-wrenching seconds, he was convinced someone had spotted him and called the cops. He climbed out, took a quick piss, and started driving.

Up ahead, he spotted the "Welcome to Texas. Drive Friendly—the Texas Way" sign. Finally relaxing, he leaned back against the seat and rolled down the window as the truck crossed the state line. He enjoyed the warm air. He was tired of the snow and the frozen ground. The deep, soothing warmth of Texas appealed to him. He'd never buried anyone in the desert before.

He reached for a bag of half-eaten white powdered doughnuts and popped a whole one in his mouth. It was dry, but a swig of cold coffee washed it down just fine. The combination of sugar and caffeine hit the spot, giving him the boost he needed.

He pressed the accelerator and turned up the radio.

Eight more hours of driving and he'd be in San Antonio.

CHAPTER FIFTEEN

*Knowledge is power. Always pays to be nice until nice
no longer serves you.*

San Antonio, Texas
Tuesday, November 28, 10:45 p.m.

After dropping Kate off at the car rental place, Mazur swung by his
ex-wife's house, hoping he had a little time with Alyssa before she went
to bed at eleven. He strode up the front walk, noting the new BMW
in the driveway. Sherry had always liked the finer things, and with this
new job she was making serious bank.

Sherry had purchased a patio-style home in a community that took
care of the lawn and common areas, provided a nice swimming pool
and a fitness center, and hosted a bunch of fancy events ranging from
wine tastings to concerts. When they'd married, they'd been so damn
much in love. He'd have bet his right arm that they'd have made the
long haul. But when he'd joined homicide the relationship frayed with
every missed meal, late night, and missed birthday. Caleb's birth hadn't
been planned, but he and Sherry had seen the boy as a second chance.
For a few months, it looked like they'd turned a corner. And then he'd
died. The grief shattered them both completely.

When Sherry asked for a divorce it hadn't been unexpected, but it had been a kick in the balls. For a long time, he'd mourned the marriage, and he would always be sorry that they'd failed Alyssa.

He rang the bell. High heels clicked in the hallway, and the door snapped open. Sherry was dressed in a fitted skirt, white blouse, and heels that made her legs look great. She'd pulled her blond hair into a twist.

"Theo," she said, smiling in a slightly uncomfortable way. "Alyssa told me you might be coming."

"Sorry I didn't call, Sherry. I only have a few minutes."

Her smile didn't waver, but the glint in her eyes turned brittle. "I understand. It's not a problem. In fact, there's something I'd like to talk to you about."

"Sure."

"Dad!" Alyssa appeared at the end of hallway. She wore sweats, an oversize Chicago PD T-shirt, and socks.

"Hey, kiddo." He wrapped his arms around her and hugged her tight. Seemed every time he saw her she was a couple of inches taller.

"We just ordered pizza. Why don't you join us?"

He glanced to Sherry, who smiled. "Absolutely. Join us. The three of us haven't eaten together in ages."

He followed them into a kitchen outfitted with white marble countertops, stainless-steel appliances, and a crystal chandelier. French doors led to an enclosed backyard and a night sky full of stars.

On the counter were two boxes of pizza. One was cheese for Alyssa and the other was pepperoni and sausage, which was his favorite. She must really have something important to say if she was trying to order his favorite.

Alyssa handed him a plate, and he dropped a couple of slices on it. "Eat up."

Sherry moved to the refrigerator and pulled out a cold soda. She popped the top and set it in front of him. "I have beer, but you said you have to get back to work."

"This is perfect."

"Great."

As Alyssa told him about her day, Sherry walked to a wet bar and filled a glass with ice and vodka. She took a sip and then another before joining them.

They made small talk for the better part of fifteen minutes. He had to give Sherry credit. She was trying, and she had never denied him any time with Alyssa, often working around his crazy schedule to make sure their daughter saw him.

When Alyssa's phone buzzed she glanced at it. "I've got to take it. It's about the math test."

"Take it in your room," Sherry said. "Dad and I'll wait for you."

Alyssa glanced up at him. "Don't leave."

"Not going anywhere, kiddo."

She hurried down the hallway, the phone pressed to her ear.

"So what's up, Sherry?"

She sipped her vodka. "I've been transferred."

He dropped the remains of his slice and wiped his hands with a paper towel. So his and Alyssa's gut reaction had been right. "To where?"

"Washington, DC."

He'd uprooted his life when he moved from Chicago to San Antonio. Now he and Alyssa were trying to make this place home, and Sherry wanted to leave again. He'd pulled strings to get the San Antonio job but doubted he had any more aces up his sleeve. "When?"

"Four weeks."

He balled up the napkin and tossed it on the counter. "Have you told Alyssa?"

"Not yet."

"You're going to pull her out before the semester is over?"

Sherry drew in a breath. "I was hoping she could stay with you. I can get an apartment there and get my bearings. The first few weeks on the job are going to be crazy."

"Of course. And then at the end of the school year, are you going to move her east?"

"I thought the end of the semester. Holidays are never great for the three of us anymore."

"And I'm supposed to just find another job?" Frustration and anger bled through the words. Sherry had had to petition an Illinois judge to take their daughter out of state, who'd reluctantly agreed.

She traced the rim of her glass with a polished nail. "I never asked you to move here. I don't expect you to move there."

"I'm supposed to watch my only living child walk out of my life."

Ice clinked in the glass as she swirled it. "I've never denied you visitation."

"No. You just keep trying to put distance between me and my kid. If I want to see my daughter on a regular basis, I'll have to move again."

A muscle pulsed in her jaw. "She's growing up. Soon she won't need either of us."

"She's not there yet, Sherry. And until she does really leave the nest, I'm going to be a part of her life." He didn't want to get into a pissing match with her, but he was finding it hard to be civil. "She can move in with me at any time."

"It's only temporary, Theo."

"So you've said. By my count, I've got a month before Alyssa and I have to turn our lives inside out again for your fucking career."

"This is a really good job, Theo. I'll be making the kind of money that will allow Alyssa to attend the best schools. She's smart and can go to any college in the country now."

He'd known from the start he'd married over his head when he said *I dos* with Sherry. She was smart and savvy, and he was always a little surprised she'd never reached for the big time. After their son had died, reaching higher kept her mind off the pain.

"When do you fly to Washington?"

"Saturday."

"You're shittin' me. You just said four weeks."

"I'm looking for a place to live and need to meet the people in the DC office." She raised her chin. "I have no choice."

"We all have choices, Sherry."

She sighed. "I don't want to fight."

He did. But with Alyssa in the other room, he'd have to find his pound of flesh somewhere else. "I'll be ready for her." His voice sounded tight. "Do you want me here when you tell Alyssa?"

She looked up, eyes filled with pain. "It's not necessary."

"Excuse me. I want to see Alyssa."

"That's it?" she asked.

"What do you want me to say, Sherry?"

She stared at him a long moment. "That you understand."

He swallowed, his throat suddenly tight with emotion. "I understand you're still running from the pain. Hell, that's part of the reason I left Chicago. But so far neither one of us has done a good job of it."

Mazur moved down the hallway and found Alyssa lying on her white four-poster bed with the phone pressed to her ear. The room was painted a pale pink, and the posters on the walls were a bunch of teenage boys he doubted he'd like if he ever met them.

"Dad?" she asked, cupping her hand over the phone.

"I've got to go, Alyssa, but we're on for the weekend." If by some act of God the murder investigation didn't spill over into his free time.

"I'll see you then?"

He kissed her on the cheek. "Love you, kid."

She hugged him. "Is Dr. Hayden going to be with you?"

"We're working a case, kiddo. If we aren't working, then there's no reason for us to be together."

"I like her." And giggling, she added, "And I think you do, too."

He did like Kate, but their relationship was professional and temporary at best. Still, he asked, "Why do you say that?"

She rolled her eyes and then glanced toward the door to make sure her mother wasn't there. "It's the way you talk around her."

"How's that?"

"Friendly. Relaxed."

He shook his head. "Maybe you should be an FBI profiler."

Her eyes sparked with interest. "Maybe I should." She kissed him on the cheek. "Love you, Dad."

"You, too, kiddo."

He gave her one final squeeze. By the time he reached her door and glanced back, she was already lost in conversation with her friend. He moved back down the hallway, wondering where it had all gone wrong.

Sherry cut around the counter. "Theo, I'm not running."

At the rate he was going, a move east would have him back in uniform working a beat or as some kind of rent-a-cop. Fuck. But if that was what it took to be in his kid's life, he'd figure it out. The fact that Kate was based at Quantico somehow softened the blow of moving again. "Could have fooled me, Sherry."

When he closed the front door behind him, it slammed shut with a little too much force. He strode to his car and slid behind the wheel, releasing the breath he'd been holding. He glanced in the rearview mirror and spotted Sherry standing at the door watching him.

Mazur drove off, grateful to return to the office. The drive went faster than he expected, and when he arrived at his desk, he was happy to see the phone records for Martin Sanchez had arrived.

He brewed a fresh cup of coffee, then slid off his coat and rolled up his sleeves. He sipped the coffee, not wincing at the taste. Kate had cleaned the pot and machine again. Thank God for small favors.

Seconds later Palmer entered the bull pen and dropped her oversize purse in her chair. "I heard those records were coming tonight. Couldn't resist taking a peek."

He dropped half the stack in front of her. "You know the drill. We'll start with the numbers he calls the most and then work our way back from there."

"What's got your panties in a twist?" she asked.

"Nothing."

"Ah, I bet you saw the ex."

A smirk on her face undercut some of his annoyance. "What if I did?"

"They do know which buttons send us into a crazy spin. It's a wonder I didn't murder mine and bury his ass in a shallow grave."

He sat down. "Might not want to say that too loud."

"He's alive and breathing, but I do have a perfect alibi when the time comes."

Mazur shook his head. "Read."

She sat and opened the first file. She read for less than a minute before she looked up and sighed. "We're partners, you know. You can tell me anything."

He could feel her gaze. "Read."

"I mean it. I'm not like the other assholes in this cowboy department."

"I know."

She muttered a curse. "Any phone number in particular that I'm looking for?"

"Lena Nelson. She's the manager of their premier showroom and a big fan of his." He rattled off the number.

"Like in ol' Marty had a thing going on the side?"

"Kate got that vibe, too."

Palmer rubbed her palms together. "Now it's getting interesting."

"Maybe."

A few minutes went by. "What's it like working with her?"

"Kate Hayden? She's smart, objective."

"I can't get a read on her at all. For a fembot, she is actually likeable in a weird sort of way."

"There's a sense of humor lurking in there, which gives me hope."

"I heard you're looking for Bauldry," she said.

"Kate and I checked his house, his brother's home, and also the family farm. No sign of him. I've put a BOLO out on him with the deputy in Medina County. He's sending a deputy to check out his house again as well as the Medina property."

"You heard about Kate's old man, right?"

"Murdered by Bauldry."

"Did you know she was this big chess whiz and so was Bauldry? They played a tournament together and it didn't end well for him."

He looked up, knowing Palmer wouldn't rest until her curiosity was satisfied. "You know a lot."

She scooted forward on her chair a fraction and leaned forward. "Maybe I'm friends with a few of the ladies in records. And I bring doughnuts when I need a favor."

"Why'd you look her up?"

"Curiosity. She's not the first who went to work for law enforcement after a tragedy." She glanced around and pulled a thick binder from her desk drawer. "Want to see the file?"

"You pulled the father's murder file?"

"I did." No hint of apology.

"Yeah, I'll have a look." He thumbed through the file, stopping on a picture taken of Kate at the age of seventeen. The light-brown hair was longer and the face a little rounder, but she had the same serious look as today.

"It's a miracle she survived," Palmer said. "The shooter hit her in the thigh and then the face. She nearly bled out."

He turned to William Bauldry's mug shot. The boy barely looked old enough to shave. His face was thin, his eyes dark and wild. But this scared kid had shot a man dead in cold blood and nearly killed Kate.

"William Bauldry," he said, reading up on the young man. "Brilliant. Controlled and very aware of what he did and why. Dated Kate for a short while. They broke up, and he became obsessed with her."

"Maybe William also became obsessed with Gloria Sanchez. Maybe he shot her?" Palmer said.

He closed the murder file. "Believe me, finding William Bauldry is at the top of my list. But I still can't rule out Sanchez. He was first on the scene, he had his wife's blood on him, and the couple was having financial problems. Not to mention the first wife died in a car accident."

"Don't forget, he was stepping out on this wife and most likely the last."

"Martin Sanchez had a lot of good reasons to have his wife die."

It took less than a half hour to spot a pattern of calls between Martin Sanchez and another unidentified number. Whomever he was talking to, they'd been speaking for over a year, daily and for extended periods of time.

"Think this is a girlfriend?" Mazur asked.

Palmer reached for her phone and dialed. "No better way to find out." She held the phone out as a recorded message played. *This is Rebecca. I'm out. Call me again, baby.* "She sounds young and sexy to me."

"Was she young and hot enough for him to want to leave his wife?" He ran his hand down his tie. "I don't suppose Gloria Sanchez had a life insurance policy."

"Funny you should ask. I've done some digging. Gloria had a two-million-dollar policy listing her husband as the beneficiary." Palmer shook her head as she absently tapped her index finger on the records. "Sanchez has a mistress, Rebecca? And he decides to kill his old lady so they can live happily ever after?"

"Maybe," Mazur said.

All the dots logically connected to Martin. Mazur should have been feeling pretty good knowing he might be on the heels of closing a high-profile case. So why didn't he?

"Everything the Samaritan has done so far could have been dug up in the papers," Palmer said. "It's all just so perfect."

"I'd like to run it by Dr. Hayden and get her feedback."

Her eyes narrowed as she studied him, and a slight grin tugged the edge of her lips. "Are you attracted to the fembot?"

"Kate?"

"No, the other fembot. Of course Kate."

He didn't quite meet her gaze as he shook his head. "That's the last thing I'd need right now."

Palmer sang, "Theo's got a girlfriend."

***

He'd lured Kate Hayden to San Antonio with the Samaritan, who had ended Gloria Sanchez's life with one shot. Now, it was time to morph into another killer from Kate's files and claim another victim, one who would not enjoy a quick and merciful death.

He stood in the shadows, waiting for the woman to leave the coffee shop that was scheduled to close soon. The street was quiet, and the back alley where she parked her car was shrouded in deep shadows.

She had dark hair, pale-white skin, and a slim, athletic figure that any man would gladly bed. If it were in the game plan, he'd do her in a heartbeat. But fucking her wasn't part of the plan.

He waited, watching her duck down the side alley that led to her car. She rummaged in a large purse as she fumbled with keys until her thumb pressed the "Unlock" button on her fob. She opened the back driver's side door, dumped her purse on the seat, and slammed the door closed.

His head covered in a hoodie, he followed her, keeping his hands tucked and his head down. He could move quickly when he put his mind to it, and speed was most important now. As he approached she was opening her driver's door. He quickened his pace. When gravel sounded under his boots, her body tensed and she turned.

Her gaze widened, startled. First, there was a flash of recognition, then fear. She gripped her keys and tried to hurl herself into her car. She was quick enough to close her door, but he was fast enough to stop her from locking him out.

He stabbed the needle into her back, and she arched back. He silenced her scream with a gloved hand over her mouth and held her close to his chest, giving the fast-acting sedative time to course through her body. She grabbed his hands with hers, desperately trying to pry open his grip. A car drove down the street, and he yanked her deeper into the dark. Cries became a moan as her muscles lost their tension and worry. She slumped back against the seat.

"That's right," he whispered against her ear. "Give in. It'll be so much easier if you just let go."

She tried to shake her head, but the movement was slight. Finally her hands dropped to her sides, her keys clinked against the ground, and her face tipped forward.

"That's a good girl," he said.

He grabbed her under her arms, and snatching up her keys, he dragged her toward the car's trunk. He opened it and placed her inside. She lay helpless before him, her head turned, her neck exposed, her full breasts pressing against a white blouse.

He laid his hand on her breast, savoring the softness. He grew hard and wondered what it would be like to strip her naked and slide into her as he pretended she was Kate.

Drawing in a breath, he squeezed her breast once more and pulled back. Rape was not on his list.

He slammed the trunk closed, savoring a rush of excitement that was more potent than any opiate. Killing was so sweet, so intoxicating; he knew he would never stop unless Kate caught him.

He slid behind the wheel of the car and started the engine. He'd already mapped out where he was going and what would happen next. It was all falling into place.

He drove through town and onto the southbound interstate, driving until he found the barren stretch of road where he had planned to finish his evening's work.

He pulled off onto the access road and wound his way along a side street past fields of scrub, rock, and red soil. He slowly drove off the road and parked.

He popped the trunk and found the woman still lying on her side. The drug he'd chosen wouldn't last long, and if he judged her weight correctly, she'd be awake in minutes.

A soft moan rose in her chest as he hoisted her on his shoulder and carried her to the spot that had been so carefully staged.

He placed her on the ground and spread her arms and legs wide. He tied her feet first and moved to her right hand. As he fumbled with the knot, she looked at him with hazy eyes and screamed. She reached out with her left hand and scraped his arm. He slapped her hard on her face, stunning her. He finished securing her right hand.

Her eyes were wide and full of fear as he carefully fanned out her dark hair. She tried to raise her head, but he hit her again. "Don't move or it'll be far worse."

"Why are you doing this?"

"Payback is a bitch."

His fingers brushed the sheath hooked to his belt, and he removed the long knife. She screamed again, and this time he jerked a rag from his back pocket and shoved it in her mouth. Tears welled in her eyes.

Straddling the woman, he carefully unbuttoned her blouse, slid the tip of the knife under her bra, and exposed her breasts. Her nipples hardened in the cool night air and made him want her so badly.

The surge of power filled him as he stared up at the crescent moon. He gripped the knife in his hand. The woman moaned and her eyes fluttered. He waited a beat, knowing she needed to see him.

The rag muffled more screams as he scraped the tip of the knife along her bare skin. She flinched. "Time to pay the piper."

She jerked hard against her restraints several times before the tight ropes cut into the flesh of her wrists.

When she stared up at him, pure panic sharpened her gaze. She would have given him anything, absolutely anything to gain her freedom.

He adored that look of shock and terror. "It's not a bad dream," he said. "It's quite beautiful."

She croaked out a strangled cry as he pressed the knife slowly into her right breast, between the rib cage and her lung. Then quickly he yanked the knife free and studied her face. It was all he could do not to come.

There was a pattern to the remaining cuts he would place on her beautiful body. This was the next item on the list.

He jabbed the knife over and over into her body, finishing at number thirteen with a slice across her neck. He was breathless, and his hands were wet with her blood. As she struggled to breathe he drew closer to her face as her last breath brushed over her lips.

He whispered, "Goodbye."

He rose to his feet and staggered away from her, drawing in a breath as he calmed his racing heart. Using the gun to kill had been exciting, but *this*, he thought, looking at the knife dripping with blood, was an even bigger high.

He sheathed the knife and moved toward the body, stepping around the pool of blood seeping into the hard red soil. Carefully he dipped his gloved index finger into the pool of warm blood and drew an eye on her forehead. Satisfied with his work, he pushed the tip of the knife into her left eye socket and dug out the eyeball. He laid the bloody prize on her chest and repeated the process with the right eye. Carefully he bagged both trophies.

He pulled out a burner phone and snapped pictures of the lifeless woman. Once he was a safe distance away, he'd call in the murder, knowing there would be no way the local cops wouldn't call Kate.

CHAPTER SIXTEEN

I've found my bait; now it is time to build the trap.

San Antonio, Texas
Wednesday, November 29, 6:00 a.m.

The shrill ring of the phone woke Kate. She sat up straight; the papers that had been draped over her chest fell to the floor. She blinked and looked around the unfamiliar room. She'd been in so many rooms like this over the years that there were plenty of times when she woke up and looked at the phonebook on the nightstand to see what city she was in.

She snatched up the phone. "Kate Hayden."

"Jerrod Ramsey. Did I wake you?"

She glanced at the clock on the nightstand, surprised she'd slept so late. "No. I was up." She ran her tongue over her teeth and her fingers through her hair.

"What's the status of the San Antonio shooting?"

"We get the ballistics back today."

"What're your thoughts on the case at this point?"

She pushed the hair from her eyes as she swung her legs over the side of the bed. She rose and rolled her head from side to side, trying to work a kink from her neck. "The victim was in deep financial trouble and had terminal cancer. Husband likely having an affair."

"And what do you think?"

She rubbed the back of her neck, chasing away an odd feeling. She moved toward the closed curtains and peeked through to check the weather. "When I've all the data points, I'll call. Evidence, not opinion, leads. Has Nevada had any luck with Sara Fletcher's abductor?"

"Not yet."

She rubbed the worn edges of the Wonder Woman bracelet. "Has she spoken yet?"

"No. Which is all the more reason why I want you back there. You've got until five your time today, and then I'm calling you in so you can work with Nevada on the Drexler hunt."

A weariness settled on her shoulders that she'd not felt in a very long time. "I'll update you today."

"Good."

He rang off, and she tossed the phone on her bed. She stripped off yesterday's clothes and stepped into the shower. She ducked her head under the hot spray, savoring the heat pulsing on her tired muscles.

She toweled off and set the coffeepot in the room to perk. While coffee dripped into a paper cup, she dressed in her last clean outfit, which was simply a navy-blue version of the other. Simplicity in wardrobe cut down on daily choices and kept her mind focused on the puzzle. Hair dried and makeup applied, she packed her belongings into her suitcase. She was sipping her coffee when her phone rang. Detective Mazur's name appeared.

"Detective. Have you gotten the ballistics report?" she asked.

"Good morning to you, too."

Blinked. Felt like a computer processing unexpected data. "Good morning."

"That sounded as if you were in pain. Pleasantries can be a challenge, can't they, Agent Hayden?"

She heard the laughter in his voice. There was a time she could have accepted good-natured ribbing about her stiff demeanor. But there wasn't anything in this day or the hours ahead that was remotely amusing. "There's a plaza in the center of the city. See you in thirty minutes."

"I'll be there."

She packed up her backpack, left her room key on her dresser for the maid, and made her way down the elevator. She checked out at the front desk and hurried to her rental car. She loaded her suitcase in the trunk and tossed her backpack in the front passenger seat. Behind the wheel, she started the engine. She paused to again familiarize herself with the knobs and buttons. Satisfied, she drove to the plaza.

She found Mazur leaning against his car. His head was bowed as he checked his phone.

As she approached, he typed a message. He hit "Send" and looked up. "I haven't eaten breakfast yet this morning. Been busy with a last-minute homework assignment with a teenager who needed a rundown on my side of the family for an American history project. There's a diner over there."

"That would be good. I'm hungry."

"So you're now eating and perhaps sleeping regularly?"

"Badly on both counts," she countered.

He pushed away from the car and walked beside her. "Seems to be a hazard of law enforcement."

"I've been terrible at both most of my life."

"Because of your father's shooting?" He slid the question in as if it were perfectly natural.

She looked at him. "Most likely. I'm a fairly easy puzzle to figure out."

He opened the diner door and as she passed said, "Your idea of easy and mine are different."

A hostess escorted them to a booth in the back. He took the seat that placed his back to the wall and faced the front door. She sat, and a waitress approached and offered coffee to both.

"How's the hotel?"

She scanned the menu. "Like a million others. Very predictable and different enough that I stubbed my toe on a chair."

"I can't imagine being on the move all the time."

The waitress filled the stoneware mugs and took Kate's order for a western omelet, while Mazur ordered pancakes. He sipped his coffee and waited until the waitress was out of earshot before asking, "Has Sara Fletcher spoken yet?"

She was oddly touched that he'd remembered. "No."

"And Drexler?"

"Still on the loose." She thought about the girl lying in her hospital bed, pale, emaciated. Her eyes had seen things that no human should ever see in a lifetime. Pivoting the conversation back to him, she said, "You seem off."

He set his cup down carefully. "My ex announced she's moving to Washington, DC."

"You haven't been here long, so I'm assuming she hasn't either."

"Another big promotion is in the works. She's one talented attorney."

"Is she taking your daughter?"

Absently he tapped his thumb on the table. "She's going to let our daughter finish out the semester here with me."

"And then she moves to Washington in January."

"Yeah."

Pain, loss, and longing huddled around the word. "You would find the area around Washington an acceptable place to live. I've connections in law enforcement there."

"I didn't say I was moving."

"You're a dedicated parent. Each time you speak of your daughter, it's clear you love her very much. I'd wager you'll be there by spring."

He shook his head. "You can't be sure of that. Hell, you just met me two days ago."

"I had your priorities figured out after the first two hours I met you, Detective."

He shook his head, a pained smile on his lips. "I'm not saying I'm going to make a move. But keep this under your hat."

"Of course."

The waitress arrived with their food, and they both sat back, each momentarily lost in thought.

"There's more evidence that Martin Sanchez was having an affair," Mazur said when the waitress left again. "He called a Rebecca several times a day for the last year. It makes sense. Man kills wife to be with mistress. But somehow I keep going back to Bauldry."

"Why?"

"Don't know. Hate to say it's a gut feeling, but that's about all I have right now. He's been out of prison eleven months. Has he contacted you at all?"

"No."

Mazur picked up his fork and stared at the stack of pancakes. "Could Bauldry and Richardson have crossed paths?"

Her brow knotted. "Dr. Richardson did consulting work with several prison systems. He studied criminal behavior and profiled dozens of serial killers."

"Did he visit Bauldry's prison?" Mazur asked.

Kate frowned. "Bauldry was in Bastrop Federal Correctional Institution near Austin. Because my father was a prosecutor, it became a federal case." She thought back through Richardson's professional associations. "I don't remember Richardson being at Bastrop. Maybe I missed something. I'll check with the detectives in the local jurisdictions who are still digging into Richardson's past and see if he visited the facility."

"I'll have Palmer make some calls." Before she could respond he pulled out his phone and typed a text. The phone chirped with a response almost instantly. "She's on it. Why did Richardson develop a taste for killing?" Mazur asked.

"He had a history of violence as a child. All his cruelty was directed at animals. He also had a history of frequenting prostitutes, who reported he could be violent."

"And Bauldry?" Mazur asked.

"There were problems of animal abuse in his past that came out at his trial. His parents did an excellent job of hiding his issues." She stared into the depths of a half-empty cup. "It's been seventeen years."

"That kind of crazy is forever. He keeps a picture taken of the two of you in the cabin." He stabbed a section of pancake. "Palmer won't get back with me for at least an hour or two, and we've got every cop in the area looking for Bauldry. Come down to Laredo. One way or another I have to prove or disprove Martin Sanchez as the shooter."

"Sure."

***

Traffic headed south to Laredo was heavy, but Mazur was glad for the time alone with Kate. He liked being with her, especially breathing in her soft scent and watching the way her brow wrinkled when she was working a case. More and more he wanted to peel off that damn suit and see the woman beneath it.

She was silent, lost in her thoughts. He was learning that silence was almost a constant condition. He sensed she was thinking a few moves ahead of herself, but right now he needed her focused on the moment at hand.

They arrived at the condo building where Gloria Sanchez kept her unit. They showed their badges to the guard at the front station. He was a burly man with thinning hair, but the creases of his uniform were sharp and crisp. He accompanied them up to her condo. It was empty. Tile floors were scuffed with bits of debris, and discarded packing boxes were scattered about.

"When did she move out her furniture?" Kate asked.

The guard stood by the door. "It was about two weeks ago, right after she sold this unit."

"When did she put it up for sale?" Kate asked.

"About six weeks ago. The plan was to clean the place for the new occupants, who show up the first of December. The cleaning lady got sick on Sunday, so she never made it by. Mrs. Sanchez was scheduled to make the final walk-through with the new buyers on Monday morning. Of course, we all know what happened. Terrible."

"We'll let you know when we're finished," Mazur said.

"Yeah, sure. I'll be at my desk."

Kate moved to the large bank of windows that overlooked the city, its green parks below, and the Rio Grande River. "The view is stunning."

"Agreed." He moved into the kitchen and found a couple of bottles of champagne chilling, cheese, and a box of crackers. The cabinets were empty. The trash can in the pantry closet was filled with paper plates, takeout boxes, and bottles of wine.

"How often did she come down here?" Kate asked as she entered the kitchen.

"About two or three times a month."

He opened a drawer to crackers and ketchup packets. "This is not the place of a woman committed to an area."

"It was supposed to be cleaned. No one was supposed to see it this way," she said. "Appearances were very important to her. The cleaning lady got sick according to the guard. We should be seeing a spotless place." Kate pulled out the trash can.

"I'll get local police to send a forensic team here." His phone chimed with a text.

She moved into the bedroom, and Mazur followed. There was an air mattress on the floor, a few rumpled blankets, and small trash can. In the can were several empty pill bottles with another woman's name on the prescription. "Oxy. She was taking some high doses of pain meds and deliberately keeping it off the radar."

"We both figured a cancer like hers would be tough to manage."

"Did Ryland find any record of cancer treatment?" she asked.

"No."

"She took pride in her appearance, and the chemo would've stripped her of her hair, health, and the ability to work," Kate said.

"But she was spared all that when she was randomly killed by the Samaritan," Mazur offered.

"I want to pay a visit to her mother's nursing home."

"According to my notes, it's ten minutes from here."

Less than half an hour later they were following the Lady of Lourdes facility manager, Sister Maria, toward the memory-care unit of the nursing home. The facility was clean and the staff friendly. Crucifixes hung on many of the walls.

"How long has Mrs. Hernandez been here?" Mazur asked.

"A couple of years."

"How often did her daughter come to visit?" Kate asked.

"We haven't seen her in over a month. And we heard the news of her death." She made the sign of the cross. "Terrible."

"Was Mrs. Sanchez current with her bills from you?" Mazur asked.

"Until three months ago she paid like clockwork. Then she wrote us a big check to cover the next five years. She said if her mother died before the five years to donate the money to someone else."

"Did she say why she paid in advance?" Mazur asked.

"No." She led them to the glass doors that overlooked the common area. "As I told you when you arrived, she doesn't communicate." She pointed, indicating a slender woman sitting in a chair staring sightlessly at her hands. Gray hair was pulled back into a neat bun, and she wore a pink housecoat with slippers.

When Kate looked at the woman, she hesitated as she stared at the lined, wrinkled face and the thick stock of hair. "I know her."

Mazur looked at her. "How?"

She seemed to search for the answer. And then, "She was the housekeeper for the Bauldry family. Her name is Anita Hernandez."

"Isabella called her Nina."

"An endearment, I suppose."

"She knew William Bauldry?" Mazur asked.

"Yes. She'd worked for the family even before William was born. He was very fond of her."

"Has anyone else visited Mrs. Hernandez?" Mazur asked.

Sister Maria shook her head. "No. Just her daughter."

"I have memories of a quiet, attractive woman with gray hair swept into a bun. But I don't remember Gloria. But by the time I was dating William, Gloria was in her early twenties and must have been married to Martin Sanchez. I never saw her at the Bauldry house." Kate sat beside the old woman. Mrs. Hernandez's head was bent, her fragile thin hands threaded and resting on an orange crocheted blanket. "Nina?"

Mrs. Hernandez's gaze didn't waver.

Kate laid her hand on the old woman's hand. "Nina, it's Katie. I used to date William. We've met before."

The old woman mumbled but didn't look up. Whatever was locked in her head wasn't retrievable anymore. "Nina, do you remember William?"

The old woman's brow knotted, but she didn't speak.

Mazur turned to the sister. "If anyone else does visit her, will you contact me?" He handed her a card.

"Yes, of course."

***

Leaving Laredo, Mazur knew this case reached way beyond a murder for hire. He and Kate drove back to San Antonio and pulled up to the criminal justice building. They made their way through the building toward the stairs to the Forensic Department. She kept pace with him as he moved quickly to the second floor.

Down the hallway, they found Calhoun sitting in front of a microscope, her blond hair tied in a tight ponytail.

"Tell me you have ballistics," Mazur said.

"I do." She looked up from the scope. "The weapon that killed Gloria Sanchez *was* used in the other five I-35 shootings."

"Are you sure?" Kate asked.

"Have a look for yourself," Calhoun said.

Kate took a seat and glanced in the viewfinder. She adjusted the focus a couple of times before she released a sigh. "Although both hollow points deform by design on impact, the copper jacket has very pronounced and identical striations that cut into it."

As she stepped aside, Mazur looked into the microscope. The markings on the bullets matched. "I'll be damned."

"I personally spoke to every forensic technician who tested the ballistics in the Samaritan murders," Calhoun said. "I also reviewed each of their findings personally. All are a match to the bullet that killed Gloria Sanchez."

She laid an enlarged photo taken of the Sanchez bullet next to images from the other five cases.

Kate stood very still. "The gun was never retrieved. Richardson was working with someone else."

Mazur's phone rang, and a glance at the display had him frowning. He answered the phone. "Palmer, what do you have?"

"I was called to a homicide on I-35. Really ugly."

He glanced toward Kate. "A shooting?"

"No, a stabbing. It's south of San Antonio not five miles from where Gloria Sanchez was found. I'm on scene now. You might want to bring Dr. Hayden. This is the kind of shit she deals with."

"We'll be there in less than an hour." He nodded toward the door. "Another murder on I-35. Palmer wants you to see the scene."

"Of course." Within minutes, they were on the interstate headed south.

As Mazur raced down the highway, Kate's phone rang. "My partner. I've got to take this." She hit "Receive." "Mike. Do you have Raymond Drexler?"

As she listened, the color faded from her face. "Thanks. Keep me posted." She ended the call clutching the phone in her hand.

"What's going on?" Mazur asked.

"Nevada received a call from a truck stop in southern New Mexico. The manager saw Drexler's picture in the news, and he swore Drexler came into his store. Said he bought a razor and shaving cream. Nevada checked the store security-camera footage, and it offered a clear shot of Drexler's face. My partner was calling me from a shower room reserved for the truckers at the site. There was hair in one of the shower stalls. Color fits Drexler. Plenty of samples for DNA testing."

"New Mexico. He could go any number of places from there. Any idea where he's headed?"

"My partner thinks he's coming south. I've been in the news, and I ruined Drexler's horror show at his farm."

He glanced toward her as she stared out the window. "Cool as a cucumber."

"Getting upset is a waste of time."

He gripped the wheel. "I've seen some bad stuff, but this guy is really twisted. I don't think I could be as calm as you."

"You would do whatever you had to do to catch him, yes?"

"Hell yes."

"Then if you needed to be calm, you would be."

CHAPTER SEVENTEEN

Fool me once, shame on you. Fool me twice, shame on me.

San Antonio, Texas
Wednesday, November 29, 3:00 p.m.

Kate struggled to stay relaxed as Mazur wove in and out of traffic. Mazur was silent as he punched the accelerator, and they traveled down the interstate at eighty-plus miles an hour with dash lights flashing.

Ahead she saw the lights and the police cars lined up along the side of an access road that ran parallel to the interstate. Dust kicked up as Mazur nosed his car behind the forensic van. They got out of the car and met by the hood as Mazur surveyed the area.

"A woman has been stabbed and dumped in this field," Palmer said as she moved toward them. She'd removed her jacket and rolled up her sleeves. Sunglasses tossed back the sun's reflection. Her black boots were covered with red dust.

Mazur accepted a set of rubber gloves from Palmer. "Do you have an ID on the victim?"

"We found her purse in the car. Driver's license identifies her as Rebecca Kendrick, age twenty-six."

"Rebecca?" Mazur asked.

Palmer nodded. "Yeah, what are the chances that Martin's alleged girlfriend would also be named Rebecca?"

Mazur rested his hands on his hips. "What can you tell me about this Rebecca?"

"She was last seen at the coffee shop where she worked. It was her turn to close. She was supposed to meet a friend but didn't show. That's not like her, so the friend called it in. A passing motorist spotted her car." Palmer looked at Kate. "Would love your take on this one."

"It's not like the Samaritan, so why call me?"

"Just have a look," Palmer said. "This shit is right up your alley."

Mazur and Kate followed Palmer across the field. Without any trees and the sun directly overhead, the warm autumn quickly cut through her dark jacket. She'd be covered in sweat eventually. As she stripped off her jacket and draped it over her arm, she noticed Mazur's attention shifted to her and then back to the path ahead.

Several officers and deputies huddled just beyond the yellow crime-scene tape, perfectly still in the motionless air, that was strung between two poles staked in the desert dirt. The forensic technician snapped pictures of the woman's body. In the dry heat the belly had already bloated. The red Texas dust never hesitated to reclaim its dead.

As Mazur and Palmer ducked under the tape, Kate remained on the outside, knowing the less contamination the better. She glanced around the open field and saw the heat rippling on the horizon.

She turned to the victim's car, which had a temporary license plate suggesting she'd bought it in the last thirty days. The license plate holder read "Sanchez Motors." It was a small, perhaps irrelevant connection to Gloria Sanchez, but it was there.

She scanned the area. Killers liked remote areas like this. It gave them the privacy and time they needed to visit with their victims. Over the course of her career, she'd seen hundreds of crime-scene photos set in areas just as remote as this one. She'd also listened to and watched countless recordings made by killers while torturing and murdering. No matter how many she captured, more would take their place.

Mazur waved toward her. "Kate, would you mind having a look at this?"

She ducked under the tape and was greeted by the heavy scent of death that would only grow more putrid by the hour. Palmer's face was solemn, and any hints of her biting humor had vanished.

When Palmer stepped aside, Kate looked at the woman who lay spread-eagle on the ground. Her hands were tied to spikes and her eyes removed. Revulsion slithered through Kate, but she refused to react as she mentally armored herself against the scene. The body was no longer a person. It was rotting meat. Evidence.

A very odd sense of déjà vu overcame her as she knelt by the slender body and studied the chest and abdominal stab wounds. However, when she lifted her gaze to the mutilated eyes and the third eye painted in dried blood on the woman's forehead, her memory tripped back to a case she'd worked.

As she studied the message the killer had sent via the body, she automatically compared and contrasted it with her case, which had resulted in an arrest.

Like the old case, there appeared to be thirteen stab wounds in total. All the cuts were near the heart, lungs, and abdomen, except for one across the throat. The mutilated eyes and the painted eye were the killer's signature.

But that killer, Michael Carter, had covered his victims with dried leaves. This woman's shirt remained ripped open, leaving her exposed to the elements. Some killers, like the Soothsayer, redressed their victims after the violence and posed them in a demure position—arms crossed over the chest, ankles crossed, and face covered. These were all signs of remorse and regret.

However, Rebecca Kendrick's arms and legs had been left flung wide and the mutilation of her eyes displayed. The killer's intent was to humiliate her and leave her vulnerable to the world.

Kate had seen this scene displayed before. "Something is not right."

"Pretty messed up, if you ask me," Palmer said.

"What I mean is that I've seen this before. There was a serial killer in North Carolina. They called him the Soothsayer."

"You didn't mention him after the briefing," Mazur said.

"Because the case is closed. He stabbed three women over the course of two years and left partly buried bodies in a field. All the women were young prostitutes. When I asked him why he cut out the eyes, he told me he was certain the women could see into his soul."

"You arrested him?" Mazur asked.

"I did. Based on a profile I drew up for the local police. His name is Michael Carter. He was a lawyer from a well-to-do family near Asheville, North Carolina. He was just convicted and sentenced to life in prison."

"He's behind bars," Palmer clarified.

"Yes." Kate studied the wounds, noting that they were almost identical to the patterns of Carter's three victims. "There is no way he could have done this."

"You were the chief profiler on the case?" Mazur asked.

"Yes."

"Two murders in three days," Palmer said. "And you worked on cases similar to both. This ain't a coincidence, Agent Hayden."

Kate stared at the body. Sadness and regret tried to breach her composure, but she wouldn't allow it. Later, when she was alone, the emotions might get the better of her, but not here at the crime scene. "No, it's not."

Mazur nudged Kate. "We need to talk."

She allowed him to guide her away from the body.

"What the hell is going on?" he asked. "I've spent the last two days following the trail on a case that appears to be a copycat of one of your cases, and now I've another killer impersonator?"

She tipped her head up to meet his gaze. "I can't explain it except to say someone is following my cases."

"Was Carter working with anyone?"

"When I did his profile I determined he was a loner who was living out his own fantasies toward women. And when he was arrested we discovered he lived alone, had lost his job, and was having his food delivered to the house. A shut-in, he only went out when the moon was full. That's when he picked up a prostitute, stabbed her to death, and left her just like this woman here. When I interviewed him after his arrest, he was very proud of the fact that he did the work alone."

"Could you be wrong about an accomplice?"

"Of course. There's always the chance. But my team checked his online profile, and though he commented often on certain occult sites, he never appeared to be in communication with anyone."

"What are the chances that I'd have two murders mirroring your cases?"

"Zero. Clearly my work and I are the common denominators."

"Who has access to your case files?"

"A few people in the bureau. And each of the jurisdictions had copies. But all those are closely guarded."

"What about boyfriends, lovers, friends, family? Ever left files out and someone got a peek?"

"No. Never."

"I want a list of all the cases you've profiled."

She shook her head. She'd worked several very grisly cases that still woke her up in the middle of the night. She wouldn't wish that list on anyone.

"Could this be Bauldry?" Mazur asked. "Could this be his way of sending you another message? Could he be following your work?"

"He would have been incarcerated at the time of the Soothsayer murders, but the case received quite a bit of press locally and some nationally. It would have been easy to research considering the case is now closed. And it's clear whoever killed this woman wanted her left in a humiliating position to send a message."

"We need to find out more about this woman."

"Start with her vehicle. It's new and it was purchased from Sanchez Motors."

***

Kate stood apart from the cops and dialed her boss, Jerrod Ramsey. He picked up on the third ring. "There's another complication."

He cursed. "I hate complications, Kate."

Her voice was steady and gave no hint to the growing worry that threatened to cloud her thoughts. "There's been another homicide."

"A Samaritan shooting?"

"No. The victim was killed like the Soothsayer's victims. She was stabbed, her eyes removed, and an eye drawn on her forehead."

Silence crackled over the line. "That case was solved."

She could take his yelling and his curses. That's what Ramsey did to blow off steam. He only worried her when he was quiet, careful. "I know."

"How much does this crime scene resemble the ones in North Carolina?"

"It's almost identical."

"*Almost* identical."

She could picture him standing at his desk now, his hand pressed to the small of his back. He'd be pacing past the multiple diplomas framed on his office wall toward the window.

"I'd like to stay and work with the local authorities. Though I'll tell you right now, they aren't pleased with me."

"No wonder." He dropped his voice a notch. "Do you have any idea what the defense for Richardson and Carter will do with this information? They'll argue you've not botched one case but two. Both legal teams will file for retrials."

So much hard work unraveling. A recreation of one of Richardson's murders had been surprising enough, but a second murder mirroring one of her investigations was not a coincidence. She pressed her fingers to her temple. "Do you have any updates from Nevada regarding Drexler?"

"Don't worry about Drexler. Nevada is on his trail."

Promises made to Sara Fletcher felt as flimsy as old tissue. But her business allowed no personal feelings or ego. You did what you could, when you could. "I'll stay in San Antonio and figure this out."

"How are you holding up? Do you need Nevada to back you up?"

"No. His priority is Drexler. I'm fine."

"Understood. Who's your local contact again?"

"Detective Theo Mazur."

"He'll shadow you for this entire investigation." No inflection at the end of the sentence. It was a statement, not a question.

Her voice dropped. "I don't need a babysitter."

"You need a partner *and* backup until Nevada can get there." He sighed. "This isn't the time to be a cowboy, Kate."

"Right."

When she ended the call she rubbed the side of her neck. Sweat had soaked through her blouse, making it cling to her skin.

Mazur answered his phone, and his mouth hardened into a grim line. He looked toward her, the phone to his ear as no doubt someone above his pay grade told him to work with her. Like it or not, they were in this together.

She approached him after he hung up, seeing no reason to delay the inevitable.

"Looks like we're joined at the hip," she said.

"Right. There's not much more we can do here. The forensic team is collecting data, and the medical examiner will be here soon to collect the body."

"What about witnesses and security cameras between here and the interstate?"

"Got it covered. I've uniforms searching local businesses. Maybe we'll get lucky."

"Maybe."

He walked her back to his car, and when he opened the door, heat washed out. As they slid into the front seat, he switched on the air conditioning, which felt good for the first few minutes. Soon it chilled her skin.

"I'll be right back," he said. "Stay put."

"Sure."

He left her and crossed to Palmer. They spoke, their heads ducked slightly toward each other, and a couple of times the two glanced back toward her. Palmer shook her head and rubbed the toe of her boot into the dirt.

Mazur returned to the car. A grim expression deepened the lines around his mouth and eyes.

"We should go through my cases," she said.

"A parade of freaks and demons. Can't wait."

***

At the office Mazur hustled Kate toward the conference room. He wondered how she contained all her emotions as she pulled out her laptop from her backpack and set it up at the head of the table.

Her expression was determined, but she didn't look the least bit tough. Sweat from the heat had flattened her hair, and her mascara now cast faint shadows under her eyes. Her skin was pink from the sun. She slid off her shapeless navy blazer to reveal a cotton blouse that now clung to her skin and nicely rounded breasts. Absently she wiped a bead of sweat from her chest.

He cleared his throat. "I need to see the chief. Don't leave this room."

"Has Palmer called Bastrop?"

"I don't think so."

"I'll do it."

"Right." He left her and ordered several sandwiches to go, knowing Palmer would be starving soon. He went to his chief's office.

"I don't like getting calls from the FBI," the chief said without looking up from a stack of papers. "It has a way of aggravating my ulcer and fucking with my day."

"I'm not fond of it either."

"What the hell is going on? Ballistics matched the Sanchez murder and the Samaritan cases?"

"That's correct."

"And that murder victim you have resembles another of Agent Hayden's cases?"

"It does."

The chief muttered several curses as he looked up. "Figure this out fast, Mazur. The press is already up my ass about the Sanchez shooting, and they're going to double down when they hear about this latest murder."

"I will."

"I gave you a shot in this department because you saved my boy's ass in Iraq. And, if push comes to shove, I'll ride the ship down with you. But I'd rather not go down with my ship."

"You won't, sir."

"Dr. Hayden really suspects this Bauldry guy?"

"We know this latest victim, Rebecca Kendrick, purchased her car from Sanchez Motors, where Bauldry worked after his release from prison. We also know Gloria Sanchez's mother worked for the Bauldry family."

He rubbed his palm over the back of his neck. "Holy shit. Where's Bauldry?"

"Right now, he's MIA. He's not been at any of his last known addresses, and his brother hasn't seen him. I've a BOLO out on him."

"His family is very well connected," the chief said. "Father died last year, but the brother is just as powerful."

"The family has cut him loose. He's on his own."

The chief studied him. "I'd be doing you a favor by tossing this hot potato of a case to someone else."

"No. I want this. There're others in the department who know the players better than I do, but I caught more homicides in Chicago in the last five years than half these guys caught in their career. Cultural differences or family history is not going to stop me from solving this case."

The chief's jaw worked as if he were chewing leather. "I refuse to retire with a loss like this."

"You won't." Promises meant little. Only results mattered. "The autopsy for Rebecca Kendrick is going to be tomorrow."

"I want a report from you right after that autopsy. Until this case is solved, I don't want you taking a piss without me knowing it."

"You're in the loop."

He knew it would be a long day and returned to the conference room. Kate was hunched forward studying her laptop and scribbling notes on a yellow legal pad. She straightened and slid on dark-rimmed glasses that framed her face in a nice way. "I called the warden at Bastrop. He's away from his desk but will call me back."

He glanced at the legal pad. She'd already made a list of twelve names with three circled. "That's some list."

The door opened to Palmer, who glanced toward Kate. "Something tells me none of us are going home for a while." She nodded toward the legal pad. "That your list of greatest hits?"

"It's the cases I've worked in the last five years. I circled the cases that put me in the eye of the media."

"Like the Samaritan and the Soothsayer," Palmer said.

"What's the deal with the eyes?" Mazur asked as he pulled out a sandwich and set it in front of Kate.

Kate recapped Michael Carter's biography. "And as Carter's paranoia grew, he believed that he was under constant surveillance from certain women who he thought were soothsayers. In Carter's mind, soothsayers could steal your soul."

"Did these women reject him in some way?" Palmer unwrapped a sandwich and slurped on a chocolate milkshake.

Kate nodded. "As far as he was concerned, yes. He had prior contact with all of the women, who were prostitutes. From what other sex workers told me, Carter's initial encounters weren't violent. But then he kidnapped each from their place of work and took them to a secluded area, where he stabbed them to death and mutilated their eyes so that the world would know their blind souls could not roam the world tempting man."

"And the wound patterns on Rebecca Kendrick's body matched the Soothsayer's work?" Mazur asked.

"I'll know better after the autopsy, but from what I've seen, they're almost identical," Kate said. "The eye extraction detail was kept from the press. I've no reason to believe it was leaked."

Mazur rolled up his sleeves as he nodded to her laptop. "Have you ever lost sight of that computer? I imagine it's full of all kinds of case details."

"I have not," Kate said. "It has several encryption levels, and when it's not with me it's locked in my hotel room safe."

"Nothing is impregnable," he challenged.

"I'm aware, that's why every measure is taken."

"Is there a leak in your unit?" Palmer asked as she plucked a potato chip from the bag.

"We're a tight-knit team," Kate said. "I trust everyone."

"What about someone who's close to the team and might have access to files?"

"Not possible. We're all very careful."

"That reporter, Taylor North, keeps close tabs on you," Mazur said. "What's the deal with him? Did he cover the Soothsayer case?"

"He didn't approach me during the investigation, though that doesn't mean he wasn't following the case. I assumed he was simply driven and hungry for a headline. Now, I don't know. I should talk to him. I'd like to know where he's been."

"Agreed." Mazur glanced toward the legal pad and noted one case was circled multiple times. "What other cases do you have?"

"There're a few that come to mind. I really hope if there's a copycat, he doesn't attempt one of these."

She clicked her computer, and three images appeared on the screen. These women were tied to a stake and burned. "They were doused with gasoline and set on fire. Their killer thought they were witches." Another image showed the bodies of five prostitutes who'd been strangled and their corpses mutilated with a knife. Those killings happened in Denver.

As she ran through the slides, Mazur was struck by the utter horror that filled her life. Every cop had to find a way to decompress, but he wondered what the hell she could ever do to cope with this.

"This last case is the most recent. I just came from Salt Lake City, where I was interviewing the victim."

"Is this the nut that puts women in boxes?" Palmer asked.

"Yes. Sara Fletcher was his fifth victim," Kate said.

"Jesus, I hope this creep is caught before he can recreate any of your other house of horrors victims," Palmer said. "How the hell do you sleep?"

"Not well," Kate said.

Mazur glanced at the picture of Sara Fletcher and then to another picture of the wooden box that had been her prison. A primal rage made it hard for him to sit still. "This guy is headed south and was last spotted in southern New Mexico."

"At this time, Drexler is not relevant to this case."

"Assuming the Sanchez and Kendrick killings are connected," Mazur said, "what theories do you have about this killer?"

"Male. Late twenties to midthirties. Educated. And he wants the world to know he's smart enough to obtain classified details, but he also wants the world to know he's his own man."

"That description fits Bauldry," Mazur commented.

"I know."

"So what can we expect?"

"The next time he murders, he might improvise. He might have his own style that he wants to show off."

***

When Mazur and Kate arrived at the Forensic Department an hour later, Calhoun had organized all the clothing articles from Gloria Sanchez's murder scene next to Ms. Kendrick's belongings. Kate scanned the items, not touching but evaluating.

"I've processed the items from the Sanchez case, but haven't had a chance to examine Ms. Kendrick's things. You can look but don't touch," Calhoun said.

"Of course," Kate said as she pulled on a pair of rubber gloves.

Gloria Sanchez's clothes were all high end and designer. The shoes were Gucci as was her purse.

"She liked nice things," Mazur said.

Kate lifted an evidence bag that contained a bottle full of oxy, then replaced it. She studied the shoes, the belt, and the earrings. And then she paused when she saw the victim's key chain. It appeared to be a brass chess piece.

She raised it up. "It's the queen, the most powerful player on the board."

"She was the Queen of Cars," Calhoun said. "She often appeared at events with a crown, a cape, and a scepter. It was her shtick."

Kate moved to Ms. Kendrick's belongings. The items weren't nearly as expensive. Faded jeans and a white blouse, a beaded bracelet, and slip-on shoes. All now stained with blood that was still sticky and damp.

She took a mental step back, banishing the image of the young woman who'd been alive and well yesterday.

As she inspected each item, she saw nothing that was out of the ordinary. Why had the killer chosen her?

"I'd like to look at the contents of the purse."

Calhoun unzipped Rebecca Kendrick's large black leather tote. She removed a spiral notebook, several pens, lipstick, a hairbrush, a leopard-print wallet, and a packet of blush.

"Is there any jewelry?"

Calhoun looked up. "Two gold stud earrings."

Kate frowned.

"What are you looking for?" Mazur asked.

"I'm not sure," she said, more to herself.

"You were interested in the queen chess piece before," he prompted.

"William and I used to play chess. It's how we met. We were our happiest when there was a chessboard between us." William would see all this as a game. He would deliberately leave her a memento so she knew it was him. "Check her purse one more time."

Mazur shook his head. "This is a stretch."

Calhoun rooted in the bottom of the purse. Seconds passed, and then she arched a brow before frowning as she removed a white bishop. "It was stuck in the bottom of her purse."

Kate released the breath she was holding, but there was no sense of relief. She rubbed her thumb against her forefinger, now worn red.

CHAPTER EIGHTEEN

I have chosen the queen, the rook, and of course the bishop. When this match is finished the king will have nothing left.

San Antonio, Texas
Wednesday, November 29, 8:00 p.m.

Mazur and Kate arrived at the coffee shop where Rebecca Kendrick had worked for the last sixteen months. A uniformed officer Mazur recognized from the Sanchez crime scene approached them as they got out of Mazur's vehicle.

"I've interviewed the owner and am going to canvas the area businesses for surveillance tapes," the uniform said.

"Good," Mazur said. "I'd like to talk to the owner."

The uniform shrugged. "Emma Gibson. She doesn't know much."

"Right."

A tall, thin woman with gray hair twisted into a bun greeted them at the front door. She wore a peasant skirt and a white top. Bracelets jangled from her wrists. She was talking to another uniformed officer, who seemed relieved to see Mazur.

"Emma Gibson," he said as he showed her his badge.

She lifted her chin a fraction. "Yes."

"I understand you own this café?" he asked.

"That's right, for fifteen years now."

"And you hired Rebecca Kendrick," Mazur said.

"That's right." She steadied a quivering bottom lip, but her tone shook. "A little over a year ago."

"What can you tell me about her?" Kate asked.

She blinked back tears. "Great gal. Had a few hard knocks as a teenager, but she was pulling herself up and making progress."

"What kind of hard knocks?" Kate asked.

"She didn't talk much about it. Health issues, which led to too much drinking and ultimately arrests. She was released on parole early last year."

"Not everyone hires ex-cons," Mazur said.

"She had solid references from a work-release program. I called her sponsor, and she vouched for her personally."

"Who sponsored the program?" Mazur asked.

"Sanchez Motors."

"Gloria Sanchez?" Kate asked.

The woman frowned. "Yeah. Jesus, do you think the cases are related?"

"We don't know," Kate said. "Did Mrs. Sanchez ever visit your shop?"

"She came in for coffee a few weeks ago. Rebecca took her break, and she and Gloria sat at a corner table and talked. It looked intense, but when they were finished Gloria hugged Rebecca."

"That the only time you saw the two together?" Kate asked.

"Yes." She leaned in. "Look, Rebecca worked hard and was talking about going back to school. The girl was smart, and if she could keep her head screwed on straight, she was going places." She bit her lower lip. "Did her past catch up to her?"

"We're still trying to figure it all out," Mazur said. "You said she locked up as expected?"

"She clocked out of the register at 11:01 just like she was supposed to do."

"Anything unusual about her last few days?"

"No. There was nothing that caught my attention."

"Did she have friends?" Mazur asked.

"Sure. A few guys and gals in her age group. They came in sometimes to see her."

"Do you have names?" he asked.

"Only a couple of first names. Steve and Patsy. The others, I don't know. They seemed like a nice group of kids. I do know they all attended that drug-addict support group. 'One day at a time,' Rebecca always said." Ms. Gibson frowned. "I did see a guy lingering outside a few times while she was working. He never came in or did anything. But him watching the place made me notice."

"What guy?" Kate asked.

"Tall, thin, dark hair. Well dressed."

"How old?" Kate asked."

"Midthirties, maybe. I didn't know him, so I asked Rebecca if he was a friend of hers. She said no."

"Did you believe her?" Kate asked.

"Funny you should ask," Emma said. "I never caught her in a lie, but that time I got an odd feeling."

"You think she knew the man?" Kate said.

"I asked her later again, but she shrugged it off. Said for me not to worry."

"Did you ever see the guy again?" Kate asked.

"No. Not after that day." Her brow knotted. "Do you think he killed her?"

"He could have just been a guy standing on the street corner," Kate said.

Mazur scrolled through his phone and found Bauldry's picture. "Is this the guy?"

Emma studied the phone a long moment. "It's an older picture of him, but yeah, I'd say so."

"You're sure?"

"Ninety percent." Emma was frowning when she looked up at him. Tears glistened in her eyes. "Did he kill her?"

Mazur knew in his gut he was on the right track but kept his voice even and his expression blank. "He's a person of interest."

A sad smile tipped the edge of Emma's lips. "I still can't believe she's gone. She had so much life ahead of her."

"Do you have security cameras?" Mazur asked as he tucked the phone back in his pocket.

"I don't. But the restaurant across the street does."

He texted the information to Palmer. "I'll have my partner check."

"She had a locker in the back if you want to look inside it," Emma said.

"Lead the way," Mazur said.

They followed Emma to the back, where she pointed to a locker with a combination lock. She rattled off the numbers before she returned to the front. "That was one of my rules. I needed access, seeing as she'd been an addict. I didn't ever look in the locker, but I could if I wanted."

Kate opened the locker and gazed at the contents, which included postcards featuring Hawaii, colored beads that looked as if they had been tossed from a Mardi Gras float, a small mirror, a hoodie, a hairbrush, and lipstick.

"She doesn't exactly fit the profile," Kate said softly. "The Soothsayer's other victims were all prostitutes and drug abusers."

"How did you catch the Soothsayer?"

"I sensed he stalked his victims before the kill. Anticipation is just as strong for males like this as the murder itself. The local cops dug through hundreds of credit card receipts from each of the businesses near where the girls worked. His card appeared multiple times at one store nearby. With that same card, Carter also bought a carving knife at a cooking store and duct tape at the hardware store. An identical knife matched the nick marks found on the victims' rib cages."

"And you're certain you have the right guy?"

"His DNA matched hair fibers we found on victims two and three. We also matched his thumbprint to the steering wheel of the first victim. We had evidence to connect him to all three victims."

"Solid work."

She sighed, rebuffing the compliment with a shake of her head. "We need to know what William was doing outside this store and learn more about his relationships with Rebecca Kendrick and Gloria Sanchez. The fact he crossed their paths is not a coincidence."

"William right now is in the wind. Let's check out Ms. Kendrick's apartment and see if she left anything behind. I want to know what Bauldry's connection is to her."

"Agreed."

***

Rebecca Kendrick lived in an efficiency in the Ridgefield Manor Apartments. Located in central San Antonio, the apartment units occupied the second level, and the first level was an open deck for resident parking. The building was covered in a dull-gray synthetic paneling, and the units' front doors were painted red.

Mazur located the manager's unit and showed the old man his badge. With little fanfare, the man took him to Unit 1C and unlocked it. Mazur thanked him and promised to let him know when he and Kate had finished.

Mazur moved inside the room while Kate held her position. Moments like this were always tense for cops. These apparently routine situations could just as quickly result in an ambush.

He checked the closet and the bathroom before he holstered his weapon. "It's clear."

Kendrick's place was six hundred square feet and included a small kitchenette. Next to the small sink was a dish rack filled with neatly stacked blue dishes. The dishtowel was neatly folded over the edge of the clean sink. The countertop had a coffeemaker, a sugar bowl, and a small ceramic utensil holder with several wooden spoons and a spatula. Inside the fridge was a head of still-crisp lettuce, a box of cookies and muffins from Emma's café, and a carton of milk that still had a week to go before expiration. The cabinets held more dishes and several boxes of sugar-coated cereals.

The brown tiled floor of the foyer led into a small living room covered in faded brown carpet. A bright indigo cotton rug added a spark of color. The avocado-green couch was draped with an American Indian blanket that tied in well with the carpet. The vertical blinds looked standard issue, and a standing lamp provided secondary light. The television that sat on a bookcase in the corner was several generations old. Stacked on top of the television were three books that dealt with sobriety, living with addiction, and positive affirmations, respectively. On top of the table a collection of sobriety chips was lined up in a neat row. One month, two months, and up to over a year's worth. The table was free of dust, and the few fashion magazines were arranged in a crisp stack.

"Sobriety meant something to her," Mazur said.

"So did order and control. But that is common in recovering addicts who are focused on the program."

Mazur removed the sofa cushions. "There's a pullout sofa, and judging by the smell, the sheets covering this lumpy mattress are fresh."

Kate picked up one of the magazines. "A couple of dozen pages are dog-eared. The articles she's marked feature makeup tips." She selected another magazine. "All about brides and exotic travel locations. I wonder who she was dreaming of marrying."

"Marrying?"

"Makeup, bridal gowns, honeymoon locations. She was dreaming big."

"Her boss said she didn't mention a boyfriend."

"She might not have spoken about him to her boss, but she'd set her sights on someone."

"Like Martin Sanchez?"

Kate entered the bathroom. "Expensive lacy undergarments hanging on the shower curtain rod to dry, and in the drawers there's pricey makeup, feminine products, and a nearly full box of condoms." He moved to the threshold to see her open the medicine cabinet. "Empty except for a bottle of aspirin, a razor, and a small can of men's shaving cream."

The trash can was filled with piles of tissues. He gingerly lifted several. "And below these tissues is a used condom and a DNA sample for Ms. Calhoun."

"It might tell us who the boyfriend was."

Mazur replaced the tissues and in the bedroom found a small dresser with an empty flower vase on top, with more expensive undergarments neatly folded in the top drawer. The second drawer held shorts and T-shirts, and the last, socks. All organized. The lone closet contained one navy-blue peasant dress, a black skirt and white shirt draped on the same hanger, a collection of a half dozen tops, and three pairs of jeans. One pair of boots, one pair of sneakers, and flip-flops.

Back out in the living room, he opened the small side table's drawer by the couch and removed more condoms, a fresh pack of chewing gum, and a collection of pictures. "She's worried about getting pregnant. Not just cautious but very careful."

Kate flipped through the pictures. The first featured a smiling Rebecca Kendrick, her arm wrapped around a young man with a haggard face and the toothless smile of a meth addict. Behind them was a circle of chairs and a cross on the wall. The next picture featured Rebecca and two young women. The smiling women were thin and pale, their eyes sunken. And the next picture captured Rebecca with Gloria Sanchez.

Mazur studied the picture. "I get the sense these two liked each other."

"Relaxed posture, close proximity, and the slightly arched brows certainly indicate that. Gloria's smile reminds me of the one I see in her car ads. Big, bold, as if she's selling something."

"No pictures of Mr. Sanchez."

"No. The background appears to be the basement of a church. No windows, and a cross on the wall. Also, there's a large coffeepot in the background and a plate of doughnuts. Ms. Kendrick was working the program."

"What was Gloria doing at the meeting? Checking up on her?" Mazur asked.

"Gloria's hair and makeup are completely done. She's dressed in a high-end pantsuit. Nails polished. Jewelry. She wasn't sneaking around and trying to hide. She expected to be photographed. Maybe this is part of her charity outreach to ex-cons. Publicity, no doubt."

"That fits. Take away the hair and makeup, and they look very much alike. They could be sisters." He pulled the small notebook from his breast pocket. "But they're not. Ms. Kendrick moved to Texas five years ago from California. She bounced around the state, living in Houston and Austin before settling here. And she did serve nine months in the Travis County jail for possession early last year." He flipped the pages of his notebook.

"Gloria is wearing fall colors and a light blazer. And if you compare this image to the commercials made last summer, Gloria's hair is longer. If I had to guess, I'd say the picture was taken very recently."

"The crucifix hanging on the wall behind them suggests a church."

"Check a three- to five-mile radius of this apartment. Recovering addicts like to stay close to their meeting sites, especially in the beginning. She would want to know she could get to a meeting quickly if she had to."

He typed the information into his phone. "There's one church within two miles of this apartment. Saint Anthony's."

"Let's pay them a visit. Maybe they've also seen Bauldry."

The drive to the parish in the modest neighborhood took less than ten minutes. The parking lot had about a dozen cars. The brown adobe exterior had arched doorways and windows with leaded glass, and a cornerstone marker dated the church to 1899. The landscape was neatly trimmed and the trash picked up.

Inside, they moved down the dim hallway following the signs that read "Office." Beside the church office hung a sign-up sheet for altar flowers. A flyer requesting volunteers for Sunday school was next to a notice that the first meeting for the Christmas pageant would be held in two days.

They entered and faced a small desk where an elderly Hispanic woman with salt-and-pepper hair sat at a computer. Her round spectacles magnified her dark eyes when she looked up and smiled.

"Police?" she asked.

Mazur reached in his pocket as Kate pulled out her badge. "You've seen the police before?"

The woman rose, pulling off her glasses. "In this neighborhood? Father Jimenez counsels many at-risk youth, so we get our share of visits from the police." She extended her hand. "I'm Maria Lawrence. I'm the church secretary. Father Jimenez is making a hospital visit now, but maybe I can help. Who are you here for?"

"Rebecca Kendrick."

"Rebecca?" The woman shook her head. "Don't tell me that Rebecca is in trouble. She's worked so hard to straighten out her life."

"You know Rebecca?" Kate asked.

"Yes. She came to us after she was released from jail and joined our sobriety group last year. She just received her eighteen-month chip."

"What do you know about her past?" Kate asked.

"She came from a very bad family situation. She lived on the streets many times growing up in Los Angeles. She's proud of her new apartment and her job at the coffee shop. She was saying they were talking about making her manager."

Mazur showed the picture of Gloria and Rebecca. "Was this taken here?"

She slid her glasses back on. "Yes. In the basement. We have meetings several times a week. And, oh my, that's Mrs. Sanchez with Rebecca. I was so sorry to hear about her. Such a lovely woman."

"How was Mrs. Sanchez affiliated with the church?" Mazur asked.

"She's a very generous contributor. She grew up in this parish, and she and her husband were married here. In fact, Mr. Sanchez called me this morning about the funeral. He doesn't have a date yet. I understand the medical examiner hasn't released the body."

"Were Mrs. Sanchez and Ms. Kendrick friends?"

"They did get along. Mrs. Sanchez liked Rebecca's fire and ambition. She even stopped by a few times for meetings, especially in the last month."

"You know why?" Mazur asked.

"Mrs. Sanchez seemed troubled. I know she wasn't feeling well, and Rebecca helped Mrs. Sanchez when she stumbled a few weeks ago."

"She fell?" Kate asked.

"They didn't think anyone saw, but I did. Mrs. Sanchez tripped, and Rebecca helped her into the ladies' room. They were in there for a few minutes, and when they emerged Mrs. Sanchez looked pale, but better."

"Did they say anything about what had happened?" Kate asked.

"Neither one of them said a word. Rebecca valued her privacy and everyone else's as well. Are you trying to figure out who shot Mrs. Sanchez?"

"We are," Mazur said. "And we're now trying to find out who killed Rebecca Kendrick."

"Rebecca." The word came out on a strangled whisper. "She's dead?"

"Yes, ma'am," Mazur said. "She was killed last night."

"How?"

"We aren't able to say right now," Mazur said. "Is there anyone in this church who might have had an issue with either of these women?"

"I know we're in a rough neighborhood, but the people who come here are good."

"But you minister to all walks of life. Did anyone seem to focus on either one of these women?"

"Not that I ever saw."

Kate pulled up a picture of William Bauldry on her phone. "Have you ever seen this man in the parish?"

"William, yes. He never misses confession and comes to Wednesday and Sunday services. He's a nice young man. Joined us about ten months ago. Keeps to himself. But is always happy to lend a hand when asked."

Kate was silent for a moment. "Would he have run into either of these women here?"

"I'm sure it's very possible."

"Did he say or do anything that would give you pause?" Kate asked.

"Why would he?" The woman's face hardened with a frown. "I've seen cops zero in on a suspect and then search for anything that will prop up their theory."

"That is not my intent," Kate said. "You didn't answer the question."

"Of course not, he never did anything to worry me. Just last week he arrived early for one of our meetings and helped set up the chairs and tables. Saved me an hour's worth of work. A good, solid man. And yes, before you say it, I know he has a prison record. But God believes in second chances, and so do I."

Mazur knew how clever these monsters could be. They hid in plain sight and either went unnoticed or were pillars of the community until they were arrested. "Do you know where we could find William Bauldry?"

"If he's not here, he's working or at home."

"Where does he work?" Kate asked.

"At Sanchez Motors. He has a job in their body shop. Gloria sponsored him when he got out of prison, and I suppose she referred him to our church."

"That job lasted only six months," Kate said. "It ended over the summer."

Mrs. Lawrence shook her head. "That's not what he told us. He said he was still working there."

"Was William close to Ms. Kendrick?" Mazur asked, shifting the conversation.

"Friendly. Nothing romantic."

"And Gloria?" Kate asked. "What was her relationship like with William?"

"They got along very well. Seemed to get each other's jokes when no one else did."

"Did they talk about anything in particular?" Mazur asked.

"They were always quiet. I could never hear."

"And was Ms. Kendrick seeing anyone?" Mazur asked.

"She was, but don't ask me who. I heard her on the phone a couple of times. I could tell by her voice it was a romantic partner."

Mazur thanked Mrs. Lawrence and left his card. Outside with Kate, he stared up at the cloudless night sky filled with bright stars.

"I need to get my car back at the station," Kate said.

"Finding a new hotel?"

"I'm going to see my mother."

He didn't speak for a moment. "I can take you straight there."

"Just drop me at my car."

"Sure."

They were on the road before he commented, "Mrs. Lawrence had pretty nice things to say about Bauldry."

"The William I remember was a very clever, charismatic man," Kate said. "And now he is out of prison, once again charming everyone around him."

"With what end in mind?"

"Self-serving. If Church Lady only knew what was walking among her flock. If anything, guys like him get more dangerous in prison. They learn from other prisoners to hide their thoughts and to become the person they need to be to get what they want."

"What else do you remember about William?" Mazur asked.

"I'm remembering how it was when I was in high school. After I broke up with him, he followed me everywhere. He called me all the time. He turned our family inside out. He enjoyed the harassment, the toying. So killing me today would be too easy. He doesn't want the game to end."

Scowling, he shook his head as he stared at her. "Jesus, Kate. How can you be so calm?"

"Between you and me, I am not calm. I'm scared. But I don't have the luxury of hiding. If I don't catch this guy, he will kill again."

His phone chimed with a text. "Palmer has footage from multiple security cameras that shoot directly on Rebecca Kendrick's coffee shop," he said. "She says William appears on yesterday's footage."

"We need to find William," she said.

"But in the meantime."

"Keep doing what you're doing. You're a good cop."

They were less than a foot apart, and he couldn't deny his need to protect her. He wanted her to know she wasn't really alone.

They made the ten-mile drive back to headquarters in silence. His gaze was locked on the road and hers focused on the passing buildings.

When they reached the lot, she stared at the cars, as if trying to remember where she'd parked.

"I've been in so many cities, so many hotel rooms. It's all becoming a blur." She raised her key fob. "It's here somewhere."

Mazur shook his head and grinned. "You can track a serial killer, but you can't find your car."

"Distraction is an occupational hazard." She hit the "Unlock" button on the fob and waited for taillights to flash. There was a distant beep and a flicker of light. "Did you see it?"

"Yes."

He drove her to the red car. "Agent, I'm astonished. Fire-engine red?"

"My walk on the wild side." She thanked him as she got out of his car, and slid behind the wheel of her rental. He saw her glance in her rearview mirror as the headlights of a marked car switched on. She might not like it, but he was going to have eyes on her while she was in his city.

***

Kate pulled out of the lot, accepting that Mazur or one of his cops would be with her while she was in San Antonio. Oddly, she didn't mind. As she drove toward her mother's house, she'd barely reached the end of the block when her phone rang. She recognized the number. It belonged to Taylor North.

She raised the phone to her ear. "Mr. North."

"I want to talk."

"You're in luck. So do I."

Kate distanced herself from strong emotions. It wasn't that she didn't have them—she simply steered clear of them. They only created confusion and were a distraction. But when it came to Taylor North, she had a hard time remaining civil. He was a bottom-feeder. He was willing to exploit people, and even the truth, for personal gain. She'd heard from her boss that there was talk of a book, and this murder was simply another notch on his belt regardless of whom he hurt.

She parked in front of a small café and stared at the blue neon "Open" sign. As she got out of the car, she noticed the marked police car and walked over to the vehicle.

The officer rolled down the window. "Agent Hayden."

"You don't have to stay."

"Mazur's orders are to shadow you until you reach your mother's."

"Fine, thank you."

Kate entered the shop and spotted North sitting in the corner. A stoneware mug in front of him, he leaned over a legal pad.

As she approached his table he glanced up, made an anemic move to stand, but she waved him back down. She pulled her chair around and sat with her back to the wall. "Mr. North."

"Agent Hayden."

He'd been covering the Samaritan case more than any other reporter and knew the details better than most of the cops. This killer was getting his information from someone. "So what questions would you like to ask me?"

"Did you arrest the right man? Is Dr. Richardson guilty?"

"He's guilty. I'd stake my reputation on it."

"So he has an accomplice?"

"Still working on that one."

"The Gloria Sanchez murder stinks of the Samaritan killings. Whoever did this must have been working with Richardson," he countered.

"Why do you say that?"

North shook his head as he leaned forward. "We're jumping the gun. My hope was that we'd use this meeting to get to know each other. To learn a little about trust."

A dark intensity shadowed his gaze. She leaned forward. "You've gathered a great deal of information on this case."

"I'm a very good reporter."

She shook her head as she traced a small nick on the table. "You've done a hell of a job of researching this killer. You have an inside track on details only the cops would know. In fact, you could have pulled off a good imitation of his murders."

A frown wrinkled his brow. "I'm one hell of a reporter, not a killer."

"Maybe too good." She let the word hang. "It's almost as if you know the killer."

He pulled off his glasses and let them dangle between his fingers. "Do you think I'm the killer?"

"I've read your articles. Your ability to climb into his mind is astonishing."

He sat back. "How am I supposed to react to a statement like that?"

"Take it however you like. Denial. Outrage. I would be upset if someone thought I was involved."

Entertained, he sipped his coffee. "I didn't kill anyone."

"You interviewed Richardson several times in prison. Did he whisper sweet secrets in your ear?"

"No. He was quite evasive. He was using me to get his message of innocence out."

She shook her head. "I think he gave you key details so you could stage this whole show. It's the why that I can't figure out."

"You're running down the wrong rabbit hole, Agent Hayden." He smiled. "Can I call you Kate?"

"No."

"Keep it formal. Maybe for the better. I reported the facts, and yes, I dug deep into a lot of facts on the Samaritan. Maybe I danced close to the line a couple of times as far as revealing too much information, but if I don't sell my articles, then I don't eat."

"That sounds dramatic."

"I live and die by the numbers."

His demeanor suggested confidence that bordered on arrogance. He gladly took shortcuts, believing the ends justified the means. One cop had said Taylor would push his own mother off a cliff for a solid lead on a story.

"Okay."

"Okay, what?"

"We've reached the end of this journey. You have nothing for me, and I've nothing for you."

He looked disappointed. "Just like that? I don't see you as the type that gives up so easily."

"I don't. I haven't. I'm just finished with this conversation."

Eyes narrowed, he shifted topics. "Gloria Sanchez doesn't fit the profile of the first victims."

"Really?"

"She's a business success and well known. Not the random low-income woman that no one would miss right away."

Kate didn't respond.

"Have you tested ballistics? Did the same gun kill Gloria and the others? You can tell me. This is strictly off the record."

She smiled. "No such thing as off the record. Didn't you learn that in PR 101?"

He drew circles on his notepad. "The killer must have crossed paths with Richardson."

She studied him, knowing he was fishing. "What other cases like the Samaritan have you covered?"

"Why do you ask?"

"Humor me."

"At least a half dozen."

"List 'em."

He drew in an impatient breath. "I've written about several cases in the last few years. The Dollmaker. The Hangman. The San Francisco Strangler. The Soothsayer."

The Soothsayer. Her mind grew very still even as her heart skipped a beat. "Which of the cases did you find the most fascinating?"

"All of 'em. They're all unique in so many ways."

"Arrests were made in each of the cases."

"What are you getting at?" he asked.

Serial killers were addicted not just to the murder but also to recreating it over and over in their memories. Who better to share information with than a reporter?

"Just trying to figure out how much you know. You would tell me if this killer contacted you, correct?"

"Are you asking if we should work together?"

She wondered how many people he'd drawn in with that boy-next-door tone. "I work alone, Mr. North. I just want to make sure you aren't withholding important information."

"I wouldn't do that."

"Really?"

"You're working closely with Detective Mazur."

North's not-so-subtle deflection told her he was paying close attention to her. "He's law enforcement. You're not."

Instead of being annoyed or put off, he grinned. "Help me and I'll help you."

This was a game to him. The victims were inconsequential. Simply pieces to be moved about as he saw fit.

She nodded to his cell. "Record this."

Arching a brow, he quickly unlocked the phone and hit the "Record" button.

She leaned in and in a clear voice said, "Whoever shot Gloria Sanchez thinks he's very clever. He thinks he can throw me off, make me guess. But he's not that smart. He's an amateur who gets his one rock off killing women. I'm going to enjoy locking him away."

"Strong words."

She rose. "Let's see what he has to say when I arrest him. Bet he cries like a baby."

"I'm going to use this."

"I'm counting on it." Kate rose, knowing the quote would win her some flak from Mazur and her boss. Fine. Playing safe rarely scored big points.

***

A car pulled into the driveway across the street from his house. He watched as Mrs. Hayden got out and walked with a clipped, urgent pace toward the house. She was in her late sixties now, but she had kept herself in great shape. He'd watched her long enough to know she took daily walks and often had friends over for book club or a girls night out.

He'd had surveillance cameras positioned in his yard, and they all pointed at her house. And when she'd been on vacation six months ago, he'd gotten into her home and posted more cameras. Living room. Kitchen. The bedrooms. All the bathrooms.

Surveillance told him she lived a clean and simple life. She played by the rules. She was the least likely person to be murdered by anyone.

And yet that was why she was so perfect. Her death wouldn't be ignored. Kate Hayden would certainly notice.

As easy as it would have been to kill Sylvia Hayden, he wasn't interested in her death. Her home was simply the bait. The one place that Kate would return to once she came back to San Antonio. Once she was in that house, he could watch her while she slept, showered, or ate.

As he sat and watched tonight, he noticed a car drive by the house. It was a beat-up truck with Utah plates. Utah. Kate had been in Utah. She'd been chasing that man who put girls in boxes. What was his name? The name danced on the tip of his tongue before it came to mind. *Raymond Drexler.*

Frowning, he leaned closer and watched the truck as it crept past. It circled the block, its red taillights vanishing. He sat back, wondering if he'd worried for nothing. He checked his watch. Waited.

A couple of minutes later the vehicle returned, slowing in front of Sylvia's house almost to the point of stopping, but not quite. The driver wore a hoodie, so he couldn't make out his face. When the truck vanished again around the block, he grabbed his keys and ran to his car. He leaned low in the seat, watching, betting and hoping that this interloper doubled back.

Sure enough, he came back for a third time. Not smart to watch so closely, but some people were amateurs.

He started his car, backed out of the driveway, and followed. When the vehicle drove back toward the center of town, he was glad for the increased traffic that allowed him to go unnoticed.

Maintaining a few car lengths, he followed the truck, and when it pulled into the parking lot of a Best Texan motel, he kept driving far enough to make it look good before he doubled back on foot.

The man was large, well over six foot five, and he had a freshly shaved head. He pushed open the door to Room 304, glanced both ways, and vanished inside.

"There's a new player in the game," he said.

He didn't appreciate poachers, and he sure as hell wasn't going to share Kate with Raymond or anyone.

But as the old adage went, keep your friends close and your enemies closer.

CHAPTER NINETEEN

My brother is anxious to get started. But I have cautioned him to wait. None of it matters unless we have a clean sweep of the board. Patience is a virtue.

San Antonio, Texas
Wednesday, November 29, 11:00 p.m.

Kate parked in front of her mother's home. She sat for a moment, hating that her heart was racing and her thoughts would not calm. Her mother had prepared the yard in what she had called xeriscaping. She'd switched to rocks and succulents, declaring she was done with the constant yard work. She'd had the house repainted and a new roof put on, but the one-story rancher was almost as she remembered it.

Kate continued to sit and think. Her father had been dead seventeen years, but his mark on this land hadn't been erased. The swing he'd hung for her still dangled under the large cypress tree. The front aggregate sidewalk was still the one laid by her brother and father. And she had helped her father build the side screened porch when she was fourteen.

The memories rushed and surrounded her. They reminded her of all that had been lost and told her to run. *So easy to find a hotel room.*

So easy to keep running. She glanced back at the waiting officer and waved before she shut off the engine.

The front porch light clicked on, and she saw the curtains move. Her mother was up and waiting, as she'd expected, and had seen her. No escape now.

She grabbed her bag and walked up the sidewalk. Her brother was good at taking care of their mother. He wore the mantle their father had left as best he could. Whereas Kate had been frozen with grief and done everything she could to avoid this place, he'd stood fast. As cold and distant as he'd been to her, he had loved their mother. She understood his anger toward her had been born in grief and fear. But, as a sister, it stung deeply.

She reached for the front door handle as she'd done every day of her childhood. She wrapped her fingers around the cool metal and hesitated. This wasn't her home anymore. Not really. She rang the bell and stepped back.

Footsteps sounded inside, and the screened door fluttered as the door behind it opened. She tightened her hand on her strap and raised her gaze to her mother.

She'd last seen her mother in May in Chicago. Kate had flown her up to the Windy City, and they'd spent several days visiting sites and eating out. It had been nice. Until her mother had invited her home for Christmas.

Her mother was tall and kept her frame trim. She wore her thick salt-and-pepper hair tied back in a ponytail and wore jeans, a loose sweater, and boots. Her mother beamed on the other side of the screened door.

"Kate. It's so good to see you." She pushed open the door and wrapped her arms around Kate. Her mother still smelled of Chanel, and her arms still held her tight when she hugged. With effort, Kate relaxed her body and raised a hand to pat her mother on her back. Her mother's grip tightened for a moment, and then she released Kate.

"You still don't like to be hugged," her mother said.

"When it's you, I don't mind." She smiled.

The marked car slowly pulled away.

"You can kid the rest of the world, but not me." She squeezed her daughter's hand. "Come inside. Your room is ready."

"I didn't mean to surprise you like this. I can go to a hotel if I'm putting you out."

"Kate, this is your home. You're not putting me out. I'm glad you came. And don't you ever ring that front bell again. Come inside!" She grinned. "When I saw you on the television, I thought you were going to sneak in and out of town without seeing me."

"I almost did."

Her mother laughed. "I do love your honesty. Are you hungry?"

"I am."

"Skipping meals isn't good for you, Kate."

"You sound like the local cop I'm working with. He's always trying to feed me."

"I like the man already." Her mother arched a brow. "Change clothes and I'll make you scrambled eggs and a bagel, no butter, light on the cream cheese."

The knot inside her eased a little. "Thanks, Mom."

She moved toward her room, passing a family picture that hung in the hallway. It was the last family picture with her father. She was smiling, but like all her smiles, it was a bit flat. The others were grinning. She remembered the day the photo was taken. Her brother had been tugging on the end of her hair, doing his best to stoke her temper. She'd yelled. Her father had said something about putting his foot up asses if they didn't settle down.

"Mitchell and Kate, knock it off."

"They're too much alike," her mother had said.

"They're night and day," her father countered.

Her brother had glanced at her but hadn't said a word. She knew he was glad they weren't alike. She'd been about sixteen with no friends or a social life outside of chess club.

Her room was exactly as it had been when she was a teenager. A simple blush quilt lay on the double bed with the wrought-iron frame. No stuffed animals, dolls, or even extra pillows. A painting of mountains she'd done in art class. Her wooden desk with a clean blotter, pencils still sharp, notebook centered as it had been in college. Her chess set remained on an end table, the pieces still in midplay.

She carefully unpacked, hung up her clothes, and plugged her phone in by the nightstand. She laid out running shorts, top, and shoes in anticipation of rising early and going out in the morning. And she set out the clothes she'd wear tomorrow. Some things never changed.

After putting on sweats and a T-shirt, she slipped on flip-flops and moved down the hallway into the kitchen. Her mother was standing at the stove scrambling three eggs. Bagel slices warmed in the toaster.

Kate sat at the table and resisted the urge to dab at a couple of stray crumbs. There'd been lots of family dinners at this table. They'd been wild, raucous affairs with her brother, and though she'd always been quiet, she could always hold her own. She glanced toward the seat at the head of the table that had been her father's. Her chest tightened. Guilt tugged at her.

"Why haven't you redone my room?"

"Don't know. Maybe I always held out hope you'd come back and would want something from it."

She'd never wanted to come back, but now that she was here, she found an odd comfort that her room had remained the same. "You should remodel it, Mom. Or better, find a new place to live. Don't you want to get out of the suburbs and live where there's more to do?"

"There's plenty to do here."

"Mom, is it really good for you to stay here?"

"I like being around my memories. Maybe that isn't the most ideal, but I like it. It's peaceful. Lots of friends."

Her mother set the eggs and bagel in front of her and sat at the table, sipping coffee and allowing her daughter to eat. Kate had loved these moments when she was a kid. Her mother understood her need for silence and yet was still content to be with her daughter.

"I saw you on the news," her mother said. "You were front and center at this conference."

"San Antonio had a shooting that was identical to the Samaritan killings. The local jurisdiction contacted me, and I've been investigating the case with a local detective."

"You arrested the Samaritan months ago."

"This killer knows intimate details of the other Samaritan murders."

Her mother studied her, shaking her head. "I was married to a prosecutor for twenty-eight years and have given birth to two cops. I know when one of you is holding back. What aren't you telling me?"

Kate sat back, doing her best to emit a relaxed confidence. "The killer asked for me by name. But given my recent media exposure, it's not unexpected. Nothing to worry about."

Sylvia shook her head. "You'd think I'd be used to all the talk about killers after all these years. But I still worry. Every day I dread a phone call like the one I received—"

The weight of blame grew heavier. "You can say it. The day my ex-boyfriend shot and killed Dad."

Her mother laid her hand over Kate's. "That boy shot you, too."

"But I didn't die."

Her brows knotted. "I never blamed you. I've told you that a hundred times in every way I could."

Mitchell had said as much, and all she could do was cower behind her logic. Never in her life had she ever found the words to express her feelings of regret and guilt.

Her mother stared at her, and she sat back and sipped her coffee.

"I pictured you as a scientist toiling happily away in your lab, not chasing killers like your brother and dad."

She was proud that she was as much like them as she could be. "Genetics is hard to fight."

"Your father was never more excited than when he won over a jury and sent a criminal to jail." She patted Kate's hand. "I thought at least one of my two children would have a little of me in them. I see so much of your father in you."

Kate traced the rim of her cup with her finger. "Then why didn't Dad and I ever spend more time together?"

"He never knew what to do with a girl. Never knew the right things to say. It's why he drove you to school for the evening chess meets. He wanted to spend time with you."

And he'd been killed.

As if sensing Kate's thoughts, Sylvia said, "Tell me about your case. Don't think you've deflected me from finding out more about this killer."

Kate smiled. Her mother was sharp. "Do you remember Nina Hernandez? She was the housekeeper for the Bauldrys."

"I saw her once or twice at the school. Her daughter was a little older than Mitchell. Nina was a striking woman. Very quiet."

"What about her daughter, Gloria?"

"I never spoke to her, but your father did. She got into trouble when she was about seventeen. The senior Mr. Bauldry spoke to your father directly and smoothed things over."

"What did she do?"

"She vandalized the car of one of the cheerleaders. A stupid prank that ended up doing quite a bit of damage to the car."

"Anything else?"

"No. Or if something did happen I never heard about it."

Kate dabbed a crumb on her plate with her thumb. "I saw Mitchell."

Her mother's posture stiffened. "Really."

"He came by my hotel."

"Did he behave himself?"

"He was very gracious. He said he was sorry."

"He is. You know him. He's not a talker. But every holiday you weren't here after Sierra died troubled him."

She shook her head. "I should accept his peace offering and move on."

"Will you?"

She'd missed her family. They'd all lost, but she'd lost her home, father, and brother. "I'll try."

Her mother waited until Kate had finished eating. "Back to this killer, Kate. Who is he?"

"Have you heard from William Bauldry?"

Her mother straightened, and the softness around her eyes and mouth vanished. "I know he's been out of jail since January 5. Has he been bothering you again?"

"No. I haven't seen him. Has he contacted you?"

Her mother's lips flattened. "No."

"No odd sense that you're being followed? No notes or letters or flowers?"

"None of that. Do you think he would do all that again?"

"No. I'm just reviewing all the angles. He was pretty obsessed with this family and especially me toward the end."

"None of us realized he'd go to such extremes."

"Do me a favor and be extra careful. I think he's close and he's watching, just like he used to."

"I'm fine, don't worry about me."

"I would like you to go and stay with Mitchell until I finish this."

"I love your brother, but I'm not staying with him. I can take care of myself."

Her father had spoken similar words before he'd been shot. "What about staying with your sister? Aunt Lydia always likes to see you."

"You're chasing a killer, and you expect me to run off like a frightened child and stop worrying about you?"

"I'm partnered with Detective Mazur. He's a good cop and has my back. I'll be fine."

"Detective Mazur sounds like a man who has sense."

"He's very reasonable." There was a calm steadiness around him she found appealing. "But I would feel better if you visited Aunt Lydia."

Her mother shook her head. "Hell no, I'm not running."

"Just for a week or so, Mom. I could send you and Aunt Lydia on a cruise."

"We don't need an expensive cruise."

"I can't afford expensive, Mom. You'd both be getting the economy cruise."

Her mother laughed. "I love your honesty. But I've made up my mind."

"You need to. I know William. If he's out there, he needs to believe he can get to me. He won't, of course. But he needs to believe it. I can't do my job and worry about you."

"You sound like your father."

"Mom, please. Do it for me."

Her mother gathered up her cup and Kate's plate and let out a sigh. "I'll drive up to Dallas and see my sister for a week or so. But I'm calling your brother and telling him what's going on. Last I checked, I'm still in charge of this family."

"Mom, William knows that the best way to throw me off or hurt me is to kill you or Mitchell without a second thought."

"No one cares about me. And your brother is a Texas Ranger and a former Army Ranger. I think Mitchell will be fine."

"Dad was a former cop and prosecutor."

Her mother raised her chin, then shook her head. "We all underestimated William back then. None of us will do that again."

"Okay. Tell Mitchell. He listens to you better than me."

"Of course. Now, would you please get some sleep? You look exhausted."

Kate stifled a yawn. "I could use more sleep. I'm still running a deficit."

"Go on. I put clean sheets on the bed when I saw you on television."

"You were so sure I'd visit."

"I hoped." Her mother kissed her on the cheek. "I'll see you in the morning."

Kate rose and walked back to her room. She pulled the comforter back; the scent of laundry soap rose up from the sheets, and it reminded her of her childhood. She checked each of her three windows to make sure they were locked and secured. Only then did she lie down and shut off her light. Moonlight cut across the white ceiling and the pencil drawing of a horse her father had done for her when she was six and afraid of the dark.

Tears filled her eyes and slid down the sides of her face. It was good being home.

***

The shrill sound of Kate's phone yanked her from a restless slumber. She glanced at her phone. The display read BLOCKED. It was 4:59 a.m. She hesitated, then clearing her throat, answered the call. "Dr. Hayden."

"Katie."

Half awake, the soft-spoken voice didn't register immediately. "Who is this?"

"You don't know?"

A familiarity in the speaker's tone sent an uneasy tremor up her spine. "Who is this?"

"This is William."

She sat up and pushed her hair out of her eyes. Her heart raced into high gear, pounding against her chest. "How did you get this number?"

"Don't you remember how good I am with computers, Katie? It's easy."

"I remember. Where are you?" She swung her legs over the side of the bed and moved to her briefcase. She dug out a minirecorder, clicked it on, and held it close to the receiver.

"I'm traveling. My housekeeper told me you came by. Why did you come to see me, Katie? Did you miss me?"

Katie. It was the nickname reserved for her family, and for the few months they'd dated, she'd allowed him to use it. "It's Dr. Hayden."

He chuckled. "You were always Katie to me."

"That was before you shot me and killed my father."

"I was terribly sick in those days. I know the way I stalked you wasn't right. I was having trouble with my medications. I paid the price."

"My father is still dead."

Silence crackled. "I sent flowers to his memorial service. I wrote that I was sorry in the card."

The memorial service had been delayed three weeks so Kate could heal. Seventeen years had done nothing to temper her pain. The thought of reliving it now with him made her sick.

William had been a master manipulator when they'd played chess. He would set traps, try to get in her head, anything to dominate her. Not now. Not ever again.

"I want to talk to you about Gloria Sanchez," she said.

"Gloria and I were old friends. Why are we talking about Gloria?"

Of course, he knew the answer. This was another layer to the game. "She was shot and killed off of I-35 near San Antonio."

"That's terrible. But I don't know anything about that." He sounded almost coy.

Her gaze steady, she was barely breathing. "It's been all over the news."

"I've always thought so much of you, so I guess I'll believe you."

"Did you shoot her?"

"Why would I kill Gloria?"

He'd not said *her* or *that woman*, but he'd said *Gloria* in a way hinting of familiarity. She pressed, "Did she do something that made you angry? What was it about her that drove you to shoot her?"

"Sounds like you've already made your mind up about me." He didn't sound upset but amused.

"Gloria's mother worked for your father."

He was silent for a moment. "Really? I don't remember."

His tone had shifted, suggesting she might have hit a nerve. "You remember everything. You and Nina were close."

"I don't remember."

That was a lie, but for her to challenge him would ensnare her in an endless loop of accusations and denial. "You enjoy manipulating people."

He chuckled. "You have a harsh view of me. But there was a time when you loved me. I still remember the feel of your naked breast in my hand."

She wouldn't allow rage or regret to overwhelm her. "How long had Nina been with your family when you were born?"

"Why do you keep asking about Nina?" His voice was soft, curious. "She's tucked away safe and sound."

"Did Gloria tell you about Nina? Did she tell you she paid for five years' worth of care in advance?"

He chuckled. "My goodness, you have been digging. That's what I like about you. You're smart, disciplined, but most of all, you're persistent. And no beating around the bush. You get right to the point."

"Why Gloria?" It was important to stay focused. "Why shoot a woman you've known since you were a child?"

"What are your theories?"

"I never saw you two together when we were younger. She was married by then. But I remember Nina talking about her daughter. She was so proud of her. Nina was also good to you. I remember how fond you were of her."

"Was I?"

She gripped the phone. He was evading her questions, knowing he was frustrating her. She tamped down her rising temper. "There was another murder."

"Another one? Terrible. Is a pattern emerging, Katie, or are you paranoid?"

Rebecca Kendrick's name had not been released to the media, and she wouldn't discuss the case details with him now. "Did you kill this second woman?"

"That's a riddle you're going to have to solve. I just wanted you to know I received your message. You look beautiful, by the way. Television suits you. Your mother must be so proud. She looks good, by the way."

She swallowed anger and fear and resisted the urge to tell the monster to leave her mother alone. "We need to meet."

He chuckled. "I doubt that would be wise now. I've no doubt Detective Mazur will be tagging along."

He was paying very close attention if he knew about Mazur. She glanced around the room almost as if she expected to see him standing there.

"I'll call again soon. I like talking to you, Katie. I've missed you."

The line went dead.

For a long moment she sat there, her heart racing in her chest. Her hands trembled. She glanced at the clock. It read 5:01 a.m. The call had lasted less than two minutes. Not long enough to trace or track. William was always thinking. But his tone suggested arrogance, as if he knew how this contest would end. Good. Let him overplay his hand.

Kate dialed Mazur. He picked up on the third ring, and when he barked his name into the phone, his voice was heavy and rough. No need to ask him if she'd awakened him. She had.

"I received a call from William Bauldry," she said.

"Kate." He cleared his throat. "When did he call?"

"Minutes ago. I taped the call."

"And?"

"I asked him directly about the murders. He wouldn't give me a straight answer. Did he or didn't he kill those women? It's a riddle as far as he's concerned."

She heard a light click on. "Do you think he did it?"

"Yes. He could have denied it, but he didn't. My accusations amused him."

"Where is he?"

"I don't know." She rose and paced back and forth. Nervous energy snapped through her body. "His number was blocked, and if he was using a burner, my guess is he's disabled it by now."

"Are you still at your mother's house?"

"Yes."

"I can be there in half an hour."

She glanced down at her trembling hand and drew in a breath as she flexed her fingers. It had been a long time since she felt this rattled and unsteady. "That's unnecessary. Get a few more hours' sleep. I don't want William to think he's under my skin. Plus, I'll need you to rest up. You're going to need it."

"You're sure?"

"Very."

"I'll see you in a few hours."

***

William stared at Katie as she paced by the edge of her bed. She was so tense and nervous. She'd acted so cool and calm on the phone, and for a moment he thought he'd not gotten to her, but he had.

He watched as she tossed her phone on the unmade bed. It didn't surprise him that she'd called Mazur. He was her partner in this case, and Katie, if anything, stuck to procedure. She was so predictable, even at chess . . . most of the time.

Thinking about Mazur irritated him. He didn't like the way the cop's gaze tracked her a little too closely. She was a unique woman, and no doubt the detective wanted in her pants almost as badly as he did.

As Kate stripped off her nightgown and moved to her suitcase to slip on her bra, he leaned in closer to the screen and watched. He grew hard and thought about what it had been like to touch those breasts and to kiss them.

When he'd first met Kate, he'd been smitten. Puppy love, some might have said. It had taken him months to summon the nerve to ask her out. And when he had, he'd been shocked when she'd said yes. They'd dated for several weeks, and she'd grown to really like him. On what was their last date, he'd walked her home and had kissed her. She'd given in to his touch and kissed him back. He'd felt her hunger. Her need. He'd been so hard.

She'd tensed, but he'd told himself that was her excitement. When she'd whispered *no* in his ear, he'd thought her a tease. He'd kept kissing her, and when she pushed him away, he grabbed her hands and pinned them over her head. She'd kicked and cried, but her fear only excited him more. He stripped off her pants, freed himself, and pressed into her, feeling her tightness and her nervous energy. That moment had been so perfect that he replayed it over and over in his head. He'd expected more from her, but after the best day of his life, she'd been cool, distant. She'd flinched when he tried to touch her. When he'd finally said good night, her father had been waiting.

He wouldn't see her again for another month. She'd been too busy. She had plenty of excuses why she couldn't see him.

Finally at a chess tournament he'd seen her. He wanted to talk to her about what they'd shared, but contact and conversation were limited. When her gaze reached his, he'd seen strain. Her fingers were tense and her body so still when they'd played in the finals.

He was so in love with her.

"Where have you been?" he'd whispered as he moved a pawn forward.

"I can't see you anymore."

"Is it because of your father? He doesn't like me."

She'd pressed the tip of her index finger on a bishop and moved it three diagonal spaces.

She didn't meet his gaze.

"It has nothing to do with my father."

"You love me. You let me be the first."

She shook her head as her fingers curled into tight fists. *"That was a mistake."*

He stared at her, barely able to think clearly. She'd stayed focused and continued to play. She was much better. This time she beat him.

After that night he walked by her house often. He would stand in the shadows and stare at her at night. Once in a while he'd see her pass in front of a window. He would stare toward her, willing her to see him, but she never did.

More and more William became convinced that she was a prisoner in her home. And it was his mission to put an end to her imprisonment.

Once his mission was clear, then it was a matter of planning. He followed her father, noting his daily habits, his moves, and when he was alone.

That night in the dark parking lot, he'd seen her emerge from the building and walk toward the car. He'd been so focused on her that he hadn't seen her father, who had shouted for him to put the gun down. He'd fired, shooting Mr. Hayden first.

Kate's piercing scream had shifted his focus. He took aim at her, determined to destroy her heart as she'd destroyed his. He fired, but she'd pivoted. The bullet had sliced her leg. When she dropped, he fired again, but this time he was more nervous and his hand shook. The bullet cut across her face. Blood gushed, and he'd thought he'd killed her.

He ran. Though when he stopped to catch his breath nearly a mile away from the scene and slid into his father's car, his body was alive with fear and a triumphant rush he'd never experienced.

He'd never expected to be so excited or to enjoy the thrill of the kill.

Later, after his arrest, he learned she was alive and that he had failed. In the courtroom, she'd been very precise when she testified against him. Mitchell had railed his frustration at the sentencing hearing, but Kate hadn't spoken a word.

Over the last seventeen years, he'd followed her work after she joined the FBI. She kept a low profile, but he paid close attention and made it a point to track her development. What case she was solving. Though he wanted to hate her, he took pride in her wins. She rose through the ranks and was one of the best agents in the country. She liked to chase killers, so he'd decided to become the ultimate killer.

He watched as she dressed in her blue slacks and white shirt. He liked the way the fabric clung to her breasts. But the pants and matching jacket were too dark and heavy for her small frame. When the time came, he would ask her to dress differently.

She paced the room. His call had upset her. Made her restless. She wanted to go for a run, but wouldn't dare in the dark.

He traced the outline of her body on the screen and smiled. "Come and get me, Katie. Find me. You know you want me."

She studied every corner of the room as if searching. For an instant, she stared toward the window. She thought someone was looking through the window, never realizing the camera and microphone were hidden in the grate.

Those pale-blue eyes cut into him. And he recoiled before he reminded himself she couldn't see him.

She thought she was smarter than he was, but she underestimated him. That would be the first lesson she would learn from him.

"Are you worthy of what I've planned for you, Katie? Are you up for the challenge? I hope you are, because I want a good fight before I checkmate you."

CHAPTER TWENTY

Keep your friends close and your enemies closer.

San Antonio, Texas
Thursday, November 30, 6:00 a.m.

When Kate moved from her room down the center hallway of her mother's home, she was careful to be very quiet. Her mother had never been an early riser, and she didn't want to wake her. Avoiding the part of the floor that always creaked, she went into the kitchen. Opening cabinets, she was comforted to know her mother still kept everything where she remembered it. Retrieving the bag of coffee that had always been her father's favorite, she made a strong pot and toasted a bagel. She selected a mug that said "Texas"—it had been hers in high school.

Sitting in silence, she ate as she checked her phone for any updates from Agent Nevada. No new texts. Not good. Drexler remained on the loose. With an altered appearance, he might easily slip through the cracks. Nevada had theorized he was headed toward Texas, but Drexler could be in Arizona and over the Mexican border or have turned north to make his way to Canada. Once out of the country, he could vanish into the wind.

She curled her fingers around her bracelet. She traced the *W* and the faded paint. She'd promised Sara he would not escape. And she never reneged on a promise.

She rinsed off her plate and set it in the sink, then took one last swig of coffee before pouring the remains down the drain. Using paper from her notebook, she wrote a note to her mother. She took extra care with her handwriting, wanting her mother to see without realizing it that she had it all under control. Nothing was further from the truth. But she was good at pretending.

She checked her watch. There was time to drive by Rebecca Kendrick's place of employment and see if there was anything the officers had missed before Mazur arrived. Chances were there wasn't, but she couldn't breathe in this house. Couldn't think.

As she closed the front door behind her, a dark SUV pulled up in front of the house. She hesitated, reaching for the gun clipped to her waistband.

When the man rose to his full six foot four inches and stepped out of the shadows, she recognized Mazur. He locked his car with his key fob and moved toward her. He was dressed in khakis, a white shirt, and dark tie.

"What are you doing here?" she asked.

"Your brother, Mitchell, called me."

"Why?"

"He said you might get up early and do something stupid like go for a run." His gaze swept over her. "Or maybe return to a crime scene alone."

"How does Mitchell know about you?"

Mazur shook his head. "So where were you headed?"

"I planned to visit Rebecca Kendrick's place of employment again but expected to return in time for the autopsy."

He moved toward her a step.

"We can go together."

Her 9 mm rested securely on her hip. "I've no intention of getting myself killed."

He jangled keys in his hand. "No one ever does. My vehicle awaits."

"You make me sound reckless," she said, falling in step beside him. "Call 'em like I see 'em."

"I'm not reckless. But I'm not afraid to take calculated risks."

The front door opened, and the porch light clicked on. Her mother opened the screen door, and huddling in a blue bathrobe and worn Uggs, asked, "Did you think you could sneak out, Katie?"

"I was coming back, Mom."

Her mother studied Mazur. "Looks like Mitchell rallied the troops."

The tone of her mother's voice caught her attention. And then she understood Mitchell's early-morning call to Mazur. "Did you call Mitchell?"

"I texted him," her mother said. "I heard the phone ring, and then I heard you start pacing. I knew something was wrong."

Aware that Mazur was watching, Kate walked toward the porch. Mazur followed. She glanced up to warn him to stay back, but he shook his head.

He extended his hand toward her mother and introduced himself. "Detective Theo Mazur, ma'am."

"Sylvia Hayden," she said, studying Mazur. "You're my daughter's San Antonio police partner, right?"

He flashed a grin that was charming. "We're working together on this case."

A smile teased her lips. "You don't sound like you're from Texas, Detective Mazur."

"Chicago, ma'am. Been here six months."

"How do you like it?"

"Mostly hot."

Her mother laughed. "Chicago's too cold for me."

Mazur winked. "The cold builds character."

"I say the same about the heat." Her mother tucked a lock of hair behind her ear.

If Kate didn't know her mother well, she'd say she was flirting. She wasn't sure if she was mortified or amused. "We have to go, Mom."

As Kate kissed her mother and moved to turn, her mother captured her hand and met Mazur's amused gaze. "Take care of Katie."

The grin dimmed. "Yes, ma'am. I've a daughter of my own. I know what worry feels like."

Kate could have pointed out she'd been an FBI agent for seven years and was quite capable. Although her colleagues and family would never believe it, she understood all too well the significance of emotions and their overwhelming effect on logic.

Kate kissed her mom again on the cheek and pulled her hand free. "Go see Aunt Lydia."

"I'll be on the road by nine." She pressed a key in Kate's hand. "I had the locks replaced a few months ago, so you'll need this. You're always welcome. Come and go as you like."

"Thank you." She glanced at the shiny brass key. "Why'd you have the locks changed?"

"A few break-ins in the neighborhood. Time to upgrade."

"Was your house broken into?"

"The back door was ajar one afternoon. I couldn't remember if I locked it or not. Nothing was missing or disturbed, but better safe than sorry."

Kate hugged her mother. "Be careful."

"And the same to you."

Kate left her mother standing on the steps of her family home, remembering that when she'd left for her freshman year of college, she'd felt such a sense of relief, she hadn't glanced back.

This time she did look back and nodded to her mother, who waved and smiled just as she had done a million times when Kate had been young and their family was still whole.

The heavy weight of her mother's gaze had her sliding into the front seat of Mazur's SUV. She settled her backpack by her feet and pulled on her seat belt. Mazur settled behind the wheel.

"Your mother is nice," Mazur said.

"Most people aren't sure I have a mother. Some assume I was spawned."

He laughed. "It did cross my mind."

His rich, deep laughter lifted some of her dark mood. She appreciated his directness. No hidden agendas with Mazur from what she could tell. A straight shooter.

As he drove, he studied the neighborhood filled with one-story stucco homes, many landscaped with desert plants and pale rocks. "You grew up in this neighborhood, didn't you?"

"We moved here when I was fourteen. We started off in Austin until my father took the job with the local district attorney's office."

"How did you handle the move?"

"It wasn't easy at first, but then you find a friend and it gets better."

"I hope the same for Alyssa. Uprooting and coming here has been hard for me, but I figure it's worse for Alyssa."

"Kids are more resilient than adults."

"In Chicago, I lived a few blocks from where I grew up. Even to this day the old-timers like to share stories of my escapades as a young man."

She angled her head toward him. "You were a troublemaker?"

"The Mazur brothers were legendary."

As an investigator, making small talk could be critical when dealing with a suspect. Get them to open up about the small things and then the big might follow. She sensed Mazur was doing this to her. "What was it like living around so much family?"

"Great times. All my cousins lived within a few blocks. Holidays and birthdays were always a blowout. Mom was usually the host. Our house was always filled with people. Laughter."

"And you gave up all your family and career to be here for your daughter?"

"In four years she'll be off to college. I'll never get that back, but Chicago isn't going anywhere."

"Have you thought more about moving to Washington?" she asked.

"I've thought about it a lot."

"Have you considered staying here and keeping Alyssa with you? Lots of single dads in the world."

He drove down the darkened streets that were only just beginning to fill up with commuters. "I have. Not sure I want to take a kid from her mother. A girl needs her mother."

"A girl needs her father, too."

A half smile tweaked the edge of his lips. "Trying not to be an asshole in this joint-parenting thing, but it's hard."

"Alyssa is lucky to have you."

They drove in silence for several minutes.

Early-morning sun cut across his face, deepening the sharp angles and highlighting his white teeth as he grinned. "FBI is a hell of a career."

"I wanted to catch bad guys. Also thought I'd get in some very interesting travel."

"How'd the travel work out?"

"Been in hundreds of small towns, back alleys, corn fields, and swamps. The full tour of America."

"I think you were just trying to figure out how to leave San Antonio with grace."

Frowning, he drove in silence for a few more minutes. "Think you can find Bauldry?"

"Yes."

They arrived at the small café located in the city center. Mazur parked across the street. This early, the shop should have been bustling with customers. But it was dark and quiet as a temporary memorial to Rebecca. However, tomorrow the café would reopen and be back in business. No matter how gripping a tragedy, the world moved on, leaving behind fading memories.

"Why here?" Kate said more to herself as they walked down the alley behind the café. "Why Rebecca? As crazy as William is, he was always methodical. And sixteen years in prison would have taught him patience, too."

They walked toward a small parking lot. "Maybe Rebecca and Bauldry had a thing, and she was breaking it off with him."

"Perhaps." She knelt down and touched the worn asphalt, wishing it could share its secrets. "His tone on the phone this morning was so smug. It's as if he had a secret he couldn't wait for me to discover. He's really proud of himself."

"You said you recorded the call."

She fished out her phone and hit "Play."

Mazur's jaw clenched. "He's done his homework. Your mother might not have seen him, but he's seen her. She said she had the locks replaced."

"Yes. Observing is what he does best. He always took his full allotment of time before making each move in chess."

Mazur checked his watch. "We need to get to the medical examiner."

She rose and brushed the dust from her hands. "Right." She paused and looked back at the scene. "William knew both the victims. Why them? Why now?"

In his car, she replayed in her mind William's phone call as they drove toward the Bexar County Medical Examiner's office.

Neither spoke as he parked and they crossed the lot. Inside, they took the elevator down to the autopsy suite, where they found the medical examiner gowned up and talking to his assistant. Between them was a body covered by a sheet.

Kate had attended countless autopsies during her seven years with the FBI. Each autopsy suite was different, but there was a likeness about them that enabled her to quickly adapt. She set her backpack aside and pulled on a gown. As she reached up behind her to tie off the gown, strong hands brushed hers away.

"I got this."

Mazur's hands were large but nimble as they tied the strands into what felt like a tight, neat bow. Before she could offer to help him with his gown, he moved past her toward the table, pulling on rubber gloves. She followed, and Mazur exchanged pleasantries with Dr. Ryland and his assistant.

The technician pulled back the sheet to reveal the nude body of Rebecca. Gashes marred her flesh. Most of the wounds were around the heart, lungs, neck, and abdomen.

The victim's eyes were removed. Cutting patterns suggested they had been gouged out of her head with the tip of a blade. Her skin was pale and clear, her cheekbones high, and her lips full.

"Rebecca Kendrick is a twenty-six-year-old Caucasian female, who is sixty-five inches tall and weighs one hundred and thirty pounds. Each eye along with a section of the extra ocular muscles has been removed. There're no other wounds on her face. Also, no defensive wounds on either hand."

"Was she alive when the eyes were removed?" Mazur asked.

"My guess is no. Otherwise, I would expect potential pain, conscious or not, would have made removing them impossible without more trauma to the face."

"Thank God," Mazur said. "Was that true for the Soothsayer cases you worked for the FBI?"

"No," she said, unflinchingly.

Mazur and Dr. Ryland exchanged troubled glances. The focus then shifted to the victim's arms, where multiple scars were clearly visible. "Her body shows signs of extensive and prolonged IV drug use. We'll run a tox screen to determine if she was using at the time of her murder."

Everything they'd learned about Rebecca so far suggested she'd been clean at the time of her death. But addicts often relapsed in their first eighteen months of recovery. And when they did, some could be quite clever hiding it.

The dead woman had three tattoos: a heart on her inside wrist, a scroll around her right biceps, and a set of teardrops over her right ankle. Her muscle tone was good. Her ears were pierced, and she had a belly ring.

The doctor held up the victim's left hand. The nails were painted a bright blue, made garish when contrasted to the pale skin, and were all neatly rounded except for the right index finger, which was broken and torn. The cuticles had already receded.

Dr. Ryland took tweezers and a scalpel and held the edge of the nail while simultaneously trimming the tip off. "Maybe she scratched him and we'll find his DNA."

The doctor pressed the tip of his scalpel to the flesh above her right breast and made a diagonal slash toward her midsection. He repeated the cut on the left side and then drew the blade down across her midsection for the classic Y-incision.

What followed was the sound of flesh pulling and the rib cage snapping as the doctor removed the bones. The wounds had caused a significant amount of blood to pool in the chest cavity, which now oozed onto the stainless-steel autopsy table. The technician wiped up the blood and suctioned the interior cavity, giving the doctor an unobstructed view of the organs.

The killer's knife had lacerated through what had been a normal kidney, stomach, and descending thoracic aorta, which was the largest artery in the body.

The doctor held up the damaged artery. "Both the jugular wound and this would have bled out very quickly. No emergency care could have saved her."

The clinical savagery of the autopsy was necessary, but knowing that didn't cool Kate's rising anger. William had known this woman. Surveillance footage confirmed he'd been in her shop the day she died. And the phone call from him early this morning cemented in her mind that William had killed Rebecca to make some kind of point to Kate. This was a game to him. If not for Kate, this woman might have dodged the Reaper.

After the autopsy was complete, the technician moved in to repack the organs and sew up the body.

"I'll get back to you as soon as I have test results," the doctor said.

"Thank you." She moved out of the suite. Slowly she stripped off her gown, wishing she could peel away her guilt as easily as the thin fabric.

She heard the doors whoosh open behind her and knew by the steady clip of footsteps that it was Mazur. He moved with precision, determination.

Mazur stripped off his gown and tossed it in the bin next to hers.

She raised her chin and met his direct gaze, careful not to let anything she was feeling reflect in her expression. "Each Soothsayer victim was discovered near an open field. The knife wounds were meant to blind the spirit in the afterlife. Simply killing in this life was not enough retribution. He wanted everlasting hurt and pain."

"What was the time difference between the killings?" Mazur asked.

"Four weeks. He thought his work was most effective under a new moon. In his mind it was the most powerful time to send his victims into the afterlife. The first victim worked as an exotic dancer in a nightclub. The second was involved in the porn industry and was a high-dollar escort."

"And they shared no other characteristics?"

"Both were Caucasian, of small stature and trim. But other than that, they didn't resemble each other. My assumption from the beginning was that the killer liked smaller women because they were easy to subdue. From there I drew up a psychological profile. It took over a year to find him. When they did he had already drawn up plans for his next kill. They found the women's eyeballs in a jar in his home office."

"Rebecca was not killed during a new moon," Mazur said as he checked his phone. "That was November 19."

"An anomaly that sets this case apart from the others. Gloria Sanchez didn't fit the victim profile of the Samaritan. Another anomaly. Both women had chess pieces found in their belongings."

"How long did you work the Soothsayer case?"

"On and off for a year. And it was common knowledge that case was very personal to me."

"Why?" Mazur asked.

"The second victim was the daughter of a friend of mine. My friend, Mimi, worked in public relations near the Oklahoma FBI office, and I knew she and her daughter, Elise, were estranged because the daughter had become a sex worker. We both led busy lives and didn't see each other much, but occasionally we ran into each other at the local gym. She couldn't forgive herself for her daughter's death."

Mazur drew in a breath. "Let's assume this is Bauldry. Who will he plagiarize next?"

"The case that has gained recent notoriety is Raymond Drexler. As I've mentioned, he locked his victims in a wooden coffin."

He slid his hand into his pocket and absently rattled change. "I don't have enough evidence for a judge to let me get Bauldry's credit cards or phone records. Nothing he said in that phone call to you was threatening, and two chess pieces are not going to get me a search warrant for his home."

"He's likely not using his credit cards now anyway and has already pulled out what money he needs," she said. "He's been in prison for seventeen years. He has had years to plan this. He won't stop until he has total control of my life."

"I don't give a shit what he wants. He's not getting it."

"He's done a pretty good job of it so far. I'm back in San Antonio chasing the clues he left for me and looking over my shoulder. Did I leave anything out?"

"It's time we stopped chasing and start hunting."

"Where?"

"We'll talk to Martin Sanchez again and suck everything out of him that he knows about Bauldry. Then I want to visit the prison where Bauldry was incarcerated."

CHAPTER TWENTY-ONE

He loves me, he loves me not.

San Antonio, Texas
Thursday, November 30, 1:00 p.m.

They arrived at Sanchez Motors and found Martin in Gloria's office. He was talking to Lena, and they appeared deep in discussion when a salesman from the floor announced their arrival.

Martin thanked Lena, who nodded to the cops before she left. He came around his desk. "I'd rather talk with Mr. Bennett present."

"That's your choice," Mazur said. "We don't want to push you. Just had a quick question about Rebecca Kendrick."

Martin's eyebrows drew together, and he folded his arms over his chest. The subtle gestures gave away more than he'd intended. "Rebecca Kendrick worked here last year after she was released from prison. She was one of Gloria's protégés."

Immediately Mazur noticed Sanchez's closed posture. "That's what we've learned. Looked like they were close, based on the evidence we found at Rebecca's apartment."

Sanchez took a small step back. "What were you doing there?"

Mazur spoke as if the woman were still alive. "We're trying to learn more about her relationship with Gloria and another employee by the name of William Bauldry."

"Bauldry? What does he have to do with all this?"

"What can you tell us about him?" Kate asked.

"Worked hard enough. I wasn't a fan of having him, but he turned out to be a good employee. He left about five months ago."

"Why?"

"Said he didn't need the money and wanted to do other things. Where's Rebecca?"

Mazur locked his gaze onto Sanchez. "She's dead."

The man's face instantly paled, and he rubbed his hand over the back of his neck. "What?"

"She was found this morning."

"How?" His face constricted with pain. "Was it drugs?"

"Had she gotten back on drugs?" Mazur asked.

"No, no," he said, shaking his head. "She swore to me she was clean. I worried about that, but she swore."

"Then why did you ask about an overdose?" Kate asked.

Martin cleared his throat. "She was doing so well. I wanted to see her succeed. But I know it was a struggle for her."

Kate leaned in a fraction. "You two were having an affair."

"What? Why would you say that?" Sanchez took another step back.

"When I first saw her I thought she could have been Gloria's sister. They look a lot alike. But they aren't related. She's simply your type. Men who stray often find a woman who reminds them of their spouse when she was younger."

Martin cleared his throat. "No. You're making assumptions." He drew in a breath as he retreated behind the desk. "I need you to leave. I'm calling Bennett."

Mazur didn't budge. "Don't you want to know how she died?"

The man stood silent, blinking.

"She was murdered."

"Like Gloria?" he whispered.

"How do you think?" Mazur pressed.

Martin lowered to his chair. "I don't know!"

"Did you hire William Bauldry so you could be with Rebecca?" Mazur pressed.

"What? No!"

"Maybe Bauldry got a taste for killing again and then decided to go after Rebecca," Mazur said.

Martin shook his head as the color drained from his face. "Get out!"

***

Kate sat silent, staring out the front window of the SUV as the endless horizon of dry Texas scenery passed by as they headed northeast. She'd received word from the warden at Bastrop that Richardson had volunteered his time at the prison. He'd never been on the payroll and had visited as part of a church group. She felt like a fool for having missed the connection. They were now driving there. As much as she wanted to remain objective, she couldn't shake the feeling that she was now responsible for not only her father's death but the deaths of Gloria and Rebecca.

"You need to get out of your head," Mazur said.

"You don't know what I'm thinking."

"You're playing the blame game," he said. "I'm a master at it. That's how I know you're doing it now."

She released a breath and looked at him. "What do you blame yourself for?"

"There're a couple of cases that went sideways that I'll never forget." His jaw tensed. "But I never go to bed now without wondering if I could have saved my son if I'd woken up the night he stopped breathing."

When he spoke, all the lightness she'd come to associate with him vanished. Kate knew there was nothing she could say.

"I'd have moved heaven and earth to save Caleb. And you'd have done the same to stop Bauldry from shooting your father."

She tugged at the center button on her jacket. "Logic and emotion never mix well."

"No, they sure as shit don't."

They made the rest of the hour-long ride in silence. At one point, he turned on the radio, allowing a country-music song to drift lazily around them.

They arrived at the Bastrop Federal Correctional Institution, and after passing through the guarded main entrance, parked. Inside, they showed their identification and secured their weapons in lockers for visiting police.

Bastrop was a minimum-security prison a little under two hours from San Antonio. The fact that William, a convicted murderer, had been placed here spoke to the influence his father had wielded. Without his old man's pull, William would have been slated for a maximum-security prison twice the distance away, with all solitary units and strict conditions.

The Bastrop warden, Jim Smith, a tall, lean man with a gray swatch of hair, greeted them on the other side of the locked doors.

Smith shook their hands. "Welcome."

"Thank you for seeing us on such short notice," Kate said.

Mazur shook his hand. "Detective Theo Mazur. You spoke with Agent Kate Hayden on the phone."

"About William Bauldry. I'll help you if I can."

"We'd appreciate that," Mazur said.

Smith guided them down a plain hallway toward an office at the end. Inside he nodded to his administrative assistant, a plump middle-aged woman, and offered each a chair in front of his large wooden desk.

The walls were covered with pictures of the warden and several key Texas politicians. There was a collection of well-read books that dealt with prison reform, psychology, and law. A plant sat in need of watering on the credenza behind his desk, but there were no personal pictures. Not surprising. Most who worked in the prison system revealed as little as they could about their private lives. Prisoners had a great deal of free time to think and scheme against their jailers.

"What do you want to know about Richardson and Bauldry?" He motioned for them to take a seat before he sat behind his desk. "Mind telling me first what's prompting all the questions?" Smith asked.

"We have two murders that we're investigating," Mazur said. "One is a Samaritan copycat; the other is a look-alike of the Soothsayer case. In both cases William Bauldry's name has come up."

"I know William committed murder when he was a kid, but he was one of the few I never saw reoffending. From day one William was one of our best inmates. And to be perfectly candid, I was worried. We don't house violent offenders, but his daddy knew important people and pulled strings. You know how it goes."

"He never gave you any trouble?" Mazur asked.

"Didn't so much as look at anyone crossways. In his last two years, he helped my administrative assistant with filing. He was a big help, and I was actually sorry to see him go."

"When did Richardson and William see each other?" Kate asked.

"They never had a formal appointment—that's why I didn't get right back to you. Took some digging to find the connection. Richardson was here to give motivational speeches. William's good behavior earned him the job of setting up for prison events. Richardson was just one of many programs we had for the prisoners."

"Did they get time alone?" Kate asked.

"Sure. There was always a guard in the hallway, but there were times when they were alone. I know William enjoyed talking to Richardson. William is very intelligent."

"Warden Smith," Mazur said. His grin was easy, natural, as if he and the warden were old friends. "We aren't here to second-guess you. We both know you run a tight ship."

"Did Richardson ever give William anything?" Kate asked.

Frowning, the warden shook his head. "That's forbidden."

"How long did Richardson visit this prison?"

"About a year. The men in his group spoke highly of him. He was very effective with the men." He shook his head. "Do I have a problem here? Are you trying to say I let something slide?"

"No." Mazur said. "We're just gathering information, sir. We're trying to connect a few dots."

The warden's shoulders relaxed a fraction, but his expression had turned guarded. "As I said, William was a model inmate. He checked books out of the library weekly, and as I understand it, he read every book we had in stock. He was one of the success stories."

Kate's temper scraped against her skin like nails on a chalkboard. She remembered how her father's body twitched when the bullets cut into his flesh. "Did William have any visitors?"

"His brother visited in the beginning but not in the last ten years. However, his sister continued to come several times a year."

"Sister?" Kate asked. "He didn't have a sister."

"Well, half sister is more like it. She said they had the same father."

"What was her name?"

He moved to his desk and checked William's file. "Gloria. Gloria Hernandez."

Gloria Hernandez, now Gloria Sanchez. As Nina's daughter, she had grown up in William's house. They had been close as kids. Were they half brother and sister, or had that just been a story they told?

Mazur scrolled through his phone and pulled up Gloria's picture. "This her?"

The warden leaned in. "Yes, I believe it is. Though she didn't wear makeup or jewelry like that. She was always modestly dressed."

"How often did Gloria visit her brother?" Kate asked.

The warden checked several pages in the file. "Two or three times a year ever since he was first incarcerated." He squinted and he checked an entry. "Five times during his last year."

"Did you two ever speak?" Mazur asked.

"Sure. I make it a policy to know something about regular visitors. She was always nice. The two of them liked to play chess when she was here."

"Chess?" Kate asked.

"She was very good. I watched a game between the two of them once. She was William's equal, if not better."

The three talked another ten minutes before Kate and Mazur thanked the warden. Outside the prison, the warm air coaxed the chill from her bones. She was silent as she and Mazur walked toward his car.

In the SUV, she released a breath. "William and Richardson were connected. And Gloria visited William on a regular basis." She could easily have taken instruction from William and made additional contact with Richardson.

"Was Gloria really his half sister?"

"My mother said Gloria got into trouble in high school and William's father spoke to my father and the charges were dropped. It's the kind of thing a father would do for his daughter."

"That's the kind of thing a father does do for his daughter."

"William never said a word to me, but I do know the family was very loyal to Nina."

He reached for his phone and typed a text. "I'm asking Palmer to check Gloria Sanchez's birth certificate."

"I doubt William's father is listed, but it's worth checking."

"Think the Soothsayer might have been a case that Richardson studied?"

"It's the kind of case that would appeal to him."

"So William could have learned about the case particulars from Richardson."

"Very possible." Her phone rang. She noted the number was blocked. "Agent Hayden."

"It looks like you're visiting my old haunts."

William's voice slithered down her spine. She looked toward Mazur and mouthed William Bauldry's name. "I did. The warden had some interesting things to say. Do you have a GPS on the car?"

Mazur raised his phone and mouthed, "Trace." He got out of the car and immediately dialed a contact at the phone company for a triangulation on the incoming call as he searched around and under the car for a tracking device.

"I don't know anything about a GPS. I wish we could talk about it, but we don't have time. I've about thirty seconds. I'm guessing Detective Mazur is already tracing my call."

Lying to him would make him angry and her look foolish. Her best play now was to make him believe he had something to prove to her. "You know how it works."

"Why are you so determined to find me, Katie?"

"There's so much we need to talk about. Seventeen years is a long time."

"A lifetime."

"I understand you and Dr. Richardson were good friends."

"I wouldn't call us friends. I helped him with this and that. Fascinating man."

The calmness of his tone stoked her anger. "But the time you spent alone with him would have given him time to tell you about the women he murdered along I-35."

"That's a stretch, don't you think?"

She hesitated, wishing she could see his face as she delivered this line. Quickly she ticked through the Samaritan case. She knew all five murders had been carried out with the same weapon, which had never been recovered. Had Richardson realized his mistake when he'd texted authorities from his secretary's computer? Had he asked William to send Gloria to take it? "Did Gloria get the gun from Richardson for you?"

He was silent a beat. "You have been busy."

The edge in his tone told her she'd struck a nerve. "She was your half sister."

He chuckled. "Sounds like you've figured a few things out."

She gripped the phone and closed her eyes, and she concentrated on keeping her tone even. "Why won't you face me, William? We can talk like adults. I know teenagers make mistakes that they regret."

"They do."

"Then tell me where you are. We can talk about your life, Gloria, and Dr. Richardson. I'd like to see you."

"I see you all the time."

A jolt shot through her nerves as she looked around the car's interior. "What does that mean?" She checked her watch. Could he see her now, or was he bluffing? "I want to talk to you in person."

"We're talking now. What do you want to know?"

Directness was a technique she used in interviews, but she understood revealing some of what she knew came with a risk. "Why kill Gloria Sanchez if she was your half sister and she stood by you all these years?"

"That's a bold question."

"Did you turn on her like you turned on me?"

He was silent for a moment. "Blue eyes laughin'," he said, quoting the Elton John song. "Remember how we used to sing it? It was our silly song."

"Why did you gun down Gloria?" She was now operating on an educated guess, doing her best to make him miscalculate.

A heavy silence lingered as she glanced down at her watch. *Either give me something or just hang up.*

"Blue eyes ain't laughing now, Katie. You're trying to get under my skin, just as you did in high school. I'm not bad. I *am* good."

The line went dead, and Mazur shook his head. He held a GPS tracking device in his hand. "Found this under the back bumper."

"He's monitoring us."

"We need to check your rental car."

"Right. What about the trace?"

"The trace wasn't successful. We have him narrowed to a few hundred miles, but that's not going to help."

"He's already on the move again." She ran her hand over her head.

"Think of this as a chess game, and you're letting him have the small pieces while you keep your eye on winning the game."

"I want to talk to Martin Sanchez again and see if he knows anything about these visits, then take another look at my father's murder file."

"Why?"

"There're notes in the files that William wrote to me. I'd like to read them again."

"Why?"

"Something he just said."

***

Kate's nerves were on edge from her earlier conversation with William when she and Mazur arrived at Sanchez Motors, where they found Martin in the back office. He was alone, sitting behind his wife's desk, staring blankly at stacks of papers that had grown since their last visit.

Martin rose. "Detectives. I've said all I'm going to say to you. You need to leave."

"I'm not here to talk about Rebecca. But I do have questions about Gloria's life before she married you. What do you know about her family?" Mazur asked.

The question caught him by surprise. "Not much. She lived with her mother."

"Did you ever visit their home?" Mazur asked.

"No. She said her mother was a domestic, and it embarrassed her. I met her mother, of course, but it was never at the house where she worked."

"Do you remember the name of the people Nina Hernandez worked for?"

"I did some asking around because Gloria was so evasive. Nina worked for the Bauldry family. They were good people."

"Gloria ever talk about the family?" Mazur asked.

"Never." He tugged on his shirt cuffs.

"What about her father? Did she ever talk about him?" Mazur pressed.

"How does this have anything to do with her death?"

"It might be critical," Kate said.

Martin sighed. "I asked, of course. She said she never really knew her father. She was born out of wedlock and was deeply troubled by that." He dropped his head into his hands. "It's not what you think about Rebecca and me."

Kate softened her voice. "How was it?"

When he looked up at them, tears glistened in his eyes. "I loved Rebecca. I wanted to marry her. But she was worried about hurting Gloria. She actually liked Gloria and appreciated all that she'd done for her." He wiped away a tear. "Who would kill her?"

"We're still trying to figure that out. Have you made funeral arrangements for your wife?" Kate asked.

"Yes." He lifted his chin a notch. "The service will be on Saturday afternoon."

It wasn't her place to judge Sanchez, but given that he'd lost two women he'd loved in a matter of days, it was hard not to acknowledge his pain. "If we learn anything new, I'll call."

Martin sank back into his chair looking lost and broken.

"Should I call your daughter, Isabella?" Kate asked.

"Isabella," he whispered. "Thank God I still have her."

"I'll be in touch," she said.

Kate and Mazur left him, neither speaking as they made their way to his car. Twenty minutes later, they arrived in their precinct conference room. Her father's murder files were waiting for them. "You sure you don't want me to go through them first?" he asked.

"No."

He angled his head. "But this is very personal."

Her backpack slid from her shoulder to a chair. She traced her finger over the murder book. "I'll be fine."

He jabbed his thumb toward the door. "I'll be right back with coffee. And if I can score a doughnut or two, I'll grab them."

"Thank you."

When the door closed behind him, she sat in front of the book. Carefully she smoothed her hand over the vinyl top. She drew in a breath and opened it.

The first page was a form that detailed the basics of the case. If she didn't look at her father's name, then she could distance herself from the facts as she had done so many times before.

When she turned the page, there was a series of sketches done by the investigators. The crude drawings showed the parking lot, the position of their car in relation to the two others in the lot, and the buildings that ringed the area. And, of course, the alley where the shooter had been waiting.

The next page was the autopsy report, and this time she could not control the rush of emotion that burned through her body. Unshed tears stung her eyes and her hands trembled as she skimmed over the autopsy pages to the notes she hoped were still there.

When she saw the two handwritten letters addressed to her, she could only stare. It took several deep breaths before her heart steadied. She read the first note:

Katie;
I love you. You're my Angel of Mrcy. Please call me. I'm not bad.
I am good. Without you, I am weak and broken.
William

Clearing her throat, she read the second:

Katie;
Your enduring silence left me in darkness; but now it makes
me angry. I know now everything you told me was a lie.
Everything we shared was an illusion. You don't deserve to
live.
William

She wasn't sure how long she stared at the precise lettering written in blue ink on white linen paper. She didn't even hear the conference door open and close.

"Kate."

She flinched at the sound of Mazur's voice. She looked up as he set down the brown to-go cup holder nestling two coffees and two glazed doughnuts.

"Sorry, I was lost in thought."

Mazur looked toward the open book and the letters. "Bauldry wrote those to you?"

"Yes."

"When did you give them to the cops?"

"Not until after my father was shot."

"Why did you keep them a secret?"

"I was embarrassed. I had thought William was so good and wonderful, and then to find out I had been so wrong. What a fool."

"Nothing in those letters said he planned to hurt you?"

"No. He never said outright that he wanted me dead."

"So you've made a career out of finding the meaning in words."

"More or less."

He pulled out a chair beside her and handed her a cup of coffee and a doughnut. "So what does the note tell you now?"

"William Bauldry sent this latest Samaritan note to the police."

"How do you know that?"

"He uses the term *Angel of Mrcy* in his letters. And just like the letter he wrote to me all those years ago, misspelled it. The use of the semicolon after my name, which isn't a common punctuation mark to use, is consistent with the letters to me. And look at the use of the contractions. He doesn't contract pronoun and verb when he speaks about himself in the positive, and when he speaks in the negative it is contracted."

"He tried to fool us."

"Or he's simply testing me. He knows this is my job. This is what I do. He's playing a game. He has now maneuvered me into this room, and I have relived the worst moment of my life."

Mazur closed the book. "I'm going to enjoy seeing this asshole behind bars."

"Not the descriptor I'd use, but I agree."

***

When Drexler pushed through the motel room door, it was two o'clock in the afternoon and he was dog-ass tired. He'd had enough energy to find the Hayden house, and as much as he'd wanted to park and wait for her, he knew that was a sure way to get caught.

He'd slept in New Mexico, but the handful of hours hadn't been enough to chase away the fatigue that had been dogging him for weeks. And now that he was in the city and around so many young girls, it would be even harder to slow down and rest.

All he could think about was making a box and locking one of the women inside. At first, they always screamed and pounded against the wood. They'd beg, plead. And finally, the pounding would soften to scratching, and then there'd be silence.

And when he finally opened the box and peered inside after a couple of days, none of 'em had much fight left in them. Instead, they were all so damn grateful for the scraps of food and the sips of water. Of course, he did put them back. Usually by the third time he took them out to play, he didn't have to ask for their compliance. They gave it willingly.

Grateful.

That's what he liked. The pure gratitude for each and every kind act he granted. And when he pulled the girls out of the box and asked them to spread their legs, they didn't fight or fuss. They were willing to do anything so that he didn't put them back in the box.

Of course, he always did. He let them out and played with them when it suited, and when they were no longer of interest to him, he just left them in the box and let nature take its course.

He sat on the edge of the bed and reclined back, releasing a sigh. As tired as he was, he was also hungry. There was a diner right across the street, but he needed to be careful. He looked different enough, but that didn't mean he was safe.

His motel phone rang and he jumped. He'd ditched his cell in Utah, and no one knew he was here. He let the phone ring eight or nine times before it stopped. He moved to the side of the bed and sat down, staring at the phone, still afraid to pick it up.

As the seconds passed and the tension ebbed, the phone rang again. Tensing, he picked up the receiver. "Yeah."

"We need to talk."

Drexler didn't recognize the voice. "Who the hell is this?"

"Someone who knows you like to watch Kate Hayden."

A jolt of fear and adrenaline cut through him. "Who the fuck is this?"

"I bet you're hungry for food and a woman."

Drexler drew in a breath but said nothing.

"And a box to put her in, right?"

"I don't know what you're talking about."

"You can't have Kate, but I've another girl for you. A very pretty blonde."

Drexler didn't speak. Cops were smart. Those bastards were everywhere. "I'm not stupid."

"You are if you drive by Kate Hayden's house again. She's off limits. But the lovely Isabella is ripe for the taking."

Isabella. A pretty name. He closed his eyes. Temptation begged him to accept, but caution kept him quiet.

"We can work together, or I can call the cops."

Drexler rose, the receiver pressed to his ear as he glanced toward his locked door.

"I have food. And I can tell you how to find the girl. And you just told me you're not stupid."

If he were real smart, he'd hang up. He moistened his lips. But the need to control was too strong. "What do you have in mind?"

CHAPTER
TWENTY-TWO

The greater the suffering, the more powerful the lesson.

San Antonio, Texas
Thursday, November 30, 8:00 p.m.

Mazur parked in front of the Texas Department of Criminal Justice offices on Guadalupe Street. He'd placed a call to Bauldry's parole officer and asked him to meet Mazur and Kate at his offices. The parole officer had yet to cross paths with Mazur and at first had not been anxious to drive back for the meeting. Mazur had done his best to cajole, but when that didn't seem to work, he'd threatened to send a uniform by his house and have him brought in.

"Let's see if his parole officer has any insights into where this son of a bitch is hiding."

Moonlight mingled with the lights from streetlamps illuminating the one-level building with the red clay mission tiles. "My guess is this man will have only nice things to say about William, who would not mess up his shot at freedom."

"We shall see."

Out of the car, the two walked to the central entrance. Mazur twisted the handle and opened the door. There was an empty reception desk and beyond it a long hallway. "Mr. Dickerson!" Mazur shouted.

A tall, burly Texan wearing jeans and a flannel shirt appeared out of the back office. He had short hair, wide-set eyes, and a dark mustache that made an otherwise forgettable face memorable. "You Theo Mazur?"

"That's right. And this is Dr. Hayden with the FBI."

"I pulled William Bauldry's file after we spoke." He motioned them into a small plain office decorated only with a metal desk, a couple of chairs, and diplomas from the University of Texas. "Honestly, I was surprised when you called, Detective Mazur." He motioned for the two to take the seats in front of his desk before he settled his large frame in his chair.

"Why's that?"

"I just saw William last Tuesday. We had a good visit."

"How so?" Kate asked.

"He mentioned he was excited about the future. He said his life was coming together." Dickerson pulled readers from his front pocket and put them on before flipping open the thin file centered on his desk. "He's been out of prison eleven months now and so far has not missed one meeting with me. He's never been late, and every time I do a spot drug test, he's clean. I wish all my parolees were like him."

Kate shifted. "He can be quite charming."

Dickerson leaned forward, resting his elbows on the desk and clasping his hands. "There's no crime in that."

"No, but he uses his charm to manipulate people."

"I recognize your name," Dickerson said. "From William's file."

She sat ramrod straight with no emotion changing her features.

"He spoke about you several times," Dickerson said. "He expressed tremendous guilt over shooting you and your father."

"Did he?"

"He had mental-health issues. But the right meds have balanced him out."

"I don't agree," she said. "I think he might have brutally killed two women in the last week."

Dickerson yanked off his glasses. "You sure we're talking about the same man?"

Mazur shook his head. "Where do you think William would go?"

"I can give you his current address. He also has a brother in town."

"We've been to both places," Mazur said. "Anywhere else?"

Dickerson scratched the side of his head. "He's from a wealthy family. Hell, he could be anywhere."

"Did he mention anyplace that he liked to visit?" Kate asked. "Anyplace that brought back good memories?"

"He's a smart man," Dickerson said. "Why would he tell me?"

"Sometimes the truth slips out. Profilers call it leakage," she said.

Dickerson sat back, expelling a breath. "He liked to talk about fishing. He said he loved to fish."

"Did he say where?" Mazur asked.

"Never said where, but once he said he had to hustle if he wanted to make it to his pond before sunset. It was spring and about six in the evening. There couldn't have been more than an hour or hour and a half of daylight left."

Mazur flexed his fingers. "Anything else?"

"Not like we had a lot of time to chat. I've one hell of a caseload, and when I realized he was doing well, I never held him long."

Mazur handed him his card. "When is he due in next?"

"Five days."

Kate shook her head. "He's not coming back."

"How do you know that?" Dickerson said. "He never missed once."

"He's finished with the charade," Kate said. "He's doing now what he's been planning to do for a long time. Dickerson, call me if you think of anything else or if he contacts you?"

Mazur heard the trepidation in her voice, and it tore at him that he couldn't find this son of a bitch for her. She protected people from the monsters, but who protected her?

He dialed Detective Santos as they stepped out of Dickerson's office. Santos picked up on the fourth ring. "Santos? This is Mazur."

"Yep."

"You know this area of Texas well, correct?"

"I do."

"Good. Palmer is doing a record search of properties owned by William Bauldry. Have a look at the list and tell her which properties might have ponds suitable for fishing."

"She doesn't need my help."

Mazur gripped the phone. "Help Palmer, or I swear I'll do more to you than piss in your coffee mug."

***

Kate couldn't shake the image of William sitting calmly by a pond, fishing, while she scrambled to find him. As they were walking back to Mazur's car, his cell rang. "Calhoun, what do you have?" He put it on speaker so Kate could hear.

"The quick DNA test of the semen found in Gloria Sanchez showed it belonged to Martin Sanchez."

"I assumed they weren't sexually active," Mazur said. "What about the DNA found in the condom in Rebecca Kendrick's apartment?"

"Also Martin Sanchez. Guy gets around."

"What about the hair samples that the medical examiner found on Gloria?" Kate asked.

"State lab is testing DNA now. I also pulled additional strands from her blouse. Thanks to the high-profile nature of the case, you might have results within a week."

"A week?" Kate asked.

"Light speed in my world," Calhoun said. "Also, there were similar hair fibers found on Rebecca Kendrick. I looked at hair samples from both victims, and they're very similar. Again, a wait-and-see until the lab gets back to me."

"Thanks, Calhoun," Mazur said.

"Sure thing."

He hung up. "The clock is running out. A week is going to be too late."

"If William is our killer, then he has a very short cooling-off period."

Many serial killers took breaks between murders. Some could only wait weeks or months, while others could wait years. He moved his jaw from side to side. "Right."

Her cell rang. It was Agent Nevada. She pressed the phone to her ear. "Tell me you have good news."

"Kate." His voice sounded heavy with fatigue.

That tone never boded well. "Where are you?"

"About a hundred miles from you." Silence rose up between them. She closed her eyes. "What happened?"

"Sara Fletcher committed suicide. She got hold of a pair of scissors and cut her wrists."

"What?"

"The staff thought she was improving. According to her nurse she ate a decent meal and then settled back into her pillows as if she'd turned a corner."

This kind of relief wasn't uncommon before suicides. Knowing death was close gave the troubled a sense of peace because they knew their suffering would soon end.

She could have discussed the whys of this girl killing herself, but right now she didn't care about the reasons. Sadness and despair washed over her.

Nevada cleared his throat. "She left a note for you."

She swallowed hard, not trusting her voice for several seconds. "What did it say?"

Silence hovered for a moment. "She said, 'Tell Agent Kate it's not her fault, but I can't live with the monsters anymore.'"

Her chest tightened, and unshed tears clogged her throat as her gaze dropped to the Wonder Woman bracelet around her wrist. "That's it?"

"That's it. I'm sorry, Kate."

Mazur was staring at her, very aware that something was wrong.

"I'll get back to you."

"Right."

Ending the call, she carefully slid the phone in her pocket and glanced at the bracelet on her wrist. "Sara Fletcher killed herself."

Mazur swore. "It's time for a break."

"I'm fine," Kate said. Tears welled in her eyes, and one spilled down her cheek. She sniffed and wiped it away with her knuckle.

"No. We're calling it a night. I'm taking you back to your mother's."

She sighed and pressed her fingers to her temple. "I can't just stop."

"I'll make calls and get a few of the detectives out there searching for this property. I don't think he's going to be found until he wants to be found."

***

When William arrived at the church, the secretary told him the cops had been there asking about Rebecca. Barely two days since he'd stabbed Rebecca, and Katie was here. He'd expected Kate to figure this all out, but not quite so soon. He would have to step up his game. Clever girl.

"I told them you couldn't have done this," Mrs. Lawrence said. "They told me to call them when I saw you."

He smiled gently down at her. "It's a misunderstanding."

"I knew it," she said smiling. "You're a good man."

"Thank you, Mrs. Lawrence."

"They told me Rebecca is dead?"

He nodded. "I know. It's terrible."

"She wasn't a perfect woman, but Rebecca wanted to be a better person."

If only Rebecca had been more loyal to the people who had helped her most. "It's a terrible tragedy."

"What should I do about the police?"

He smiled. "You will have to do what you think is best. Now I have to see the priest."

She frowned. "Of course."

William ducked into the confessional and waited a few minutes before the small door separating his booth from the priest's opened. Though the screen was supposed to hide the identity of the penitents and the priest, he always knew who sat on the other side as soon as they spoke.

"Bless me, Father, for I have sinned," William said.

"How can I help you, my son?"

The faint New York accent gave Father Tim away immediately. Young and idealistic, he believed prayer really was effective.

William cleared his throat. "It has been five days since my last confession. I have been having impure thoughts about a woman from my past."

"I see."

"The woman I'm thinking about is Katie."

"Katie?"

"I love her."

Silence emanated from the priest's side. "I understand police were here asking for you."

Just as he'd recognized Father Tim, the priest had recognized him. "I know."

"Can you help the police with Rebecca?"

"No. I can't help them at all."

***

Kate knew her detached silence troubled Mazur as he drove to her mother's house. She knew she looked pale, exhausted, and heartsick. But as much as she wanted to pretend she could handle this one alone, at this moment she could not.

He walked her up to the front door. "You need a good night's sleep."

She unlocked the door and flipped on the lights. He followed her inside, and then checked each room and closet before joining her in the main room.

For a moment she was quiet, doing her best not to allow her gaze to roam over him. She liked looking at him and wondered what it would feel like to touch him. "Do you want to stay?"

"Stay?"

She took his hand in hers and rubbed her thumb against the calluses on his palm. "I'd like you to stay."

He angled his head as he closed his fingers over hers. "I know words are your thing, but I want you to tell me exactly what you want."

She cleared her throat, more nervous than she had been in a long time. She'd been around Mazur enough the last few days to know he liked her. She'd noticed the way his gaze lingered an extra breath on her body. She took a half step toward him. Inches separated them. "In our line of work we deal with death." She hesitated, wondering why words, which were always her ally, had abandoned her.

A smiled tugged at the corners of his mouth. "Tongue-tied?"

She cleared her throat. Her heart thudded in her chest, and her body tingled with anticipation. "Sex is one of the few ways to really feel alive."

"I've heard that." His tone had dropped and his smile vanished.

Kate shifted and drew in a breath. "I know I can be quirky. And I'm not very good with people." And then before she had a chance to change her mind, she said, "I'd like to have sex with you."

He stood still, staring. His gaze didn't waver, and he didn't speak. Her heart tripped, and she feared if they didn't enjoy each other in this precious pocket of free time, she'd return to her life and he to his and that would be that.

And then he cupped her face in his hands, angled his head, and kissed her. Her lips parted, and he very expertly slid his tongue into her mouth. Her body warmed to him instantly, and rising on tiptoe she wrapped her arms around his neck. Without breaking the kiss, he banded his arm around her waist and pulled her against him.

When he broke the kiss, she was breathless, excited, and afraid of how much she wanted not just the sex or temporary escape, but him. Her chest was tight with desire, and even if she could have pulled in a breath to speak, the words had now abandoned her.

He studied her face closely as if trying to read her thoughts. He rubbed his finger along her jawline. "You sure about this?"

She drew in a breath, savoring the thrill that shot through her body. "Yes."

He cupped her face with his hands and carefully traced the scar on her face with his thumb. Her work brought her so close to evil that she'd forgotten a touch could be soft and gentle. She could almost believe in happy endings and good winning out over evil. The reality of life would remind her of life's bitter truths, but for now, she had the illusion of hope.

He tipped his head forward and lightly kissed her on the lips. Again, he traced the scar on her face with the edge of his thumb. The utter gentleness nearly made her flinch, and if she had not wanted to forget the darkness so badly, she'd have pulled away.

She pressed her palms to his chest and slid her hand under the folds of his jacket so that she could feel his heartbeat. It was steady, even. She rose up on tiptoes and deepened their kiss, promising a passion that went beyond gentle lovemaking.

She wasn't interested in polite right now. She wanted her body to explode with wanting and desire so intense that the world would vanish for a little while.

Her breasts rubbed against his chest as he banded his arms around her narrow waist. His heartbeat jumped. His erection hardened and pressed against her.

He broke the kiss and laid his hand on her shoulder.

"You're reacting to the news."

"That's part of it." She kissed him again. "I've had too many days like this and too many nights spent alone. Not tonight. Can't we just enjoy each other? I won't get weird about it later."

His brow wrinkled as he studied her, and then shaking his head as if this was all against his better judgment, he kissed her. This time the touch wasn't gentle or tentative—urgency vibrated as his hands slid from her shoulder to her breast. He palmed the soft flesh, making her nipples harden.

She shrugged off her jacket and let it fall to the floor. "There's a room down the hallway."

He glanced down the hallway. "Not the room you lived in as a kid."

She chuckled. "No. A spare room. Neutral territory."

He arched a brow. "And you're sure about your mother not coming home?"

A playfulness she'd not felt in so long bubbled. "When's the last time you asked that question?"

"Too long ago." A wry grin twisted his lips. "And I can't believe at thirty-nine I just asked it."

She took him by the hand and led him down the hallway to the room at the back. Her mother always kept this room for anyone who happened to visit.

Kate pushed open the door. She didn't switch on the light, preferring the moonlight that leaked in through the blinds.

Mazur shrugged off his jacket and laid it on a chair across from the bed. Slowly he unknotted his tie, tugging it back and forth until it loosened. She kicked off her shoes, amazed at how much she wanted and anticipated this.

As she reached for the top button on her blouse, he shook his head.

He looked as if he had all the patience in the world. "No. I want to do that."

Her heart jumped. But she let her hand fall to her side, and she slowly walked toward him. He reached for the top button and slid it free. He went to the second and then the third. The *V* of the blouse now showed the full swell of her breasts peeking over what was a very plain and practical bra. She never took time for clothes beyond what was utilitarian. Normally it didn't matter, but now it did. She wanted him to desire her as much as she now wanted him.

He ran his finger along the shoulder strap. "Did the FBI issue this?"

She smiled. "Wait until you see the panties."

The smile faded from his eyes as fire kindled behind his gaze. "I can't wait."

He unfastened all the buttons on her blouse and slid it off her shoulders. It fell to the floor by her feet. He ran a calloused thumb along the bra strap and over the swell of her breasts, then reached for the clasp between her breasts. With a small click it unhooked and she spilled free.

He leaned down and kissed the top of her breasts and then suckled her nipples. Somehow she shrugged out of the bra, and it too fell. She closed her eyes, and for a moment, the darkness filled with the cries of the victims begging her for help. She tried to push back, but the screams grew louder, threatening to override her sexual excitement.

"Open your eyes," Mazur said. "It's just you and me here. No one else. No one."

She found him staring right at her with an intensity that allowed her to believe that it was just the two of them. There was nothing else. Only them. Only now.

Each removed their sidearms. She placed hers on the nightstand on the right side of the bed. Without a word, he laid his on the left nightstand, along with his cuffs and phone.

When he came back around the bed, she reached for the buttons of his shirt, and he let her slowly unfasten each as he caressed her breasts with one hand and skimmed his other along the waistband of her pants.

She fumbled with one button, and it took her a couple of tries to get it free. He grinned as he watched her clumsy attempts.

"Am I making you nervous?" he teased.

"Yes."

She pulled off his shirt. He then tugged off his undershirt, revealing a small gold crucifix that dangled from a chain. She traced the crucifix with her finger, wondering if he were religious or just too superstitious to ignore it.

He had a lovely chest. Firm. Covered in a mat of dark hair that tapered to his narrow waist.

He reached for his belt buckle, and she reached for hers. He slid off his pants with no hesitation, but she paused.

"Let me see you," he said as he now stood naked before her.

She drew in a breath and slowly unhooked the waistband of her pants. He brushed her hands aside and slowly slid her pants over her hips.

"Let me. I can't wait to see the FBI panties. Do they have a logo?"

Heart hammering in her chest, she sucked in a breath. "Of course."

His brow rose as her pants fell to her ankles. He stared at the white cotton panties and brushed his finger over the front panel. He then traced his finger along the front. "Where's the logo?"

She moistened her lips. "I might have exaggerated."

He pushed the slip of cotton to her ankles, and she stepped out and put her hands on his waist.

The teasing had allowed her to momentarily forget the jagged scar that ran along her thigh. It was raised and pink.

He studied it, not seeming to be repulsed, but curious.

"He shot me twice," she whispered, unwilling to say the other's name for fear it would shatter all this.

He kissed the scar. "It's part of you, and I like what I see."

He guided her toward the bed and jerked back the comforter before pressing her into the crisp white sheets. She scooted to the center, and within seconds he was beside her running his palm over her flat belly and to the nest of curls at her moist center.

"Wet," he said. "That for me?"

She gulped in air and nodded, unable to articulate a word.

"Good."

He rubbed gentle circles, and she hissed in a breath as she fell back against the pillows. The sensations shot down to her core and grew quickly into a white-hot need that shoved her toward climax. But just as she was about to come, he drew his hand away.

"Not yet," he said. "Not yet."

He smoothed his hand up and down her leg and cupped her buttocks. He kissed her breasts, licking and teasing her nipples until they were hard peaks.

She tensed and slid her hand down along his belly until her fingers touched his erection. She wrapped her hand around him, enjoying the ripple of tension that swept over his muscles. If he wanted to torture her with excitement, she would do the same to him.

He paused and allowed her to move her hand up and down his shaft. He closed his eyes, tipping his head back, groaning as she teased the tip of his erection.

He pulled back, leaned down, and kissed her on her thigh. He began to lick her center. A whimper escaped her lips, and she knew she would not be able to hold off her orgasm much longer.

As if sensing this, he climbed on top of her, careful not to rest his full weight on her. His erection rested against her center, but he made no move to enter. Instead, he leaned forward and kissed each of her breasts and then slowly pressed more kisses along her belly. She nibbled her bottom lip, anticipating what would come next, but he pressed those lips to the scar on her thigh.

She was barely hanging on.

"You're beautiful," he said, and kissed her lips, then trailed his lips down her throat and over her breasts. He suckled each nipple until they were hard peaks. His hand trailed along her thigh as he straddled her. Their gazes locked as he entered her.

She wrapped her hands around his hips and pulled him toward her. He pushed inside of her, stretching her tight body and making her savor every sensation that was exploding in her body.

He moved inside her, slowly at first. Her breath quickened, and a whimper escaped over her lips. Her hand slid to her breast, and she squeezed the tender flesh. Desire and need swirled and collided around her until this time her body exploded with sensations.

Kate arched, and grabbing her breast tighter, let out a moan. He pushed hard once, twice, and then his body shuddered as he found his own release.

Mazur didn't move immediately. He smoothed his hand over her ass, next cupping her breasts as his breath slowed. Finally he dropped into the spot beside her on the bed, curling close. He draped his arm over her body.

Without thinking she laid her hand over his. She was content to stay as she was and allow this moment to linger as long as it could. Mazur also seemed to be in no rush to end this moment. The two drifted toward sleep.

***

Kate ran toward the open field, the tracking hounds and police officers right behind her. The cool air burned in her chest and her side ached from the running, but she kept moving, pushing through the tall grass toward the outbuilding.

Inside the shed was the wooden box. Inside the box was Sara Fletcher. Naked and trembling, her pale body was desperately thin and skin raw with sores. Her hair was matted and twisted.

Sara didn't open her eyes immediately, and her hands covered her face. When Kate touched her, she screamed and jerked away.

"It's okay, Sara. I'm with the FBI. You're safe."

"I'm not safe," she said. "I'm alive, but really I'm already dead. He killed me. And he's going to kill you, too."

Kate startled awake, her gut tight with regret, loss, and shame. Shadows slashed across the unfamiliar room, and for several beats she didn't know where she was.

She'd not been good enough to save Sara.

Mazur roused. "You okay?"

The sex with Mazur had been great, but it had been a temporary fix to the problems she faced. As soon as they left this house, the hunt for William and Drexler would take over her life again. "Yes, I'm fine."

He smoothed his hand over her back, and she flinched. He stopped rubbing but didn't remove his hand from her skin. "Is this your idea of not getting weird?"

The sound of his voice and his touch settled her and chased away the doubts and regrets. "What do you mean?"

"You said you'd not get weird after sex. Withdrawing into yourself might be a little weird."

She sat up in bed and leaned against the headboard. "Sorry. It's the safest place I know."

"Is it? Judging by what woke you up, I'd say differently."

"I can control it."

"Really? Even nightmares?"

She glanced toward him. The cross on the gold chain around his neck dangled. "You sound like a psychologist."

"Aren't all cops part shrink?"

"Yes."

"What was the nightmare about?"

Absently her fingertips went to the worn toy bracelet around her wrist. She wouldn't be a coward now. Not in light of what Sara had suffered. "I was dreaming about the day we found Sara. As long as I live I'll never forget her. She didn't look human. But I wanted to believe that we had made it in time and that she would be all right."

"Sometimes victims can't be put back together again. No matter how hard we try."

"I'm supposed to be so smart. I wasn't good enough to find Sara Fletcher faster."

"You did what no one else could do. You found her."

"But it wasn't enough." She wanted to fly back to the funeral and pay her respects, but right now she felt too ashamed.

He rubbed his hand over her leg. It wasn't sexual but an absent, familiar thing lovers did. And oddly, more personal than sex. She stiffened, uncomfortable with a touch that felt so intimate.

"What's wrong?" he asked.

"It feels too personal."

"And personal never ends well, does it?" There was a bitter bite to the last word.

"No, it doesn't." She looked down at his hand brushing her scar. "People like us don't get happy endings."

"Why not?"

"We see too much. It ruins us for the normal people in the world who don't believe in monsters."

"Maybe." He ran his hand up her thigh. "Maybe we should stick to our own kind."

She glanced toward the digital clock behind him. They'd slept for an hour. Soon they'd have to be back to work, but for now, they still had a pocket of time that was all their own.

She slowly climbed on top of him. This time she straddled him, and just a few strokes of her fingertips against the tip of his penis and he was hard and ready.

The last time he'd teased her. Now it was her turn to taunt him just a little. She lowered her lips to the tip of his erection and then took all of him into her mouth and throat. He hissed in a breath and ran his fingers through her hair.

"Jesus, for someone who comes across as repressed, you sure aren't."

She licked her tongue around his shaft, kissing and teasing. "We all have a hidden side."

She saw his belly twitch and the muscles in his neck strain. She released him and positioned herself on top. Slowly, very slowly, she lowered onto him, filling herself and capturing him.

She moved up and down, cupping her breast.

"One hell of a hidden side," he groaned.

***

Rage filled William as he sat by the monitor and watched Kate whore herself out to that cop. "Why are you cheating on me?" he shouted.

He'd not liked Mazur from the moment the cop had set foot on his property. He'd watched from a closed-circuit television as his housekeeper had sent them away. Even then, he'd considered the cop a trespasser.

Now the cop was more than an annoyance. He was a threat. A thief. An intruder who endangered seventeen years of planning.

"Steal from me, and I'll take twofold from you, Detective Mazur."

He reached for one of the cells he'd bought with cash from a box store. He dialed the one number he cared about now.

Drexler's voice was groggy when he answered the phone. "What the fuck do you want?"

"How much have you had to drink?"

"I haven't been drinking."

"Don't lie to me. I cannot save you if you lie."

"A few. But I didn't get drunk. Half the case you brought is still unopened."

He still sounded as if he were drunk. "Make yourself coffee and take a hot shower. We have work to do."

"What kind of work? You said to lay low. To stay out of sight."

"I thought you wanted to build another box?"

He hesitated. "I do. But you said I had to wait."

"Well, time's up."

He cleared his throat, and bed springs squeaked. "Why the hell should I trust you?"

"I'm feeding you. And if I'd wanted, I could have called the cops, but I haven't. I'm the closest person you have to a best friend right now. If you want me to bail and drop a dime on you, say the word. Otherwise, stop acting like a little bitch."

"Okay. Okay. I get it."

"Goddamn right, you got it. Right now you need to shower, shave, and change into the clothes I left for you in the room."

"And then we get to go hunting?"

"Oh yes." William turned to a stack of photographs he'd taken of Isabella. He traced the line of her jaw in a picture he'd snapped while she was shopping at a local boutique. She was supposed to be next on his list. It was important to stick to the plan, but strategies sometimes required modifications.

He shifted to a computer screen and pulled up a picture he'd taken today. These pictures were of the lovely Alyssa. She was younger than he preferred, but he would make an exception.

He traced his thumb over the outline of her smiling lips. "You're going to like this one, Mr. Drexler. She's just your type."

CHAPTER
TWENTY-THREE

My must-do list: Gloria. Rebecca. Isabella.

San Antonio, Texas
Friday, December 1, 5:00 a.m.

Mazur woke to the still darkness. Rubbing his eyes, he glanced at the clock and realized he'd slept a few hours. Though he couldn't really afford the shut-eye, it would ensure his brain clicked on all cylinders for a couple more days. His hand slid to the other side of the bed. It was empty. Cold. Kate was gone.

He checked his phone. Three bars. Enough. And no calls from Alyssa. He never went to sleep without the phone by his bed in case she needed him.

Out of the bed, he switched on a light and went into the bathroom. Afterward he gathered his clothes and dressed. He clipped his gun, cuffs, and badge on his belt. A look back at the rumpled sheets coaxed a smile.

Tie dangling around his neck and his coat slung over his arm, he moved down the hallway and paused at a series of pictures that hung on the wall. He switched on the overhead light and studied the images, not the least bit concerned about sticking his nose into the life of a woman who didn't want anyone poking around.

There were several family pictures. The first was Mom and Dad and toddler Mitchell. The next frame captured the addition of the second child. A chubby-faced little girl with curly blond hair and a gap-toothed smile.

There were more pictures of Mitchell, but his interest zeroed in on Kate's life story. Moments captured during soccer, birthday parties, chess, and graduations showed the progression from a cute toddler to a gawky teenager and then to the serious FBI academy graduate.

Absently he rubbed his fingers together as he remembered the rough skin of the scar on her leg. It was a wonder the bullet hadn't hit the femoral artery or the second shot hadn't slammed into her brain. Jesus.

The scent of coffee drifted down the hallway, luring him from the pictures. In the kitchen, he found Kate fully dressed and sitting at the kitchen table. Beside her was an empty cup.

Scattered before her was a collection of files and crime-scene photos. She didn't look up. "I made a fresh pot of coffee. Mugs in the cabinet above. Milk in the refrigerator."

He made himself a cup and poured in a splash of milk. "If your mother left you fresh milk, my guess is there's food."

"Bagels in the bread box."

He kissed her on top of the head. "And good morning to you."

She looked up. "Good morning."

As he moved to find the bagels, he asked, "Do you always wake up this productive?"

"Sometimes." She ran her fingers through her tousled hair she'd yet to tie back. "When a case is bothering me."

He pulled out two bagels. "You want yours toasted?"

"Yes."

"So what has your mind buzzing today?"

"I would bet money Drexler's headed to San Antonio to find me. I'm the one who found Sara and the other bodies. I'm the one who ruined his good time."

"Are you that easy to find?"

"Unfortunately, yes. Or at least my mother's home is easy to find."

Mazur's gaze roamed the kitchen. "And she's in Dallas with Aunt Lydia, correct?"

"Yes." She shook her head. "With William and Drexler out there, she's better off in Dallas."

"This isn't your fault."

"Of course it is. Given my work, I should have never come here."

He reached for her mug, refilled it, and set it in front of her. "It's a matter of time before Nevada catches him."

"He's completely shaved. His own mother wouldn't recognize him."

He moved to the toaster, set the bagels on a plate, and placed them in front of her. From the refrigerator he dug out butter, cream cheese, and strawberry jelly. "We eat first."

"I can't eat now."

"Yes, you can. We have thirty minutes. Then we'll head to the station. Eat."

She looked toward him and then back at her computer.

"Is this the part where you get weird?" he challenged.

"I'm not being weird. I'm being normal. This is how I am all the time."

"Which is a little weird, Kate. In a good way."

The acceptance in her expression was almost sad. "It's amusing to you now, but in the long run it'll drive you crazy. I'm not an easy person."

"Neither am I. And don't you think we have to be a little odd to do what we do?" he asked. "But we found a few perks of the job last night."

She grinned slightly. "I really enjoyed those perks last night."

He raised his cup. "To more perks."

The idea made her frown. "We can't be lovers and work on this case."

"Why not?"

"Because sex taints relationships."

"Taints?"

She pressed her fingertips to her temple. "That's not the right word."

He shook his head. "Words are your specialty."

"You're right. *Taint* is the word I meant to use. I've been to a few shrinks. The consensus is that I was intimate with William Bauldry and it destroyed my family, so since then I associate sex and closeness with trouble."

"Do you like being alone?"

She dusted the bagel crumbs from her fingertips. "I understand the practicality of it."

He shook his head. "Classic deflection, Dr. Hayden. Do you like it?"

"No. Not really. But it works for me."

"How much longer do you think it'll work?"

"I don't know. For as long as I can take it, I suppose."

"Why don't you allow yourself a damn personal life?"

A brow arched. "With you?"

"Sure, why not? There's a good chance I'll be in Virginia by the end of the year. I'd like to see you again."

She stood, moved to the sink, and poured out the coffee. "Like I said, once you get to know me, you're going to be disappointed. I'm a workaholic, and I don't leave my work at the office."

He moved to within inches of her and leaned in a fraction to set his coffee cup on the counter next to hers.

She stiffened but did not pull away. "There are two monsters out there, and they both want to kill me. I don't want you to get killed, too."

Mary Burton

"I'm a big boy. Besides, I hope ol' Willie or this Drexler make a play. Nothing would give me more pleasure than to bring them both down."

She laid her hands over his. "You're cocky."

"I'm confident. Big difference." He kissed her.

She leaned into the kiss, and he could feel the fresh coat of ice melting. She pulled back. "We have to get to the station."

"I know." He glanced at the clock. "We still have half an hour."

"A whole thirty minutes?"

"Yep."

She smiled.

***

Drexler was glad to get out of the city. He couldn't breathe around all the buildings and people. But under an open sky he felt free. He followed the directions William had given him. As he moved down the barren stretch of road, he saw in the distance the gates that seemed to open to nowhere. Nothing in Texas was nearby. No telling how many miles he'd drive once he turned onto the property.

Dust billowed around his tires as he came to a stop. The name of the ranch was The King's Castle. A smile crooked the edge of his lips. Even he got this one.

"King's Castle," he said as he drove down the lane. More red dirt kicked up around him as he made the two-and-a-half-mile trek to the two-story brick home with a wide front porch. A couple of hundred feet beyond that was an outbuilding. He headed straight to the back barn.

He parked and got out, stretched his back a few times. He'd been on the run for days now, and it was beginning to take its toll.

He moved to the barn door and lifted the latch. He glanced back at the house to make sure no one was watching before opening the door. Inside to the right of the door was a light switch. He flipped it on.

286

The lights cast a warm glow and brightened his mood. Centered in the room was a stack of lumber, sawhorses, nails, hammers, and saws. All the supplies he needed to build one of his boxes.

Drexler skimmed his hand over the fine lumber. These weren't discarded scraps, but oak that had been milled to a smooth finish.

He shrugged off his jacket and tossed it over a sawhorse. A scan of the room revealed a cot made neatly with white sheets and a green blanket, a sink, open cabinets stocked with canned goods, a hot plate, and a refrigerator. He looked behind a wooden partition to find a toilet. Bauldry was good with the details.

He opened the refrigerator and found it packed with beer. Pinned to the beer was an envelope. He studied the note a beat but reached for a beer first.

He popped the top, drained it, crushed the can, and tossed it toward the trash. He missed. Grabbing another beer, he opened the envelope. There were two images inside. The first featured a young girl. She had blond hair. Whoever took the picture captured her hair blowing back in the wind. She had a blush to her cheeks and perfect white teeth. She was petite, likely not more than five feet tall.

The picture behind the first featured a familiar face. The woman was Kate Hayden. She wore her dark badass FBI jacket, jeans, and boots. She was staring off into the distance.

He took a long swig as he continued to study the images. The lumber pile beckoned him. It was just enough for two boxes.

"Nice."

CHAPTER
TWENTY-FOUR

New Year's resolution: burn it all down.

San Antonio, Texas
Friday, December 1, 11:00 a.m.

Kate was in the conference room reviewing her notes on William when a uniformed officer knocked and entered. "Sorry to bother you, but there's a Mark Westin here to see you. He said he's the attorney for Charles Richardson."

She let her pen drop and for a moment didn't speak. "Where is he?"

"He's in the front reception."

"Right. I'll be right there."

When the door closed, she rolled her head from side to side trying to work some of the stiffness out. She'd dealt with Mr. Westin when Richardson had been arraigned, and the judge, based on her testimony, denied bail. Richardson had been furious, but Westin had taken it in stride, knowing there'd be other opportunities to help his client.

She slid on her jacket, pulled a brush from her backpack along with lipstick. Chin up, she closed her laptop, shoved it into her backpack, and dropped it in Mazur's cubicle. He was on the phone. She mouthed, "Can I leave this here?"

He nodded and cupped his hand over the phone. "What's going on?"

"Richardson's defense attorney is in the lobby."

Ignoring his frown, she wove through the cubicles toward the elevator and rode it down to the first floor. The scent of cologne greeted her as she stepped into the lobby. The room was buzzing with activity. In one corner, a mother and child were waiting. In another, a couple of cops were in a heated discussion. At the front desk a man in jeans, an old plaid shirt, and worn boots was shouting at the police sergeant behind the desk.

Westin stood by the front door. He wore his trademark handmade suit, white monogrammed shirt, red tie, and polished Italian wing tips.

She crossed the lobby. "Mr. Westin."

He studied her. "Agent Hayden. We need to talk."

"What do you want to talk about?"

"You have a Samaritan killing right here in San Antonio. Considering you were instrumental in making sure my client didn't get bail, I'd say this murder is proof positive that Dr. Richardson is not your man."

"Wrong. I have Richardson dead to rights, and you know it." She glanced around the noisy, chaotic room and then back at him. "But you know this. You know no judge will give Richardson bail. Why are you here?"

Westin stared at her, silent, and she knew he was weighing his words carefully.

She opened her phone and showed him a picture of William Bauldry. "This guy. William Bauldry. When did you see him last?"

"I've never met him before," Westin said.

"I don't believe you," she said, bluffing. "I'd bet money Richardson has mentioned him."

Westin's jaw clenched and released. "Why would my client tell me about this guy?"

"Because this guy and Richardson crossed paths at Bastrop prison multiple times. They had the opportunity to discuss Richardson's shootings and, I'd bet, to plan the murder in San Antonio."

"Richardson is in jail. He had nothing to do with this case."

"The gun Richardson used is still missing. Where is it?"

Again Westin was silent, weighing his words. This man knew how to deal.

"What do you want?" she asked.

"Take the death penalty off the table."

She nodded as understanding dawned. He'd come here to offer her information, but he didn't give anything for free. "You'll be the high-priced lawyer that keeps a monster like Richardson alive. Granted, Richardson will spend the rest of his life in prison, but he will be alive."

"It's not a perfect victory but the best I can get."

"The final sentencing is a promise I can't make, but I would speak to the prosecutors about it."

"That's not much of a guarantee."

She shook her head. "Best I got. Have you been in contact with Bauldry?"

"Not *him*."

The added emphasis on the pronoun caught her attention. He'd not seen Bauldry, but he was opening the door for her to ask about others. She scrolled through the pictures on her phone to Gloria Sanchez. "What about this woman? Have you seen her?"

Westin looked at the picture. He shifted his stance, and his left hand flexed into a loose fist. "She was the woman shot."

His tone changed just enough for her to know she was on the right path. "She was also William Bauldry's half sister. And she visited him in prison quite often. Is she your client?"

"No."

"So no privileges will be violated."

He drew in another breath. "I was in possession of a key, most likely to some kind of locker. My client said if anyone came by asking for it to hand it over. She came by my office six months ago and asked for it."

She thought about the missing gun. Richardson had stashed it somewhere. "What was in the locker?"

"I don't know. I only gave her the key."

She couldn't prove it, but she could reasonably argue that Richardson had stashed the gun in the locker, told Bauldry about it, and Bauldry had sent Gloria to retrieve it.

"That's it?" she asked.

"That's all I have."

"All right."

"You'll speak to the prosecutors?"

"I will." She left him in the lobby, and as she climbed the stairs she glanced at her phone. One missed call from Nevada. She dialed his number.

Nevada answered on the first ring. "I think you're right."

"What do you mean?"

"I tracked Drexler to a motel room in San Antonio. We just got in the room, and I'm staring at what he left behind. You need to come see this," Nevada said.

"Give me the address," she said. "I'll leave right now."

Kate relayed what was happening to Mazur, and minutes later they were in his car headed across town. When they rolled up to the motel, there were three black FBI SUVs nosed in at the far end of the parking lot.

She stepped out of the car, headed toward the room that was now roped off with crime-scene tape. She hurried toward the yellow barrier and, flashing her badge at an agent, ducked under it.

Nevada's tall frame and broad shoulders dominated the small seedy room furnished with a low double bed, a faded brown comforter, and a box television. Pizza boxes were scattered around the floor along with a dozen crushed beer cans.

"Nevada, what do you have?" she asked.

"He was here. No one seems to know when he left, but the clerk said he's paid up for the motel room through tomorrow, so he might be back."

Kate shook her head. "He's not coming back."

"The manager said he had a visitor yesterday. While he was inspecting the ice machine down the hall, he saw a Caucasian male, early thirties, dark hair, at Drexler's door with a couple of pizzas and a twelve-pack of beer," Nevada said.

"The description could be William," she said. "But they don't know each other. The description could be any one of a thousand other guys in this city."

"If William has been watching you," Mazur said, "he would notice if someone else was stalking you."

Nevada nodded. "He spotted Drexler."

"They're both interested in the same woman," Mazur said.

"There's one way to find out," Kate said. "Where's the manager?"

"Over there." Nevada nodded toward a slim man with graying hair and a full mustache.

She hurried toward the man and introduced herself. Not caring about small talk, she showed him a picture of Bauldry. "Have you seen this man?"

The manager sniffed as he studied the picture. "That's the guy I saw."

"You saw this man talking to Mr. Drexler?"

The manager shifted his stance. "I don't know no names. I just know that's the guy who brought the pizza and beer to the man the Feds are looking for."

"Thanks." She returned to Mazur and Nevada. "He just identified Bauldry."

Mazur's jaw tightened. "How the hell would they hook up?"

"I don't know," she said. "But we need to assume they're working together now."

"I can call a forensic team and have them here ASAP," Mazur said.

The forensic team could pull Drexler's and possibly Bauldry's DNA from the room. No one came into a room or left it without leaving trace evidence. But forensics took time. And in a hotel room there would be dozens of DNA samples from other guests as well as the maid service. Days to collect it and days to analyze it.

The hotel room telephone rang. Kate crossed the room and answered it. "Yes."

"This is William." His voice was soft, almost a little breathless.

"William," she said, loudly enough to get Mazur's attention.

Mazur moved toward her and had her tip the phone out a fraction so he could hear.

"Where are you?"

"I'm back in San Antonio, Katie. What's the problem?"

"How did you get this number?"

"Is that the most burning question you have for me?"

Mazur moved out of the room, his cell pressed to his ear as he requested a trace on the call.

She hesitated. "Tell me where you are."

"What's the fun in that?"

"William," she said, dropping her voice. "This has to stop. We have to meet. I want to see you. It's important for me to be with you. There was a time when we loved each other."

Silence crackled over the line.

"William, are you there?"

"You drive me crazy, Katie. You always have. If I could just put my problems in a box and bury them, I might feel like myself again."

The words *box* and *bury* rattled in her head. She met Mazur's gaze as he came into the room. "I need to be with you, William."

"Maybe tomorrow, Katie," he said. "Come by my house in the morning."

"What's wrong with now?" she pressed.

"I'm tired. And I have work to do. In the morning."

The line went dead.

"What the hell does he have to do?" she whispered. Her gut tightened, and she could feel her core temperature drop. "He said he wished he could put his problems in a box and bury them."

"What's that supposed to mean?"

"William and Drexler are going hunting."

***

William watched as the young girl left the private Catholic high school. Like all the other girls she was dressed in her plaid skirt, white shirt, knee socks, and ugly brown shoes. She crossed the lot to a waiting dark Lexus and tossed her backpack in the backseat. She was laughing when she slid into the front seat.

He tried to imagine Katie at that age. He remembered the way her plaid skirt had brushed just below her knees. Those horrendous brown shoes all the girls had to wear looked terrible on most, but she somehow made them look cute and seductive. He wondered if she still had her uniform. Just the idea of seeing her in it made him hard.

The Lexus drove off, and he waited a beat before he followed, making sure to stay a couple of car lengths behind. The car wove through town and within fifteen minutes pulled into a gated community. He couldn't follow or he would be noticed, but she'd be back out soon. There was a football game tonight.

William pulled away and drove toward the school. He took time for dinner and did a bit of shopping. He bought a petite white dress and size five white shoes. Then he stopped at a florist and bought flowers. It was going to be a good night.

By the time he'd returned to the high school, the sun was low on the horizon. The new moon would soon leave little light to navigate by. Not the best night for hunting, but he knew it was now or never. Drexler was working on the two boxes he'd commissioned, and he needed bodies to fill them.

The pregame show was an explosion of noise and confusion. So many young ladies running around giggling and huddling close as they whispered secrets. The boys postured as if they were men, but none would be able to stand up to him if he had to take one of them out. However, a group of them could be a problem because of the attention it would draw.

So he needed to be careful. And like the spider in the web, wait for his juicy little bug.

He moved toward the concession stand, doing his best to look like someone's big brother or uncle, not a guy who was patiently waiting to kill.

At the concession stand he ordered a hot dog and a soda, and then as he bit into the dog and its very dry bun, Alyssa bounded up to the stand and ordered a diet soda.

Standing this close to her he could smell her soft, sweet perfume and see the natural highlights in her hair. The top of her head barely reached his shoulders, and if he had not promised her to Drexler, he might have kept her for himself.

"Carrie, I've got to run to your mom's car," Alyssa said to a friend he'd barely noticed. The other girl was tall and slim, but her limbs were gawky and unattractive. To fit nicely in one of Drexler's boxes, she'd have to be altered. "Didn't she leave the keys with you?"

Carrie fished keys out of her oversize purse and dumped them in Alyssa's hand. "She did. I'll wait for you here, and then we can order something to eat. Mom said she'd give us each a burger."

"Sounds good." Alyssa sipped on her soda and turned to the lot.

He didn't follow right away. To separate from the crowd again would draw attention to himself. So he watched as she wove through the crowd toward the south fence.

He tossed his hot dog and soda in the trash and moved through the crush of people. The home team scored a touchdown, and immediately the people around him jumped and shouted. One boy knocked William with his elbow. The accidental blow set his teeth on edge, and in another time and place he'd have reacted differently.

William kept moving, cutting through the wall of loud and shouting people until he reached the gate, and nodding to a volunteer parent in a red apron, he stepped out into the packed parking lot.

For a moment, he didn't see Alyssa and thought he might have lost her. Damn. He scanned the lot illuminated by large overhead lights. He heard a car's beep and saw taillights flash to his left where Alyssa was opening the trunk.

He hustled across the lot, jogging, knowing if he moved quickly enough he had a chance to take her without an incident.

Dodging right, he moved down a row of cars. His heart beat faster as the cheers of the crowd roared around him. A pivot and he was only a few car lengths away from her.

A glance behind proved no one was watching. He barreled right up behind the girl and jabbed a syringe in her side with one hand as he wrapped the other around her mouth.

The plunger sent the sedative into her system. She struggled, her screams muffled as she went limp. Her keys dropped to the ground.

He placed her body into the trunk and closed it gently. Casually he scooped up the keys and slid behind the wheel of the car. He started the engine, and though his nerves danced and jumped with adrenaline, he drove carefully through the lot, even waving at a couple passing by. At the stop sign, he turned on his right blinker, pulled out, and headed toward the main road.

Excitement raced through him. Now that he had Alyssa it would be easy to get Kate. Checkmate was close at hand.

***

As the FBI agents collected evidence from Drexler's room, Mazur and Kate spent the afternoon tracking William, who had not returned to any known hangouts. As they left William's church, Mazur's phone rang. Ducking his head, he moved away, saying, "Hey, kiddo."

His expression immediately turned dark. "Alyssa, what's going on? Where are you?"

Nevada flexed his large hands.

Kate moved toward him so that she could hear.

"Dad, I'm in a car. A tr-trunk." The girl sounded groggy, as if she could barely form the words.

Deep lines furrowed around his brow and mouth. "It's going to be all right. Who took you, honey?"

"I don't know," the girl said.

The line went dead.

Mazur immediately redialed his daughter's phone, but there was no answer. He dialed again. Nothing. "Shit."

"Track her phone," Kate said.

He hit the find-phone feature, but no signal appeared. "Shit. Her phone had to be disabled for this not to work." He punched the button again and again. "Shit!"

Gently she took his phone from his grip. "Where was she supposed to be tonight?"

He clenched his hands into fists. "At the football game. She's spending the night with a friend."

"What friend?"

"Carrie. Carrie Scott."

"Do you have her number?"

"Yes." Immediately he dialed, but there was no answer.

"Let's start moving now and head to the game," she said. "That's where the trail started, and that's where we begin."

"Right."

Mazur's next call was to Palmer, and he advised her of what was happening with clinical precision. He ended the call, and as he redialed Carrie's number, said, "Palmer is sending police to the game and to Bauldry's brother's house. Every cop car in this city is going to be looking for her."

He pressed the phone to his ear and cursed. "Carrie, this is Detective Mazur, Alyssa's father. Call me immediately. This is an emergency."

She wished she could tell him that it would be okay. But the grim statistics already were stacked against finding Alyssa alive.

They hustled down the stairs and out the back door toward his car. She had to run double time to match his stride. In his car he started the engine, and tires squealed as he backed out of the spot.

"Jesus, she was at a football game. She's a smart kid. She doesn't walk off with strangers," he said.

Kate didn't look at him as a colleague any longer. He was a parent and a terrified man who knew he was on the verge of losing everything.

His gaze cut to her. "What kind of monster are we looking for? Could this be Bauldry? Or that psycho, Drexler?"

"I hope not."

He smacked his hand against the steering wheel. "Tell me about Drexler."

"The less you know right now about Drexler, the more focused you'll be."

"To hell with that!" Mazur shouted. "I want to *know*!"

Pure anguish deepened the lines around his eyes and mouth. She'd brought the monsters into his and Alyssa's life. "If it is Drexler we have some time."

"Meaning he doesn't kill them right away."

"Yes."

He dialed Carrie's number. This time she answered.

"Carrie, Alyssa is missing." He listened. "When's the last time you saw her?" He glanced at his watch. "That was twenty minutes ago. Okay. Stay by the concession stand. I'll be there in ten minutes, and other police will be there soon."

He listened. "Your mother's car is also missing?"

"Do you have the license plate?"

He glanced at Kate. "Alyssa went to the Scotts' car to get her sweater, and she didn't come back. Mrs. Scott's car is also missing. It's new and has GPS. We might get lucky."

He called the company, identified himself, and the operator promised to get back within five minutes. Then he called Palmer. "Tell me you have a location from Alyssa's phone." He listened and then, "Damn it. Are you sure? Right." He dropped the phone in his lap and he quickly rounded a sharp turn. "There's no signal from the phone."

Drexler was smart and knew enough to destroy the girl's phone. But just the fact that Alyssa had called suggested William was behind this. He wanted Mazur afraid and off his game. She thought back to what William had said. He wanted to put his "problems in a box." William was giving Alyssa to Drexler. She looked at Mazur and saw the thinly cloaked anger and fear. If she told him this now, it would be impossible for him to concentrate. He wasn't thinking like just a cop now. He was going to react like a panicked father.

They arrived at the football game to a dozen cop cars with lights flashing in the parking lot. Palmer was already on the scene, and she'd spoken to the principal, who had located Carrie and her mother, Kelly Scott. The girl and her mother were pale.

When they approached, Palmer introduced them.

Mazur extended his hand to Mrs. Scott. "I'm Alyssa's father."

Mrs. Scott's frown deepened. "I just saw Alyssa with Carrie a half hour ago. Detective Palmer tells me she might have been kidnapped."

Carrie's red-rimmed eyes filled with fresh tears. "Mr. Mazur, I'm so sorry." Understanding her through the sobs was a challenge. "I thought she was just going to the car to get her sweater."

"Carrie, it's okay." Mazur laid his hand on the girl's shoulder, and she quickly hugged him. He looked up at Mrs. Scott. "This is connected to a case that I'm working."

The woman leaned toward him. "I told the girls to stay with the crowds."

Mazur pulled the girl away from him. "Carrie, I need you to focus. Did you see anyone lingering around?"

"No. No one that looked weird," she said.

Mrs. Scott drew in a breath. "There was a man by the concession stand."

"Who?" Mazur asked.

"Midthirties, dark hair. I noticed him because he wasn't old enough to be a parent and too old to be a student. He just didn't fit here. And then he tossed out a perfectly good hot dog." A sigh shuddered through her. "God, do you think it was him?"

Kate moved in front of Mazur, introduced herself, and showed Mrs. Scott a picture of Bauldry. "Is this him?"

The woman leaned in and studied the picture. "I can't say for certain, but it does look like him."

"Did he say anything?" Kate asked.

"No. He was extremely polite and put a twenty-dollar bill in the band-fund jar."

Kate turned to the girl. "Carrie, you need to stop crying. I need to talk to you."

The girl stopped sobbing and turned toward Kate. She wiped her eyes with the sleeve pulled down over her hand.

"You're really FBI?"

"I am." She looked at the girl's mother and nodded.

"You come when there's been a kidnapping or murder."

"That's right. You need to listen closely, because we don't have a lot of time. Can you focus for me?"

The girl sniffed. "I-I'm so rattled."

"I don't care how rattled or upset you are," Mrs. Scott said. "You need to focus and help the police."

Carrie nibbled her lip. "Yes. Yes. I can do that."

"Good. Did you see anyone lurking around you tonight?"

"No. We were just enjoying the game."

Mazur's phone rang. "Detective Mazur." He cradled the phone between his shoulder and ear, pulled out a notebook, and scribbled down notes. "Great. Thank you." He looked at Kate. "They've located the Scotts' car."

"Go," Kate said. She held out little hope that whoever had taken Alyssa left some kind of evidence. "I want to talk to some of the people here. See if they know anything."

"Right."

Mazur and Palmer left, leaving Kate alone to talk to Carrie and her mother. She watched as his car drove off, so sorry she'd ever met him or Alyssa.

"How long have you known Alyssa?" Kate asked.

Carrie sniffed. "A couple of months. She's new, and it's hard to make new friends in this school. Most of us have been going here since kindergarten."

"But you're her friend."

"She's cool. And she's nice. We have fun together."

"Is Alyssa dating anyone? Would she have left with anyone?" Sometimes a missing child had not been taken but had left with a friend. Kate had experience with girls like Carrie. They wanted to protect their friend and at this stage feared the parents more than the police. In their naïveté, they didn't believe monsters were real.

Carrie leaned in a little. "She does like a guy. His name is James. They've kissed a few times."

"Where is James?"

"He's one of the football players." She pointed to a tall, dark-haired kid whose football uniform was covered in dirt and grass. "He's really nice. And he couldn't have left with her during the game."

"Okay, honey."

Needing to cover all her bases, Kate cut through the crowd and made her way up to the young football player who was headed to the locker room for halftime. He stood at least a foot taller than her. She held up her badge. "James, I need to talk to you."

The boy's face paled, and as the two cut away from the crowd, he asked, "What's going on?"

She studied his face, suspecting almost immediately he had no relevant information. "You and Alyssa are dating?"

"Not exactly dating. But I want to. I like her."

"When's the last time you saw her?"

"In school yesterday. She decorated my locker."

"You've not seen her since?"

"No." He ran an unsteady hand over his short hair. "What's going on?"

She didn't have the heart to tell him Alyssa had been taken or that her chances grew slimmer by the moment. The truth was, girls who had been abducted were often dead within the first few hours. "I can't say right now." William was already several moves ahead of her, and time was running out. Drexler wouldn't kill right away, but that was little solace for what she knew was in store for Alyssa.

She dialed Nevada.

He picked up on the third ring. "No sign of Drexler yet."

"I think we have a bigger problem now."

CHAPTER
TWENTY-FIVE

All I want for Christmas is . . . revenge.

San Antonio, Texas
Friday, December 1, 8:00 p.m.

Mazur and Palmer arrived at the dimly lit box store parking lot ten minutes after William's call. The car he'd stolen was parked in the darkest part of the lot nosed in at an angle toward a stand of small trees.

Both detectives were silent as they drew their weapons and approached the white Lexus. No one was in the front seat, and the trunk was ajar.

Mazur moved directly to the trunk while Palmer walked around the front to make sure it was secure. Normally Mazur would have waited, but he needed to see the inside of the trunk. He'd once bargained with God to bring back his son as he held the boy's still body in his arms. But those pleas had gone unheeded. Still, he hoped, and struck a new bargain. *I'll do anything.*

He lifted the trunk lid. It was empty. No Alyssa. He stepped back; the swell of fear and relief nearly made his knees buckle. "She's not here!"

Palmer stepped forward and inventoried the trunk's contents.

There was a spare tire, a trunk organizer with flares, and an open first-aid kit. But shoved in the very back was Alyssa's blue sweater.

"What's it doing crammed up there?" Palmer asked.

"She did it. She wants us to know she was here."

With trembling hands he holstered his weapon and pulled on latex gloves. He picked up the sweater. Under the sweater lay her bracelet. She'd left it for him so he'd know she'd been here, just as Kate advised. His daughter believed he could save her.

When Caleb died, he thought he had shouldered all the anger and sorrow a man could. Now he realized there was so much more of both that could be waiting for him.

Palmer searched the front and back seats. "There's nothing here."

"Get Calhoun here now. I want this entire car dusted for prints. There's a chance the kidnapper didn't use gloves."

"I'm on it."

***

Kate had a uniformed officer drive her to her rental car, which had been checked and judged clear of tracking devices, and then she drove straight to Bauldry's house, where three squad cars were now in position, lights flashing. The front door was open, and the housekeeper was talking to a police officer.

Pulling her badge, she hurried up to the front door. "Where's William?"

The housekeeper looked panicked and afraid. But a quick glance over her shoulder said she was more afraid of her employer. "He's not here."

"We're not here to arrest him," Kate lied. "We need to talk to him."

"Please," she whispered. "I can't help you, Miss."

Kate could play by the book until moments like this when doing it by the book stood between her and saving a life. She pushed past the housekeeper and screamed, "Bauldry!"

"Miss. Miss," the woman said, hurrying after her. "You can't come in the house. Mr. Bauldry doesn't see people."

"You said he wasn't here." Kate searched deeper into the house and scanned a dimly lit sitting room. It was clean, pristine, but there was no sign of William.

The housekeeper shook her head. "You have to leave."

Kate bounded up the staircase, shouting, "Where are you, Bauldry?"

She opened the first door in the hallway as she heard the housekeeper on her phone calling someone. As the woman spoke in rapid-fire Spanish, Kate ran to the second room. Nothing.

Her phone rang. The number was blocked. She ran down the steps. "This is Kate Hayden."

"You always sound so frantic," William said.

She looked toward the housekeeper, who slid her phone back in her pocket. "William."

"Katie." He drew out the word as if she were a naughty child. "How are you today?"

"I'll let you know when it's over. Where's Alyssa?"

"You have exactly twenty-six minutes to make it to the address I'm about to text you. Then I'm going to introduce sweet Alyssa to Drexler and see how they hit it off. He's quite the ladies' man, but he's distraught you took his other toy away. But, thankfully, Alyssa has graciously agreed to help Mr. Drexler forget about his lost toy."

She gripped her phone. "You want me, not her, William. She's not a part of this. I'm coming to you."

"Remember, no cops, Kate." His voice had a singsong, happy quality.

305

His type loved moments like this. They savored the attention, fear, and domination.

"I won't be nice to you if you hurt her."

Ignoring her threat, he said, "I'll know if you call anyone, Katie. I always do."

Her gaze met the housekeeper's, who stared at her with a mixture of fear and longing. "Understood."

"Ready or not, here comes the address."

The line went dead, and two seconds later her phone dinged with a text. She read the address and plugged it into the map on her phone. According to the directions, if she drove full speed she might make it. She ran past the stunned woman. Kate desperately wanted to call Mazur, but knew somehow that William did know what she was doing.

Kate crossed back to the housekeeper and barely whispered, "He's watching?"

Brown eyes widened with fear.

The woman's body language screamed what she suspected. William was watching. "Do you have pencil and paper? There is an address I have to remember."

The housekeeper handed her a pen and paper. Kate scribbled down the address she'd just been given, plus Mazur's phone number and the word *Emergency!* She ripped off a blank page from the notepad's bottom and handed it back to the woman.

The woman accepted the pad and glanced quickly at it. "Yes, Miss."

If William witnessed her mutiny, she was betting he'd not kill the girl. She was a bargaining chip. And logic dictated if Kate didn't reach out for help, there was a good chance she and the girl wouldn't get out alive.

Kate ran back to her car. Her tires squealed as she backed out of the driveway. She wove in and out of traffic, punching the accelerator. On the interstate she clocked over one hundred miles per hour until she saw her exit, which led into the countryside.

Her phone rang. BLOCKED appeared on her display.

"You're behind schedule," William said. "Ticktock."

"I hit traffic. I'm driving as fast as I can." The countryside sped past her.

"Drexler said the box is a little small this time. He measured wrong. You know what that means. Snap. Crackle. Pop."

The line went dead.

She pressed harder on the accelerator. She was driving so fast that when the GPS told her to turn she nearly missed the hard right. Brakes screeched, gravel kicked as she skidded and turned down the rural route to the gates at the entrance. They were swung wide open in silent invitation.

She barreled down the driveway, hoping she didn't blow a tire.

***

Restless energy and raw fear burned in Mazur as he paced by the abandoned car. His phone rang. It was Santos. He cursed. "Tell me you have good news."

"I looked over the list of properties associated with William Bauldry. I have two locations with large enough water sources for fishing."

As Mazur scribbled down the addresses, his phone rang with a second call. Without a word, he took the other call. "Detective Mazur."

"Police, police!" the frantic woman yelled.

"Who is this?"

"Police. This police?"

"Yes. Who is this?" In the distance he could hear traffic and a horn honking.

"Miss Kate said to call. Said to give you this address." She read off an unfamiliar address.

"Give me that again."

She repeated it as he scribbled onto a notepad. "Who is this?"

"I work for Mr. Bauldry."

He snapped his fingers to get Palmer's attention. She turned and moved toward him. "You're his housekeeper, Mrs. Lopez?"

"Yes. The FBI lady came by the house and couldn't find him. But he could see. And then he called."

Adrenaline cut through his body. "Where are you now?"

"In the city, at my brother's bar. This is his phone. I'm not going back to Mr. Bauldry's. Miss Kate is going to that place I told you about. She wrote *emergency*."

His heart tightened. "She said *emergency*?"

"Yes, sir."

Jesus. "Are you sure about these details?"

"Yes, I think so." Her voice trembled, and she paused to mutter a prayer. "Yes, I'm certain. That is what she gave me."

He didn't dare hope. "How long has Kate been gone?"

"About fifteen minutes. She's very brave, I think."

And she was just crazy enough to go after Bauldry alone.

"Where's your brother's bar?"

"Don't tell Mr. Bauldry."

"I won't."

She rattled off the address.

"Stay at your brother's bar, okay? I'm sending Detective Palmer. She'll take care of you."

"Yes, sir."

He hung up and looked at the addresses he'd scribbled down. One was a match. He had a target.

"Palmer, I need for you to go to this address and find a Mrs. Lopez. She works for Bauldry."

"What's going on?" Palmer asked.

"While Kate was at Bauldry's house, she received a call from him. He has Alyssa. I'm going to follow this lead, but call Santos and have him check out the other location."

"Consider it done."

"Good." Mazur got in his car, backing out so quickly he nearly hit another cruiser. Pressing his foot on the gas, he flipped on his lights.

***

William lifted the groggy girl out of the back of the 1971 Buick that he'd swapped for the Lexus. The old cars were some of the best. Granted the gas mileage was terrible and their safety records questionable, but there was no GPS. He yearned for the simpler days.

She moaned, and her smooth brow wrinkled as she tried to open her eyes. "My dad will come."

"Ah, you're awake." He held the girl close, enjoying the way she felt in his arms. "No, no, he won't. But Agent Kate is riding to the rescue."

"Kate?"

"My Katie is headed our way right now."

She tried to wriggle free, but she was still too groggy. She slumped back in his arms. If only she knew that tomorrow she would awake inside a box.

The door to the barn opened, and light silhouetted Drexler's tall frame. "Is that my girl?"

"It will be soon."

Drexler hurried over to him. Sawdust peppered his freshly shaved scalp and his plaid shirt. "Where's the other one? You said to build two boxes."

"She'll be here shortly."

Drexler studied the girl's body, running his hand along her thigh to her ankle. "The dimensions you gave me were too small."

"You've worked around that problem before."

Drexler smiled. "Yes, I have. Can I have her now?"

He held back. "Not just yet. It can't be a party until Katie arrives."

***

Kate killed her headlights, using starlight to maneuver slowly down the dirt road. Dust kicked up around the car; gravel crunched under her tires. In the distance were the lights of a ranch-style house.

Her tire hit a rut, jarring her and forcing her to grip and turn the wheel to keep the car on the road.

She looked in her rearview mirror at the endless stretch of darkness behind her. This house was a needle in a haystack, and without an address, impossible to find quickly. She could only hope that Mazur had received her address and her message.

And as much as she wanted to wait for him, the image of Sara Fletcher's face flashed in her head. Waiting gave the monsters more time with Alyssa.

Kate simply couldn't live knowing that child had suffered because of her. She was ready for this to be a one-way trip if it meant nailing these two beasts before they got to Alyssa.

CHAPTER
TWENTY-SIX

Revenge is a dish best served cold.

—*Gloria's proverb*

San Antonio, Texas
Friday, December 1, 10:00 p.m.

Kate shut off the engine, drew her weapon, and got out of the car. She stood in the cool night air as the gentle breeze reminded her of a calm before a storm. She stared at the lights glowing from the windows of the simple outbuilding constructed of weathered gray wood and a tin roof. A male figure passed in front of a large window, and then the door opened. William Bauldry stood in the doorway. He flashed her a wide grin when he saw her.

"Katie, you made it," he said, as if this were all friendly.

"William."

He waved her closer. "Come. Alyssa and Drexler are inside, and they're just getting acquainted."

"What have you done to her?"

"She's fine. Still in one piece for now." Again he motioned her forward. "Come on. I won't bite."

She drew in a breath and took her first step. When she approached him she stopped. "You go first."

"Sure. You can never say I wasn't a good host." He backed away and extended his hands.

Her gaze shifted to him, and she made sure he was at least ten feet away before she glanced around the room. She spotted Alyssa immediately. The girl was in a chair, her chin slumped forward.

Drexler looked more menacing with his long hair and beard shaved. With no distractions from the cold black eyes, his smile looked lifeless. He gently stroked the girl's hair. "We've been waiting for you. And for her to wake up. William said she'd be awake by now, but she's a real sleepyhead. She has to wake up. It won't be any fun if she sleeps through it all."

Sara's scream echoed in her mind. "William, I know why Drexler does this. What's your reason?"

"I've been dreaming of a day like this for seventeen years," William said.

Her heart raced, but her voice was steady and even. "But you couldn't have known Drexler."

"A happy accident. I saw him circling your mother's house. I realized we might be of help to each other."

A chill trailed up her spine. "You were watching my mother?"

William leaned toward her a fraction. "Did you know I installed monitoring equipment in your mother's house?"

When he'd called her that night at her mother's, he'd been stating fact, not toying with her. "Mom said there'd been a break-in, but nothing was taken."

"It was me. I even rented the house across the street from her."

She maintained a calm facade as her mind raced. *Buy time. Buy time.* She only hoped Mrs. Lopez had called Mazur.

William regarded the girl. "I had an entirely different scenario in mind. Alyssa wasn't on the original list. She and Drexler are . . . improvisations."

"Who made the original list? Charles Richardson?"

He shook his head. "No, Richardson was just another instrument."

William had been using Richardson all along? "You realized what Richardson was when you met him in prison, didn't you?"

"Funny how people like you and me can see the darkness in people. That's a special gift we both have."

She hated the idea that they shared anything, but he was right. They both could see the monsters. "You must have told Gloria during one of her visits to the prison that Richardson was gunning down women."

He grinned. "Why would I do that? You and I aren't the trusting sorts."

"You trusted Gloria. She was your half sister. You grew up with her. She knew everything about you, didn't she?"

He winked and touched the tip of his nose. "She did."

"I think you also cared about her."

"I did."

"Why kill her?"

He moistened his lips as if he'd tasted a delicious morsel. "When I told her about Richardson, she was fascinated, as I knew she would be."

Gloria had been more like William than she'd ever imagined. "Richardson was more than a curiosity, wasn't he?"

"Using what he'd done and this was all her idea," he said. "Of course, she never envisioned *this* particular scene, but she carefully planned the first two murders."

"She wanted you to kill her." The pieces clicked into place. "She knew she was dying of cancer, and she found out about her husband's affair with Rebecca."

"She found out about the tumor and Rebecca on the same day. That kind of shock would have killed a lesser woman, but not my sister. She knew if she was going to leave this earth, she'd do it on her own terms and she'd take people with her."

Drexler tugged at Alyssa's hair. "She's not waking up."

The girl's jaw remained slack and her eyes closed.

William didn't turn toward Drexler or the girl. His gaze remained on the gun in Kate's hand. "She will wake up. A few more minutes won't matter."

"Who was next on Gloria's list?"

"Isabella Sanchez. Martin's lovely daughter."

"Why her? Is killing her another way to punish Martin?"

"Yes. Gloria is not a woman you cross. If she wants you to suffer, you will."

Gloria had intended to strip away everything good in her husband's life: herself, the business, his lover, his daughter, and perhaps even his freedom. This kind of cold, calculating plan suggested she was not a novice to killing or with getting away with murder. "She killed his first wife."

He laughed. "She did! She wanted Martin from the moment she first saw him. I don't know what she saw in the man, but she wanted him. But as much as he said he loved Gloria, he would not leave his wife."

"She worked in the dealership then and learned about cars and brakes."

He winked. "Anything that got in her way had to go bye-bye. When she told me about Martin's affair with Rebecca, I told her about you and how I had not forgotten our special bond. She said there might be a way we could both get what we wanted."

"She picked up Richardson's gun from the bus station locker, didn't she?"

"Richardson always kept his gun there. Weeks before you arrested him, he visited the prison and told me where it was. He said he couldn't risk getting it. So I sent Gloria to his lawyer's office to get the key and then the gun. She was more than happy to run the errand because she knew the gun could be of use."

Kate tightened her fingers around the grip of her gun. "And you knew a Samaritan shooting would bring me to town."

He laughed. "I knew it would get your attention. I knew if I could just get you in the game, I could keep you engaged to the end." Darkness shuttered over his eyes as he clapped his hands. "I'm having fun, aren't you?"

She didn't respond.

William laughed. "What about you, Drexler?"

"I'm getting excited." He gently kissed Alyssa on the cheek. The girl didn't move or flinch. "She's going to have fun, too."

"Kate?" William asked.

"This is between you and me. Alyssa is not a part of this."

He arched a brow. "She is now. Seeing you and the detective made me so mad. I watched as you two picked up Alyssa from school. I couldn't follow you into the gated community, but I got the idea for taking Alyssa. I just want you to know what happens to her in the next few days is all because of you." The smile vanished from his lips. "You need to put the gun down."

When she didn't, he raised his hand, and Drexler pulled Alyssa's head back and pressed the tip of the blade to her jugular.

"You know how this works," William said.

It took the human brain at least a second to process what was happening, so regardless of whom she shot first, she might have a millisecond to shoot the other.

If either man dropped his guard even a fraction, all the better.

Setting her trap, Kate lowered her weapon, the Wonder Woman bracelet slipping down. Her gaze dropped in apparent defeat as her heart thudded in her chest. Time slowed to a crawl. Seconds felt like hours. From under hooded eyes she watched Drexler relax his hold on Alyssa's hair a fraction. A victor's smile tugged at the edges of William's lips. Who to shoot first?

Then she drew in a breath and rapidly raised her gun and fired. Her bullet struck Drexler in the center of his chest. He staggered back a half step, wearing an almost comical expression as he stared at the bloodstain blossoming on his chest. He lowered his weapon and dropped to a knee.

Praying for one more second, she shifted toward William. But he must have anticipated the move because as she turned to shoot him, he dived toward her and slammed his body into hers. He grabbed her wrist and banged her hand hard against the ground. A bullet exploded from the chamber and struck the wall behind them. His fingers crushing the bones in her hand, he again smashed it on the floor. Pain shot up her arm, and as hard as she tried to hold on to her weapon, her fingers released it.

He pinned both her arms over her head and straddled her body. His breathing was hurried and excited. His vice grip on her wrists snapped the plastic Wonder Woman bracelet, breaking it in two. "I knew you'd go for him first. You couldn't risk Alyssa's life, could you?"

She spotted a flutter of movement in the corner of her eye as she struggled. "Let her go, William! This is between you and me."

"You have no idea how long I've waited for this. How much I've dreamed about showing you just how much you underestimated me."

He shifted his grip so he held both arms with one hand, then with the other reached for the snap of her pants and tugged hard. Fabric ripped.

A bloodcurdling scream cut through the barn as Alyssa stumbled across the room and jumped on William's back. She pulled his hair and bit his ear.

He reared up and threw the girl off him. She hit the ground hard and tumbled. The delay was enough for Kate to stagger to her feet.

William picked up the gun, and when Alyssa rose up a second time, he slapped her hard across the face, splitting her lip and knocking her to the ground.

Fists clenched, Kate watched in horror as William raised the gun and pointed it at Alyssa's head.

Kate charged.

***

Mazur turned off his lights as soon as he made the last turn off the deserted road and barreled down the driveway. He gripped the wheel, funneling his fears into action. If he dwelled on the stakes, he'd risk overthinking and making a mistake. He still hadn't heard from Santos about the second property and prayed he'd arrived at the right place.

When he saw lights glowing from a large shed, he hoped he was on the right track. When he saw Kate's rental car nosed in behind a silver four door and a green truck, he said a prayer of thanks. He jammed on the brakes and threw the car in park. Pulling his gun from the holster, he ran across the graveled drive toward the door on the left. As he reached for the door handle, he heard a woman scream.

Tightening his hand on the grip of his weapon, he pushed through the door and took a split second to survey his surroundings. Alyssa was cowering, her hands in front of her face. She was whimpering, but appeared okay. Another scream drew his attention to the right just as Kate plowed into William, who was holding a gun.

Kate didn't have enough body weight or momentum to knock him over, but when her frame slammed against his arm, she created enough force to push it just as the gun fired. The bullet slammed into the wall, just feet from Alyssa's head. Immediately Bauldry recovered and landed a right hook on Kate's jaw. She took a half step and fell to her knees.

Mazur leveled his weapon, breathed out, and squeezed. His bullet burrowed through the side of Bauldry's cheek. The man's head snapped back as he staggered, gun still in his hand. Blood streamed down his face, staining his shirt. Dark eyes narrowing, William raised his gun toward Kate.

Mazur fired a second and a third time. These bullets caught Bauldry in the arm and chest and propelled him back. He dropped his gun. His expression was stunned as he dropped to his knees. He looked toward Kate as she rose up and glared at him.

"I love you," Bauldry said before he collapsed to the ground.

Mazur ran toward Bauldry, grabbed his cuffs, and hooked Bauldry's limp arms at the base of his back. He retrieved the gun before he looked to Kate, who had stumbled to her feet. Her face was red and already swelling.

"Kate?"

"I'm okay. Go to her."

He ran toward his daughter. He scooped up his little girl and held her so close. She cried as her fingers clutched his shirt. In one second, relief washed over him, but as he looked down at the bloodstains on the side of her face, his heart broke. Nothing would ever erase the painful relief of this moment for him for as long as he lived.

He cleared his throat when he saw the blood around her mouth. "Are you hurt, Alyssa?"

"I left my bracelet in the car."

"I found it."

"And then I pretended to be asleep. When they weren't looking I jumped on his back and bit his ear."

He tipped her chin back and wiped the blood away. He studied the dark, angry bruise on her cheek. His girl had followed the advice Kate had shared when they had picked her up from school. "Shit."

Mazur held his daughter close and watched as Kate swayed on her feet. He wasn't sure what to say to her. He was relieved she was okay and wished he had the words to thank her.

Alyssa wiped away a tear. "Kate saved me, Dad."

"She's fierce. A warrior."

Kate worked her jaw and rolled her neck, then stumbled toward Drexler. She rolled him on his back and checked for a pulse.

"Is he dead?" Mazur asked.

"Yes," she said. Her voice was hoarse and rough.

"Kate shot him," Alyssa said. "He had a knife to my throat."

Mazur looked at his daughter and then past her to the constructed wooden box. Waves of emotions collided. *Jesus.*

Finally he cleared his throat and met Kate's gaze. "Thank you."

Kate lifted her chin. "Of course."

She shoved a trembling hand over her head as she stared down at William.

"Are you really okay?" he asked.

Outside, the sirens of multiple cop cars approached through the night. Seconds later, there were cops everywhere.

"I'll be fine."

***

Kate leaned against the paramedic's bay, fingering the broken pieces of the Wonder Woman bracelet as she watched the flashing blue lights from a dozen cop cars mingle with the spotlights on the forensic van.

Yellow crime-scene tape had been strung around the bodies of Bauldry and Drexler, which still lay where they'd fallen.

It had been three hours since Mazur had raced to her and Alyssa's aid. Once backup teams arrived, he'd driven his daughter home, leaving Kate, and now Nevada, on the scene.

Nevada approached her, his expression pleased. "The medical examiner will be here soon to take away the bodies."

"Good."

He folded his arms and hesitated as if searching for the right words. "You all right?"

No. She could barely stand, her head throbbed with pain, and for as long as she lived, she would never forget the look of fear on Mazur's face as he'd hugged his daughter close. "Never better."

"It's got to feel good. This is a win in anyone's book. You brought down the bad guys and saved a kid."

"I wish it could be like this every time."

Nevada shook his head. "Enjoy the wins when you have them."

Gravel crunched under the tires of an approaching vehicle, and she saw Mazur rise out of it. As he strode toward them, she looked up at Nevada. "Mind giving us a minute?"

"Sure."

Mazur's face was drawn and pale under his thick stubble, which now darkened his jaw. He pulled Kate into his arms, and she willingly went. "I'm sorry I had to leave."

The fingers of her good hand clutched the folds of his jacket as she allowed herself to relax for the first time in what felt like years. "Is Alyssa okay?"

"Sherry's with Alyssa now. Alyssa is shaken up, and I know there'll be more emotional fallout from this later."

Kate looked up at him. "I don't know what would have happened to us if she'd not been so clear headed."

He looked down at her balled fist and uncurled her fingers to find the broken bracelet. A pained expression crossed his features before he met her gaze. "After all this has settled, I want to see you again."

Personal ties in this business were so difficult to maintain that she'd not even bothered to try since she'd joined her team. But now for the first time, she wanted more than the chase and the darkness. She rose on tiptoe and gently kissed him on the lips. "I'd like that."

EPILOGUE

Quantico, Virginia
Three weeks later

"Are you sure you want to do this?" Nevada asked Kate.

The box centered on her desk was filled with the few items she'd kept during her seven years with the bureau. "I'm very sure."

"What are you going to do?"

"Take a vacation," she said.

He leaned against the edge of her cubicle, fumbling with a rubber-band ball. "And then what? You'll miss the work."

"I'm taking a leave of absence, not retiring." She took the ball from him and put it in the box. "You're the one who has been after me to take time off."

"Yeah, but like a week in Cabo or a hike in the Catskills. Not a year off. You're too good at what you do."

"You might be right. I could get very bored. But I want to see what it feels like."

He shook his head. "You won't like it."

"I'll always be available for a consult. And you've got my number."

He took the ball out of the box and tossed it in the air. "It won't be the same."

She snatched the ball in midair. "Nothing stays the same. It's the one constant."

He grinned. "Ah, Yoda, you're so deep."

She smiled. "Yoda. That my new code name now?"

"Seems fitting. Yoda is almost as smart as you."

She reached for the box, but he took it. She followed him to the elevators and down to the lobby. The last time she'd left her home for college she'd known her life would never be the same. She had that same feeling now.

It had been three weeks since she'd left San Antonio, but in many respects it felt as if it were a lifetime ago. She and Nevada had searched Bauldry's house the night he died. After Mazur took Alyssa to her mother and she'd fallen asleep, he had joined the search team in the house adjacent to the large metal shed.

In the third room they'd found a room filled with computer monitors that showed not only her mother's house but also Rebecca's apartment and Isabella's room. William had been watching all the locations for months. They'd assumed it was all William's plan.

And then she'd found the small yellow notebook on William's desk. Nearly every page was filled with scrawled notes. She'd recognized immediately that the handwriting was not William's but belonged to a woman.

When love is betrayed, there is nothing to contain the demons.
The pills make the days' oppressive routines possible.
The bait will be too enticing to resist. Get more flies with honey than vinegar.
Her smile is sweet, and she thinks her sins are a secret. But I know them all.

Later, forensic analysts identified the handwriting as that of Gloria Sanchez. William had told the truth. She had planned all the killings out of revenge. On the heels of finding out she was dying, she'd also discovered Martin's affair with Rebecca was more than a passing romance. He was in love with Rebecca and wanted to marry her. She'd recruited William, enticing him with a dual plan to bring Kate back to San Antonio.

Though the Sanchez dealership had no record of Gloria checking out the white four door she'd been driving when she died, Calhoun had taken apart the backseat of the vehicle and found a gas receipt for a station near Westin's Dallas office. The receipt backed up Westin's claim she'd retrieved the locker key where Richardson had most likely stashed his murder weapon.

Gloria had mapped out the steps in her notebook, and William agreed to follow them. He'd written in his journals he didn't want to kill Gloria, but she'd insisted. She was leaving this world on her terms.

What Gloria had never anticipated was that William would deviate from the list. He'd not killed Isabella as he'd promised, but had shifted his attention to Alyssa when Kate slept with Mazur.

Other pieces of the puzzle had tumbled into place. One of the police sketch artist's drawings given by a woman who'd reported being spared by the Samaritan looked remarkably like William. The DNA pulled from hair fibers found on Gloria's and Rebecca's bodies matched Bauldry, and the semen sample in Rebecca's apartment matched Martin.

After Kate's and Mazur's final report to the chief and the bureau had been made, they'd slipped away for a night. He'd driven her to the airport the next morning, they'd kissed, and she'd flown to Salt Lake to attend Sara Fletcher's funeral, which had been held on a mountaintop where her parents had spread her ashes.

Kate had given Mrs. Fletcher the broken bracelet and told her Drexler was dead.

Mrs. Fletcher hugged Kate. "I am grateful to you. Without you, I would never have seen my little girl again."

Kate had relaxed into the embrace, accepting her gratitude. She'd left the bracelet in the mountains with Sara.

Neither Kate nor Mazur had reached out to the other in the last couple of weeks. She'd been caught up in a whirlwind of paperwork and debriefings, and she guessed he'd been pulled back by the demands of his own life.

All her life she'd enjoyed solitude, but for the first time, she felt alone.

Now, crossing the lobby, she was surprised when she looked up and saw Mazur. He was wearing jeans, hiking boots, and a thick winter jacket. His hair was a little longer, and he looked thinner. His expression was unreadable, but his gaze was locked on her. She tucked a curl behind her ear and smiled. He winked and moved toward her.

Nevada leaned toward her. "Want me to run interference?"

She shook her head. "Thanks, I got this."

"You sure?" Nevada asked.

She took the box and winked at him. "I can handle it."

Nevada smiled. "See you soon, Yoda."

"I'm on leave."

"Won't last."

She moved toward Mazur. "You look good."

"So do you." His voice was deep, ripe with emotion. "Bruises are gone."

"Right as rain. How's Alyssa?"

"The kid is amazing. She bounced back and is now talking about being an FBI agent."

"Really. Good for her."

"God help me." He glanced at her box. "Where are you going?"

"Don't know. I have a year's sabbatical."

"You quit?"

"Just taking an extended break."

"Let me at least hold the box."

Their fingers brushed when he took the box. Electricity snapped up her arms. "Thanks. My car is this way."

He followed her out the front door to her silver two door. She popped the trunk, and he set the box inside. "I'm out here for a job interview with a security company. Sounds promising."

"So you're going to move?"

"I go where my daughter goes."

"That's great, Mazur. She's lucky to have you." She fished her keys out of her purse.

"I'm sorry I haven't called," he said.

"You have your hands full."

"That's no excuse. You saved Alyssa."

"I brought the monsters into her life."

"Maybe, or maybe they'd have come anyway. The point is that you saved her." He shook his head. "How was Sara Fletcher's funeral?"

Her throat tightened with emotion. "Heartbreaking."

"I read Drexler's file. You were right. If I'd known all that before Alyssa's rescue, I'd have lost it."

"You're a good father."

"Can I take you to dinner tonight?" he asked. "Or if you have plans, another time when it works."

"I'd like that."

He took a step toward her and kissed her on the lips. "Thank you."

"Is this a thank-you dinner?" She wasn't interested in a payback.

He grinned. "I'd rather think of it as a date."

She rose on tiptoes and kissed him on the lips. His arm rose and gently rested on her hip. She'd missed him far more than she'd realized. "A date sounds nice."

ABOUT THE AUTHOR

Photo © 2015 Studio FBJ

New York Times and *USA Today* bestselling novelist Mary Burton is the popular author of thirty-two romance and suspense novels, as well as five novellas. She currently lives in Virginia with her husband and three miniature dachshunds.